# In Search of Honor

By T.S. Dawson

## Acknowledgments

Thank you to all of my friends and family who have aided in the process of writing this book. Without you I likely would have never started this process and I certainly would not have continued past chapter one of Port Honor without your love and encouragement. I really appreciate each and every one of you.

Again, I would like to thank my husband, Terry Dawson, and son for allowing me the time it took to be able to write these books. I would especially like to thank my husband for helping bring Gabriel and authentic male voice. I love you both very much and appreciate all that you do for me.

I would also like to thank my parents, Linda and John Bryan, for their love and support in this process. A special thank you goes out to John for working so hard on my website and entertaining all of my special requests. Thank you also for helping me to format the book for publishing.

I would like to personally thank Donna M. Goss for continuing to be my first editor. You have been through so much this year and you still had time to encourage me and keep me moving forward with this book.

Thank you to Annette Saunders for sticking with me and helping to edit this book as well. You and Donna are invaluable when it comes to listening to my ideas for the characters and plot.

Thank you also to Susie Taylor and Christie Johnson for your editing skills. Susie is the queen of commas and Christie rocks at grammar.

Thank you to Jill Rowland, Dottie Harper, Greg Dinsmore, Christie Johnson (again), Tammy Pardus, Rachel Holcomb, Phyllis Aycock and all of my friends that have helped me try to get the word out about my books.

Thank you the staff at The News and Farmer for interviewing me and putting me on the front page of the newspaper in the town where I grew up. What a thrill that was for me.

Thank you to Amanda Castro of Channel 11 in Macon for my four minutes of fame. You were my first ever interviewer and what fun it was!

Thank you to every last one of you who is and has given your time to my writing. I sincerely hope you are entertained by my stories. For those of you who have written reviews, thank you so much and please keep them coming. If you like it, let me know and, if you don't, let me know that too. I sincerely appreciate your feedback.

While some locations referenced in this book do exist, the characters are based solely on my overactive imagination. Any similarities to actual people are due to your own imagination.

Thank you for reading and enjoy!

Sincerely,

TS Dawson

Our own heart, and not other men's opinions, forms our true honor.

-Samuel Taylor Coleridge

They would not let me sit with the family. In fact, they said I should count myself lucky that they let me attend at all. They said she deserved better and I deserved nothing, not even the kindness of being allowed near her now.

The song "Nearer My God to Thee" was being played on the church organ and the room was cold and full of the smell of carnations. The sermon was done, but I still sat there. I had endured the entire thing with all of the murmured whisperings behind me. I was small for my age, but I wasn't deaf. I could hear all of them.

I was only seven. I was wearing a navy blue, hand-me-down suit because I did not own one of my own. My parents weren't church going people so I had never needed one before, but I did for this day. It was March 20, 1975, the day that my parents and my sister were laid to rest.

*They* were the relatives of my mother and friends of my grandmother. Grandmother was their leader and the instigator of the grudge that the entire family seemed to have against me.

"They say he did it," the voice of one old lady said. The voice was shrill. I recognized it. She was one of my grandmother's dearest friends. They went way back.

"I heard that too. I don't know what they're going to do to him," said another. I recognized her as well. I had interrupted their Bridge Club once and she was the main one I remembered that day. She was my grandmother's Bridge partner.

"You know, Virginia can hardly stand the sight of him," added yet another.

I knew them all and they had been kind to me in the past, but they did not dare challenge my grandmother or stand up for me. They just kept going on and on with their speculation and gossip. The truth was, I did not know what they were going to do with me either.

5

Virginia Verde was my grandmother, my mother's mother, and that lady whispering behind me was right. My grandmother couldn't stand the sight of me ever since the police officers told her what I had done. She had beaten me a minimum of three times per day for the last three days just to make sure I understood how little she cared for me and that I knew I must pay for my sins. What she failed to realize was that I got the message after the first beating and she really did not have to waste her effort.

Here I sat on the front pew of the First Baptist Church of Gainesville, Florida, and before me were two coffins. My father was in the dark brown wooden one and beside it was a pale pink one. The pale pink one was the color of the only strand of pearls that my mother owned. It had white ovals of ivory with pink roses painted on them at every corner and it held my mother and my sister. My grandmother insisted they be buried together.

I focused on the coffins the entire time, stared at them in an effort to keep from crying. Grandmother threatened me. She said if anyone had a right to cry it was her and if she saw me shed one tear she would make me sorry. I was already sorry. I envied my sister inside that coffin.

I did everything I could to distract myself from crying, but awful thoughts keep creeping into my head. I could not help but think how embarrassed my mother would be to see me. No one had helped me with my hair and my cowlicks were ever present. The suit was two sizes too big for me, but the gift of it was about the only kindness I had been shown. The patent leather dress shoes were too big as well and they looked like I was playing dress up. My mother would have been mortified that I looked as if I had been thrown away and I was on the very verge of being just that.

My mother would have also been hurt that anyone would have put her in anything pink. Everyone who knew her knew she hated that color and it would have hurt her to know that my grandmother, her own mother, did not know that about her. My father brought her pink flowers once and she cried for a week because her opinion was he did not care enough about her to remember she despised that color.

6

"Nearer My God to Thee" continued to play until the pallbearers started carrying the caskets away. I could not bear it anymore. I missed my mother and father and even my sister. I looked back to my grandmother. She was sitting with my grandfather and all of the rest of my mother's family on the opposite side of the aisle. She glared at me and if looks could have killed, I would have gotten my wish about not being left behind by my parents. I had no bearing then for what a really evil woman she was other than that she was the basis for every villain in every Disney movie. She probably had a coat made of puppies stashed somewhere in her house.

The look my grandmother gave me terrified me and I broke. The caskets were nearly all the way down the aisle and to the front door of the church when I leapt to my feet. I struggled to run in the slick bottom shoes that flopped on my feet with every step. I screamed as I struggled to keep the shoes on and chased after the men carrying my parents away. "Mommy, don't leave me! Please, I promise I will be good! Please!"

I grabbed the handle of my mother's casket and I held on, pulling to stop them from taking her. "Please, don't leave me!" I sobbed and sobbed. "I'm so sorry. I'll be a good boy."

\*\*\*

I have relived that day in my dreams night after night. I awoke drenched in sweat and tears and in utter darkness, both realistically and figuratively. I carried their opinions of me as if theirs were the only ones that mattered until she came along. Amelia was the light in the darkness that had been my life. I did not realize I was searching until I found her.

# CHAPTER 1

"I don't bite you know...unless it's called for," Mrs. McMillan said, just above a whisper, as she leaned across the bar that I was wiping down.

I glanced sideways at her from my end. "Excuse me?" I asked and tried to pretend I had not understood what she said.

"It's a quote from Audrey Hepburn's character in the movie 'Charade.' Her pick-up line," she said off-handedly while propping her head up with one arm. Her white blouse was unbuttoned a little too far down and flopped open from the way she had positioned herself nearly laying across the bar. I was wiping up from the far end toward her and could not help but notice what she seemed to be offering; rather remarkable tits for a woman of nearly fifty. I looked away as quickly as I had noticed.

"So Gabe, why are you here so late tonight?" asked Mrs. McMillan.

"The Germans won gold today so we had to wait around to serve them dinner," I replied as I continued my chore and tried not to look in her direction. "What brings you in this evening?"

A group of German businessmen purchased Port Honor just before I was hired last year. Since the purchase, the club had been completely revamped for the sole purpose of hosting and housing the German Equestrian Team while they were competing in the '96 Olympics.

Mrs. McMillan responded with an exasperated sigh, "Harry phoned and said he would not be down until tomorrow morning, so I thought I would hang out with Andy and nurse a few drinks. However, it appears he's not working tonight."

Mr. and Mrs. McMillan were members at Port Honor, the club where I had been a manager for two weeks shy of a year. He was a named partner at some accounting firm and she was a third grade teacher in Duluth, Georgia. They owned a second home in the neighborhood that surrounded the club. They were successful, but not so much so that their home was on the lake. It was on one of the

8

interior lots that abutted the golf course. The house was expensive by some standards, but not over the top like some of the others around the course or on the lake. I only knew all of this because she had hired us to cater Mr. McMillan's sixtieth birthday party this past March and what I did not learn about them then, other staff members told me.

It struck me as odd that Mrs. McMillan had specifically included Andy in her response when she had just propositioned me. Perhaps I was her second choice or she was just casting a line to see who would take the bait. Beyond the great job done by some plastic surgeon on her chest, she had likely had her eyes lifted and things tightened a little around her chin and neck. The work was remarkable and no expense was spared. In fact, the only reason I suspected she had had work done at all was because I had seen her six months ago. She looked firmer, but not necessarily younger.

"Yeah, Andy worked earlier and Matt was on tonight, but it appears you already know that," I said having observed that someone had been serving her drinks already.

The Germans had just left the dining room. They had gone up to the inn for the night and the remaining servers were resetting everything for those who had to return for the breakfast shift the following morning. Matt agreed to help them so we could all finally go home. I had only gone up to the bar to collect the till, but seeing the rings from glasses on the bar top, I decided to wipe it down while I was up there.

We had all been working doubles since the equestrian team had arrived for the Olympics about a week ago. There was hardly a one of us that was not utterly exhausted, but we still had another week to go until the closing ceremony and the departure of the team.

"I just hate being in the house alone." Mrs. McMillan was trying to be subtle in her offer, but I knew it was an offer all the same.

"I know how that can be. As old as I am, I still feel like flipping on every light in the house when I get home late like this." I acted oblivious to her suggestion.

It had been since April for me, but I was not breaking the streak for a club member, let alone a married woman whose husband was a decent guy by all accounts. Plus, if I were to ever have another one night stand, it would be with someone that I did not have to face at work on a regular basis. I did not need another Kimmie in my face all the time, reminding me of my lapse in judgment. Not to mention, there was only one person I wanted and I had probably ruined that for good. In addition to all of those excuses for the use of my better judgment, I had to get home to relieve Mrs. Allen, Gabby's sitter.

"Do you need one of the girls drive you home on their way out?" I asked Mrs. McMillan.

I tried to give the impression that I was oblivious to her advances as my way of politely declining her without having to actually decline. She seemed to get my meaning and leaned back from the spot where she had been draped across the bar. With clear disappointment on her face, she began to button up her blouse. As she did so, she noticed the TV playing on the wall behind my head. Suddenly, she found something sobering on the television. Something had caught her attention. Her voice became serious, "Gabe, could you turn that up?"

I turned to get a look as I reached for the remote. "They were doing an interview with one of the American swimmers that had won gold earlier and then something happened in the background," Mrs. McMillan described before ordering me to "Turn it up!"

I turned up the volume to hear the broadcasters explaining that "something" had just happened behind them in the park and all of the glass in the pavilion where they were had been shattered. "People are running everywhere. Stay with Channel 11 as we bring you live events from Centennial Olympic Park."

A dreadful feeling came over me and I felt nauseous for a moment. I was sure it was nothing, just exhaustion. I shook it off and handed the remote over to Mrs. McMillan. "I will send the girls up for you when they get ready to leave. You feel free to turn up the volume or change the station if you like."

10

I then opened the cash drawer and took the tray from the register and headed to the kitchen.

***

It was still dark and I struggled to come to. It was as if all of the bells of Saint Peter's Cathedral were going off in my head all at once. I did not know whether to answer the alarm clock or hit the snooze on the phone.

All of a sudden, I did come to and realized it was indeed the phone ringing. A cold chill rushed over me as I noticed the red numbers shining in the dark signaling what time of night it really was. No one calls at 3:00 a.m. unless someone is dead or on the way to the hospital. Not to mention, I had only been asleep for a little over an hour.

In the pitch black, I searched the nightstand with one hand for the cordless phone and with the other I tried to find the pull cord for the bedside lamp. The phone stopped ringing just shy of the answering machine kicking on. As quickly as the ringing stopped, it started again and I was no closer to finding the lamp switch or phone than I had been when it stopped.

Scores of obscenities rolled under my breath and off my tongue. I feared the ringing would inevitably wake Gabby. Just as I spouted off the third "mother-fucker" under my breath, I finally had a hand on the phone.

"Hello!" I demanded as quietly as I could still trying not to compound whatever problem the caller was about to lay on me with the wailing and screaming of my three week old daughter.

A sobbing voice on the other end of the line gasped my name, "Gabe! Gabe! You have to help me!"

I recognized the voice. It was Cara, one of my employees at Port Honor. I could hardly understand her words through her crying.

"I will do what I can, but you have to calm down and tell me what's wrong." She was clearly upset, but if she did not calm down there was no way I would be able to understand or help her. I was

11

scared to know what was going on as displays of emotion like this were uncharacteristic of Cara. She was the tough one of the bunch of servers at the club and I had never seen any customer even slightly ruffle her feathers.

I had been walking through the hall toward my daughter's room to make sure she had not woken up when Cara said the words, "I can't find Millie."

I may not have understood too much else that Cara had said, but those words came across the line as clear as day. My heart dropped and I could feel the blood drain from my face. My voice was stern and I responded with a touch of panic, "What do you mean, you can't find Millie?"

I leaned against the door jamb of the hall bathroom as my knees went a little weak. As soon as Cara had said the words I remembered two things all at once. I remembered that Cara had been given tickets to the equestrian events by the German Equestrian team members who were staying at Port Honor during the Olympics. I also remembered glancing at a breaking news report that there was a bombing at Centennial Olympic Park that night before I left the club.

My mind was quickly headed toward the conclusion that Cara verbalized. "Gabe, I can't find Millie." Cara repeated herself and continued through tears, "I could not hang on to her. It is complete chaos here and I can't find her. I don't know what to do. I tried calling Jay..."

"Calm down and tell me what happened." I was telling her to calm down, but I was struggling to remain calm myself.

"They are saying there was a bomb. We were just standing there. Talking. A flash, a boom and suddenly people were running everywhere. Millie was injured. Shit, Gabe, the pay phone's about to cut off. I don't have any more change. Shit!" Cara snorted and cried and the volume of the phone was already starting to go.

"Cara, call me back collect. I'll accept the call," I instructed her.

12

I anxiously awaited Cara to call back. It seemed like forever between the calls and I tried to pass the time without losing my mind. I looked in again to make sure the baby was still sleeping and she was, but that wasn't enough to keep the bad thoughts out of my head as I waited.

All of my regrets and fears were coming to the surface. Where was Millie? I told her I would come for her once I had sorted out everything with Beth and Gabby. I had a plan and I was working on that plan, but I had been so busy since Gabby was born and things had been derailed by the business at the club with the Olympics. I could think of a hundred reasons, but they were just excuses for self-preservation. I was terrified to tell her that I needed more time. Terrified I would lose her for good and now what if I never saw her again? What if something had happened to her and she did not know how I felt about her? Dear God, when is the phone going to ring again?

I took the cordless phone and the baby monitor to the garage. It was the only place I could think to go so that I could speak freely without risking waking Gabby. I paced back and forth in the space along the side of my car and the garage wall. It was nearly five minutes between hanging up with Cara and the phone ringing again. Those five minutes were an eternity.

"You have a call from; caller say your name," the operator instructed.

"Cara Price."

"Sir, will you accept the..." I completely cut off the operator.

"Yes! Yes, I'll accept the charges," I responded urgently.

The operator was gone and Cara spoke again. She was still crying and she sniffled in between her words and sentences. "Gabe, I don't know what to do or where to look. There are police everywhere and FBI. They told me to go home, but I can't leave her. I know she's injured."

"Cara, you're no good to her as long as you are hysterical. Are you sure she was injured and you didn't just get separated from her? Have you gone back to where y'all parked to see if she is just waiting on you there?" I tried to comfort both Cara and myself with thoughts that they had just lost one another in the rush of everything.

"No, Gabe, she got hit with stuff from the bomb or whatever it was," Cara explained before starting to fully sob again. "Millie got hit and blocked me from getting hit. There was blood everywhere on her back and on her hands. I have her blood on me. Oh, God, I've got her blood on me! I tried to hang on to her, but the people just kept pushing past us. I tried Gabe, I swear."

I was sick to my stomach. Thoughts of Amelia being alone, scared and hurt were nearly more than I could stand. I didn't know what to do, but I knew I had to go and help try to find her. I had to do more than try; I had to find her.

"I tried calling Jay, but I can't get him and I don't know her Aunt's number..."

"Cara, I will call Amelia's aunt and as soon as I can find someone to keep Gabby, I'll be on my way. Where will I be able to find you?"

The line was silent for a moment. I am sure Cara was trying to think and suck up tears, "I don't know if you are going to be able to drive down here. I don't know where to tell you to meet me. I just don't know. I am so sorry."

"Can you see the Westin Peachtree Plaza Hotel from where you are? It's a building that is shaped like a tall cylinder. There'll be a ring of lights around the top of it."

I could hear Cara wipe her nose before she acknowledged, "I see it!"

"Good. Go there. Find a place to sit in the lobby and I will find you there. I'm on my way." I was already back inside searching the kitchen for where I had placed the note with Amelia's aunt Gayle's number on it by the time Cara agreed to meet me at the Westin.

As I searched the kitchen, I tried dialing her apartment in hopes that I would find Jay, Amelia's roommate. They were like brother and sister and I would have loved to pass off the call to Amelia's aunt to him. Plus, he would want to know what was going on with Amelia and probably insist on helping.

Jay did not answer and this was not a message I wanted to leave on their answering machine. I hung up just as the machine kicked on and I found the scrap of paper with Gayle's number. I dreaded making the call, but it had to be done.

I dialed the numbers and steeled my nerves. I headed back to my bedroom to get dressed as the phone rang on Gayle's end. Time was of the essence and I had to multitask all of this. There was an urgency that was taking over me that I had to get dressed, make the call, get Gabby packed and find someone to take care of Gabby while I was gone.

Gayle answered within two rings. She sounded exactly as I had when I answered; urgent and demanding with her greeting. "Hello?!!"

"Gayle, it's Gabriel." Amelia always called me by my whole name and that's how her family would recognize me.

"What do you want?" Gayle questioned. I understood her tone. She was resentful of the pain I had caused her niece, the niece she had raised as if she were her own daughter. I am sure I was the last person she ever wanted to hear from again.

"Did you hear about the bombing at Centennial Olympic Park on the news before you went to bed?" I asked her.

"Gabriel, it is 3:30 in the morning and Amelia is not here and if she were..."

"I know she's not there. Did you see the news?"

"No, I did not and what does this have to do with Amelia or me and why are you calling?" Gayle was losing what little patience she had left for me.

"Amelia was at the park and there's been a bombing," I squeaked out the words past the lump in my throat.

I could hear the rustling of the covers as Gayle sat up in her bed. "WHAT?!" she gasped.

"I just got a call from one of Amelia's friends from the club. All I know right now is that they were at the park when the bombing happened and Amelia is missing." I was getting dressed to go down there as I explained to Gayle. I did not want to tell her Amelia was injured since I was not sure of any details.

"Oh my God!!!" Gayle gasped again and again.

"Gayle, I'm headed down there and I am going to find her. I just thought you should know." I slipped on my shoes. "I'll call you as soon as I know anything. Gayle, I will find her."

"I'm getting up now. I can't just wait here," Gayle replied and again I could hear her covers rustle through the phone as she got out of bed.

"You must wait there in case she calls. I promise, I'll check in with you and let you know as soon as I know anything; as soon as I find her. I promise. Now, I have to go."

By the time I hung up with Amelia's aunt I was finished dressing. I had to focus on Gabby now. While packing the diaper bag and mixing a couple of bottles of formula I tried calling the natural choice to take care of her, her mother, Beth.

Gabby was three days old when she was released from the hospital to come home. Beth was released the same day. She handed the child to me and told me she was going to her mother's to recuperate. I was astonished, but even though I knew nothing about babies, I was glad to be free of Beth. If she were leaving the baby, this was the perfect time for her to do so. Better she leave before Gabby was able to miss her.

I dialed the number to Beth's parents' house in Atlanta and waited. No answer beyond that of the machine. I left a message.

"Beth, it's me. I need to you to call me." I was not about to elaborate and give her the satisfaction of finding out that something might have happened to Amelia.

16

I hung up and dialed Mrs. Allen.

I had hired the grandmother of one of my employees at the club as a nanny. Ever since Beth left the baby with me, I had needed all the help I could get caring for her and Mrs. Allen was a godsend. Without her, I am not sure Gabby and I would have survived the last few weeks.

As the phone rang, I reflected on how I came to hire Mrs. Allen. It was because of Amelia and the fact that she was always looking to help others. She was always thinking of others even when they did not deserve a second thought from her. I was one of those people. I did not deserve her, but in these moments since Cara phoned, I knew that I had to find her. I had to get her back.

Amelia was the one person beyond my parents that had ever truly loved me and what might be happening to her right now or what might have happened to her, I shuddered to think. I shoved the negativity out of my head and pushed on with packing the diaper bag.

It took two calls before Mrs. Allen finally answered. Like the rest of us, her initial greeting was that of being a little put out by being phoned in the middle of the night.

"Mrs. Allen, it's Gabe. I am sorry to disturb you, but I have an emergency and I need help with Little One. May I please bring her to you? If I had anyone else..."

When Mrs. Allen responded, her tone had completely changed. In the calmest voice I had heard since leaving the club that night, Mrs. Allen answered, "Of course dear. I will get up right now and put the light on for you."

"I'm on my way and again I am so sorry to trouble you. I will explain more when I get to your house."

"You don't have to explain anything to me honey, just come on and bring that sweet baby to me." I knew I did not have to explain to her, but I wanted to. I was certain that Mrs. Allen was a good, God fearing, praying woman and Amelia might need all the prayers she could get.

I did not need to get directions as I knew where Mrs. Allen and her grandchildren lived because I had given her oldest, the dishwasher at the club, a ride home on a number of occasions before I helped him find a car. They lived just off of the next exit down on I-20 in Siloam, Georgia. Mrs. Allen typically stayed with the baby at my house on the nights that I worked and even though Siloam was in the opposite direction of where I needed to go to try to find Amelia, I had no right to ask Mrs. Allen to come to me at this time of night. Plus, she would have had to make arrangements of her own for her young grandchildren. It just made more sense to take Gabby to her.

I tried not to wake Gabby as I moved her from her crib to the car carrier. Although she was gaining weight on schedule, she was still so tiny; tiny with a huge set of lungs. The last thing I needed right then was for her to wake up and wake up hungry. She had her mother's temper and it really showed when someone woke her up or when she was hungry. The rest of the time she was a great baby and she took it easy on me.

I looked down at Little One as I loaded her in the car. She was sleeping soundly; all pink pajamas and snuggled in. She sucked her little thumb, something she had been doing since I first saw her in the sonogram pictures. She was beautiful and I hated myself every time I left her. My favorite time of day was feeding her.

I thought about her mother leaving her and I just did not understand it. I would never understand it. I often thought about Amelia's stories of her mother when I looked at my daughter. Beth left with the understanding that she would be back. She did not give any indication as to when she would be back, just that she needed some time. The honest to God's truth was that I did not want her to come back. I would rather Gabby have no mother and no memories of her at all than have a mother like Amelia described hers; someone who never really wanted her. Amelia always put on a stern face when talking about her mother, but I know it hurt her and I did not want that for any child, let alone my child.

I made a promise to my daughter that I would never leave her and I meant to keep that promise. I also made a promise to Amelia that I would sort out the situation with Beth. I had been working on something, but it was continually getting put on hold.

Perhaps all of this was meant to force me to sort things out not just for me or for Amelia, but for Gabby as well.

***

It was almost 4:00 a.m. by the time I pulled into Mrs. Allen's driveway. The headlights of my Acura shown across the yard and among other things, they lit up the flower bed made from a painted tractor tire. The drive was of beaten down dirt and ruts, which I hit like speed bumps. Immediately I looked back to the car seat. She was still sleeping despite the earthquake inside the car.

The headlights lit up the house as well. It was a modest house of cinder blocks that were painted white like the tractor tire in the yard. In the daytime, you could tell that the shutters were a royal blue color and the front door matched. You could also tell that the yard was well kept; nothing like the landscaping of the houses in the neighborhood surrounding the club, but clearly someone put effort into it, if not money.

I knocked lightly on the front door so as not to wake everyone. She had turned on the front porch light for me and had the wooden door propped open. I could see Mrs. Allen seated just inside the door waiting on me as I knocked.

"Gabe," she said as she opened the door to me, "come on in."

I stepped inside the house and was relieved to see its condition. I knew they were poor. I had been poor the majority of my life and the one thing I had always understood is that one could be poor and still be clean. Mrs. Allen's house was a reflection of that belief as well.

"She's still asleep," I said as I glanced down at Gabby. "I packed some bottles for her. I last fed her a little before 2:00 a.m. so she won't be ready for another until around 5:00. I think she would be all right to sleep in this carrier, if you want to leave her in here for now."

I sat the carrier down on the floor next to the chair where Mrs. Allen had been seated.

"I don't want you to worry about anything. Baby girl is going to be just fine with Nanny." Mrs. Allen always referred to herself as Nanny. I think she treated Gabby as if she were just another of her grandchildren, which I liked. To me, it meant she cared.

"Mrs. Allen, I really appreciate you taking care of her for me and I won't forget this." I ran a hand through my hair and hung my head as I began to tell her just what the emergency was tonight. The gravity of what might lie ahead was starting to set in. It's not that I was unfeeling or uncaring, but I was not a crier. I could not recall the last time I cried. I plugged my tear ducts with my index fingers and held back the tears.

"There was a bombing at Centennial Olympic Park tonight. You were likely in bed already when it happened, but it is all over the TV now. Amelia, I mean, Millie, was there with one of the other girls from the club, Cara. It appears Millie and Cara got separated in the chaos. Millie is missing and we believe she was injured, but we don't know how badly."

Mrs. Allen placed a hand over her mouth as I spoke. I could hear her words through her hand, "Oh Lord, dear Lord. Miss Millie just has to be all right."

Tears began to fill Mrs. Allen's eyes and I could tell she was genuinely worried for Amelia. I reached out and hugged her. "If you could pray for her I would appreciate it."

"Of course. Mr. Gabe you sure are a good man going to help Miss Millie." Mrs. Allen wiped her eyes as she stepped back from me.

I am certain she did not know the whole story of me and Millie, but I was glad someone thought I was a good man because I certainly did not feel like one right then. All I could think about was that if I had not let Millie go then she would have been safe with me tonight.

I kissed Little One gently on the forehead as she slept, "Daddy loves you and will be back as soon as he can. You be a good girl for Mrs. Allen and I will see you in a little while."

I took one last look at the house as I backed out of the driveway. Mrs. Allen waived at me through the screen door. I suppose I could have called Joan and she would have taken Gabby for me. In the time since Gabby was born and since Beth left for her so called recuperation, Joan had offered on a number of occasions to help me out with Gabby if I needed her. Despite her many offers and despite that Joan and I had gotten along well in the past, I just had a feeling that she was not sincere. I don't know why I felt that way, but I was secure in my decision to leave Gabby with Mrs. Allen.

I had not cut on the radio while on the way to Mrs. Allen's, but I turned it on as soon as I got onto the road headed back to I-20 outside of Siloam. Even Dock 100, the local station out of Greensboro, was broadcasting events of the evening. I figured I would get better information if I could get one of the Atlanta stations to come in so I turned the dial to Star 94.

I was nearly to Greensboro when the station first came in clear enough that I could hear it. There were two DJs and they were up in arms about reports.

One of the DJs reported, "We have received confirmation that the incident at Centennial Olympic Park tonight was the result of a bomb."

The other added, "We have also received word of at least one fatality, a woman. Her identity has not been released pending notification of her next of kin."

I gripped the steering wheel to the point of having white knuckles. Again my thoughts raced. Oh my God, what if it was Amelia? I refused to believe it. I assured myself that just because she was lost in all of the commotion did not mean she had been killed. Surely, I would have felt it if something had happened to her. Perhaps I did feel it. Perhaps that was what the nausea was when I first heard of the bombing on the news earlier.

The DJs went on with one adding, "We are receiving reports from witnesses including newscasters from other stations around the city that they first thought they were just seeing pyrotechnics that were a part of the concert."

I could not take hearing witness accounts or any more talk of the bombing. It just made things harder and harder to swallow and it was as if they were snuffing out my hope of finding Amelia. I turned from station to station searching for anything. I did not feel like jamming or rocking out, but I needed something to distract me from the doom and gloom of the morning news. I came across a station that was still picking up out of Augusta, WBBQ. I caught the tail end of "Unbreak My Heart" by Toni Braxton. I narrowly escaped that one, but I was even worse.

"You've got to be fucking kidding me!" I said out loud

The song was "I'll Be There" by the Escape Club. I prayed to God that this was not a sign, a song about death and how the person will be watching over you from above.

"I do *not* need this shit right now!" I screamed as I violently turned the radio off.

In the silence, with nothing but the wind and tire noise, my mind wandered to thoughts of Amelia. Memories of my time with her haunted my drive. They were laid out in visions lit by my headlights across the road in front of me.

CHAPTER 2

How it all began...

"It's me. Give me a call when you get in." There was no mistaking the voice on my answering machine. It was Beth.

Beth Reed and I had been an on again-off again item since college. We were off right now, but still friends. I am sure she was calling for an update on how things were going at the club. Beth had pulled some strings and called in a few favors. I am not sure now, but she had essentially gotten me the job as the chef and dining manager at Port Honor, a golf resort on Lake Oconee, outside of Greensboro, Georgia.

I grabbed the phone and took it with me as I went to get out of my work clothes. The dinner special had been fried catfish and I reeked of it all the way to my bones. All I had thought about the majority of the evening was getting free of that odor. Well, I thought of one other thing that night.

I dialed the number from memory and it was ringing by the time I made it down the hall to my bedroom door. There were three full rings and I was beginning to plan the message I was going to leave on her machine when Beth picked up.

"Hello, dear," she greeted me from the other end of the line.

One might think she answered as if she knew it was me, but that was not the case. Since I had known her, Beth had always answered the phone that way. She said it was her signature greeting. I had heard it so many times over the years that I nearly rolled my eyes every time she answered now. I had tried to explain to her that it was actually an insincere way of trying to make someone on the other end feel special. My efforts were in vein. As with everything else, Beth was going to do what Beth was going to do.

"Hey, I'm sorry it's late. I just got in," I explained since it was after 10:00 p.m.

"Well, if you want to talk to me, you are going to have to make it quick. I am in the middle of getting dressed to go out," Beth responded. Had she forgotten that she called me? Probably.

"I am returning your call from earlier. Was there something you wanted?" I let a bit of my own attitude fly back at her in my voice. The older I got, the less patient I was becoming with her air of superiority.

She was getting dressed and I was getting undressed. She had an attitude toward me for interrupting her evening and I reciprocated. There once was a time when the thoughts of us getting dressed or undressed would have been mutually titillating, but those days were long gone. I had known Beth Reed since college. We had dated for a long time, but now we were just friends. In fact, I was likely her best friend, maybe her only friend.

It was a week night and as I recalled Beth had a job, an early morning job. I called her on it. "Don't you have to work tomorrow?"

"Yeah, so? That does not mean I can't have a life." Beth paused for a moment. I could hear her on the move through the house and out a door, likely the one to the back yard. "Hold on, I have to let the damn dog out."

I think she put her hand over the phone, but I could still make out her yelling at the dog. "Shit and get it over with already!"

I also heard the dog yelp and whimper. He was still a pup, a tiny little Yorkie she had named Beatle after the band. There was no telling what she had done to him. He was sweet, but Beth had no patience for him.

"How was your day?" Beth inquired as if she genuinely cared. Her demeanor was like night and day. Once back on the phone with me butter would not have melted in her mouth. Although I had cautioned her about being cruel to Beatle in the past, tonight I acted oblivious to her tantrum. I did not feel like receiving a dose of what he was getting.

I replied with one word, "Long."

"So things are picking up at the club?"

In the time since I started at the club, I had tripled the business and I had done it on a skeleton crew. I had recently been granted permission by the higher-ups to hire a real wait staff.

"They are," I responded. "I actually had another girl to interview for a server position today."

I was already visualizing a portion of the interview and formulating my answer before Beth even asked, "Really? How did it go? It had to be better than the last."

I squelched my true reaction to her observation. I refrained from saying, "Oh it was," in a tone that would surely suggest inappropriate thoughts about the college girl who applied for the job. Instead my answer was more low key.

"It started off rocky. She was thirty minutes late. Apparently there was a cattle crossing..."

Beth snickered and mocked the situation openly, "A cattle crossing? Now that's not an excuse you hear every day! So, it *was* as bad as the last."

"No," I corrected her and continued. "It ended better than I expected."

Thoughts of Amelia Jane Anderson bending over at the side of the piano clouded my mind as they had done all evening. I caught myself before I let Beth in on that detail.

"In all honesty, I was a real jerk to her for being late and when I first laid eyes on her I thought she was going to run."

"Who knew you could be intimidating?" This time Beth mocked me. Of the two of us, it was always Beth that was intimidating.

"Well, she did not run and she held her own against me. She's feisty." I chuckled at my last comment.

"And you like that." Beth did not ask a question. She made a statement.

Suddenly, I was guarded. If Beth and I were friends, why did I feel the need to hide my thoughts? Our days of dating had been over for a while so why did I feel the need to spare her feelings and hide that another woman had turned my head?

The answer was that we had agreed to be one another's backup plan. "If we aren't married by age thirty, then I will marry you," she once told me. At the time it sounded like a good plan.

I scoffed at my own internal description of my reaction to Amelia. Turned my head, that was the understatement of the century. I felt like a bit of a pervert for the thoughts that ran through my head when I first laid eyes on her waiting for me in the bar. It had only been a month since I had last been laid and maybe depravity was starting to take hold of my mind. Upon sight of this girl, all I could think about was having her.

I turned from stilling the swinging door that led from the kitchen to the bar and there she was. I had never had that sort of immediate reaction to anyone before. Sure, there were women that I had been attracted to, but nothing like this. She had risen from the chair where she had been waiting for me. She had on a suit and heels. She was not a tall girl, but the short skirt and the height of the heels made her appear to have legs for days. As soon as I had laid eyes on her, the visions that danced in my head were not sugar plums. I immediately looked away and could not make eye contact with her for a good ten minutes especially after shaking hands with her.

I shut those memories out of my head and denied that there was anything more to it when I replied to Beth's accusation.

"You do like her!" Beth was more adamant the second time around. "So, are you going to hire her or what? I have got to get going."

"I am not going to hire her. The members would eat her alive." Well, that's what I was told by the Port Honor office busy bodies: the secretary, accountant and the membership director. As soon as Amelia left they all aired their opinion that the husbands would love her and the wives would hate her. Not to mention, I likely needed to avoid her for my own selfish reasons, but mostly, I was just telling Beth what I wanted her to hear for the time being. No firm decision has been made as to whether or not I would hire Amelia.

"Good. Then that's settled. My ride is here and I need to go. Ciao, for now!" I could hardly say goodbye before I heard the receiver click on Beth's end of the line.

I continued on to the shower. The day had been long and every muscle in my body ached, but I could not shake the image of Amelia or the feeling I felt when we touched. I hung my head and let the water run over me. The water was hot and had a bit of a bite. The sting from it went no deeper than my skin, but it reminded me of the feeling I got each time I had touched the girl. From shaking hands with her to offering my arm to steady her as she put her shoes back on after working the pedals on the piano, that sting ran all the way to my core. I had never felt that before. It was quite a sensation.

I did not know much about Amelia Anderson from our one meeting, but I did know she was a sharp contrast to Beth Reed. Beth was tall and Amelia was nearly a foot shorter than I was. She looked so young and delicate and Beth was like a gale force wind, icy and driven.

I know the application asked for her date of birth, but I could not recall what was in that blank. I knew she was in college, but I really was puzzled as to how old she was. She was beautiful and, my God, what was wrong with me? There was just something about her.

That night I dreamt of her. The entire interview replayed in my dreams. I awoke the next morning with the image of her leaving so fresh, as if I had only just seen her. Her eyes were green and flakes of gold sparkled in them. I would guess that her hair was naturally straight. It was long, hanging down midway of her back, and it was thick. It appeared she had tried to curl it, but it fell in the heat. The color of it was not blond, but it was not brown either, it was something in between and what appeared to be natural highlights shown in the afternoon sun as she turned to look back at me one last time while walking to her car. And, the way the burgundy suit she had chosen for the interview fit her was just snug enough to accent her proportions. The best was her smile that gave away how striking she was and yet she was completely oblivious to that fact.

She had insisted on being called "Millie," but to get a rise out of her I had addressed her as Amelia as was listed as her given name on the application. In return, among her parting words she addressed me as "Gabriel" and no one had called me that since my mother. In the dream, her parting words were different and I awoke to those words. It was not the alarm clock that woke me, but the whisper of her words as if she were right there in the room with me, "Gabriel, did you feel it too?" I had felt it, whatever *it* was.

***

I passed the Greensboro exit on my way back from Siloam and dropping off Gabby with Mrs. Allen. I glanced in the rearview mirror back to where Gabby's car seat was sitting just a little while before. How different would all of our lives have been had I not made the call to Beth the night I met Amelia? How different would our lives be if I had not met Amelia? I would not trade Gabby for anything and I was done trading Amelia.

I continued on down I-20 toward Atlanta on my mission to find Amelia and the memories kept coming. One of my favorites came to mind next, the night on the front porch of her old apartment...

The whole night had been an error in judgment on my part, but it was as if I could hardly help myself. I had just entered the bar through the swinging door from the kitchen and I could hardly hear myself think from the squeaking and ringing back and forth of the door. As usual, I moved to still it when I overheard Andy bragging to one of the members at the other end of the bar.

"Guess who my little brother's going out with tonight?" Andy asked as he prepped the bar for the dinner shift.

"Do tell," the older man replied. He appeared to be a man of about sixty, salt and pepper gray hair, distinguished looking, but highly interested in Andy's gossip. His face had lit up with his response like a blue haired old lady seated in her local salon chair as opposed to a patron at the clubhouse bar at the golf course.

28

I did not recognize that particular member, but Andy had been there forever and knew everyone as well as their drink of choice. On one hand he was an asset, but on another he was just an ass.

"The piano player. Yeah, little bro will be the first here to tap that ass I suppose. Makes me proud and envious." Andy looked like the Cheshire cat as he held up the conversation and polished rocks glasses at the same time.

I did not know his brother, but my blood boiled at the thought of him being anything like Andy and laying a finger on Amelia. More to the point, my blood boiled at the thought of anyone laying a hand on her, but me. An image of Amelia from her interview came to mind and a shiver ran over me at the thought of her touch. I recalled first laying eyes on her and what thoughts ran through my mind and I cringed at the thought of anyone else thinking of her like that. Accompanying the attraction or pull I seemed to have toward her, there was this underlying need to protect her. Did she have that effect on everyone?

Since she had been hired, I had avoided Amelia and purposefully scheduled her for shifts that were opposite my own. I did this because I knew for me to give into the pull toward her was inappropriate as long as she worked at the club. I did my best to fight whatever it was that was drawing me to her, but the thought of her with someone else set off a feeling in me that I was unaccustomed to, jealousy.

Just as I was about to intervene in the conversation and put the kibosh on talking about co-workers as Andy was, another of the new servers came prancing into the bar. She did my work for me, ending the chatter with her drink order for the dining room patrons.

I had interviewed Cara three days after my interview with Amelia. Unlike Amelia, I hired Cara within moments of meeting her. In fact, I spent a fair portion of her interview rehashing my meeting with Amelia. It was as if I could not help myself. Cara did not seem to mind my rambling, but I fear I may have embarrassed myself.

"I need a Dewar's and water and a glass of Fetzer Sundial Chardonnay. Thanks!" Cara said to Andy as she laid down the ticket for the order on the bar in front of him. She cut her eyes at the gentleman to whom Andy had been gossiping. Without saying it aloud she told him to put his eyes back in his head.

Andy rolled his eyes at her interruption, but made the drinks all the same. I continued to watch and go unnoticed until Cara mentioned that we should all go to Cameron's after work. Cameron's was a college bar in Milledgeville. Although I was not in college, I had been with the crew a couple of times.

"Count me in Cara. Why don't you call Millie and see if she would like to meet us there? I will get you her number." I said to Cara who had already mentioned to me that she met Amelia in the parking lot on her way in that afternoon.

Cara agreed to call Amelia before leaving the bar with the drink order.

Andy failed to realize that I had heard his conversation or think that I noticed when he shot a look at the member. While Cara exited the bar back into the dining room, I proceeded to the end of the bar and introduced myself to the man with whom Andy had been chatting. "I am Gabe Hewitt. I don't believe we have met."

I offered my hand and the man took it. "Harry McMillan," he replied as he shook my hand.

"Good to meet you, Mr. McMillan," I replied before turning my attention to Andy. "Will you be joining us at Cameron's tonight?"

Again, Andy shot a look at Mr. McMillan while handing him another drink and responding to me. "Sure. Count me in."

"Great. Well, y'all will have to excuse me. I need to get that number for Cara," and I turned and left for the kitchen.

It was not long after giving the number to Cara that she returned and explained that she had gotten the answering machine. Despite only being able to leave a message, Cara relayed confidence in her opinion that Amelia would likely meet us at Cameron's. I relied on that confidence and continued with my plan to go to Cameron's with hopes of seeing Amelia.

While Andy and Cara locked up I went home, showered and changed. I returned to the club and followed the two of them to Milledgeville. We had agreed to meet at the bar at 11:00 p.m., but I went ahead and hung out at Andy and Matt's apartment while they got ready. Their apartment was within walking distance of the bar and the three of us set out on foot about five minutes 'til eleven and arrived there about five after. We found Cara waiting on the sidewalk outside of Cameron's. She was being ogled at by every guy that passed, and although they did not pass, Matt and Andy joined in the ogling. Cara was dressed in jeans and a red tube top that left little to the imagination.

Upon opening the door to the bar, the smell of cigarette smoke hit us like a ton of bricks. Smoking had never been my thing so, I am sure if anyone noticed my face, I appeared put off by the smell. I had been to that bar about three times prior to that and it was always dark, smoky and loud. This particular night was no different. It was dimly lit by a disco ball, a dozen or so neon beer signs and a few candles placed here and there. The floor was tacky and every step I took I struggled not to leave my shoe fixed to the floor. It was a typical college bar.

I stopped just inside the door. There was a cover band playing Jimmy Buffett songs and I could see them from where I was standing, but I could not see Amelia anywhere in the crowd.

"Gabriel, come to the stage with us?" Cara asked me while trying to take my hand and pull me with her.

I eased my hand from hers. "I think I'm going to grab a drink at the bar. I'll come find y'all in just a bit."

"Okay. Suit yourself." No sooner had the words left her mouth did Cara bounce away into the crowd.

I found a seat among all of the college kids at the bar. The bar was packed and the two bartenders were working feverishly to attend every raised hand and yell in their direction. It took about five minutes, but I finally managed to get the attention of one of them. I ordered a shot of Jose Cuervo Gold. I downed the shot as the bartender sat another drink in front of me. The drink was pink and fru-fru looking and all that was lacking was an umbrella. It was not at all something I would order for myself and my face likely told that story.

"It's a pink panty dropper." I looked at the heavily pierced bartender almost sideways at the name of the drink. She continued, "It's from the girl four seats down."

I could not recall ever having a drink purchased for me and was shocked to look down the bar to see Amelia precisely four seats down from me. I suppose Andy was wrong about his brother and Amelia since here she was sending me drinks at the bar. I know it would have been wise to refuse the drink, but what man in their right mind would have refused anything called a pink panty dropper from someone that looked like her? Especially from one that smiled in their direction the way she had just smiled at me?

What was it in her smile that gave the impression that the whole world would go dark if she stopped? It wasn't that she gave a wide, white toothy grin that caught and reflected light. She hardly opened her mouth at all. The light came from her eyes and coupled with her dimples they were the perfect combination of cute, sweet and sexy.

Sexiness exuded from her and she had not the faintest idea. From where I had been seated, I could hardly see what she was wearing. My heart fluttered at the sight of her face. Amelia was utterly irresistible to me and I was a dog. The images of having her rushed my mind and like everything else that pertained to my thoughts and actions regarding her, I could not help myself.

I did not send the drink back. In fact, I left my seat and headed in her direction. There was a bit of banter back and forth. I toyed with her, teasing her when she told me her roommate had bought the drink for me and I headed toward the very tall, dark haired girl that was giving Amelia the thumbs up from the dance floor. The toying ended when she reached for my hand and pulled me back.

It was when I turned back to her that I got the full view of what she was wearing. As soon as our hands touched that shiver, or explosion or whatever it was, went all the way through me. It begged the question, how could I get chills and a shock just from her touch?

32

I think she felt it too since she trembled a little and almost recoiled. Instead, she gripped my hand a little tighter and with her other hand she brushed her hair back over her shoulders and appeared to shrug off the sting of whatever that fascinating feeling was.

Her hair had been long and flowing and wrapped around her neck falling to cover her chest. With her hair brushed back, Amelia's shoulders were bare except for the tiny white straps of her tank top and her tank top was so tight that it hugged her every curve. I envied that tank top.

I ended up paying the lush sitting next to her twenty dollars for his stool. I wanted to be near her, to have her attention, to impress her. She said I could have had the seat for less. She was right. I could have had the seat for free if I had just bowed up at the smarmy little drunk. He was hardly the size of Amelia and I could have sent him scurrying with little effort, but I wasn't sure how that would have gone over with her. Some girls are impressed with the flexing of a little muscle. Others are impressed with the flexing of a little cash. I still could not read which would work on her, but what she could not read about me was that I would have paid more, quadruple that if the dude had refused the twenty.

I ordered another round of drinks for us. A Coke for Amelia and another pink panty dropper for me. I offered her a sip of mine and she took it. Everything about her was a turn on including the lack of inhibition she had for drinking after me. She tried to hide it, but she was clearly unaccustomed to the burn of alcohol.

As we started to nurse our drinks, I could not help but inquire as to how the date had gone. "So, I heard you had a date tonight. It could not have gone well since here you are here with your roommate."

Amelia's eyes lit up as if she were embarrassed that I knew about her outing. "It was just dinner with some new friends." She tried to assure me. I believed her because if it had been a date surely he would have been here with her and he wasn't. I was.

"So you won't be going out with Andy's brother again?" I am not sure how well I hid the fact that I was pleased.

33

I could recount the entire conversation from her reasons as to why she would not be going out with Andy's brother again to when she asked me about my girlfriend. It appeared even then she knew about Beth. I should have taken that point in the conversation as a sign and excused myself, went back to avoiding her right then, but I just couldn't. My will was not my own around her.

We talked and talked that night as if we had known each other for years. There was hardly a moment when our hands were not joined. I often caught myself stroking circles on the back of her hand with my thumb. I tried to stop it by interlocking our fingers. I could not explain it, but letting down my guard was easy with her and that in itself made me nervous. The conversations with Amelia that night were the most emotionally intimate I had ever had with another human.

It was nearly 1:30 a.m. when I noticed the time.

"Do you have a way home?" I asked her.

"Our apartment is right around the corner and I can walk."

"Your roommate left about twenty minutes ago, remember? I can't let you walk home alone." Shit, I had just offered to walk her home. Dare I kiss her? Lord knows I wanted to and more. The night had already been perfect just holding her hand and I know I sounded like such a girl just thinking that way.

In the glow of the street lights, I got a full view of what Amelia was wearing. The jeans she had on were ripped here and there, but the rip that caught my eye was the one running just under her ass cheek. I could see skin as plain as day where I should have seen underpants. Surely she had on underpants, perhaps a thong.

The night air was cool and I could see chills on her shoulders as soon as we stepped out onto the sidewalk. I was so distracted by the thought of her underwear or lack thereof that it took me a few minutes of walking with her to calm down enough to offer an arm around her to stave off the chill bumps. It had been all I could do not to pull her close, kiss her and run a hand across to search for the line of panties.

Her apartment really was only about a block from Cameron's and the walk was not nearly long enough. I would have walked to Macon with this girl, but at the same time, reality started to set in again. I was her boss and all of this was highly inappropriate.

I stopped shy of the steps and let go of her hand. Amelia continued to the stoop before turning back to me. "Goodnight and thanks for walking me home. I had a great time tonight."

There was an awkward pause while I continued to fight the urge to kiss her and decide how to tell her goodnight; with words or with a hug and words. I told myself it was alright to hug her. That would be enough for me, just to hug her once. Friends hug and we could be friends and work together.

I stepped forward and leaned down a bit to her. She stood on her toes to reciprocate. With hands at the small of her back I pulled her close, probably a little closer than a friend hug, but through the smell of cigarette smoke from the bar there was still a hint of strawberries. With a whiff, resisting a kiss became more challenging.

I moved my hand from her back up to her hair. I just had to touch her hair. Run my fingers through it just once. I buried my face in her hair. I said it aloud, but in a whisper, "I'm not going to kiss you."

I could feel Amelia sigh against me. Were my words as disappointing to her as they were to me? I took hold of her hair in my hand and gave a gentle tug tilting her head back as I removed my face from where it had been resting. I looked her in the eye, but had to break the connection or I would give in.

I said it again as I dropped my face and ran my nose gently against her neck, "I am not going to kiss you tonight because if we start, I won't stop."

Amelia pressed herself into me. She was so tiny up next to me and so hot. I turned my face and slid my nose across her skin to the far end of her shoulder and I continued to whisper, "I would kiss you here and here and here and here."

35

I wonder if I did the things to her that she was doing to me. I had never seduced anyone without seducing them before, but from the heat coming off her skin, this technique was working even though it could not go anywhere. I was not saying the words just to hear myself talk; I was saying them to tell the both of us that this could go nowhere.

"I am not going to kiss you tonight, but if I did..." I paused before pointing out each and every spot I would kiss on her.

Amelia went weak beneath my touch. I could feel her every breath as she held on tight around my neck, digging her fingers in. Some sort of instinct took hold of me and I remembered the rip in the indecent jeans. I had been making circles with my fingertips on the small of her back, but I inched down from her back to her hip and down farther until I found bare skin. Through the rip, I felt the crease where the back of her leg began. Amelia gasped ever so slightly and tightened her grip around me.

I whispered to her again and pulled her tighter to me while I stroked that spot, "And here."

She then surprised me as much as I had surprised her when I stroked the skin through the rip of her jeans. Amelia transferred her weight to one foot and balanced as she slid her leg up mine. I was on fire for her.

"So I am not going to kiss you tonight. Do you understand?"

"Yes," she panted breathlessly. My God, I wanted her, but I wanted to keep my job uncomplicated, too.

"If we ever kiss, I will ask your permission first, Amelia." I began to loosen my hold on her and as I did, Amelia ran her hands up my neck and just into my hair.

"You smell like heaven," she said and I almost snickered until I felt her lips graze my neck.

I replied as if telling her a secret, "You still smell like strawberries."

I looked her in the face and that feeling, like ringing a bat, but in a good way, was there all through the hugging incident. This was torturous and maddening and exhilarating all at once.

This time I spoke to her directly, looking her in the eye. "I am not going to kiss you tonight and we are not going to talk about this at work. We are not going to talk about this at all. Do you understand?"

She looked down as if she was disappointed, but I needed her to answer. I asked again, more serious, "Do you understand?"

"Yes," she whispered.

"I am going to release you now." I looked down at her and I could see that every inch of her skin that was bare from her chin, down her neck to her chest and the top of the tank top was on fire with hives.

We stood in silence for a while before I broke the silence, "Amelia, you know this is wildly inappropriate and that's why we can't do this."

She was coy with me. "All we did was hug."

"We are going to pretend this did not happen." I wanted to be clear.

"If you insist." She dropped my hands and started fishing in her pocket for her keys. Was I reading her right? Was she disappointed? Oh, I did not want to ever to do that, but this was trouble.

"I do insist. Now goodnight, Amelia, and I will see you at work."

"Goodnight, Gabriel. Thanks for walking me home." And then she turned to go in the front door of the house.

I continued to watch as she started toward the door. I couldn't help but notice those jeans were perfect. I did not want the night to end on a sour note. I knew what I had just said to her, but that did not mean I did not want her to think about me, dream about me. I knew I had no right, but I said it anyway. I gave her another slap on her ass and teased her, "Don't let me catch you in public with those jeans on again, young lady." In all honesty, I did not want anyone else to see her the way I did.

The smack stung my hand as much as it stung her rear and she jumped and backed the rest of the way through the door. I waited for her to get inside before I took my leave. Once Amelia was safely inside the door of the old house that held her apartment somewhere inside, I made my way back across the yard.

It was nearly 2:00 a.m. when I passed beneath the limbs of the pecan tree at the corner of Amelia's yard and continued on to the sidewalk. Under the street lamp, I glanced back once more. I am not sure what I expected to see. Perhaps I was just taking one last mental picture of the night. When I glanced back, through an upstairs window, I saw a light pop on.

I could see her only in shadow form, but it was most definitely Amelia. It looked as if she was changing clothes; first pulling the tank top over her head and then I looked away. I shook off the urge to run back, throw caution to the wind and finish what I had told her to forget.

My attention was immediately pulled away as a truck with a multitude of college girls riding in the bed pulled up along the curb near me. I turned to get a look at the commotion just as one of the girls leaned over the side and threw up as the others giggled at her misfortune. There was nothing like the sight of a girl vomiting to kill a mood. I guess that was exactly what I needed.

As soon as the girl was back up right, they sped away and I came to my senses. I began my walk back through the streets of downtown Milledgeville to my car. I was satisfied and somewhat thrilled to know that my attraction to Amelia was not a one way street. Unfortunately, there was nothing to be done with that knowledge.

\*\*\*

Crossing the I-20 bridge over Lake Oconee, I barely noticed the lights from houses shimmering across the lake from the Morgan

38

County side. I continued driving at breakneck speeds, pushing the Acura Legend to its limits. This was most certainly the fastest I had ever driven the car, perhaps the fastest I had ever driven any car. I noticed at least twice that the needle on the speedometer had pegged out, before I backed off on the gas. The Legend showed no signs of strain at those speeds. It was as smooth of a ride as ever and gave off no sounds beyond those from the radio. Neither noise nor tail lights of the few cars I sped past distracted me from my thoughts or my mission.

All in all it had only been about twenty minutes since I had dropped off Gabby with Mrs. Allen, but it seemed like time was standing still. I squirmed in my seat. I was restless and anxious at how long it seemed to be taking to get to Atlanta.

The memories kept coming as the miles drug on.

CHAPTER 3

The point where the Atlanta skyline becomes visible when traveling on I-20 from the east was just as one topped the hill right before the intersection with I-285. Dawn was yet to break, but the Westin Peachtree Plaza hotel was within sight. I had first started looking for the hotel, the lights around the rim at the top of the cylindrical building, as soon as the cityscape became visible.

The Westin was just another of Atlanta's many landmarks and it was still at least twenty minutes away. The hotel stood out as one of the tallest buildings in the city and had once been the tallest, but that claim to fame had since passed. It remained known for the revolving Sun Dial restaurant that occupied the top floors. One floor of the restaurant made a rotation every sixty minutes and another floor made it in thirty minutes. I knew all of this because Beth's parents had thrown her a twenty-fifth birthday party there and flown me in for the occasion.

As much as I could while driving, I kept my eyes on the lights in the sky. More memories played in my head and I remembered the night at the Georgian Terrace with Amelia. The way she charmed Mrs. Von Bremen and the other wives was priceless. From her soft southern accent, to the way her hair hung in ringlet curls down her back and the grace with which she moved, she mesmerized them with all that a modern Southern Belle was.

For one of our stay-at-home dates, Amelia planned a night of watching Gone With the Wind. Neither of us had seen it in its entirety and it was her opinion that one was not a true Southerner until they had watched the movie start to finish. We were now true Southerners by her standard.

Even before we watched the movie together, Amelia was well versed in quotes from various scenes beyond that of Rhett Butler's most famous line. My personal favorite was when she mocked Jerry about how his waist must be eighteen inches again and enlisted Daniel to reenact the entire scene of Mammy helping Scarlett get into her dress for the bar-b-que at Twelve Oaks.

"You are no Scarlett O'Hara," Jerry huffed with embarrassment.

Amelia responded without a specific quote, but still within the context of the movie, something to the effect of him being jealous and an old maid.

After seeing the movie, I could understand the draw of Mrs. Von Bremen to Amelia. She was a combination of the characters of Scarlett O'Hara and Melanie Wilkes. It was as if her grandfather and her aunt had used the book and the movie as a how-to guide to raising the perfect combination of sweet and feisty.

This was not the first time memories flooded my mind of Amelia. There had not been a day since our break that I had not thought of her. On a daily basis I missed the way she made me laugh, the way she made others laugh, the way she laughed. I missed everything about her.

The nervousness of what I might be in for today was beginning to return as I pulled onto Peachtree Street and began looking for the entrance to the parking garage at the Westin Peachtree Plaza Hotel. There was no use trying to use the skyline as my guide. At that point, I had to keep an eye out for the sign on the outside of the building.

The Westin sat at the intersection of Peachtree Street and Andrew Young International Boulevard and for once the grid system of one way streets on which Atlanta was laid worked to my advantage. I did not have to over shoot the building by two blocks and come back around. I was able to turn onto Andrew Young International at the traffic light and the entrance to the hotel's parking garage was right there.

I pulled through the garage, palms sweaty and white knuckling the steering wheel all the while. The garage was dimly lit and packed. Round and round I crept along passing by what seemed like a thousand spaces, all full. There were tags on cars from all around the country and a few from Mexico and Canada. Undoubtedly, the hotel was filled to capacity with guests in town for the Olympics.

I was beginning to think this was going to be yet another sign of how difficult the day was going to be when parking took this much effort. Just as I was making the turn toward the exit I spotted a black town car with Texas plates backing out. I whipped into the spot and let out a deep breath, gathered my nerves and opened the car door. I braced myself for how I might find Cara.

The elevators from the garage to the lobby were clear across the lot from where I had parked. I picked up my stride while making my way up the incline back toward the elevator. Once at the elevator, I pressed the up button and waited impatiently for the car to return. When the doors opened I jumped on and when the doors opened again I jumped off like Pavlov's dog at the ringing of the bell. I quickly noticed I was still in the parking deck, just on a higher level. I turned to get back on only to find the doors closing with the two Japanese looking tourists that had entered as I had exited the elevator. They were staring back at me.

I called up what little of the language I knew from my days of being stationed in Osaka, Japan, while in the Navy. I did my best to ask them to stop, but it had been so long that God only knows what I said. From the looks on their faces, whatever it was, it was either offensive or frightening. Either way, the doors closed in my face as the two tourists took a step back toward the back wall of the elevator.

Feverishly, I pressed the button for the elevator to return. I paced in front of the series of three doors while I waited. I looked at my watch, the Rolex that Amelia had given me for Christmas. I had not taken it off since the moment I unwrapped it. It was not only the most expensive gift I had ever received, but the most thoughtful as well.

Despite its age, the Rolex kept time like a champ. According to it, it took five minutes for the next elevator to return and in those five minutes I had recounted every moment of Christmas with Amelia and her family. I would have never expected things to have turned out like this. I had never felt family like that before or the feeling of belonging as I did when I was with them. Now, I worried that I had lost everything.

When the doors of the elevator opened, I nearly ran over two uniformed hotel workers as they were exiting. In passing them, I had the presence of mind to ask which floor was the main lobby.

"Get off on the next floor up," the male employee said as the female waited a few steps away.

"Thanks man," I called to him as the doors were closing.

Within moments I had found the lobby of the Westin and began my hunt for Cara. I exited the elevators and had already forgotten which way the staff member had told me to go. I was not worried since from the hallway that contained the elevators I could see a gift shop at one end and what was likely the lobby at the other.

At the end of the hallway where it opened up to the lobby, I looked around to take it all in. There was swag for the Olympics everywhere. Had I been there under different circumstances I would likely have made mental notes of everything in the hotel and compared it to the inn at Port Honor. As it was, I was in such a daze that I hardly noticed anything at all.

Had I continued straight out of the hallway I could have run into a set of escalators leading to and from the next floor. From my vantage point I could see another set of escalators on the next floor up that led to another floor. I looked to the right and there was a series of attendants for guests to check in and out. Only one of the clerks was occupied with guests. I could not see Cara anywhere so I continued my harried hunt.

To my right I could see a few areas for guests to sit and lounge or wait. I could not see Cara in any of those waiting areas. I decided to walk to the left. The building was shaped like a circle, so I would just keep going around and surely at some point I would find her.

The most noticeable thing on the left side of the lobby was the booming business that Starbucks Coffee was doing even though it was still only 5:00 a.m. As soon as I saw the Starbucks I spotted Cara slumped over on the arm of one of the chairs. I was surprised to see her asleep and amazed that she had not been asked to leave.

43

I had not ever seen her without her make-up or in any sort of disarray, so this was a first. Cara looked as though she had been through the ringer. Even though she was asleep, as I approached her I could see her make-up was streaked down her face from crying. If waking her had not been absolutely necessary, I would have just left her to sleep.

"Cara," I said her name barely above a whisper and gently touched her, but she was startled all the same.

Cara gasped and jumped to her feet so quickly that I scarcely had time to stand back up to avoid our heads crashing together. She did not have to say anything. I could tell she was exhausted, utterly spent from the events of the night. No sooner had she regained her breath from the fright of waking up disoriented did she fall into my arms and sob uncontrollably. It was difficult to understand her through her gasping as she gave one apology after another for having lost Amelia, for having not been able to stay with her or get her help.

"I am so sorry, Gabe. It was my idea to go to Centennial Park. If we had just gone home...I am so sorry." What was I to do but hold her and stroke the top of her head and try to comfort her as she cried? She had to get it out of her system or she would be no good to me, Amelia or herself.

"No one blames you," I assured her as I continued to run my hand down the back of her hair. "I know Amelia wouldn't want you to blame yourself. I am sure everything is going to be fine. We are going to find her and you'll see."

It took about ten minutes before Cara started to ease up on the crying and get a hold of herself. In that time several guests as well as a couple of the Westin employees approached us to see if she was alright or if we needed assistance. The last person to speak to us was a member of hotel security.

No one else had bothered to ask, but the officer did. In a no-nonsense voice he asked, "Is that blood on her?"

The officer was a dark man with a deep voice. His name tag said Anthony. Anthony was a really big dude, about six inches taller than I was with broad shoulders. His body language and the way he

44

carried himself suggested that he was not a man to be messed with. I became a little nervous just at his question. I hoped he did not think I had done something to her to put her in this state. That would just be the cherry on top of the way my day was going.

Before I could really get my back up, Cara eased her head from my chest and looked at her hands. "It's Millie's blood," Cara uttered through her sniffing to clear her nose and held out her hands for me to see.

She shook her head and a few tears continued to stream down her face, "I hadn't noticed before."

The officer looked on as my heart sank at the sight, so much blood. Cara's palms and fingers were completely stained. They appeared the color of rust as the blood had dried in the hours since she had last seen Amelia. She started rubbing her hands together feverishly as if she were trying to wash it off without soap or water.

My view expanded to take in the whole picture of Cara. The blood stains were not just limited to her hands. There were spots of it on her pink T-shirt, several of substantial size. There were also a couple of streaks of mud and blood and patches of grass stains on the shirt as well. The overall picture was as if Cara had been run over and drug for a distance.

Anthony leaned in as if to look Cara over to make sure she was not injured. While looking her over, he began to question, "Millie is your friend? Where is she now?"

I was in a bit of shock, still staring at the volume of blood on Cara. I had heard on the radio that a multitude of people had been injured. I tried to convince myself that it was not just Amelia's blood all over her. She had told me over the phone that they had been separated in what I understood to be a stampede of panicked people who were running for their lives. I know it sounds cruel to even think it, but maybe not all of this was Amelia's blood. It could be the blood of others that were injured and crossed paths with Cara.

Doe eyed, Cara answered Anthony, "We were at Centennial Park when the bomb went off. She is my friend and she got hit by..."

she paused. "I don't know what she got hit by, but she fell and I tried to hang on to her, but..."

I interrupted, "They got separated right after the bombing and now we have to find," and for the second time in the last twenty-four hours I referred to her as "Millie." There was no sense in confusing the officer.

"Are you two guests here at the hotel?" he continued with questions as other patrons, especially those visiting the Starbucks, passed by us and gave Cara a good looking over.

"No sir," I answered as I began glancing around for signs of a restroom where we could get Cara cleaned up. She was still rubbing her hands, but getting nowhere.

"I cannot have y'all standing around in here with her looking like this." I was certain he was politely asking us to leave.

"We were just going," I said as I put an arm around Cara and took a step leading her. We needed to get on with the task at hand anyway, finding Amelia.

"Wait a minute man. I'm not kicking you out." Anthony explained as he moved to block us. "I am retired APD..."

I knew exactly what he meant, but Cara asked, "What is APD?"

"Atlanta Police Department. I had twenty-three years with them before retiring. I still have some contacts on the force." Anthony held out his arm and gestured as if to escort us. "They have given us security officers courtesy rooms for the duration of the Olympics. Y'all can use my room while I make some calls."

I reached out and offered my hand. "Thank you so much! I don't know how we'll ever repay you, but I will try to find a way," I said to him as I shook his hand. This was certainly generous of him and the very definition of a Good Samaritan. Cara joined in with thanking him and not satisfied with just a handshake, she gave him a giant hug as best she could to the nearly six foot seven man.

Anthony led us back to the elevators and pressed the button. "What's your friend's name?" he asked.

I answered, "Most everyone calls her Millie, but her given name is Amelia Jane Anderson. That's what's on her driver's license."

All of a sudden, Cara started searching her pockets. She snatched a driver's license from her back left pocket and stated, "Shit! Shit! Shit! If she were at a hospital, they could not identify her. She did not have pockets in her shorts so she gave me her ID and cash to keep for her. How will we find her now?"

"May I see that?" Cara responded to Anthony's request by handing him the license.

While we waited, Anthony began to question Cara as to where she had last seen Amelia, what she was wearing.

"She had gotten wet by the fountains so she bought a souvenir shirt and put that on. I can't remember whether it was purple or hot pink." It appeared as though she were going to go hysterical again as she tried to remember. "I just cannot remember, I'm so sorry. I know it has Izzy on it. And khaki shorts. She had on khaki shorts."

"That's okay; it was a hot pink or purple shirt that had the Olympic mascot on it. That's good. Now tell me what your friend looked like." He tried to encourage her to keep her calm and it was working. He turned Amelia's ID back to Cara and showed it to her. "Has her appearance changed or is she the same as she was in this picture?"

I wanted to take over for Cara and describe Amelia, but what did I know? I had not seen her in three months and that was a truth that jarred me. She could have cut her hair, colored it or any number of things that girls do and I had no idea. I shook off the depressive thoughts and did my best anyway.

"She is about five foot five inches tall and probably weighs about a hundred and five pounds," I began.

47

Cara cut me off, "She has gained a little weight. She probably weighs about one fifteen. Her hair is long, and a dark blonde, some might consider it light brown."

The elevator doors opened on the twenty-fifth floor and Anthony escorted us out. "To the left a little ways, room 2510."

As we continued down the hall toward the room, I picked up on Amelia's description when Cara stopped to take a breath. "She has blue-ish green eyes."

"Right," Cara agreed. "And I last saw her near the sound stage where Jack Mack was playing. It all happened so fast. I tried to get back to her, but by the time I got free of the crowd the police were swarming. I could not see her, I could not find her and they would not let me back near the stage."

Cara searched our faces for understanding, confirmation that we believed her, "I promise I went back for her."

Anthony stopped just shy of room 2510 and spoke plainly to Cara, "You need to accept there was nothing you could do then. Neither you nor anyone else in the area could have known for sure that there was not another bomb or something in the area. There was nothing you could do for her. You are doing what you can now and that counts for something. I will help y'all find your friend."

When he finished speaking, Anthony opened the door and allowed us into the room. It was neat and tidy. What appeared to be his civilian clothes were folded and lying on a chair. Even though he apologized for the condition as if it were a pig sty, it was clean, like eat off the floor clean.

Cara and I stopped just inside of the doorway. I suppose she felt the same as I did, as if we did not know what to do with ourselves.

"The washroom is over there," and he pointed to the door to the left. "I am going to leave you and go back downstairs. I am going to make some calls and I will be back in just a little while."

Cara started toward the restroom, but I could not help asking. "You are just going to trust us with your room?"

48

"You parked in the garage here right?" he asked.

"Yes."

"First of all there's nothing in here of value, second there are video cameras that see every inch of this building except in this room. If you parked in the deck I can have your tag number with the flick of my wrist and 300 photos of your face from the time you exited your car until you entered this door and more when you leave. So, there's nothing to take and before you could make it back to your car, I would know your life's history. And, third, you have on a Navy shirt. You serve?"

"Served in the Navy, yeah," I replied, glancing down at the anchor and emblem on my shirt.

"Right. And you look to be about the age to have served during Desert Storm?"

"I was in during that time period.

I was still a bit confused about where this conversation was headed until he extended his hand, "I would like to thank you for your service."

No one had ever thanked me for my service before. I felt the need to clarify my position in the Navy as I was no hero. "Thank you for saying so, but my service in Desert Storm amounted to being the pastry chef to the Admiral on the Aegis cruiser USS San Jacinto in the Red Sea."

"You were stationed on the ship that fired the first Tomahawk missile on Iraq?" He took off his cap and scratched his head. "That in itself is something to talk about."

That was not a piece of war trivia that the average person knew. It was beginning to dawn on me that Anthony might have been a fellow Navy brother. "Are you a brother?"

"More like a cousin," he replied. "I was a Marine reservist."

"Did you see action in the war?"

49

"Nope.  Discharged just shy of catching a ride to the action from you Navy boys due to a knee injury while playing football in the yard with my son.  I was in the reserves and then I wasn't."

"Oh, sorry about that.  And your knee is fine now?"

"It's good enough.  Thanks for asking.  Now, let's find that girl of yours.  So, I am going to go and make some calls.  You can lie on the bed, watch some TV, use the phone in here, whatever.  I don't think you'll make me regret helping you, will you?"

"No, sir."

"Alright then.  I'll be back in a little bit."

As the door closed behind him, Cara stuck her head out from the restroom.  "Do you think he would mind if I took a shower?  Do you think I have time?"

"I don't think he'll mind and I'm sure we have time."  I flopped back on the bed as I replied to Cara.

As soon as my head hit the pillow it occurred to me all of the calls I needed to make.  I sat up immediately and made one call after another.  First, I called Alvin to make sure he could handle the brunch shift without me.  I called Joan to let her know where I was and what had happened to Amelia as best I knew at that point.  I called Daniel and asked him if he would mind picking up Gabby from Mrs. Allen once he got off from working at the club.  Everyone was agreeable and very concerned about Amelia.  Daniel even agreed to stay over with Gabby if I needed him to.  I also called Mrs. Allen to check on Gabby and let her know that Daniel would be picking her up that afternoon.

My last phone call was to Amelia's aunt.  The phone did not even fully ring before she snatched it from its receiver.  It appeared she might have been sitting directly on top of it when it rang.  I suppose if I were waiting at home on word as she was, I would have been attached to the phone as well.

"Gabriel?!!" Gayle shrieked.

"Gayle, I haven't found her yet," I said as calmly as I could, hoping her tone would mirror mine.

I barely finished that statement when she cried out. "Dear God, where is she?!!" My tone had no effect on her.

I stood and paced as I continued to tell her what little progress I had made in finding her niece. Back and forth in front of the floor to ceiling windows I went. On any other occasion, I probably would have noticed the incredible view of the city that the hotel had to offer, but this particular moment nothing about the room or the view caught my attention.

"The good news is that I found Cara and someone that can help us find Amelia." I explained about Anthony and that he had allowed us to use his room while he tried to use his contacts to give us a start on finding Amelia.

"I have called all of the hospitals, but no one by her name has been admitted. Tell me what else I can do to help find her. I can't just sit here and do nothing." Gayle was understandably beside herself.

"Pray," I beseeched her. I dared not tell her the volume of blood Cara was currently washing off. I just knew that if that was only Amelia's blood on her, we would need all of the prayers we could get.

"You think it's bad, don't you?" I could hear in her voice that she did not want an honest answer.

"Let's not jump to conclusions. I'll call you as soon as I have something more to tell. In the meantime, would you mind continuing to try to reach Jay? I'm sure he would want to know. I am going to go now."

Cara must have heard me get off of the phone because it seemed like as soon as I said "Goodbye" to Gayle, Cara stuck her head out of the bathroom door.

"Are you wearing an undershirt?" She asked and it seemed like a strange question until she began to elaborate. "I don't want to put this shirt back on with all of the blood on it. I want to throw it away, but I don't have anything else to wear."

Cara was not even finished asking when I stripped out of my shirts and gave her my white undershirt. With that came another memory of Amelia. I blinked and behind my eyelids I saw Amelia in nothing but my undershirt the night we came back from The Georgian Terrace and she slept in my guest room. I had wanted to kiss her that night more than I had ever wanted to kiss anyone. I wanted to taste her lips on mine and bury my face in her hair. Her hair always smelled like a field of strawberries just waiting to be picked. Again my heart broke at the thought that I had let her go. I should have fought harder for her.

I was brought back to reality when Cara thanked me for the shirt. "I wonder how much longer Anthony is going to be?" Cara said as she re-entered the room fresh faced; same jean shorts, but wearing my white t-shirt and looking more like herself.

"I don't know. I'm sure he'll be back any second."

It wasn't much longer before Anthony opened the door and nearly filled the whole frame. I had let Cara have the bed and I had taken the arm chair. We both leapt to our feet at the sight of him.

"Did you find her?" Cara asked as I was opening my mouth to do the same.

"Not quite, but there are two unidentified Caucasian girls that match her description. One was admitted at Atlanta Medical Center and one at Grady. You will have to go to the hospitals to confirm if either of them are your friend. The bright spot is that we have narrowed this down to two of the ten or more hospitals around the city. The not so bright spot... "

"Is that people don't go to Grady who just have some scrapes and cuts," I interjected as I started to pace again.

Cara grabbed my arm forcing me to turn in her direction, "Yeah, but she could be at Atlanta Medical, so let's go find out."

I thanked Anthony profusely for all that he had done to help us. We swapped phone numbers and I insisted he call me the next time he had a weekend off.  I promised that I would treat him and a guest to a mini vacation at the inn at Port Honor and all they could eat at the clubhouse.  I also told him that as long as I worked there, his money was no good.

Amelia once told me that she knew as soon as she met Cara that they were going to be the best of friends. I did not understand at the time, but now I did.  I knew how she felt because that is exactly the same way I felt about Anthony.  I had only met him an hour ago, but I knew I had made a friend for life.

Anthony walked us all the way to my car in the parking garage  He gave us directions to Atlanta Medical Center and Grady along the way. "Go to Atlanta Medical Center first and if you don't find her then go to Grady.  Good luck and you call and let me know when you find her.  I hope she knows what a lucky girl she is that y'all are looking for her."

Both Cara and I shook Anthony's hand and thanked him again before we got in the car.

***

I found the exit to the parking garage of the Westin with little effort since I was right at it when I had finally found a parking spot. I was well onto Peachtree Street before Cara spoke.

"Do you think we should even bother with going to Atlanta Medical Center or should we go straight to Grady?"  Cara stared out of the passenger side window as she uttered her question.

I just looked at her until she finally turned to me.  "I know there was a lot of blood on me from Millie and I know the reputation Grady has for trauma.  I also know you don't want to hear it, but I think we should try there first."

I finally replied, "I think you are right."

We continued to ride in silence until again Cara initiated the conversation.  "You didn't happen to bring a photo of Millie with you?  I know we have the one on her driver's license, but you know how those are. They are always the worst picture of the person ever. It doesn't even look like her."

"Shit! I didn't think to," I banged my head on the steering wheel, feeling so stupid. Then it occurred to me. "There's one in the glove box."

Quickly Cara opened the glove box and pulled out the small framed photo of Amelia and me from her twenty-first birthday party. Cara turned the photo to me and for the first time that morning I saw her smile.

"Score!" she said.

As I glanced at Cara, I also glanced at the photo. That was taken the night I finally gave into the temptation to kiss Amelia. It was the night of her twenty-first birthday party. Amelia gave me the photo a week after the party and I had kept it on my desk at work until just recently when Beth saw it and threw it in the trash. I retrieved it from the trash and put it in the glove box of my car for safekeeping. There's no way I would have ever thrown that photo away. It was one of the few I had of us together.

Upon sight of the photo, I could feel Amelia against me again and I was back in that moment. I remembered thinking about kissing her from the moment she answered the door wearing that red dress until she returned me to that spot at the end of the night. In all honesty, I had thought of kissing her from the moment I had laid eyes on her at the club the day of her interview.

There was a tight foyer just inside the building that Amelia and Cara lived in. The foyer held three doors in addition to the main door into the building. It was in that foyer, as Amelia was walking me out at the end of the night that I kissed her. I warned her I would ask permission and I did. In the seconds between asking and receiving her answer, I said the first prayer I had said in years. I asked the Lord to please let me have just one kiss from her. Both my request and prayer were quickly answered.

Gently, I pulled her close to me and I leaned into her. For a moment I just looked at her. She was the most beautiful girl I had ever seen. The kind of girl that was beautiful without trying. Her eyes were greener that particular night than I had noticed before and her hair fell in wisps near her cheek bones. She was so lovely that I could not imagine that I had resisted the pull to her this long.

I eased one of my hands around her face and she leaned into my touch. Her skin was so soft. I closed my eyes and inhaled deeply in anticipation of what was coming. Finally, my lips met hers. My heart pounded and I was terrified she was going to notice. I could actually feel it beating in my ears, but that did not distract me. What was it about her that made this the kiss of my lifetime?

Deeply, madly, passionately, I kissed her. My mouth completely explored hers and Amelia reciprocated. Kissing was an art and one that she had mastered whether she knew it or not.

Before I even touched her, I assured myself it would be just a simple goodnight kiss, but I became carried away in the moment. I tilted her head back with the tug of her hair at the base of her skull. There was no protest, so I indulged myself kissing her neck. I could feel her heart beat as the blood coursed beneath the skin and her neck arched backward.

I also eased a hand around from the small of her back to her hip. As I had moved my hand, I felt her leg ease up mine. Sweet Jesus, did she know what she was doing to me? Did she want me as much as I wanted her? My God, she was damn sexy and I wanted her. I could not help myself; I eased my hand from her hip down her leg. Her leg was so smooth and I caught her behind the knee. I wanted her to understand what she was capable of doing to me. I pulled her knee higher and pressed my erection into her.

With one word from her I would have carried her back up the stairs of her apartment and taken her. On one hand I wanted her to be that kind of girl and on the other I mentally begged her not to be. Wow, how my head had spun that night! I had never been a delayed gratification kind of guy, but there was something special about this girl and I wanted more. I did not want to just have one night with her. I had known that from the moment we first touched and that was among the many reasons that I had fought giving in until I could fight no more. Amelia really had been the definition of irresistible to me.

"Gabe! The red light!" Cara screamed as she braced against the dashboard and I was snapped back to reality.

"Damn it!" I slammed the brakes and we slid to the middle of the intersection. Luckily, it was still early morning and there were no cars coming.

The light quickly changed back to green and we were on our way again in the direction of Grady Memorial Hospital. I tried to remain focused on the road for the duration of the ride.

We found parking in a deck just past the hospital. There was still that sense of urgency and Cara and I nearly ran to the entrance of the hospital, but the enormity of the building looming and the unknown factor of what we might find inside stopped me in my tracks. Cara almost had hands on the entrance door when she realized I was not behind her.

The sun rose in the morning from behind the building and I just froze there in the shadow of Grady Hospital. There were vans from every news station in the tri-state area camped along the sidewalk in front of the hospital and several were already conducting their morning updates as the sun came up. This was a big deal to the whole world. For them, it was an attack on the Olympic Games, but for me it had been an attack on my very foundation and I was shaken.

Every smell from the city floated by me on the breeze and I felt nauseous. My hands went to my head and I turned around and paced back and forth for a moment. I needed to settle my nerves, my stomach, and get a hold of myself. I had been afraid of what I was going to find earlier, if I would find her at all, but now I was petrified of how I would find her. I just needed a moment to get myself together.

Cara returned to where I had stopped and took my hand. Perhaps she read my mind. "You can do this. You've got to do this. Come on, let's go find her."

Cara took my hand and we went inside.

\*\*\*

I dialed the number and again it was snatched up on the first ring. "Gabriel?"

56

"Gayle, we found her. You need to come quickly. We are at Grady Memorial Hospital in downtown Atlanta." I gave her brief directions before getting off the phone with her.

"Oh thank God, she's alive. They are saying on all of the news stations that at least one woman is dead," Gayle cried, tears of relief I am sure. I hated to tell her that her relief might be premature so I didn't. I only reiterated that she needed to come quickly.

"Cara and I will wait for you to get here in the hospital chapel," I explained. I was relieved Gayle did not press me on why we would not be waiting in Amelia's room.

It had taken us until almost 9:00 a.m. before we could confirm that Amelia was a patient there. Due to patient privacy rights and the fact that she had been listed as a "Jane Doe", things had been far more difficult than simply asking if they had her.

Cara was Catholic and she enlisted the aid of a nun that happened to be volunteering in the hospital chapel to help us in our quest to find Amelia. The nun took the photo and Amelia's ID and agreed to speak with the staff on our behalf. Cara and I waited in the chapel for Sister Mary Louise to return.

She was guarded with the answers she gave to us. "Your friend is here," Sister Mary Louise began, "but the staff cannot tell you any more since neither of you are family members."

"He's her fiancé," Cara lied. A lie with which I was completely fine. A lie that I had always intended would one day be the truth.

"A fiancé is not family. I'm sorry." Sister Mary Louise was polite as she corrected us on the definition of the word "fiancé". Perhaps she knew Cara had lied.

"Sister, is there anything you can tell us about her condition? Anything?" I begged.

"I am not allowed to disclose patient information to nonfamily members. Again, I am sorry I cannot be of more assistance."

57

"Please. Anything." Cara took over in the begging.

"From what I gathered she is in surgery," she replied.

I gasped, "Surgery?!" I ran both of my hands over my face and through my hair.

Cara covered her mouth, but I could still make out her question. "Could we see her when she gets out?"

"You can wait in the chapel for now and we will pray." She then escorted us to the altar where she and Cara lit a candle and knelt.

I believed in God and I had already prayed several times that morning, but I was no Catholic. I could not remember the last time I had been to a church of any denomination. Regardless, I lit a candle and knelt with them. I prayed and my prayers were all of the usual prayers that we sinners send up when in a bind. The usuals were made up mostly of my attempts to bargain with God.

It had been after my series of prayers that I made the call to Amelia's Aunt Gayle to let her know that we had found her. It was also during my prayers that I realized we needed Gayle, Amelia's family, so that we could find out her condition. I needed her because I desperately did not want Amelia to wake up in this place alone. My heart broke at the thought of her waking up, in a strange hospital with God only knows what's wrong with her and all alone.

When I returned from calling Gayle, I found Cara alone in the chapel. She reached for my hand to join her as she continued to kneel at the altar.

"I think we should keep praying," she said as I squatted down beside her.

"I will pray for the both of us. Why don't you lay down on one of the pews and get some rest?" I had no sooner made my suggestion than did the good sister return.

"I cannot offer specific details, but it appears your friend is likely going to come through the surgery," she explained.

After giving Sister Mary Louise an account of her night and asking if she may lay down on one of the benches, Cara fell asleep on the front row next to where I knelt. I stayed true to my word about praying until Sister Mary Louise insisted that I lie down on one of the other benches. Although they were as narrow as normal church pews, they were heavily padded and not as hard. They were nearly comfortable, but unlike Cara, I could not doze off.

Since we still did not know what exactly the surgery was for, I had not known how worried to be about Amelia being in surgery to begin with. I was worried, but I had not been any more worried than I was before we found her. Until the moment Sister Mary Louise told us she was coming through, my level of concern had remained virtually unchanged. In fact, the level had not decreased that much and likely would not until I saw Amelia with my own eyes.

It wasn't even ten minutes before I gave up on trying to get some shut eye in the chapel.

"I'm going to get a cup of coffee. Could I get you a cup as well, sister?" I sat up from the bench and straightened my shirt as I asked.

"I am fine, dear. I'll wait with your friend." Sister Mary Louise had been seated on a pew near the back of the room, but moved to sit at the end of the one with Cara as I left.

From the time I left the chapel until the time I finally found the cafeteria it seemed as though I walked a mile within the confines of the hospital. For all I knew they could have been on top of one another and I was wandering aimlessly from one corridor to another until I finally saw a sign marking my intended destination.

Along the way I passed a collection of people from all walks of life and doctors and nurses that were rushing everywhere. It was obvious by the Olympic brand attire that many were there for reasons similar to my own. Some were bandaged and some were waiting and milling around the halls and waiting rooms. Some even seemed as lost as I was.

There were televisions placed sporadically throughout the building, all airing the latest coverage of the night's events. Nothing really caught my eye until the TVs in the cafeteria. I did not feel like eating, but I decided to get a couple of items for Cara for breakfast and the unwanted coffee for Sister Mary Louise. While waiting, I watched the plethora of stations playing around the room. From local news to CNN and Headline News to ESPN, each was represented and had their own brand of the up to the minute, late breaking news.

"We have unconfirmed reports that the FBI is investigating this as an act of terrorism," one newscaster stated.

"The President of the Olympic Committee is scheduled to issue a statement. Preliminary reports are that the games are to go on as scheduled," another reported.

There were other stations that were providing interviews with eyewitnesses. One in particular gave virtually the same account as Cara. "There was smoke, a flash and then the sound of the explosion. Then people were running from everywhere to everywhere and it was just mass chaos."

The station that really caught my eye was one that was already issuing a statement credited to President Clinton, "We cannot allow terrorists to win." Already they had determined this was an act of terrorism?

During my walk back to the hospital chapel, I could not stop thinking about what the news quoted by the president. They had not released the name of the woman that had been killed and I was certain I would not know her, but I thought about what her family might be going through. I thought about what Amelia and Cara had been through and I thought about what I would give for just one moment alone with whoever had done this. The fear I had felt since I first picked up the phone and heard Cara's panic stricken voice, the sorrow, the dread, it all turned to rage.

I left the cafeteria carrying the three coffees, a biscuit and an apple for Cara. I squelched the need to hit something or someone just so I could manage the load without throwing coffee all over myself or any poor soul around me. By the time I found my way back to the chapel, I had put the rage aside and told myself this was not the time or place and acting like an ass right now really would not help Amelia.

Back at the chapel I found Sister Mary Louise and Cara exactly as I had left them, Cara asleep on the pew and the sister sitting patiently down by her feet. I approached them and set the items for Cara down on the floor next to her.

I handed the cup of coffee to Sister Mary Louise and explained as she reluctantly reached to receive it, "It's not a bribe, I promise."

"That's alright. Your friend is out of surgery. She's not awake, but she's being put in a room. It might be as little as an hour before you can see her."

I nearly leapt at the news. Although Cara had slept right through it, it was the best news we had gotten all morning. We were on our way to seeing Amelia and I could hardly wait! I tried to keep with the decorum of the chapel, but I could not help myself. I barely raised my voice, "They are going to let us see her? Thank you! Thank you! Thank you!" I gushed.

"I thought that might brighten your day a little," she calmly replied.

It was a long hour, more like an hour and fifteen minutes, but a nurse finally came to get us. I had been seated at the opposite end of Cara from Sister Mary Louise and I nudged her. Cara sprang to her feet and this time she was not nearly as confused about her surroundings as she had been at the Westin.

The nurse began by asking us our relationship to Amelia.

"He's her fiancé," Cara reiterated the earlier lie.

The nurse then directed her attention to me. She was a serious woman and her tone indicated that she was all business. "Have you notified her next of kin?"

I tried to match her level of seriousness with graciousness in my voice for all she was doing for us and Amelia while answering her question. "Yes, ma'am. They are on their way from near Augusta and should be here any minute."

"Great. In the meantime, do either of you happen to know your blood type and are you willing to donate?" Again, business only, but was she trying to tell us that Amelia had lost a lot of blood without coming right out and saying it?

"I am type O." I replied. "You can have all of it if it will help her."

"Awesome. Universal donor; that will help everyone. And you?" She turned to Cara glazing right over my chivalry.

Cara replied shyly and hung her head, "I am sorry. I don't know, but if I am a match you can have it."

"It's not just for one person, you understand. There have been a great number of people injured in the bombing. They can use your help as well and the hospital appreciates your generosity." The nurse then led us to the hospital's blood bank.

CHAPTER 4

"Your niece has suffered some of the more serious injuries we have seen from the bombing. It is a miracle that she has come through it," a fairly young looking gentleman in scrubs, clearly a doctor, explained to Amelia's Aunt Gayle.

Cara and I were returning to the intensive care floor from giving blood when we overheard the doctor speaking with Gayle. They were in the hallway outside of the room that we had been told Amelia would be in when we returned. Gayle had her back to us, but it was obvious to me that it was her.

Gayle had been cordial to me over the phone during the night and on into the morning, but I was skeptical as to how welcoming she was going to be toward me in person. I knew the pain I had caused her niece and that she was none too fond of me for it. She could very easily have me tossed out, but I prayed she would not do that. I still had yet to lay eyes on Amelia and I needed to see her desperately.

Gayle had brought another of the family members with her, their Aunt Dot. Gayle still did not see us as Cara and I took positions standing just behind her so that we might hear what the doctor had to say, but not intrude. Aunt Dot had always been my biggest fan in Amelia's family and despite knowing what had gone on; she reached out and took my hand. Aunt Dot was the epitome of Southern ladies. If she was mad with you, she might simply say her peace followed by the phrase "bless your heart," which had many translations.

This morning as Aunt Dot took my hand, she leaned in to me and whispered, "It's good to see you, Gabe, bless your heart."

I think today's translation was "It's good to see you, asshole." One could just tell in her tone and I deserved it. Saying I never meant to hurt Amelia meant nothing. These ladies would need actions and a great deal of them to ever forgive me. They did not know it now, and I did not know exactly how, but I would spend the rest of my life setting all of this right. That was one of the bargains I had made with God as I prayed, "Dear Lord, if you let Amelia live, I

63

will spend the rest of my life doing right by her." He had held up his end of the bargain and I intended to hold up mine.

The doctor continued, "From what we are removing from victims such as Miss Anderson, the bomb was likely made of a basic PVC pipe with nails, screws and other various pieces of metal. When it detonated, it sent pieces of the pipe, the crude shrapnel of nails, screws and what not, plus the bench that the backpack was under and God only knows what else, flying through the air. All of these things are what hit the bystanders such as your niece. She's a very lucky girl. If she had been standing any closer to the detonation; it's likely she would not be with us. It also appears she was standing with her back to it when it went off."

Cara interrupted, "That's right. She had her back to it and blocked me from getting hit by anything. Before she went down, she swatted a place on her neck as if she had been stung..."

Everyone turned to look at Cara and that's when Gayle noticed my presence.

"Right, she likely felt like she was being stung by an entire swarm of bees," the doctor went on. He pushed his glasses farther back up on the bridge of his nose before he started to speak again. "As for her neck, it wasn't exactly her neck that was hit. In layman's terms it was more like the base of her skull. We had to cut some of her hair to get to the spot, but there was a piece of a screw imbedded in..." and he turned and demonstrated on his own head, "this part right here. We took care of that the surgery. Let me be clear, the screw did not penetrate her skull so there was no surgery to her brain. We only went in enough to remove it, but the CT scan showed a slight hemorrhage inside and a little bit of swelling. It does not appear to be significant, but anything of that nature is a source of concern. She will stay in ICU and we just have to wait for now."

The doctor had pointed to the spot to the left of his head at the base just before the skull meets the spine. I reached and ran my fingers across the same spot on my own head. I had always heard that the forehead was the thickest part of the skull, but this spot seemed rather thick as well. What did I know? I only knew what the doctor was telling us and that the skull was not penetrated and that was a good thing. Ultimately, her skull did what it was supposed to do; it protected her brain.

The doctor was only catching his breath and did not appear to be finished speaking when Gayle began to question. "During the surgery, you said there was more to it than just retrieving a screw from her skull."

"That's because there was." Again his glasses had slipped and he pushed them up his nose and started to speak once more. "It wasn't a screw or a nail, but chard of metal pierced her back and embedded in her right pelvic bone. We were able to remove it, but there's going to be a little scar, nothing a bikini won't cover. Now the bigger issue that you are likely wondering about, so I will just go ahead and put your minds at ease, none of this has affected the pregnancy. The baby is fine."

Gayle and Dot shrieked in unison, "The baby?!!!"

I fell to my knees. I had no idea. Cara dropped to my side.

"You all did not know?" the doctor seemed embarrassed.

Gayle looked around in my direction, but directed her question to the doctor. "How far along is she?"

"Approximately thirteen weeks."

"I don't think she knew she was pregnant," Cara interjected.

"Why would you say that?" Gayle snapped.

"Because she got drunk on the Fourth of July and if she had known she would not have done that. Millie is way more responsible than that. Plus, she would have told Gabe." Cara looked back at me. "She would have told you."

During all of this, I could hardly think beyond the doctor's words indicating she was pregnant. The words rang in my ears over and over. Pregnant. Pregnant. Pregnant.

Gayle shot daggers at me, "Are you proud of yourself? You may have really ruined her future now. That's all she damn needs is to be pregnant by a man who just had a baby with someone else."

I did not figure Gayle to be one to drop the F-bomb, but there in the halls of Grady Memorial Hospital she told me what a real "mother fucker" she thought I was. "Get out!" she screamed.

I stumbled, but stood up. I got to my feet as she started toward me. Gayle landed one good slap across my face before Cara jumped between us and Dot grabbed and restrained her. The slap stung, but if I were her I would have behaved the same way. Not that I was worried, but the consolation in all of this was that she had no doubt that the baby was mine. The doctor looked on bewildered.

"I did not know! I'm so sorry! I didn't know! I swear!"

Gayle fell into Dot's arms and sobbed. "Make him leave," she repeated several times over.

Dot stroked Gayle's hair and tried to comfort her, "We can't make him leave or Millie would hate us forever and I know you don't want that."

The doctor stepped forward. "You all need to get a hold of yourselves. I know this is a lot to take in, but the girl really does not need to be upset. She nearly died today and this will not help her recovery in any way."

"Can we see her?" Cara asked.

"We have decided that it would be best to keep her sedated for now due to the hemorrhage, but yes, you may see her. Not all at once," the doctor cautioned. "I am going to send nurses by to check on you all and if I find out that any of you have made a scene, you will be removed from this hospital. Do I make myself clear?"

We all agreed to behave ourselves for Amelia's sake. The doctor then excused himself, "I have other patients to attend, but I will be watching. Now, if you will excuse me." The use of the words "you all" instead of "y'all" signified the doctor was not a Southerner, but regardless he seemed to be a likeable guy and explained Amelia's condition in terms that the average person would understand.

The doctor turned to walk away and I followed. I could not let him leave without knowing his name and without thanking him.

"Sir," I addressed him and he turned back to me. "Please forgive all of us for our behavior here. I'm Gabriel Hewitt and those are the kindest ladies I have ever met and they are just looking out for their niece. I'm sure if they were thinking clearly and not in shock of all of this they would thank you for all you have done for Amelia. Please accept my apologies and my sincere gratitude. Thank you for saving her."

"Dr. Eric Andrews and it's my pleasure. That's what we do here at Grady and don't worry about them offending me."

I stuck out my hand and the doctor took it. I shook his hand, "Thank you so much for everything."

"She is not out of the woods yet so you all need to do your best to get along for her sake," the doctor cautioned as he let go of my hand. He then gave his parting words and took his leave, "Hang in there and congratulations on fatherhood."

"Thanks for saving both of them." I concluded and then returned to wait outside of Amelia's hospital room, praying they would let me in to see her soon.

Cara was seated on the floor with her back against the wall outside of the door. She had waited on me to come back.

"Did you see her?" I asked as I stooped down to take a seat next to her.

"No. They asked if I wanted to come in with them, but I told them I would wait for you." Cara reached over and patted me on the back as she spoke. "This too shall pass. That's what my mama would say in a situation like this."

"This is quite possibly shaping up to be the best and worst day of my entire life," I shrugged. "I just can't believe all of this. I don't know how much longer I am going to be able to wait to see her."

Cara reached over and took my hand, "You know she would have told you if she had known."

"Remember the night we all first went to Cameron's?" I asked.

"Yeah."

"We talked as if we were best friends for the first time that night. I don't know how the conversation came about, but at one point she told me that if she ever got pregnant and she wasn't married she would not expect the guy to marry her. Her exact words were, 'I see no reason to compound one problem with another.'"

"Gabe, you're not her problem and I know she won't see this baby as a problem. You can't think like that."

"What I'm saying is that if she knew, there's no guarantee that she would have told me. What if she does not want anything else to do with me? What if she gave up on us?" Just saying the words, I felt as if I had been slapped again.

I hung my head in my hands just as Amelia's Aunt Dot stepped back into the hallway. "Gabe, you can come in and see her."

I sprang to my feet and that was enough of an answer for Dot to hold the door open for me.

"Brace yourself. It does not look like our Millie lying in there." Aunt Dot cautioned as she stepped aside to let me through.

I looked back to Cara to see if she wanted to come in too. "I'll just wait here. You go ahead. Just tell her I'm here." Cara replied.

I was nearly through the door when it occurred to me that in all of the chaos, no one had thought to thank Cara for calling us, for not quitting until we found Amelia. I turned back and dropped to eye level with Cara. "Thank you for calling me and not giving up until we found her. If it weren't for you, we would not even know she was missing. You are the best friend she could ask for."

68

Cara dropped her head into her hands halfway through my words and began to cry. Aunt Dot heard everything and she too dropped to the floor where Cara was sitting and she pulled Cara into her arms.

"It is going to be alright dear and we do owe you a huge debt for finding her," Aunt Dot said as she pulled Cara closer to her chest for comfort.

Aunt Dot shooed me away, "I have got her, Gabe. Go on in."

I stepped in the door. The room was dimly lit, but I could see Amelia's outline in the covers of the bed. My gaze started at the foot of the bed and continued upward. She was lying on her side and her Aunt Gayle had pulled up a chair next to her and was holding her hand, a hand pierced by the needle of an IV. My eyes continued to travel up. The covers stopped at her waist and through the gap where the hospital gown tied in the back, I could see the bandages covering several places on her back and I could also see little wounds that were left uncovered. Even before I saw her face or the white gauze covering the place on the back of her head where they removed the screw, my heart broke for her. The line of the IV, likely a tube from a catheter, the bandages, the tube the size of a garden hose for oxygen, the monitor hooked up to her, seeing all of that brought a realization that I had not felt since New Year's Eve. It was not just a feeling, but a knowing that I might actually lose her. That knowledge brought tears to my eyes.

"You know I don't like you too much right now," Gayle said to me as I made my way to the edge of the bed where she was sitting.

"I know," I said just above a whisper as I wiped my eyes.

"I might forgive you one day, but not today." Gayle paused as if to gather her nerve to complete her train of thought. "Anyway, you did a wonderful thing coming to find her."

She did not look at me, but Gayle reached up and took my hand. Amelia was just lying there. She was so pale. Her head and face were swollen, but nothing too severe. I could hardly bear to look at her and coupled with the words from her aunt, I broke down.

69

"She's the love of my life..." I sniffed to try to breathe as tears fell down my face and my nose filled. "I love her and if I could take all of this away, I would."

I leaned over and kissed Amelia's forehead. "I've loved you since the moment I saw you and you have to come back to me. I am not giving up on us."

When I kissed her, the familiar spark was there. It was as fierce as ever. My joints tingled and my knees went weak.

***

The hours rocked on and we waited for Amelia to wake up. I don't recall when, but I pulled up a chair next to Gayle and we each held one of Amelia's hands. Dot was parked on the small couch in front of the window. At some point, Dot invited Cara in and she took a seat in the window sill. No one ever said anything about too many of us being in the room.

The nurse visits were frequent, every fifteen minutes that morning, but between lunchtime and 2:00 p.m. they tapered off to every thirty minutes. Shortly after 2:00, Gayle finally caught one of the nurses and asked the question that was on all of our minds, "When should we expect her to wake up?"

"It won't be any time soon ma'am," the nurse responded as she checked Amelia's vitals and changed out the various bags running from the tube lines to her hand.

"Days?" Cara sought clarification of what she had heard. She wanted the term "anytime soon" defined.

"I am not sure," the nurse repeated as she headed toward the door.

Not long after the nurse left, Gayle and Aunt Dot began discussing among themselves that Gayle would stay over that night and Dot would take the next night. They spoke as if Cara and I were not in the room. I did not expect any more from Cara and I knew she needed to be getting home, but there was no way I was leaving Amelia alone at Grady for one moment and I said as much. I hated the thought of leaving her at all even if Gayle or Aunt Dot were going to be there, but the practicality of everything was that I had to get home to Gabby.

"I will take the day shift. I can be back here tomorrow morning by 8:00 a.m. to relieve you, Gayle," I added.

"That really isn't necessary," Gayle said as she began to pace the room. I was back to being dismissed by her.

Aunt Dot was more reasonable. "Tomorrow morning is fine, Gabe, and I will relieve you tomorrow afternoon."

At 2:30 p.m., Cara and I left the hospital. I hated leaving. Aunt Dot promised to call me if there were any changes. I dropped Cara off at her car at the Indian Springs MARTA station where they had parked the day before and then followed her all the way to the Greensboro exit off of I-20.

On the way home I could barely hold my head up. I was exhausted; mentally, physically and emotionally drained. Once at home, I found Daniel had picked up Gabby from Mrs. Allen's as I had asked him and he was feeding her when I walked in. I took over the feeding and within minutes Gabby was finished with her bottle and fast asleep.

As soon as I laid Gabby in her crib, I gave Daniel the play by play of the day. Most significantly, I told him that Amelia was pregnant. I knew he had been keeping in touch with her all summer, more than I had, and perhaps he could shed light on whether she knew she was pregnant or not.

"Would she have kept that from me or did she not know?" I asked him while I walked around and around the couch in the living room. I was tired, but I could not seem to sit still.

Daniel flopped back on the couch in disbelief. "I'm certain she did not know. She mentioned to me last week that she threw up every morning, but as soon as she threw up she was fine for the rest of the day. She thought it was just nerves or something."

"So she was having morning sickness and did not know it? She thought it was nerves? How is that possible?"

"She's not stupid if that's what you are implying." Daniel had a tone signaling that he was offended for her at my implication.

"No, no, I didn't mean that." I scratched my head and flopped down on the couch next to him. "I just don't understand how she could've been that far along and not known."

"She found out that you moved Beth in the house with you."

I cut Daniel off because that's not how it went. "I did not move Beth in the house with me!"

"Schematics! She moved in and you allowed it!"

"She showed up with a suitcase and said we were on baby watch."

The banter was getting a little heated as Daniel called me out at every turn. "Baby watch for six weeks? Who does that and where was her mother then? And when did she tell you the baby was due anyway?"

"I don't know who does that! I don't know where her mother was and she told me she was due toward the first week in June."

"Yet she did not give birth until the first week in July. No doctor allows a woman to go a month over her due date." Daniel rolled his eyes and let out sighs of exasperation.

"What was I to do?"

"Grow a pair! Stop being a victim to that bitch! That's what you should do. What was your plan? What is your plan now?" Daniel really let me have it.

"The plan is for me to get custody of Gabby."

"Are you serious?" Daniel sat up on the couch and gave me my second slap of the day. Luckily, this slap was not across my face and only across my arm. "She does not have the child, you do."

"That was just luck. Ever since Beth first told me she was pregnant, I knew this was something I had to do," I replied.

"Maybe you should've let Millie in on that plan." I knew Daniel was right.

He went on, "You wonder why she would have thought it was just nerves? You stopped calling her. The last time she saw you was on your birthday and all you wanted was to fuck her. You sent her a card and flowers on her graduation day and yet no call, no visit, no nothing worth mentioning. Screw the card and flowers, you should have been there! Of course she found out Gabby was born and never once did you call her. She should've heard that from you, not from Cara or me or anyone else from the club."

The bells and whistles all went off in my head. I sat straight up on the couch. "Right, my birthday! Thirteen weeks ago was April 27. All I wanted for my birthday was her."

"And since then, what have you wanted?" Daniel asked.

"Always her."

"Really? I know she told you she would wait and I know she trusted that you were coming for her, but it's not like you were doing anything to keep her faith in you secure. You were slowly breaking her heart, hence the issue with nerves. Do you understand you are dangerously close to not deserving her?" His words stung.

"What am I going to do?" I asked him.

"I don't know, but it seems like Beth does not want you until she finds out you are interested in someone else so you really need to figure out how to cut her loose and implement this plan of yours. You need to be done with Beth once and for all."

"I won't give Gabby up. You know I tried to call Beth this morning before calling Mrs. Allen and no one picked up. Look over there at the answering machine. No messages. She has not bothered to call back." I pointed to the machine and shook my head in disgust.

"Have you talked to an attorney?"

"Yes."

73

Daniel and I continued to talk about what I had accomplished so far. Daniel agreed to help me any way he could and that included staying on with Gabby while I ran to the club and helped with dinner for the Germans. Alvin had everything prepared and we did a buffet that night of prime rib. Since we weren't typically open on Sunday night, it was just the equestrian team and no members. Things ran smoothly and I was back home within two hours.

Once I was back, I phoned Mrs. Allen to inquire as to her watching Gabby for me again the next day. The club was usually closed on Mondays, so normally Mrs. Allen was off.

The first thing Mrs. Allen asked after she recognized it was me was, "How's Miss Millie?"

I gave her the details of Amelia's condition before asking if she could keep Gabby for me tomorrow.

"Oh, Mr. Gabe, I wish I could, but I have scheduled three doctor appointments for tomorrow. If I could cancel them now, I would, but it's too late."

I could tell from her voice that Mrs. Allen genuinely wanted to help out, but was in as much of a bind as I was. I did not want my problems to be hers, so I tried to ease her mind. "That's fine. I will figure something out even if I have to take her with me."

"I can still keep her on Tuesday if you need me." Of course I needed her, now more than ever.

I finished up with Mrs. Allen and I still did not know what I was going to do. I gave the number to Beth's parents' house another try. I hated dialing that number. I hated the thought that I might have to beg Beth to help me out with Gabby. In one regard, I suppose I was lucky there was no answer other than the machine.

For all I knew of Beth's whereabouts, she might be at their house on the lake. Wouldn't that just be something, Beth being less than three miles away and not bothering to check in on Gabby? It was obvious; she really could give a shit.

74

I noted all of these calls in the journal Attorney Ellis instructed me to keep.

Gabby was asleep in her crib again and I was about to cut the bedside lamp off when the phone rang. I came close to ignoring it, but it occurred to me, what if it was something to do with Amelia? I answered it because it could be Gayle or Aunt Dot calling to let me know she had woken up.

"Gabe, it's Jay." I would have recognized his voice even if he had not identified himself. He was more than a roommate to Amelia; they had been best friends since childhood and he sounded panicked.

"I'm guessing you just found out," I replied.

"I just got home and Cara met me at my car when I drove up." I could hear in his voice that he was scared and probably choking back tears. "I'm sorry I wasn't there to help find her last night."

"Hey, don't worry about it. Amelia's safe now and that's all that matters," I did my best to assure him while I yawned.

"Yeah, but I should've been there for her. I saw her car parked in the carport when I drove up just now and I expected her to be home. I just can't believe this has happened. I just can't believe it!" I could hear he was as upset as the rest of us and likely crying a little.

Perhaps now was not the time, but I had to ask, "Jay, did you know she was pregnant?"

"No!" He answered as calmly as he could while changing the direction of his thoughts. He was clearly stunned by the question.

"Do you think she knew?" I continued with my questions.

Jay's voice was beginning to return to its normal tone. "I know more about her than I likely should, so I can tell you her period has always been a little on the hit and miss side. It is possible that she did not know. She had been throwing up a little lately, but we

75

thought that was just nervousness from everything that was going on and that she was starting law school soon."

"Oh my God, I had completely forgotten about law school. That's what Gayle meant today when she said I had really ruined her future now."

Despite the fact that I was thinking out loud, Jay kept up with the conversation. "Yeah, she is supposed to start at Mercer sometime in mid-August. What if..."

I stopped him before he could finish the question. I knew where he was going with that. "We are not going to think like that! She is going to be fine in no time at all."

"I'm sure you're right. I should let you get some sleep. I hear you are going back down there tomorrow. I will likely see you there."

"Yeah, I can't stand the thought of her being alone in that place. Thanks for calling and, if you pray, then you should probably pray for Amelia tonight.

Then Jay said something that I would not have expected from him. I had seen him go into attack mode to protect Amelia in the past and I had expected him to feel the same about me as Gayle, but I was wrong.

"You know she loves you," he said. He did not say any more than that he would see me at the hospital tomorrow and I did not press him.

Again my mind went back to Amelia's statements the night at Cameron's. She might not have expected me to marry her, but I know she would have told me she was pregnant. Plus, I had no doubt she would have told Jay if she had known.

According to the alarm clock, I had only turned out the lights ten minutes prior to the phone ringing again. I felt around in the dark. I was determined to answer just in case it was someone calling with an update on Amelia. This time I did not recognize the female voice on the other end of the line.

"Gabe, its Stella, from family dinner at The Jefferson. I just saw Jay and he told me about Millie."

For the third time that night I gave an account of Amelia's condition at the end of which Stella asked if there was anything she could do to help.

"I don't suppose you have any experience with babies? I hate to ask, but I could really use a sitter tomorrow." I had met Stella on a number of occasions and knew she was responsible so being able to leave Gabby with her would be helpful.

"Sure, anything," Stella quickly agreed.

"I will be glad to pay your gas money to get out here plus seventy five dollars for your time. Will that be enough?"

"You don't have to pay me. What time do you need me there?" Although she refused to take the money, I intended to pay her anyway.

I asked her to be at my house by 6:30 a.m. and then gave her directions. I went to sleep relieved that I had everything sorted out for Gabby.

I could not remember falling asleep, but Gabby's 3:00 a.m. feeding arrived within what seemed like a minute of me having shut my eyes. I did not know much about babies, but I was certain Gabby was one of the best. It was as if she was barely awake to take the bottle and then down again for the rest of the night.

The alarm clock went off at 6:00 a.m. Stella arrived ten minutes early and I had just finished getting dressed in time to let her in. Gabby was fed and awake to meet Stella before I left.

"I left a list of instructions and the number to the hospital in case you need me," I explained to Stella as I scarfed down my breakfast and gave her the tour of the house.

Stella carried Gabby as we went through the house and they seemed like a natural fit. I think Gabby might have even had her first smile that was not related to gas while Stella made faces at her.

Stella was lighter skinned than Alvin, but they had the same green eyes. If they were to someday tell me they were related, I would believe it. Stella's hair was jet black and shiny. Her short ringlet curls flopped and bounced around with her every movement and when she made faces at Gabby, the baby seemed almost tickled by the sight. I had been trying for three weeks, everything I could think of, to get Gabby to smile for me and nothing, but Stella accomplished it within five minutes of meeting her. Some might have been jealous that Stella got the reaction they had been hopelessly trying to achieve; not me. I was just happy to see Gabby smile.

CHAPTER 5

I was out of the house by 6:45 a.m. and this trip down I-20 was unlike the mad dash of the night before. I did not feel the urgency of the prior morning, but I was still anxious to see Amelia. This time I did not drive at record breaking speeds even though I would have given anything to have said "Beam me up, Scotty" and to have been transported there.

Again the time in the car meant time to think and reminisce about my time with Amelia. I had barely made the turn out of the gate of Port Honor before the car was on autopilot and the road before me was little more than a daydream.

In the hours since I learned Amelia was pregnant, my attempt to indulge in the memory of the weekend we conceived was cut short by one interruption or other. As soon as Daniel and I had realized the date, I saw flashes of the weekend. Throughout the remainder of the night little bits and pieces came to mind, but each time I tried to really settle into the memory Gabby cried or the phone rang. Now, alone in the car, there was nothing to keep me from reliving that weekend.

"Hi," Amelia greeted me before asking the obvious question. "What are you doing here?"

I could tell by the look on her face that she was shocked to see me there. I could also tell that she was not entirely displeased by the sight of me. I knew her class schedule and what time to expect her home on Friday afternoons, so I arrived early and waited for her. I was sitting on the front porch of The Jefferson when she came walking home.

In the weeks since we began what I referred to as our "break," I believe she had made it a point to have little to no contact with me. I, on the other hand, could not help calling her. I had tried to abide by her wishes for me to sort out things with Beth before continuing on with her, but I faithfully called her once a week. I had to know she was alright. I had to hear her voice.

79

During my calls, Amelia was always herself, but now there had been an air of caution to her. I suppose it was for her own self-preservation and if I had any sense at all, perhaps I would have been the same way. After all, what if I could not sort out things with Beth and the baby? What would become of Amelia and me?

On this particular occasion, I threw caution to the wind. I had to see her. I wanted to see her. I needed to see her.

"Tomorrow's my birthday," I said as I stood up and brushed off the seat of my pants.

"Really?" She looked me up and down as she continued to take steps toward the porch.

"Yeah, April 27, that's the big day," I replied. "Happy Birthday," she continued with the slightest of hesitation in her voice. "You did not answer my question. What brings you here?"

Amelia bit her bottom lip and appeared a little fidgety as she awaited my response. I was distracted by how amazing she was and how much I had missed her. It had been a while, nearly a month, since I had seen her. Everything inside of me was fighting the urge to grab her and kiss her and tell her that all I wanted for my birthday was her. I knew better than to attempt that as I could feel a bit of a tension coming off of her. It was a vibe as if I would be overstepping if I touched her before she invited it.

"I wanted to ask you something." Amelia wasn't the only one that was hesitant in our current encounter. I wasn't sure how this was going to go, but I had a plan in mind of what I wanted.

"Well?"

It was hard to ask what I wanted to ask because I was so terrified that she was going to refuse me. There was an awkward silence as I gathered my nerve. Finally, Amelia reached her hand to me and gently touched my shoulder. She let the mask of preservation slip and she spoke my name. "Gabriel, you can ask me anything."

I seized the moment and kind of blurted it out, "I want you to come away with me this weekend."

I continued on as if I could not contain myself. I took hold of her hands and her eyes went wide as I explained, "It's my birthday and I am turning twenty-nine. I have taken the whole weekend off. I can't remember the last time I had a whole weekend off. I just want to spend it with you. All I want for my birthday is to hang out with you. We can do whatever you want. We can stay here. We can go somewhere. We can go anywhere you want. I don't care. We can do anything or we can do nothing. It's totally up to you."

I suppose I would have gone on indefinitely until she stopped me, which she finally did. "Gabriel, I ca..."

"Don't say you can't. You are the freest person I know Amelia."

She took her hands back and ran them over her face and through her hair before bringing them back and covering her mouth. From under her hands she started, "What abou..."

"What about what? It's just you and me if you say the word. The car's right there. We can go anywhere and I promise I will have you back home in time for class on Monday morning."

She just looked at me like she did not know what to do.

"Please, Amelia, come with me. Let's get out of here."

Amelia sighed a giant sigh before she gave her consent. "Let me pack a bag and leave a note for Jay. Come on, you can wait inside."

I stepped to the side and allowed her to pass. In the foyer, while I waited behind her to unlock the door, I thought about our first kiss. It had happened in that very spot on her birthday. I tried not to let my mind wander too much as I did not know how much I could control myself with her in my head and this close to me.

Amelia was as nervous as I was. I could tell as she fiddled around trying to get the key in the lock. I wondered if she was thinking of our first kiss as well. I leaned into her just enough that I could smell the scent of her hair. She was still using the strawberry shampoo that I loved so much. My chest has just barely brushed against her back when the lock freed and the door swung open.

81

"Help yourself to the remote. I will try to be quick." No sooner had she spoken the words did she close the door to the room behind her.

I turned on the television and tried to occupy myself by watching The Young and The Restless. It seemed like a flash and Amelia was back. Who knows what Amelia packed or if she kept a bag on stand-by because she returned in fifteen minutes ready with small suitcase in hand.

"I just have to leave a note for Jay," she mentioned as she passed behind the couch where I was sitting. She dropped the bag by the door and continued on toward the kitchen where she proceeded to leave the note.

I carried her bag and loaded it into the trunk. "Where would you like to go?" I asked her as I closed the lid.

"Do you like the mountains?" she asked me.

"I guess. I wouldn't say I've spent much time in the mountains."

"I went to school up there and I loved it. Maybe we could drive up that way?"

"Whatever you want is fine with me."

Amelia gave directions and we headed out Highway 441. Although her mood had changed and her skepticism seemed to have dissipated since she first saw me that afternoon, we were nearly to Eatonton before I worked up the courage to take her hand.

"Name" by the Goo Goo Dolls was just starting to play the radio and Amelia was singing along. I could barely hear her and from the corner of my eye I could see her lightly tapping her foot. She was patting her hand against her leg as well. She seemed a little distracted looking out of the window and singing until I reached over and touched her. She looked back at me and smiled. Undoubtedly, she felt the spark as well. The radio continued to play, but I did not hear a sound from it. We seemed to be back to ourselves as we bantered back and forth.

In a town called Cornelia, Amelia had me stop at the Ingles grocery store. It was the first time we had ever been grocery shopping together. I carried the shopping basket and followed Amelia through the aisles as she picked out breakfast items, sandwich fixin's and her favorite potato chips. She loved Lay's Salt and Vinegar chips more than any other even though they made her face pucker with every bite. This activity and these thoughts reminded me just how much I loved being domestic with her. There was never a dull moment as long as I was with her.

Once back on the road, Amelia had me take Historic 441 and we continued through Clarksville toward Tallulah Gorge. According to the road signs, we were outside of Hollywood, Georgia when Amelia asked something that I wished she knew the answer to without having to ask.

"Gabriel, do you still love me?" Her voice was soft and unsure when she asked.

I clinched her hand a little tighter and brought it to my chest. I held it across where my heart is. "It's yours. Always," I replied and I meant it. I am certain there was a conveyance in my voice that I did not understand why she was asking. I suppose I took for granted that she knew how I felt about her. There was hardly a second of any day that passed that I did not think of her, that I did not miss her with every part of me.

Again, she smiled at me. It wasn't a big giant smile, but subtle, filling her cheeks out and showing her dimples. "Would you mind turning at the next road to the left? It's kind of a fork onto The Orchard Road."

I made the turn as she asked and then another and another until we were on Bear Gap Road and what I considered to be deep in the mountains. The shadows were hanging from the trees. Although it was only about 5:00 p.m. and a bright sunny day, the lack of sunlight breaking through the trees made it seem much later and cloudier.

"We're about there," she assured me. "Just a couple more turns."

"Where exactly is 'there'?"

"You'll see."

Shortly after the last turn, the pavement ended and we traveled less than a half mile before I saw an old wooden building on the edge of the road. It was painted red like a barn with white trim that made up the rails of the porch and the eves. It was an enormous building with porch over porch that stretched the length of both the first and second floors. It sat in a valley among pine trees along the road and a meadow in the back. It was beautiful.

Before I could ask, Amelia began to explain, "It's an inn and I figured we could have dinner there. My treat."

"Are we staying there and how did you find this place?" I asked her while I slowed the car to make sure I was getting a good look.

"When I went to school in Hiawassee, one of my friend's parents had a house on Lake Rabun. It's just down the road a little farther. Anyway, when I came over to their house they treated all of us to Sunday brunch here. Seriously, some of the best food I have ever had at a restaurant."

I looked over to her and raised an eyebrow.      Amelia knew exactly what I was getting at.

"Oh, you know yours is better," she reassured me about my cooking at the club.

We continued down the gravel road. I was not typically a nervous driver, but this was a little nerve racking. The mountain was on one side and a severe drop off into a ravine of trees was on the other. With each turn, I feared we would find another vehicle facing us on the other end of the curve. We were fortunate that we never did meet anyone.

Just after taking the last fork in the road, the mountains opened up and the road traveled along the edge of a lake. The water was the color of turquoise and there were boat houses scattered along the far shoreline. It wasn't a wide lake so I could see every detail of the boat houses across the lake. I could also see that most were little replicas of the houses that dotted the mountain behind them.

I was lost in thought and observation when Amelia spoke again, "Gabriel, you are going to need to take the next driveway to your right."

"To the right?" I questioned her as to the right was what looked to be a drop off into the lake.

"Yes, to the right."

Of course she knew what she was talking about. The road curved back and about a tenth of a mile from when she spoke; there was a driveway to the right. I turned off as she had instructed and thank goodness for brakes as the driveway was straight down. It made a turn and continued under a large carport.

At the end of the driveway was a substantially sized house. In all of the Lake Oconee area, I had not seen anything like this house. It was beyond comparison as far as I knew. I dare say it was the definition of a mountain lodge.

I barely had the car in park when Amelia opened her door. "I'll get the key while you get the bags."

I grabbed the bags and went to find Amelia. The door was open and she was already inside.

"Amelia, this isn't another piece of your inheritance, is it?" I asked her as I took in my surroundings; giant, floor to ceiling rock fireplace, leather hobnail couch and matching chairs, vaulted ceiling with exposed beams of sewn timber.

"God, no!" She replied as if she were flattered that I would suspect this might be hers. "It's my friend Mary's parents' place. I called her while I packed and asked if I could borrow it. Her parents are in Hawaii for spring break."

"Spring break is only a week and it was at the beginning of the month," I commented as I continued to look around.

85

"Their spring break lasts the entire month of April. Gabriel, my inheritance is a drop in the bucket compared to Mary's family. Mary's dad is a TV producer and they only come here a couple of times per year."

"How do you know her?"

Amelia walked toward the fireplace and picked up the remote. The fireplace was not a true fireplace, but had gas logs that were cut on with the flick of Amelia's finger as she spoke.

"I know her from school at Young Harris. She was one of my roommates. She liked vacationing in the North Georgia mountains so much that when it was time to select a college she picked one here so she could be on vacation all the time. I always thought that was funny coming from a girl that was born and raised in Southern California."

"This place is amazing," I commented as I joined her in front of the fireplace. "I cannot believe it just sits here, unused like this."

Amelia reached down and took my hand as we stared into the fireplace. We stood in silence for a few moments before I could not take it anymore. I had wanted to kiss her since I had laid eyes on her earlier in the afternoon.

I pulled her hand closer to me and turned to her. "May I?"

Amelia looked up at me and the look on her face was enough of an answer for me. I eased a hand against her cheek. Her skin was so soft, so smooth. I pulled her with the other around her waist, pressing her against me. From her cheek, I found the hair at the base of her skull and my fingers slipped right through it until I took hold. I gave her hair just a little tug, pulling her head back for better access to her lips. She tasted so sweet and reciprocated every move I made.

My fingers ran through her hair and found her neck again, so did my tongue and my lips. At the same time I bent down and scooped around her backside with my other arm. My memory of how light Amelia was, how easy she was to lift and carry, was all too vivid. It would have been nothing to pick her up and carry her to one of the two couches in the room or to scoop her up and take us both to the floor.

From the move of my hands, Amelia anticipated what was coming next and stepped back. She broke our embrace, but I slid her hands into mine as they fell from her and she backed away.

"Not yet," she said as she continued stepping backward. I wasn't ready to stop and I countered her movements to close the gap between us.

Amelia was quick to give a sly smile and turn on her heels while releasing one of my hands. She pulled me with her as she started across the room. I gave only slight resistance.

"Amelia, I've missed you so much and it's my birthday." I may have sounded as if I was begging. I wanted her so badly. I was not above a little begging.

"It's not your birthday yet." Amelia was playful in her denial and the glance she shot over her shoulder at me. "Just come with me."

We went through one of the back doors of the house onto a massive deck. From the deck I could see the lake through the dense woods that made up the back yard. From the deck we were nearly level with the tops of those trees nearest the lake.

Amelia continued to lead me past the bentwood patio furniture and rock fireplace the furniture sat around to the far end of the deck. We went out of the screened door and down a pathway of stairs that wandered down hill through the backyard. The walk wasn't so much long as it was steep, but it finally leveled out near the edge that dropped off again to the lake.

The level part of the path was made up of beaten down pine straw and it led to a boathouse. Like the other boat houses I had seen across the lake on the drive in, this one was perched over the turquoise water below and appeared to be a tiny replica of the house.

We entered the boathouse on the top level, a covered deck within the pitch of the roof. This portion was decorated as another outdoor living room much like that we had passed through on the deck. It was complete with matching rock fireplace, the third I had observed on the property thus far.

Beyond the covered deck was an open area with two double lounge chairs where couples might sunbathe. Each lounger was as big as the futon that I had slept on most of my teen years. This whole place was the definition of opulence. I nearly had to pinch myself that I was here and with Amelia.

We had bantered back and forth on the way down the stairs, but nothing any more than "watch your step" and laughing over what the walk back up was going to be like. The first words of significance came from Amelia when she turned back from the railing we were leaning on looking over the water. She looked back where the loungers were and then to the living room as she casually offered, "Under there now or out here under the stars tonight?"

Initially, my jaw hit the floor. I was stunned by her offer. I never thought her a prude, but I never would have taken her for one to risk exhibition either. The offer itself was sexy as hell and exhilarating to be allowed a glimpse of her fantasy. I had never had sex outdoors before. I had done it once in a restroom at an outdoor theater in Atlanta with Beth during a Joni Mitchell concert, which we were at with her parents, but that was the closest I had ever come. I was a red-blooded American male so it went without saying either way would fulfill a fantasy of mine.

It did not take long for me to give a response. "Decisions, decisions. Can't I have both?"

"Maybe, but not in the same day." Amelia took a seat one on one of the loungers.

"Which would you like first?" I was curious as to what her choice would be.

Amelia looked to the sky for a moment. "It's getting late. Let's go to dinner." She made a choice without answering me directly. I could hardly wait for dinner and dessert.

We made the trip back around the mountain to Glen Ella Springs where we had dinner. I was hesitant to order the Mahi-Mahi due to the question as to how fresh could that type fish be when served in the mountains. I went for it anyway at the insistence of the tongue-tied waiter who guaranteed the "Maui-Maui" was the chef's specialty.   It was remarkable.   The lemon dill sauce was just the right touch. Amelia had the bacon wrapped filet. I tasted hers and it was equally impressive.  None of that mattered; all I could think about was getting back to the boathouse.

The drive back in the dark was more unnerving than the trip around in the daylight, but finally we arrived back at the house. Amelia waited in the car for me to come around and open her door for her.  I extended my hand and the anticipation struck in that current that she sends through me when we touched.

"I am going to grab some things and I will meet you by the lake.  There are a couple of flashlights in the kitchen.  Look in the third drawer on the island closest to the refrigerator and get one," Amelia instructed before heading upstairs.

I grabbed the flashlight and the bottle of wine we had picked up at the grocery store and two glasses before setting off on my hike down the stairs to the boathouse.  There was a bit of a breeze in the air, but nothing unbearable or worth derailing the rest of the evening over.

I wasn't down there long before I heard Amelia's footsteps as she stepped from the path onto the deck of the boathouse.  I had been leaning against the rail watching the lightening bugs shimmer above the lake when I heard her. I turned back to find her standing just under the roof where it ended and the deck opened to the sky above.  The moonlight reflecting off the lake was just enough to illuminate her.  She was wearing a black silk robe and her hair was flowing in the wind. I could hardly breathe.

"You become more and more beautiful all the time," I said admirably.

Amelia bit her lip, hung her head and looked shyly away.

"Come here."  I held out my arms to her and Amelia made slow strides toward me.

No more words were needed. I lifted her chin to me and took her in my mouth. It was our second kiss of the day and it put the first to shame.

Amelia's hand slid up my arms, light like feathers, sending chills down my legs. Instantly I was hard. I missed all of the sensations that she gave me.

I turned us to where Amelia was against the railing with her back to me. With my right hand I pulled her to me and pressed against her. With my other, I gently pulled her hair to one side as she let that side of her robe slip, exposing her shoulder. She leaned her head back and brushed her cheek against my head as I planted kisses from her neck to the far end of her bare shoulder.

"I would like to bend you over the railing, Miss Anderson," I whispered.

Amelia sighed, "Happy Birthday, Mr. Hewitt." Amelia pressed harder into me as she bent so slightly over the railing. Was she really giving me the go ahead?

I was so close to taking her from behind against the rail in the moonlight when logistics set in. We typically used condoms and it suddenly occurred to me that the ones I had with me were all the way back up at the house. I hated to kill the mood, but I had to confess it to her. I expected to be sent back up to the house to retrieve them.

"Gabriel, it's alright. I've never completely felt you inside me and I'm..."

I stopped her, "Are you sure?"

Her answer came in the form of her turning completely around to me and beginning to unbutton my shirt. She helped me remove it and my undershirt before she pushed me back to the loungers. As soon as I felt it against my legs, I sat and Amelia climbed on top of me, straddling me. I grabbed her ankles, she locked her knees and I lifted her slightly to adjust my position under her while she ran circles around my Adam's apple with her tongue. I exhaled sharply. She was damn hot and I did not know how much more foreplay I could take.

As she kissed me, I fell back on the lounger. Amelia nearly fell forward on top of me, but caught herself. My eyes were nearly to the back of my head with ecstasy when I felt her index finger run the length of my torso, all the way down my happy trail and to the button of my jeans. Her weight shifted off of me and I opened my eyes to see and feel her begin to unbutton my pants. I could also see her robe had gaped open below the tie around her waist. Courtesy of the moonlight I could see the black lace panties she had on. Sometimes a little bit of clothing went farther than full on nakedness when it came to my arousal.

While Amelia unzipped my pants, I ran a finger around the collar of her robe and down the lapel, just between the robe and her skin. I expected to hit a point where I would feel a bra that likely matched the lace panties. I found nothing but skin. I eased back the robe to confirm what my touch was telling me. She was bare chested and I buried my face in her.

With little to no effort, my pants were unbuttoned and unzipped. I could not take it anymore. Foreplay was over. I did not want a quickie by any stretch of the imagination, but I had to have her. I leaned up and with the flick of my finger I moved her panties to one side. Again my eyes rolled while I felt her glide over me. I did my best to hold back the inevitable for as long as possible, but it had been a while since I had been with her.

Amelia's hands were firmly on my chest as we moved and her nails dug slightly, like pleasure mixed with the sting of pain. In the throes of passion, she arched her back and the robe fell completely around her waist and her wrists. Naked under the moon, she was like a white light atop me in the open night air. Making love outside and with Amelia was a double fantasy come to life. This was heaven.

I did my best to pleasure her first, but failed. I only failed because I could not hold out any longer. I tried to distract myself with thoughts of sports, her Aunt Dot, cold water and cats. Nothing worked. When you are ready to come, it's damn hard not to.

"Jesus Christ!" I screamed while I was in her. That was quite possibly the best I had ever had.

91

Amelia fell across me and laid there for a moment while we both took the time to catch our breath.

"Twenty minutes and then again," I told her.

I had more stamina the second time and it was all about her. Not once did I worry about neighbors seeing. In fact, from what I remembered of the view from earlier, the nearest neighbor was about a tenth of a mile through the woods and up the hill and another was of equal distance across the lake. There was no one within shouting distance and that was perfect since Amelia lost all inhibitions when it came to verbally letting me know how well I was doing. She screamed a lot and in a good way.

For the longest time we laid there under the stars in silence. My mind was clear and I was so in the moment with her that everything else faded away.

Amelia's head was on my chest and I could feel her every breath against me. I stroked my fingers through her hair and reflected on what had just happened.

"You cannot begin to imagine how much I love you," I said softly to her. I could feel her exhale as if she were relieved to hear it.

The silence continued until I broke it again. "I also love your friend Mary for loaning us this place. I could get used to this."

"If I could pick anywhere on Earth to live, but I was limited in my choices to places that I had already been, I would pick here." Amelia's head stayed firmly in its spot on my chest as she spoke.

"You could live here if you wanted."

"Chalk mining and harvesting timber could never pay for this." Amelia made reference to her inheritance. "Not even if I sold everything."

"Who are we kidding anyway; you would never give up Seven Springs."

"You're right, but it's nice to dream about living here." Amelia shifted slightly to get more comfortable and pull up her robe to cover us like a blanket. The dew was beginning to fall, but she was no more ready to go in than I was. Not to mention, we had to rest up before we could make the hike back up the stairs to the house.

"You know, I did not mean this exact place when I mentioned that you could live here. I really just meant the general area."

"Maybe one day, after law school and establishing myself I could afford something a little smaller." She lifted her head and looked at me before she finished. "The minimum requirement would be a boathouse just like this."

I reciprocated her smile. "I say forego the house and just get the boathouse."

Amelia laughed for a moment and then returned her head to my chest.

The silence continued until she broke it. "If you could live anywhere on Earth, where would you pick?"

I know it sounded like a kiss-ass thing to say, but it was the truth. "I would live anywhere that you are."

Upon my response I could feel Amelia squeeze me. "When will all this nonsense be over with..."

Before she could say Beth's name, I cut Amelia off. "We are not ruining this perfect weekend with talk about her." I did not even answer her question. I changed the subject.

"Tell me about the stars," I said to her.

"What?"

"You took astronomy last semester, so tell me about the stars."

Amelia sat up and faced me. She pulled the robe up and wrapped it just enough to cover her chest. "Let me tell you about that class," she began.

I could almost always count on Amelia for a good story.

"So, my first day of class, I am sitting there with about twenty-five other students and the teacher arrives so late that five of them had already left. He took another ten minutes to organize his pencils and books before he asked who would like extra credit. Everyone left in the room raised their hands. Then he asked, 'How many of you are good strong swimmers? Keep your hands up.' Half of the hands went down. 'How many of you can stand cold water? Let me see those hands.' It went down to four hands still in the air before he went on. 'Alright, I am going to need you four to meet me out at my house on Lake Sinclair tomorrow morning at 5:00 a.m. I've got some piano wire and I need for one of you to swim it across the lake. Another is going to swim across too and fasten it up in a tree about this high.' He gestured to about his neck. 'The others of you are going to be the look outs. We are going to take care of the problem I'm having with the damn jet skis in my cove scaring off the fish.' Most of us knew it, but one student, a girl, shrieked, 'You're going to decapitate someone.' He responded, 'That's the plan sweetheart.'"

I could not help but laugh. "He was kidding right?"

"Well, he said he was, but for all I know, someone might have gotten a hefty extra credit grade."

I snickered as Amelia again adjusted her head on its spot on my chest. "It was a fun class, but I did not really learn anything much. I can spot the big dipper, the Dog Star, the seven sisters and Orion most of the time, but other than that, I'm lost."

It wasn't too much longer before I began to get cold and if I was cold, Amelia was likely freezing. I brushed my hand down her arm and felt the chill bumps.

"Are you about ready to go inside for the night?" I asked her.

"Not really, but I suppose we should," she said as she sat up and pulled the robe on.

94

I followed in sitting up and grabbing my pants. I saw no need to get fully dressed for the walk back up to the house. I just slipped on my jeans and grabbed my underwear, shirts and shoes to carry up.

"You are a mighty fine man, Mr. Hewitt," Amelia commented as she reached for my hand.

Once she took my hand I pulled her back to me and into an embrace, "For as long as I live, I will never forget this night."

The rest of the weekend was on par with that night, but the remainder of the weekend we went back to taking precautions. It was the absolute best birthday I had ever had. I did not know it then, but there was no way that I would ever be able to forget that weekend as the living proof of it would arrive with us in about twenty-four more weeks.

CHAPTER 6

By 8:00 a.m., I was back to reality. Reflection on the night we conceived was still fresh in my mind. That was all I thought about from the time I left the gates of Port Honor until I pulled into the parking deck.

I had parked and was making the walk to the front of the hospital. I almost dreaded seeing Amelia's Aunt Gayle that morning. I was certain it was likely just going to be the two of us when I got there and I was right.

I greeted her as I approached Amelia and before asking the question I was dying to have answered. "Good morning. Any change?"

Amelia was still lying on her side as she had been the day before. She looked as though she had not moved a muscle. The swelling in her head and face was almost gone and she no longer looked like a baby Sumo wrestler. I was a little relieved.

Gayle answered as I leaned down and kissed Amelia's forehead. "No, not yet. It's so frustrating. I thought she was just sleeping, but as it turns out they had given her something. They eased off on that this morning and the doctor performed some tests."

"Really, what sort of tests?"

"Dr. Andrews asked her to make a fist. She made a fist. He asked her to raise two fingers and she did it. He then did another CT scan, the bleeding was still there so he put her back on the Propofal."

"Moving her hand, that's a good sign, right?" Surely it was a good sign. He had said the hemorrhage was slight and not enough to operate, so what was the big deal. This was just a waiting game, but Gayle was right, it was frustrating. Amelia did not stir at all when I kissed her.

"I hate to leave her here," Gayle said as tears started to pool in her eyes. She dabbed the corners of her eyes to try to stifle the tears.

"Don't worry about anything. I am going to be here with her." I tried to comfort her about leaving, but I could tell from the look she cut at me that the fact that I was with Amelia was little comfort.

"You have my number. You call me if anything changes. Do I make myself clear?" Gayle asked as she straightened the room.

"I understand. I promise I will call you if anything changes. Are you sure you are alright to drive? Are you awake enough?" Gayle looked as if she had not slept at all.

"You don't have to concern yourself with me." Gayle picked up her purse and eased past where I was standing near the bed to kiss Amelia's head. She then started toward the door. In the door frame she turned back to me. "Aunt Dot or I will be back here by 2:30."

"I'll be here when you return. Don't worry. She's going to be fine."

As Gayle went out the door, the first nurse of the morning came in. She was a different nurse from any that I had seen the day before.

"Good morning. I am Sherry. I'll be with y'all until noon. If she starts to move or anything, you press this call button here," she lifted up a cord with a button on the end of it like the buzzers on Jeopardy, "and I will come running."

"Yes, ma'am," I replied.

I paced around the room as Sherry took Amelia's vitals.

"How long do you think before the swelling goes down?" I asked her.

She glanced up from her watch while trying to take Amelia's blood pressure. "I really couldn't say."

"Her aunt mentioned this morning that she was on something called Propofal. What exactly is that?" I shook my head "no" while I spoke.

97

"It keeps her asleep, a medically induced coma. It's just a precaution until the swelling on her brain goes down."

The words, "medically induced coma," were hard to hear and I covered my mouth with my hand as she said them.

I tried to refocus. "Do you think she can hear me?"

"One never knows. I know it can't hurt to talk to her." Nurse Sherry jotted down numbers in a little notebook as she spoke.

"Do you think it would hurt her if I laid down next to her?"

"You mean you want to spoon with her?"

I was a little embarrassed at her response and hung my head, "Never mind I asked."

"It's okay. It's not exactly hospital policy to allow such things, but I think people do it all the time. In this case, I cannot condone it because her wounds are to her back."

I really did feel stupid for having asked. Nurse Sherry had a remarkable bedside manner. Before leaving she came over to me and patted me on the back, "She's going to be right as rain and you will be able to spoon with her again before you know it."

As soon as Sherry was gone, I decided that I would not completely lie down next to Amelia, but I would sit on the bed and stroke her hair. I was finally alone with her and although I had preferred she were awake, there was so much I wanted to say to her.

I was careful of all of the tubes as I eased in next to her. I began by explaining how badly I needed her to wake up. "I would much rather tell you all of this with your full attention on me. I am dying to see your eyes. You may not think I notice, but I do. I notice that they change colors depending on what you wear and if you have been crying. When you cry, they are the definition of ice blue and they are amazing even then."

"More important than the color of your eyes is the way you look at me. I have loved the way you look at me from the first moment I laid eyes on you. When you look at me, it is like the world

98

stands still and it nearly takes my breath away. I have never told you, but I have always hoped you knew."

I continued to lightly stroke her hair, making sure not to touch anywhere near where the bandage was on the back of her head. "You know you are the center of my universe and I am sorry if I have not let you know that lately. I am so sorry and you must wake up and allow me the opportunity to make it up to you."

There was a lump in my throat, but I carried on, "You don't know it yet, but we are going to be parents and I need you to wake up so I can tell you how very happy I am about that news. It's hard to be happy with you like this so you have to wake up so we can be ecstatic together."

The lump in my throat was joined by tears in my eyes. "I've loved you since the moment I first saw you. I have told you that before, but what I have not told you is that I have loved our child from the moment the doctor first uttered the words yesterday. I know we conceived the weekend of my birthday and short of the day I met you, that was the best day of my life. You have given me the best birthday present ever and you have to wake up so I may thank you properly."

As I went on, Amelia did not budge. Tears streamed down my face. "Your Aunt Gayle feels this has ruined your future, but I won't let it. This is our future. It always has been. It's just coming a little sooner than I had planned, but it was always a part of the plan. If you want to go to law school, this won't stop you. I won't let it. If you want to rebuild the hotel at Seven Springs, we'll do it. We'll do it together as a family, you, me, baby and Gabby."

"I know I am asking a lot, but you have to get better so you can meet Gabby. You are going to love her when you meet her. She is the sweetest thing and you are going to make a wonderful mother to her and our baby. I just know it. You are the kindest person I have ever met and I want Gabby to be just like you. I want her to squash everything in her of her mother and if there's anyone who can teach her to do that, it's you, Amelia, and I pray you will do that for me, that you will do it for her."

I continued to stroke her hair all the while I spoke.

"I am begging you, come back to me. I have never told you before, but I need you. I need you more than anything. I'm not me without you. I'll do anything if you will just come back to me." I openly wept and poured my heart out.

I was only taking a breath when suddenly Amelia moved her left hand up and stopped mine where it was in her hair. Although I had been begging her to wake up, I was shocked when she moved. My shock was immediately turned to excitement and with my free hand, I snatched up the cord with the call button and started pressing it like ringing a fire alarm.

Even though I knew the button was not a speaker for me to talk to the nurse's station, I did not know where that button was, I started screaming at the button as if it were. "She moved! She moved! She moved her hand!"

I suppose Nurse Sherry got the picture with the button or perhaps she could hear me screaming all the way down the hall. Either way, Nurse Sherry came running. I think she was at a full sprint when she threw open the door to Amelia's room. Upon sight of her, I continued with my excitement.

"She moved!" I tried to refrain from shouting, but it was hard not to jump up and scream. "I was talking to her and she moved."

"Okay?" Sherry seemed skeptical.

"Amelia moved her hand. It was lying on her side, but she moved it up. Look here. I have not moved this arm and see her hand here on my hand. I am telling you, she moved. She's coming to right?"

Nurse Sherry then took one of those slurping deep breaths through her teeth like she had some not so good news. She then answered while she started checking Amelia's pulse. "Not necessarily. Movement is a good sign, but I told you earlier, coma, remember? See this right here?" She asked, pointing to the bag that fed one of the tubes running to the IV in Amelia's hand.

Sherry continued to explain, "It's the knockout juice, that's not the medical term, but you understand. Sorry."

100

"Well, I think it's a good sign and it's better than nothing," I replied.

"Let's try moving her hand back and seeing if she moves it again. Let me get it. You've got to be careful of the IV."

Nurse Sherry was on the opposite side of the bed, the side Amelia was facing and I was on the other. She reached up to where Amelia's hand was still on mine and she moved it back to her side. We waited and Amelia did not move. I started to stroke her hair again.

"Is that what you were doing before?" she asked.

"Yes and talking to her."

"Well what are you waiting on? Talk to her." She motioned her hand as if I needed to get on with it.

"I'm not going to give up on you. I'm going to keep asking you to come back to me until you give in. Your Aunt Gayle was here earlier and she is worried sick about you. She's coming back this afternoon and I am sure she would love to hear good news about you. I promised her I would call so, come on, and give me a reason to call her."

I felt a little awkward professing my love to Amelia in front of a virtual stranger, but I sucked it up and went for it. "You know I love you and I am going to tell you every day all day long for the rest of your life. I would rather tell you when I have your full attention."

I ran my hand all the way down the length of her hair, still mindful not to touch the area near the bandage, and had just returned it to the top of her head to start again when she moved. Amelia reached up and placed her hand on mine again. This time, Nurse Sherry saw. Although she did not make a sound, she jumped and threw up a hand to high-five me.

"Amelia, I have never been more thrilled about holding your hand!" After high-fiving Nurse Sherry, I leaned over and kissed Amelia's hand that was again resting on top of mine.

"I'm going to go and let Dr. Andrews know that she moved."

"Okay. We will be right here," I joked. This was the most lighthearted I had been since prior to receiving the call from Cara the night before.

It wasn't long before Nurse Sherry returned with Dr. Andrews. He proceeded to tell me all about the possibilities of Amelia's progress and how he had never seen anyone pumped full of drugs move like that before. He confirmed that this was a good sign and he was hopeful that she would recover, but only time would tell.

The doctor did not stay long and when he left so did Nurse Sherry. "Just press the button again, if anything changes. Otherwise, keep doing what you are doing."

While Dr. Andrews was in the room, I had stood up, but they were hardly out of the room when I returned to the spot next to Amelia on the bed. As soon as I started to stoke her hair Amelia moved her hand back to mine. It seemed to be almost instinctual.

The day passed as I sat there with my hand resting on Amelia's head and her hand on top of mine. Some might have complained about sitting in the same position for so long, but not me. I could have sat there with her hand on mine for days if it meant I could be there when she woke up or that it was helping her to return to me.

By noon I was almost tired of hearing my own voice. I longed to hear hers and after three hours I was running out of ways to beg her to wake up. Amelia always knew there was something about my past that I was keeping from her. She had begged me time and again to let her in, but I always managed to put her off. There would come a day when I would not be able to get out of telling her. Having exhausted all "pleases and I love yous," I offered full disclosure if she would only roll over and look at me.

I waited, but it was as if I had made no request at all. Amelia did not move. I sat in silence, propped up on her bed, for at least ten minutes. In that time I gave up on her accepting my bribe, but decided this might be the perfect opportunity to practice telling her that I had killed my entire family.

I cleared my throat and started, "It was the spring of 1975. I was seven and my sister was ten. We had been to visit my Grandparents, my mother's parents, who lived in Gainesville. Normally, we would have taken my dad's Jeep, but it had been raining for days and my mother wanted to show off her new Volvo to her parents.

"The Volvo was the first new car anyone in her family had ever owned. My parents had saved and saved, five years they saved for their dream car for the family. It was a 1975 Volvo 264 GL and it had all the bells and whistles. My dad did all of the research and it was supposed to be the safest thing on the road at the time.

"It was 9:00 p.m. when we left my Grandparents' house. It was still raining cats and dogs when we started back to our house in Chiefland, about an hour away. My sister and I were tired and cranky."

I began to tear up at the thought, but I continued with my story, "To this day, I hate saying it, but I hated her and she hated me. My parents set the best example I have ever seen of a couple in love and they loved each of us more than anything, but the love did not extend between my sister and I. There wasn't a day that went by that we were not at each other. Separately we were great kids, but together we were like oil and water. We fought so much and with such viciousness toward one another that other parents in the neighborhood forbid their children to play with us. Name calling would have been polite for us."

"Anyway, we were hardly ten minutes into the drive home when we started arguing. I don't remember exactly what it was that set us off, but as always our parents demanded we stop. Thirty minutes into the trip and we were still at it. Dad warned us he would pull the car over and my mother turned around and threatened to spank the next one that passed a lick."

"I remember most everything so clearly. My dad was driving and Mom was in the front passenger's seat. I was in the backseat behind Dad and Ella, my sister's name was Ella, she was in the seat behind Mom."

"Ella quickly punched me in the top of my leg with the back of her fist so mom could not see. She counted on me hitting her back and Mom seeing so I would be the one in trouble. That was classic Ella. I thought I would outsmart her this time, so I snatched up her Mrs. Beasley doll that was on the seat between us."

"I can still see that doll, blonde hair, blue dress with white dots. Ella loved that doll and she had carried it everywhere and slept with it every night. The doll was a year older than I was and the years had not been kind."

"I thought I was really going to teach Ella a lesson about messing with me without hitting her back. Ella had turned her head and I could see her smiling in the reflection of the window she was looking out of, pleased with herself for getting the last lick on me when I snatched up that doll. 'Ella, Mrs. Beasley has a headache,' I taunted her as she turned to see what I was talking about."

"I used all of my little seven year old muscles and I snatched that doll's head off. I threw the head in the floorboard of the car at Ella's feet."

"If the story ended there then it might be one of those fun stories that my family would tell about Ella and I, like the one your aunt told about you and the Christmas pageant, but the story did not end there."

"Ella shrieked in terror and tore off her seatbelt and dove to the floor to try to get the head. Still holding the body, I gloated. I had never seen or heard my parents so pissed with me."

"'Why would you do such a thing?!!!' my mother screamed at me. She had never really raised her voice at me before. She had unbuckled her seat belt and was coming over the seat. I thought she was coming for me, to spank me right there in the car."

"I tried to defend my actions. 'You said not to hit her and you didn't see her hit me.'"

"I began to cry, but not nearly as hard as Ella, 'Mommy, he killed Mrs. Beasley. I can't find her head. I can't find her head, Mommy!'"

"The head had rolled under the front seat. My mother wasn't coming for me as she leaned over the seat. She was trying to help Ella find Mrs. Beasley's head. I was crying, Ella was crying, and Mother was digging under the seat. The last thing I remember is seeing my Dad's eyes as he glanced back in the rearview mirror at me. He was shaking his head in disappointment. Everyone who knew my Dad says I have his eyes."

"As best they could figure, a deer ran out in the road. When Dad glanced back at the road, he immediately swerved to avoid the deer. There were no skid marks, no witnesses, no nothing, but the aftermath. He lost control of the car. I really don't remember how it happened, maybe it was a deer. I don't know."

"Regardless of how, I was the why. If I had just let the doll be maybe..."

I wiped my eyes. There was no use going on about what might have been. I began my story again. "The car flipped end over end. The front end of the car was crushed when it flipped. It came to rest on its roof. It slid backward down an embankment and into what they said would normally have been a dry creek bed, but the rain had caused the area to flood.

My mother was killed instantly and the front end of the car went under water. My father's legs were trapped and he drowned when the water from the flooded creek rushed in. They found him clutching my mother's body.

Somehow, Ella had been thrown through the back window of the car when it went end over end. They think she was killed instantly, but they called me a miracle. I was the cause of all of it. I have no idea how I got out of the car. They found me the next morning asleep on the ground next to Ella. I had little more than a few scratches on me, but I was no miracle."

When I was finished, I leaned over, kissed Amelia's forehead. I had removed my hand from under hers to steady myself for the kiss. Once secure, I rested all of my weight on my right side and propped on my right arm. I kissed her once more and caressed her cheek. Careful not to put any weight on her, I leaned forward to see her face. Her eyes were not open, but tears had fallen down her face. Was this even possible? Had she heard me?

I did not want to keep crying wolf when they had already told me not to expect a miracle, but I went at it with the call button again. Nurse Sherry had mentioned earlier that her shift ended at noon so this time, another nurse came running.

All in all, Amelia was making progress. It was likely she had heard me. Although the doctors and nurses did not want me to continue to make her cry, they did ask me to keep doing what I was doing. After everyone left the room, I started talking to her again.

"Let's talk about happy times, shall we?" I asked her as if I really expected an answer. Crying wolf or not, if she had answered, I would have been buzzing that call button like a Jeopardy champion.

"What would you like to talk about?" I asked rhetorically. Of course no answer came.

"Alright then, I will pick the subject, the pearls I gave you for your birthday. I told you they were my mother's, but what I did not tell you is that they were stolen. That's right. She stole them. She did not mean to, but my Aunt Mary, who was not actually my aunt, but my mother's first cousin, told me the story."

"My mother and Aunt Mary were the same age and grew up just down the street from one another. As little girls they read every single Nancy Drew book they could get their hands on and when they had read the latest book again and again until the pages were worn, they pretended to be Nancy Drew. They invented mysteries and pretended to solve them.

"There was an elderly lady, a widow named Mrs. Harper that lived a block over. Mrs. Harper had the largest house in the neighborhood. She was also the first person to have a car in the neighborhood and the first woman in the county to drive. Mrs. Harper was likely the wealthiest person any of their parents knew. Her husband had made a fortune in shipping before retiring to Florida. He died shortly after they moved down and Mrs. Harper inherited everything.

"Anyway, as young girls they got it in their head that Mrs. Harper was hiding something. They were sure of it. For weeks during the summer, they watched her comings and goings. They followed her on their bikes, tailing her every move. Mrs. Harper had no idea they were following her and they were quite proud of their prowess. Everywhere she went, they went. If she drove faster, they pedaled harder.

"Finally, they had her movements down to a science and one Wednesday afternoon, they decided that it was time to search her house. It was time to uncover what Mrs. Harper was hiding and again, they knew she was hiding something.

"They counted on her getting her hair done every Thursday afternoon. At 1:00 p.m. she left for Mrs. Flossie's beauty parlor and she never returned home before 4:00. That gave them almost three hours to turn the house upside down and inside out.

"Back then, no one locked their doors so they waited in the bushes out behind Mrs. Harper's house until they saw her drive down the street and she was out of sight. Then, they crawled across the yard attempting to keep the neighbors from seeing. When they came to the back door, they found it open and slipped inside.

"Mom and Aunt Mary borrowed my grandmother's stockings and wore them for gloves to avoid leaving finger prints as all of the real detectives in the movies always wore gloves. It was Florida, so they had no winter gloves to wear and they had to make do.

"Once inside, they searched and searched from room to room. Finally, they found themselves in Mrs. Harper's bedroom. Although they did not find anything of a suspicious nature, they did find all of her jewelry and furs that she brought when she moved from New Hampshire. Mother was busy trying on her jewelry and Aunt Mary was in her closet trying on the furs when they heard the screen door slam.

"'Did you hear that?' my mother whispered to Aunt Mary.

"Without saying a word, my mother knew from how big Aunt Mary's eyes got, that someone was in the house with them. Aunt Mary said she was frozen with fright. Footsteps were coming closer to them and Mother tried to move her, but she could not budge. There was no way out of the room other than from the direction of the footsteps.

"The footsteps kept coming and Mother shut the door on Aunt Mary leaving her hiding in the closet. Mother dove under the bed and waited. From where she hid she could see Mrs. Harper's Mary Jane's as she clopped closer and closer until she slipped the shoes off by the bed.

"Aunt Mary said she just knew they were dead meat. She heard my mother gasp all the way inside the closet and the slap against her face when Mother covered her mouth. Mrs. Harper should have been the spokesperson for a campaign against high heels. She had bunions for days and the most gnarled feet my mother had ever seen. Aunt Mary said that from then on they called Mrs. Harper 'Creepy Feet'.

"They had not counted on Mrs. Harper coming home, crawling into bed and taking a nap. Aunt Mary was stuck in the closet and my mother was stuck under the bed. As Mother waited under the bed she could see the mattress above her heave with every breath and every snort that the elderly lady took and it jolted once or twice when she had gas. Aunt Mary said it seemed like hours and hours that they were trapped there as the woman napped. In actuality, they waited three hours before mother worked up the courage to get out from under the bed, grab Aunt Mary and bolt.

"The two girls ran through the house, out the screen door slamming it behind them and never looking back as they pedaled as fast as they could all the way home. In all of the haste, my mother had totally forgotten that she was trying on Mrs. Harper's pearls when she heard the lady come back home. As they parked their bikes Aunt Mary noticed. 'Oh my God, you still have on her necklace.'" Aunt Mary pointed out. "We have to go back."

"'I am not going back now!' my mother protested.

"'You have to. You stole it and we could get in big trouble. My mother would beat us if she got one whiff of us having stolen something.' Aunt Mary was always so mindful of absolutely everything.

"They argued and my mother finally agreed to take it back the following day. The plan was to sneak in and just put the strand of pearls back where she got them, but she refused to go alone. Reluctantly, Aunt Mary agreed to go for the second time.

The following day, they were on their way to return the pearls. Pedaling along with my mother in front and Aunt Mary behind, they were almost there when a car did not stop at a stop sign while they were crossing. The car barely missed my mother, but Aunt Mary got hit and skipped across the hood of the car. Mother recognized the car as they had been following it for several weeks. It was Mrs. Harper. Aunt Mary was fine, just a couple of bruises, but the story is that the wreck scared the life right out of Mrs. Harper. She was ninety and had no business driving and there was a difference of opinion as to how Mother came to keep the pearls. Aunt Mary said Mother stole them, but as Aunt Mary told it, Mother said she inherited them.

The afternoon progressed on with me telling Amelia one story after another until my relief came. Even though it was a one sided conversation, I had enjoyed being with her as much as one could while wishing and praying that she would just snap out of it.

CHAPTER 7

It was Friday morning and what I thought was the alarm clock went off entirely too early. I was exhausted and it was not the alarm clock, but the phone ringing. As was becoming my norm, I jumped to grab the phone thinking it might be word that Amelia was awake.

Again, per the new norm, it was nothing about Amelia. It was Mrs. Allen calling at 6:45 a.m. to tell me that she could not keep Gabby today. Two of her grandchildren had pink eye and it was highly contagious. She did not want to pass it on to Gabby.

Mrs. Allen felt terrible, but I assured her, "These things happen," and everything would be fine.

Once off of the phone with Mrs. Allen, I dialed Stella. She had given me her number when she kept Gabby earlier in the week and told me to call her anytime. Unfortunately, the phone rang and rang. There was no answer.

Perhaps it was that I was exhausted or perhaps I just was not thinking straight that led me to decide to take Gabby with me to the hospital. What idiot would take Gabby, a month old baby, to a hospital for any reason other than to have the baby seen about?

Amelia's Aunt Gayle was taking the night shifts except for the one Jay took the night before last. Her Aunt Dot had been taking the afternoon shifts. I had been taking the 9:00 a.m. to 2:30 p.m. shift and then coming home and going to work. I had not missed a day of sitting with Amelia or feeding the equestrian team at Port Honor in the evening. I had hardly seen Gabby at all and I felt guilty about that. The poor thing did not have a mother and now her father had gone MIA as well.

On Wednesday, Dr. Andrews had a CT scan performed on Amelia to check the status of the swelling on her brain. The swelling had gone down, so he started weaning her off of the Propofol, formerly known as knockout juice. Another reason for weaning her off was that the prolonged use of a drug induced coma ran the risk of side effects, one of which was pneumonia. The doctor did not want to run the risk of Amelia getting pneumonia and then having to be treated for that. Plus, even though she was thirteen weeks into the pregnancy and technically out of the first trimester, Dr. Andrews did not feel that any of this was good for the baby.

Although the doctor carefully explained that he was reducing the medication. He never once said, as I recalled, that he was firing off a fog horn in her face to wake her up. Nonetheless, everyone and their dog, even those who had already visited, were storming the castle to be there when Amelia woke up. In fact, almost everyone she knew had been to see her; Jay, of course, Stella and Travis, Cara and Megan, Jerry and Daniel, Alex, Andy and Matt plus all of her family members had made the trip and a vast array of friends and neighbors from Jefferson County. They had all come in the first few days of her being at the hospital, but since Wednesday morning, most all had returned at least once. I suspected there would be more of them today.

Dr. Andrews explained to us that they would be performing another CT scan on Amelia today to find out if the swelling had gone down any more. From the discussion he had with us on Wednesday, we had every reason to believe that the swelling might be back to normal very soon as the swelling was so slight that it hardly registered on the scan. We were all very relieved at the news.

Little mention was made of Amelia's pelvic injury. Of course I asked about it, but the doctor all but stated it was the lesser of the two evils. I had been included in all of the discussions of Amelia's condition since day one. That had been at the urging of Aunt Dot. She said I had every right to know her condition as Amelia's condition was one in the same as that of the child inside her, my child. I was thankful to her for including me. I was thankful to the doctor for allowing me to ask the questions as her aunts simply hung on his every word.

"She is a remarkable girl. I have never seen someone with such a will to live as your niece. Several signs that I myself witnessed indicate just that and it has been a first for me. I have never seen anything like it." Dr. Andrews laid compliments heavily on Amelia. "She is clearly a strong willed girl. Y'all should be proud."

When I replied, "We are." It had not occurred to me that I would be out of place to respond, but it clearly was as evidenced by the roll of Gayle's eyes.

Apparently, the little signs that we had been seeing, were cause for hope. It looked as if she was just lying there sleeping day in and day out and all the while she was fighting to return to us. The Olympics were slated to end on Sunday, August 4th, so there was an end in sight for that and we had every right to hope that Amelia's recovery was in sight as well.

***

The ringing of the phone had awakened Gabby and she was hungry. There was no going back to sleep then. I fed her, changed her and dressed her. I picked out the cutest pink pajamas that she owned. I was no fashionista, but I matched Gabby's pink pajamas with a crocheted pink cap that Praise had made for her. I had found there was no need in dressing her in anything other than pajamas at this point in her young life.

While I dressed Gabby, I tried calling Stella once more. Still there was no answer. Finally, the diaper bag was packed and loaded in the car with Gabby in her carrier and we were on our way. I did not know what else to do, but take her with me.

As I drove past the hospital on my way to the same parking deck I had used all week, I noticed that the news crews that had been camped outside of Grady all week were finally starting to dwindle. There had been a barrage of reporters attempting to question most anyone that entered the hospital. I had been approached by at least three every day that I had been to the hospital. It was a relief not to have them slowing me down while carrying Gabby and all of her gear.

Gabby had slept all the way from Greensboro to Atlanta. While getting her out of the car she opened her eyes just for a split second and glanced up at me. I swear she smiled at me before drifting back off. Taking care of Gabby had been a good distraction. If I did not have her, I would have been consumed by the situation with Amelia. I had heard that babies could sense things so I did my best to keep my mood in check and not allow Gabby to sense that there was anything wrong. So far so good.

Through the doors and up toward Amelia's floor we went. Everyone we passed stopped to peek in the carrier at her. Gabby did not notice. She just kept sleeping.

I made it almost all the way to Amelia's door before one of the nurses stopped me. She stood from behind the nurse's desk as I passed by and asked, "Excuse me. Are you planning to take that baby in there?"

"I am," I replied as I turned back to face her.

"Babies are not allowed on this floor," she began.

"Right. You see I am going to that room right over there. You have seen me come and go all week," I pointed to Amelia's door. "And if you do not mind terribly, I am going to take my daughter to see sleeping beauty."

The nurse blushed a little and waived me on into the room. "If I hear a peep out of you, I will have to ask you to leave, but for now, I have not seen a thing."

It was Nurse Sherry and she was way nicer than the other nurses. She was a little more relaxed than the others that were all business and by the book.

Quickly, I made for the door to Amelia's room. I eased open the door and carried Gabby in.

"Gabe is that you?" Gayle called from the private restroom in the room. She alternated my name back and forth. Sometimes she referred to me as Gabe, sometimes Gabriel. I tended to answer to both.

"Yes, ma'am."

"Alright. I'll be right out."

I proceeded to sit the carrier down on the little couch in front of the window and the diaper bag on the floor next to it. The sleeping beauty phrase re-entered my head as I watched Amelia still lying there. She was exactly as I had left her the day before. I figured what could it hurt and everyone needed a little magic every now and then, so I leaned over and kissed her. This time I did not just kiss her forehead. Her lips were soft and the spark was absolutely electric. As I kissed her, I prayed for her to reciprocate. The kiss was cut short by Gayle's return from the restroom.

"You did not seriously bring that baby in here?" Gayle was not pleased.

"I could not get a sitter," I tried to explain.

"Where on earth is the child's mother?"

"I wish I knew."

"What do you mean you 'wish you knew'?"

I then proceeded to fill Gayle in on the details of Gabby being left with me.

Gayle's facial expression turned from anger at the nerve of me bringing what she had likely considered a thorn in the side of her niece's happiness to compassion and concern. "You mean to tell me she just abandoned the child as soon as she gave birth?"

I had not used the term 'abandoned' in relation to what Beth had done to Gabby, but the term did fit. "That pretty much sums it up."

"And you haven't heard from her since and it's been three weeks?" Gayle continued with her questions as she walked over to get a better look at Gabby while I took a seat in the chair that was pulled up next to Amelia's bed.

"Not one word. It's been closer to four weeks and I've left messages for her. She has not even bothered to call back."

"She's pretty, but she doesn't look a thing like you," Gayle voiced her observation. It was not the first time I had heard that. Most everyone who met Gabby said the same thing.

Jay entered the room just as Gabby was waking up and Gayle and I were still talking. Gabby fussed just a little so I got up and began to remove her from the carrier. While I tended to Gabby, Gayle turned her attention to Jay. She hugged him, thanked him for coming and then proceeded to fill him in on the latest concerning Amelia's condition.

"They're saying that we just have to wait. They don't appear to be concerned that she hasn't woken up yet."

As I changed Gabby I could hear their whole conversation and began to participate in it. "Did they mention what we might expect next?"

"No," Gayle answered. "They just seem to want to wait and see."

Jay asked, "What if we tried to wake her?"

"Dear, we have begged and begged her to wake up. I don't know what else we might do." I wondered what they were up to and should have intervened.

Nothing about this was normal, but normally Gayle would have left shortly after I arrived. There was still tension between us over Amelia being pregnant, which is something that we had yet to really discuss. This particular morning, she stuck around even after Jay arrived. I think she was trying to wait for Amelia to wake up, but no one seemed to understand or accept that there was no firm time table on this.

Jay did not come right out with what he had in mind, but he walked over to the tray where the pitcher of ice water was sitting and picked it up. Gayle and I watched, wondering what he was going to do. The nurses had turned Amelia and she was lying on her left side. Jay walked around to the left side of the bed.

"She hates water in her face," Jay said.

I don't know how I did not know that, but of course Gayle knew. "You aren't about to throw that pitcher of water in her face are you?"

"God, no!" Jay said as the poured water in his cupped hand. "Not the whole pitcher." And he dipped his fingers in the pitcher and then flicked the water in Amelia's face.

"I can't believe you just did that!" I was shocked, but tried not to raise my voice since I was holding Gabby.

We all saw Amelia flinch a little as the water ran down her face, but she still did not wake up.

"I thought surely that would do it." Jay was disappointed and fell back into one of the guest chairs in the room letting his face fall in my direction.

For a moment we all sat in silence. Initially, I thought they were each trying to come up with some other form of torture to try to wake Amelia since Jay's waterboarding technique had not worked. Gayle might have been having those types of thoughts, but not Jay.

Jay rose up from the chair. "May I hold the baby?" he asked as he held out his hands to take her.

"Okay." Not sure what he was up to, but we did the gentle exchange of Gabby. Jay was clearly experienced with babies as he knew exactly how to cradle her neck and head in the exchange.

Jay made faces and what not for a few minutes before he spoke again. "Your daughter has brown eyes?"

"Yeah."

Silence followed for another few minutes until Jay spoke again. "I only saw Beth that one time, but I could swear she had green eyes."

"She does," I replied. This got Gayle's attention and she sat up and took notice of me.

"Your eyes are blue," Gayle observed as she got up from the couch and walked over to where Jay was holding Gabby. It was as if she wanted to have a closer look at us for herself.

"Yes..." I was beginning to wonder where this conversation was going.

Gayle then turned back to me and sought confirmation. "The child's mother has green eyes?"

"Yes. What's this about?" They clearly knew something I didn't.

"And you were not there when the child was born?" Gayle asked and she took Gabby from Jay. She was obviously getting a better look at Gabby.

"No. Seriously, what's this about?" again I asked.

Before Gayle could say anything else, Jay spilled it. "You are not this child's father."

I was taken aback by that statement, "What do you mean?"

"I'm only a vet and I'm no doctor, but one of the lessons in basic biology for humans is that a blue eyed person and a green eyed person cannot have a child with brown eyes. A brown eyed child, whose mother has green eyes, has a father with brown eyes." Gayle explained.

"You are not serious!" I exclaimed. I got up and took Gabby back from Gayle. "This is not funny!"

"You are right, it's not funny!" said Jay. "Hold on, I will get one of the nurses in case you don't believe us. You can ask them."

The room was starting to spin a little for me and I paced with Gabby as Jay left the room. He returned with three nurses. He did not give a detailed explanation, just asked their opinions.

"No chance of parents with green eyes and blue eyes, mother green and father blue, having a brown-eyed child, right?"

The first nurse just stood there and the other two answered in unison, "No chance."

My world was spinning as the nurse at the door clarified her answer, "Almost always, brown eyed children have at least one parent with brown eyes."

"That will be all. Thanks so much." Jay escorted the nurses out and shut the door behind them.

"You need to get a blood test on this child," Gayle said.

"Blood test or not, DNA or not, you are mine," I looked down at Gabby in my arms. She was cooing at me and smiling. How could I ever let that sweet face down? I couldn't.

I looked back to Gayle and Jay and their eyes conveyed that both were surprised by my words to Gabby. "She's got no one else." I said to them. "And I won't just throw her away."

Gayle reached in her purse and pulled out a card and handed it to me. "You are going to need a lawyer and this is the finest one in the tri-county area."

I took the card and looked at it: Reggie Bell, Attorney at Law. Along with his name was his address and phone number. This was the Mr. Bell that Amelia had mentioned, the man who helped with her inheritance. "I already have an attorney."

"You already have an attorney?" Jay seemed surprised.

"I told Amelia I would come for her and I was working on that," I explained as I handed the card back to Gayle.

"Getting custody of the child has been your plan all along, hasn't it?" Gayle asked.

"Yes. I know I should have told Amelia, but everything has just gone so off track lately with work and the attorney advised me to distance myself from Amelia a little bit until we had the case against Beth more solid."

I knew I would have to explain my actions to them, but I was having a hard time focusing on that when I was still confused as to why Beth would insist that Gabby was mine, name her after me, leave her with me and disappear. Why would she turn my entire life

118

upside down for a child that wasn't mine? All this time wasted with Amelia; keeping me from her, breaking my heart and hers. Why?

Everything Beth had done to me paled in comparison to what she had done to her own child. The only bond the poor child had with anyone on this earth was with a man who was nothing to her.

"Millie told me everything about Beth. She told me about the night Beth showed up at your house when she showed up drunk and broke in and Millie told me about the photos of her that Beth left at your house, the photos where she was stalking Millie. I don't understand that woman at all and I don't begin to understand how someone could abandon their child. I didn't understand how Millie's mother could let her go so easily and I don't even know this woman and I don't understand it." Gayle reached over and gently took Gabby from me. She walked and rocked her. It was easy to tell that Gayle was a natural mother even though she had never had children of her own.

Gayle continued as she cradled Gabby in her arms. "Some people should never have children. I know you love my niece and I know she loves you, but you have more to think about than yourselves. You have to think about the child she is carrying too and your responsibilities to it. If you want custody of this child, you are going to have to fight for her, for Millie, for your child with her. To be quite honest with you, you seem to have taken the easy way out at every turn and been a coward when it comes to this Beth woman..."

"I think what she's trying to say is you need to get mad and grow a pair," Jay interjected.

Gayle turned Gabby's head so she could not see her face and she covered her ears as if Gabby might actually understand what she was about to say. "I am saying you need to get mad as Hell! I am mad as Hell! Until New Year's Eve, I thought you were a decent guy. All this time, I have been so furious with you for breaking Millie's heart. So absolutely furious! I think we have all realized it's not you that broke Millie's heart. It's the mother of this poor thing. I think it's time for you to stop being a decent guy and start fighting back. "

I bent over to the diaper bag and took out one of the bottles I had brought for Gabby and started to prepare it. I thought about what they said. "Fighting back, huh? I have been fighting for longer than y'all know. What's funny is that I have been building a case for custody of a child that we now know isn't mine and I don't intend to stop. This has just made me more determined. And, I am mad as Hell. I have been mad as Hell for a long time, but showing it outwardly really won't help any of us."

"What do you mean building a case?" Gayle asked as I handed her the bottle.

I went on to explain to Jay and Gayle that I had hired one of the club members, a local attorney named Jack Mathis. Mr. Mathis had been in practice in Greensboro for twenty years. He was well respected around the club and I had met him on a number of occasions prior to having retained him.

"I know y'all have likely heard that I let Beth move in with me. That's not exactly how it went and one of my meetings with Attorney Mathis was for me to figure out how to remove her from my house because she had refused to leave. Do you know how it made my skin crawl to think that she was in my house and Amelia wasn't? Let me be clear, she was never in my bed while she was there.

"Anyway, Jack said not to worry about Beth moving in since it allowed us to prove that Beth was now a resident of Green County, giving us home field advantage when we filed for custody against her. Beth has lived in her parents' home off of West Paces Ferry Road in Atlanta all of her life and her father is a big time developer in Fulton County. If we filed the suit for custody against her in Fulton County, she and her family would more than likely have that advantage."

Gayle and Jay continued to listen as I went on. "He also advised me to keep a journal on Beth and on Gabby. How Beth behaved and the names of people other than myself that witnessed her in the months that she was pregnant. That's the primary reason I did not run her off from the club. The more she came in and the more people that saw her, drinking while pregnant and the way she treats people, well, the more she helped me. You know how it goes, keep your friends close…"

"And your enemies closer. It appears you are not quite the coward I accused you of being," Gayle commented as Gabby finished the bottle.

"No, there has been a method to my madness and I am sorry I did not include Amelia, but in all honesty, I kind of wanted Amelia in the dark. Attorney Mathis called it plausible deniability. Should Beth call Amelia into this, he wanted Amelia to be able to say we had not been involved."

"Now you are here and everyone at the club knows what has happened to Amelia, so no more deniability when she wakes up and no more deniability from witnesses at the club who know where you have been the last week. Have you thought about how you are going to get around that now if Beth does counter sue and bring that up?" Gayle seemed to be coming around to my way of thinking.

"I have not given it much thought yet. All I can say is let her bring it on."

Jay was always Amelia's go-to guy for advice and he was sly enough to swipe The Jefferson and wheel and deal for Amelia to buy it so it was not that shocking when he presented a plan to speed up this entire process. "You need to draw Beth out and cause her to do something stupid. She seems to do stupid things when she is flustered. Her finding out she was pregnant, then getting drunk and breaking into your house is a prime example. That time it landed her in jail. I think you need to ruffle her feathers."

Gayle seemed to follow, "My daddy would say, 'You need to give her enough rope to hang herself.'"

"And how do you propose I do that?" I definitely wanted this sped up, but what could I do?

Amelia's room was on the front of the hospital building. Jay walked to the window, fiddled with the blinds until he had them open and looked to the street below, "The news crews are still out there. Why don't you give them what they have been asking us for all week?"

"What's that?" I still was not sure what he had in mind.

"Go down there and when the news crew asks you again if you were visiting one of the survivors from the bombing, tell them you were visiting your fiancé. Even if Beth doesn't see it, someone who knows her will and they'll tell her. I'd be willing to bet that she would be on your door step before you get there." I approached the window as Jay pointed, "Look, the CNN crew is still down there, perfect!"

"But we were trying to keep Amelia out of this," and telling the world she was my fiancée would not accomplish that.

"Amelia's not going anywhere and keeping her out of it, well, that's a pipe dream," Gayle insisted. "You let us worry about Amelia, but I think you really need your ducks in a row before you alert the media."

"I should probably call Jack and let him know about Gabby not being mine so as not to blindside him."

"That's probably a good idea. It might behoove you to find out who the real father is. Do you have any clue who it might be?"

"Not really." I scratched my head and tried to think, but no one was coming to mind.

"Amelia came home right before Christmas and repeated gossip that Cara had told her," Jay began. "Cara had told Amelia that she had a friend that worked at one of the other clubs. The friend told her that Joan from your club entered the dining room at lunch one day and confronted a young woman in front of the entire room. She confronted the woman about having an affair with her husband..."

Gayle gasped, "You don't think?"

"No way, Dick and Beth!" I was shocked as well.

"Amelia said Cara never said who it was that Joan confronted, but it was quite the amusing story. Apparently, Joan told the woman, 'Let me know when you are ready and I will clean out the guest room for you because I could use some help cleaning his dirty drawers and raising his children.'"

Gayle snickered, "That's priceless." It was the first time Gayle had cracked more than a half smile all week.

"That would certainly explain the vibe I have been getting from Joan since Gabby has been born," I admitted.

"We can't just go around accusing people of being the child's father," Gayle was the voice of reason.

It seemed too easy, but what if it were Dick? I thought about the time Amelia and I fought about Beth keeping her hands off of me. Gayle and Jay both noticed the look on my face and required an explanation.

"I am sure Amelia told y'all about the day we had the car chase. She came in off of the beverage cart and found me seated at a table in the dining room, laughing it up with Beth and Dick during Sunday brunch. It did not strike me as odd then. I thought they just arrived at the same time, coincidence, but now, I think they arrived together. Amelia was right, Beth was flirting with me, but I thought nothing of it."

"This was after the night she broke in, but before Joan confronted the girl at the other club." Jay seemed to be making a timeline.

"Right. What if she was..."

Gayle chimed in, "Flirting with you not for Millie's benefit, but for Dick's and Millie was just the cherry on top."

"Beth and I had a joke when I left for Japan with the Navy and we broke up. The joke was that we would always be one another's back-up plan," I shook my head in disbelief at how she had tried to keep us to that plan. "What she has failed to realize is that I didn't need or want a back-up plan and what I failed to realize is that it wasn't a joke to Beth especially if she was knocked-up by a married man."

"Joan has been acting weird to you since Gabby was born? I think we are on to something, but what do we do about our suspicions?" Gayle continued to walk the room with Gabby even though Gabby had been asleep since shortly after she finished her bottle.

"What's also amusing is that Joan has always hated Beth and this would explain so much." I thought out loud, but did not answer Gayle's question.

Jay answered Gayle and glazed over what I was saying. "I think Gabe needs to tell Joan that he knows Gabby is not his child and see what she says."

"I also can't believe Joan would let all of this happen to Amelia. Joan's always been the nicest person. She loved Amelia..."

"I think Jay is right. You need to see what Joan has to say. Don't tell her you suspect Dick or anything, but just let her know you are looking for the child's father. Talk to her like the two of you used to talk." Gayle was just as good at plotting as Jay was.

"You know what else you should probably do?" It was clearly a rhetorical question as Jay immediately answered himself before anyone else could. "You need to get the medical records on Gabby from when she was born. Find out if there were any drugs in her system."

Gayle turned and patted Jay on the back, "Good point."

"Okay," I agreed. When I first arrived at the hospital that morning, I dreaded seeing Gayle. The day had taken quite the turn and she and Jay were becoming my closest allies in the fight for Gabby.

"I think you were right about needing to let your attorney know about all of this. I think we should also wait before you give your statement to the news outside. I think you need to talk to Joan tonight and then get the baby's medical records tomorrow and then we should go from there." Jay was quite the schemer.

"I can't believe y'all are helping me like this." I just had to say it.

Gayle was the first one to respond. "You have been here all week long for Millie. I thought for a while that you might have just

124

been using her or toying with her. I thought you were a real scoundrel. This week you have really proved me wrong. You could find Beth and give this child back to her, be free to go about your life with Millie, but even after finding out today that the child isn't yours you are still willing to fight for her. You have no idea how Millie is going to feel about the child, yet you seem willing to risk her to protect the child and if that's not honorable, I don't know what is."

I had not cried in years until this week and again tears filled my eyes. I tried to hold them back at the same time I stood and hugged Gayle. She reciprocated.

Our discussion of what all I should do about Beth continued throughout the morning. Finally, Gayle laid Gabby on the bed next to Amelia and the two of them slept as Gayle, Jay and I strategized. I could hardly take my eyes off of them as they laid there. It was as if Gabby had cuddled up to Amelia and the both of them were perfect together. With the exception of the surroundings; hospital gown and the room, this was the picture I saw when I thought of the mother of my child.

Thanks to Jay and Gayle's help, I had a much better plan and felt as if I stood a chance of gaining custody of Gabby. I allowed myself to believe that I could be free of Beth and have the picture before me.

I was happy to be back in the fold of Amelia's family and I believe Gayle was equally happy to have the distraction. All week we had all been consumed with Amelia's well-being. Seeing Amelia like this and the uncertainty of her condition had taken a toll on all of us, but I am not sure who took it harder, Gayle or me.

By lunchtime we had revisited the idea of what to do with the information regarding Gabby's father. We all agreed that that would be the final blow delivered to Beth. We came to the conclusion that I was in a better position to gain custody as long as most everyone believed I was the father.

Jay backtracked on his opinion for me to seek custody of Gabby. He was more interested in Amelia's happiness and thought I would serve Beth right to have Gabby to deal with all on her own. He was in favor of taking the easy way out. Gayle quickly set him straight about how the easy thing to do is rarely the right thing or the honorable thing.

Ultimately, Jay came back around but not before making his own case. "I know we have always teased Millie about being an overachiever, but has anyone thought about what she is in for when she wakes up?"

My first thought was, "What if she wants nothing to do with me and what if she wants even less to do with Gabby?"

Jay started to speak again, but Gayle cut him off. "Don't be a fool!" she said to me. "I can't tell you how many times she and I have fought over my recent opinions of you. Millie would hear none of it. I don't think her taking you back is going to be an issue."

"Gayle's got a point, but that's not what I meant." Jay shut down the turn the conversation was taking. "I mean she is going to wake up to find that we have all planned her future without her. She's not only going to wake up to be told that she's pregnant, but by the way 'you are also the new mother of a one month old baby that's not related to anyone you really know and don't forget you start law school in two weeks and have to pick a general contractor to rebuild a small hotel. Good luck with the pregnancy'!"

Jay paused only for a moment to catch his breath and he was right, he did have a point. That was a lot for anyone and it was concerning to me.

Jay started again, "I suppose you will ask her to marry you the moment she wakes up so let's go ahead and add planning a quickie wedding to the list. And, if that's not enough, she will likely want to be involved in aiding you in the custody fight plus she still has to recover from all of this," and he turned, threw out a hand and pointed at her.

The look on Gayle's face conveyed a clear lack of amusement as she addressed Jay's concerns. "The last I heard he's not asked and that's between them. Everyone's been calling him her fiancé, but he's not..."

I cut her off, "I plan to ask as soon as possible..."

Gayle threw up her hand in the "shut-up now" gesture as she continued on. "Until you ask and she accepts, you are not and that's between the two of you. Second, he already has a nanny that helps with Gabby, so that's sorted out. Third, a pregnant girl can attend law school. She's pregnant, not crippled and they have said nothing about this bombing having crippled her. And, not to burst any bubbles, but I have always been the one in charge of the contractor and I am not going anywhere."

Gayle had directed her statements at the both of us, but the last part was Jay specific. "She also has you and you have always been more of a brother to her than a friend. Nothing has ever kept the two of you from accomplishing anything you set your minds to. Just look at that building y'all bought and what you've already done on the property at Seven Springs. Don't stop having faith in yourselves now."

She then changed courses with the conversation. Gayle glanced at her watch and walked over to where her purse was sitting. "I am starving so enough about all of that."

Gayle leaned over and picked up her purse and both Jay and I stood. "I am going to head home."

It was nearly lunchtime. Jay was still in class for the rest of the summer so he had a project to complete and needed to get back to Milledgeville. He and Gayle left together, but not before each kissed Amelia and Gabby goodbye.

Apparently Gayle's words got through to Jay because when he leaned up from kissing Gabby he whispered to her just loud enough for me to hear. "You can call me Uncle Jay and that's going to be your mommy right there and we all love her very much and you are going to love her, too. I promise."

Jay stood back up and they both hugged me and said a few parting words before they left. Gayle told me she was so sorry for all of this, meaning what had happened to Amelia and me.

"Aunt Dot will be here at 2:30 p.m. to relieve you. We all hate leaving her, but we understand you also have a job to do and that's okay. Millie would not expect you to skirt your responsibilities on her account. Anyway, tell Aunt Dot I'll see her sometime tomorrow."

"Thanks for everything," I said. "Amelia's very lucky to have you."

Gayle let go of me with her left arm and pulled Jay into kind of a group hug. "She's lucky to have both of you," Gayle said as she hugged both of us at once.

When Gayle let go of us, Jay held out his hand to me. We shook as he explained, "I just want the best for Millie and I hope you know that. I'll do whatever I can and between all of us. Your former girlfriend is not going to know what hit her."

"Thanks, man, and I sure hope you are right."

\*\*\*

As soon as Jay and Gayle were out of the door I removed Attorney Jack Mathis's card from my wallet and dialed his number from the phone in Millie's hospital room. I managed to catch him as he was heading out for lunch. I told him everything I had learned that morning and he, too, thought I was crazy for wanting to keep a child that was not mine. By the end of the conversation he was pleased with my progress and agreed to proceed as I would like. He also cautioned letting anyone know I was not Gabby's biological father as I really would not have a leg to stand on if Beth fought back.

I was hanging up the phone with Attorney Mathis when Jay reappeared in the doorway of the hospital room. "I brought you lunch."

"Thanks!" I stood and took the brown paper sack he was offering.

"I've been thinking," Jay began. "What do you think Beth will do when she finds out about all of this?"

"I don't know," I shook my head and shrugged my shoulders.

"I think we need to know what she's going to do before she does it."

"What exactly do you have in mind?"

"After you gather the information and get all of the ducks in a row, that's when you need to talk to the reporters outside. Call your friend Daniel and the lady you said was Gabby's nanny and have them meet you at your house that afternoon. Have them be there when you get there. You will need witnesses and if there's any way you can have one of the sheriff's deputies in the area, you might want to do that as well."

"Okay."

"You need her to attack you and if you can accomplish that, with witnesses and everything else you have; you might be able to go beyond getting custody." Jay seemed to always know a little something about every subject and I did not know how.

"What is beyond custody and how do you know?"

"You might be able to have her rights terminated altogether. How do I know this? I know it because my Dad had a daughter from his first marriage. I've never met her. It's a long story, but last I heard she lived in North Carolina with her mother. To sum up, her mother was a Turkish woman that he met while serving in the army. She wanted a ride to the states, but once she got here, being queen of the single wide trailer was not the American dream she had in mind. It also did not help that my father was pretty wild back then and did some stupid things, so did she, but she was just smart enough to be dangerous. My dad does not talk about it because he has always been ashamed that he let this happen to him and his daughter."

"I did not even know I had another sister until I found pictures in his chest of drawers when I was searching for cigarette money when I was sixteen. I asked my mother about the photos because the woman with the baby in them, wasn't her. It took some real pressing, but my mother finally told me."

"According to my mother, my dad's first wife told him it was her brother that was visiting from Turkey, but my dad came home early from work and found them together in bed. He said some choice words and then he took his daughter and left. After he left, they called the police and told them that her brother had come home and found her, beaten and the baby was gone. They staged the whole thing, she allowed the man to rough her up pretty good and the baby was gone so what were the cops to think?"

"They found my dad on the way to my grandmother's house and arrested him. He was charged with beating his wife and kidnapping the baby. He tried fighting the charges, but no one believed him. He could not afford an attorney and he did not think he needed one. My dad's a little simple so he just told the truth. Anyway, to avoid jail time, he took a plea deal and with it his parental rights were revoked. He is ashamed that he did not understand that giving up his rights was a part of the plea."

"Unlike Beth, my dad may be simple, but he's a great dad."

CHAPTER 8

I was running late from leaving the hospital and that made me later to work than I normally arrived. Gayle had run into Aunt Dot as she was turning onto Hadden Pond Road headed home and Aunt Dot was leaving to head to Atlanta. They stopped and chatted through the car windows. Gayle filled her in on all of our discussions of the day. By the time Aunt Dot arrived at the hospital she could hardly be contained and it was almost impossible to get away from her.

Until I met Amelia, I had been at the clubhouse of Port Honor morning, noon and night. I had no life to speak of so I had no place else to be. During the months that we were truly together I cut back on my hours, but while we were apart I had picked back up on my old habits. Although Beth was at the clubhouse regularly, it was still a bit of a safe haven for me from her.

I typically arrived at 4:00 for the dinner shift and prior to this week I was there during the lunch shift from about 9:00 until 2:00. I took a break from 2:00 until 4:00 when I returned for dinner. That afternoon I arrived at 4:30. As soon as I entered the back door, I found my chef's coat hanging in my office where Praise always put it after she ironed it. I paid her a little extra on the side to take care of my laundry and she did a fine job. My coat was pressed and starched like usual. Unlike usual there was a note clipped to the pocket of my jacket. It was from Dick.

The note was handwritten on his personal stationary and it read, "I expect to see you in my office as soon as you arrive." It was signed Richard D. Thompson, III. He was the general manager of Port Honor and my boss.

I thought nothing of the note, but proceeded to his office as soon as I buttoned my jacket. Dick's office was upstairs and at the far end of the hallway, on the opposite side from the men's locker room. I topped the stairs on my way and noticed that Joan was already gone for the day. It was Friday, so I really thought nothing of it as I made the turn and headed toward the hall.

All of the name plates appeared to have been freshly polished and his was the last one on the right. The door was closed, so I knocked. Dick had a deep voice, much like a radio announcer and stern had always seemed his normal speaking tone. I could hear the booming sound of his answer through the door. "Come in."

I still had no idea there was anything amiss other than the thoughts running through my head that he might be Gabby's biological father. I tried to squelch those thoughts and keep in mind that this was only a theory as I opened the door and spoke. "I had a note that you wanted to see me."

"Yes, have a seat." Most people would have said, "Please have a seat," but he did not. There was a thickness to the air in the room and all pleasantries seemed to have been lost.

There were two chairs in front of his desk and I chose the one closest to the door as opposed to the window. Dick was a tall man who loomed over his desk. The thought of him being Gabby's father jumped back into my mind as I took my seat. He had salt and pepper gray hair, which could have been brown in his younger years, and his eyes were a light brown color.

I was hardly in my seat before Dick began to berate me about my punctuality. "I am going to need you to start taking your duties here at the club more seriously. This coming and going as you please had better stop."

"Excuse me?" I was completely caught off guard. Since I had been at Port Honor no one had ever watched my comings and goings. There had never been one complaint against me other than the ones levied around the attack on Amelia.

"Did I stutter?" Dick snapped.

"No, but I am not sure what this is about." I was polite in my response as I really did not know where this was coming from. Dick had always been friendly with me in the past, but I was getting the feeling that this was strictly business.

An image of Gabby jumped in my head. She had brown hair and light brown eyes. I shook it off and tried to focus on what he was saying to me.

Dick started again and his voice was even more stern than before. "Let this be a warning to you, the Olympics have been a very big event for the club and you have been indisposed all week. You work here at my pleasure. My wife may have saved you from the board once before, but that won't happen again. My wife will not be able to save you this time. Do I make myself clear?"

What the fuck was this all about? I thought before I spoke aloud, "I am not sure what I have done..."

Dick completely cut me off. "It isn't what you have done. It's what you haven't done. You need to find out where your priorities lie and that's your job son. And, you might start acting a little more grateful to the one who got you this job by showing your appreciation. I know where you've been all week and I have not told Miss Reed yet, but I doubt she would be very pleased to find out."

Was he seriously threatening to tell Beth on me as if I were some child that had gotten out of line? I thought about Jay's words from earlier today, "You need to grow a pair." Little did they know I had had a pair all along. So many things about Dick's rant pissed me off, from the way he spoke to me, calling me "son," to the way he acted as if he had Beth on speed dial. I could feel the veins in my head throbbing.

Amelia had once said I had a "tell" and that was it. She said I would never last in a poker game because my thoughts were always written on my face. I could grin and bear it all I wanted, but the veins in my head were a dead giveaway that I was fuming. I clinched my teeth as I stared at him. As if what he said to me was not infuriating enough, he had the same brown eyes as Gabby. Suddenly, the theory of him being Gabby's father did not seem so far-fetched anymore. I could contain myself no longer.

"You are welcome to call Beth if you like and while you are on the phone you might tell her that I have something that I think belongs to you, but if you would like for me to continue to keep it then I would rethink that call if I were you." That's right; I threw caution to the wind. If he thought he could pick up the phone and call Beth, then let him do it. I was certain Gabby was his child and I was certain he knew it. I was equally certain that this was his tactic for keeping me in line as a part of his agenda to keep Beth quiet.

133

Dick's face turned. I think he was shocked that I was fighting back. Before he could say anything, I stood from my seat. I placed both knuckles on his desk and leaned forward toward him. I bowed up like any man with a pair would do and got in his face. "You call Beth Reed, I dare you, and I will be on your wife's doorstep before you can say the words 'adulterous bastard' letting her know that I have your child and I don't mean one of the ones she gave birth to either!"

All of the color drained from Dick's face. He did not have to say anything else. The look on his face said it all. I knew he was Gabby's real father. He leaned back in his chair to keep from going nose to nose with me as I continued to lean across.

Dick tried to protest, "I really wouldn't know what you're talking about?"

"Really? I think you know exactly what I am talking about and I'm done being played with. Mark my words; if you want your eight pounds thirteen ounce secret kept, you will get off my ass."

I came close to walking out right then, quitting, but despite my threat, I did not want Beth to know yet. I wanted things to remain the same until I had all of the pieces of the puzzle in place to get custody of Gabby. I wanted everything to remain on course for the plan we had laid out earlier today.

It all became clear to me. Beth did not want me, she wanted him. She wanted him, but Dick was not leaving Joan. As long as Beth was playing house with me then she could stay close to him. He wanted me in line because as long as I was in line for Beth she was in line for him. I was just a pawn here.

I started to the door, but stopped just shy of it and turned back. "Don't you ever threaten me again, you asshole. And, don't you ever call me son again! That implies you are some sort of father figure and, I can assure you, are not!"

"The nerve of that man! The fucking nerve!" I left Dick's office wringing my fists and shaking my head in disgust.

Down the stairs I went. I could feel my chest heaving and I could feel my heart racing and beating against my chest through to my undershirt. I was sweating like a whore in church. It crossed my mind to march back up the stairs and deck him.

Were it not for Dick getting Beth knocked up and not fulfilling whatever nonsense he had likely told her about leaving his wife, I would be single mindedly celebrating the pregnancy of the love of my life. Instead, I was plotting and scheming to take someone else's child, a child that over the last month I had grown to love as my own. In all honestly, I wasn't taking anything that I had not already been given. It had been a month and it's not like Beth had come back for her and her father was clearly denying she was his.

Dick could have come after me and fired me, but until he did I was determined to stay my course. I returned to the kitchen and did my best to carry on with my night as if nothing had gone on. I could not shake the thought, "The nerve of that man!"

I survived the night with the new sous chef and was thankful for him, but I missed the familiarity I had with Alvin. We sent Andy to the Inn to deliver a tray of pastries for the staff up there to put out for breakfast for the equestrian team. It was the strangest thing. He left at dusk and we had not seen him since. I had been manning the bar and likely would have gone to look for him if it had not been the busiest Friday night I had seen in who knows when.

As tired as I was, I took pride in it being an extremely busy night. I liked to think that business had not only picked up because everyone wanted to get a glimpse of a gold medal winner in person, but also because my hard work was paying off. I had once told the men who attacked Amelia on the course that this was my house and tonight I was feeling it. This was my house. Yeah, Beth had gotten me the job here and Dick had hired me for whatever reasons, but I had rebuilt this place and Dick could put that in his pipe and smoke it. I had completely turned business around at Port Honor, so let him fire me and we would see who had to answer to the board. I did not need this job and I certainly did not need the shit that seemed to come with it. All these things ran through my mind as I made drink after drink and schmoozed with one guest after another.

"Another Dewar's and water, Mr. Goss?" I knew their names and I knew their drinks. I knew their wives' names, Evelyn in this case, and their children's names. Most of the time, I even knew their pets. Sometimes, most times actually, I often knew their mistresses' names, but in the case of Mr. Goss, there wasn't one.

Mr. Goss looked surprised and pleased that I remembered him as I made his drink before he even answered. I put out the beverage napkin on the bar and set the drink on top and inched it toward him.

"How's Mrs. Evelyn doing? I haven't seen here in the club in a few weeks," I continued with the personal service.

"Gabe, she's tired. She's been packing the twins for college and keeping our grandson. She's a saint. I have not heard one complaint from her. I don't know how we'd get along without her." Mr. Goss slowly sipped on his drink as he heaped the compliments on his wife.

"Tell you what, I will personally go to the back and pack you up something to go for her, every dessert we have," I explained as I slid a refill to Mr. McCann that was seated next to him.

"Thanks, but I can't take home one of each because after thirty years I would not have her thinking I did not know what she likes," he explained.

"Good point, Mr. Goss, but if you take her home one of each it shows that you cared enough to take the best and all we have is the best," I countered.

"Well played, Gabe. You are smooth. You could probably sell ice to Eskimos."

"I will take that as a compliment."

"Good because I meant it as a compliment. You know, we've been members here at Port Honor since it opened and I think you might be the best thing that's ever happened to this place."

"I sure appreciate you saying that, but if you would not mind letting Dick and Joan know, I would sure be grateful." With every compliment I received from a member, I asked them to please let my boss know what they thought of me.

I excused myself from Mr. Goss to respond to Mrs. Heath that was seated three stools down. "Good evening, you did something different with your hair. I like it."

"So good of you to notice, Gabe," Mrs. Health blushed. "I changed beauticians. I dare say the last one was blind in one eye and could not see out of the other, bless her heart."

Mrs. Heath raised an eyebrow and continued as I mixed her usual Long Island Iced Tea. "I'll be damned if I am joining the blue-haired ladies club yet."

"A lady of your youth with blue hair, that's not possible." She was every bit of seventy years old and had the wit of Amelia's Aunt Dot. I liked her, so I flirted harmlessly.

"Gabe, you say that to all the girls," Mrs. Heath laughed and slipped me a twenty. I turned and put in the jar for Andy.

"Mrs. Heath, you let me know if I can get you anything else. And by the way, if your new girl does not work out," I took out my wallet and gave her the card of the guy that cuts my hair in Milledgeville. "I know Milledgeville is a bit of a drive, but all the college girls swear by John at Another World. He cuts my hair, too. The best is the massage he gives when washing your hair, cured my headache the last time I was in there."

"Oh sweetie, I could just eat you up," she said as she took the card.

"If you like the service please let Dick and Joan know. They like to hear it when the members are happy. Now, you are going to have to excuse me. I have to run to the back for Mr. Goss, but I will be back to get you a refill in just a few minutes."

At the rate I was going Dick was likely to be bombarded with calls from the members about how much they loved me on Monday morning. One of the things I liked about the members is that if they said they were going to do something, they did it.

As I went through the swinging door from the bar to the kitchen I could see straight to the back door of the kitchen. The door swung open, Andy was on his knees and then he fell to the floor.

137

I ran to see about him. Everyone in the kitchen heard the commotion and ran as well.

Jerry was cleaning up the salad cart at the walk-in cooler when Andy landed in the middle of the walkway just inside the back door. He was the closest to the back door and made it to Andy first. "Oh my God, are you alright?"

Jerry leaned over to help get Andy up and Andy whimpered upon being touched. "Didn't you hear me out there?"

Andy cringed and rolled onto his side in the fetal position. "I was screaming for help out there for the last hour and a half and no one came."

"Do we need to call someone for you?" I asked as Jerry stood back up.

"What happened to you?" asked Rudy as we all noticed Andy was holding himself.

Andy struggled to speak. He was clearly in a great deal of pain. "I fell in the manhole!"

"You what?" I gasped.

"When I went to the Inn it was still daylight out and when I came back it was dark. I have walked that dock a thousand times." Andy writhed in pain as he tried to explain. "I was walking along when the next thing I knew my right foot went down and my left foot hit me in the back of the head and oh god, my balls..."

Andy clutched himself more before he continued, "My balls caught around the rim of the manhole."

Each one of us covered our mouths in the horror of how that might feel. I think mine even drew up in me a bit at the thought of the pain of catching that part of my body in such a way. The thought of falling in a manhole alone is awful enough let alone being saved by my nuts.

Eddie, the new sous chef, finally stepped forward and said, "Oh yeah, Gabe, I meant to tell you about the situation with the sewage this week."

Andy shrugged off us calling an ambulance or anything for him. Jerry got him some ice, but he would not accept help past that. While everyone else tried to sort out Andy, Eddie went on to show me this light that had been going off on the back wall of the kitchen all week.

Eddie pointed to the light and began to explain, "It started going off on Wednesday afternoon. I asked Alvin about it and he said he would mention it to you. It was still going off yesterday and Alvin said he had forgotten to ask you. We asked the guys in the pro-shop if they knew anything about it. They said it wasn't their job to know anything about anything in the kitchen. This morning it became their job when they arrived to work and found raw sewage floating a foot deep through the cart barn."

With the thought of that, I nearly threw up. I couldn't imagine being one of the guys that had to clean up all of the golf carts that were covered in raw sewage. Luckily, I wasn't one of them.

Eddie went on, "As it turns out, the light is an indication that the septic tank is full and needs to be pumped. They told Joan and she called the septic pump guys, but they could not get out here until this evening."

Once Andy finally was able to get up off of the floor, he walked with a limp the rest of the night. Just before I left, Andy described more of his ordeal. "I was walking along and then my front foot disappeared and when I said my left foot hit me in the back of the head, it did. I don't know how I managed it, but one leg was down in the manhole and the other one was kind of doing a split on the ground. It hurt so bad that I fell over and cried."

Andy shook his head with embarrassment at the retelling, but he continued. "I have not cried since I was ten years old, but that shit hurt. Where the fuck was the manhole cover?!! I yelled for help until I think I passed out for a while. When I finally regained my strength to pull myself out of the manhole, I fell over and screamed for help, but still no one came. I can't believe no one heard me or came to look for me."

I tried not to laugh, but the mental picture; Andy was the definition of a strapping dude so to think of him lying out there crying was almost too much. The idea that he thought someone would have come to check on him, "It would not have crossed our minds to check on you. I feel pretty safe in saying I have never thought anyone would get you and this was a fluke." I barely stifled a snicker.

"Go ahead and laugh damn-it! I had to belly crawl to the back door before any of you even realized I was missing." Andy huffed.

I apologized, but I was dying with laughter inside. "I'm sorry this happened to you."

I clinched my jaw and tried not to let on that this was the funniest thing I had heard in weeks. I tried to sound sincere, but a thought popped into my head; I can't wait to tell Amelia about this. I would definitely have to tell her about this once she woke up. She did not much care for Andy and although I would not wish an injury like this on any man, I knew she would get a kick out of this. There would be so much to talk about once she woke up, so much seriousness and after everything she had been through, I am sure she would need a good laugh once she woke up.

It was nearly 11:00 p.m. when the last guest left and I was able to head home. Leaving the clubhouse that night, I knew I had had the best night in quite a while. The trouble with Amelia still hung heavy on me, but we did more business than we had done since the New Year's Eve party. The club was beginning to be profitable again and that pleased me to no end. I also took comfort in the fact that Dick would arrive to work with a dozen calls and messages from the members about how much they liked me.

I arrived home just in time to feed Gabby. I loved the way she stared at me as she sucked down the bottle. I fed her and she fell fast asleep shortly thereafter and apparently so did I.

I woke up in the glider in Gabby's room at 3:00 a.m. with her still sleeping on my chest. I did not have the blackout curtains in her room as I did in my own so the moonlight shown through the room so brightly that no lamp was needed. I leaned down and brushed my cheek to the brown peach fuzz on the top of her head. When I moved back to look at her, I could see the skin on the soft spot of her little head move with every breath she took and every suck she gave her little thumb. She was so sweet and I was completely wrapped around her little finger.

Any moment, I felt sure Gabby would wake up for her bottle, so I waited. I did not put her in her crib, I just continued to hold her and rock her while she continued to sleep against my chest. The next thing I knew it was 6:00 a.m. and I was still in the glider. Gabby had slept through the night for the first time. Another milestone had been reached and Beth had missed it.

I had to write a paper about quotes once in high school and one that stuck with me was by Rose Kennedy. Mrs. Kennedy said, "Life isn't a matter of milestones, but of moments." Either way, Beth was missing the milestones and the moments. I enjoyed these moments with Gabby so much, her sleeping on my chest, watching her sleep, feeding her, seeing her first smile. I could go on.

I could not imagine giving Gabby back to Beth and what sad life might be in store for her if that happened. She would have a companion for commiseration in Beatle, the Yorkie puppy, if Beth did not kill him first, but what a sad, lonely life she might lead. I could remember every cruel thing she ever did to the puppy and if I did not feel bad enough for the dog, my heart broke at the thought of Gabby suffering for one moment.

Gabby was just beginning to stir when I heard the phone ring through the house. The cordless was in my bedroom on the night stand, so I took Gabby with me to get it and to make her bottle.

"Gabriel, it's Gayle. She's awake!" That's what I wanted to hear, but instead it was Stella.

"Jay gave me your message and I am on my way. I am leaving Milledgeville now and will be there as soon as I can."

I had almost forgotten I asked Jay to see if Stella could keep Gabby for me today. I had resolved myself to taking Gabby with me, but this would work out perfectly. Although Grady was the best trauma hospital in the southeast, it was no place for an infant. I was also desperate for Amelia to meet Gabby, but springing so much on her the instant she woke up was not the wisest idea.

In what seemed like a flash Stella was ringing the doorbell. Her greeting that morning was not, "Good morning" or anything like that. Her greeting as soon as I opened the door was, "Have you heard they have a suspect in the bombing?"

"What? No." I was stunned.

"Yeah, it's been all over the news the last few days." Stella came on inside as I held the door for her with one arm and I carried Gabby in the other.

Stella proceeded to the kitchen where she laid her purse down on the island. I had followed Stella to the kitchen. No sooner had she put her things down did she turn and offer to take Gabby.

"I have got to get my shoes on and grab a few things from the bedroom, but keep talking. It's been such a whirlwind yet I still can't believe I haven't heard anything about this." I turned and headed down the hallway leaving Stella in the kitchen with Gabby.

Stella began again and I could tell from the volume of her voice that she had followed as far as the entrance from the living room to the hallway. She was not yelling or anything while holding Gabby, but she did project enough for me to clearly hear her. "I guess you have not seen the AJC in the last couple of days."

AJC was the abbreviation for the Atlanta Journal-Constitution, the foremost in newspapers in the South, especially in Atlanta. I typically picked up the leftover copy at the Inn, but since I had been up and headed to the hospital all week, I had not been by the Inn to get a copy and I had not taken the time to pick one up elsewhere.

Stella continued, "They have named a suspect according to the paper, but WSB is just saying he's a person of interest, whatever that means."

142

Person of interest; it meant they did not know what he was and they did not have anyone else. That's what it meant.

"Really? So soon?" I guess I should not be surprised. After all, they got Timothy McVeigh within three days last year in the bombing of the Murrah Federal Building. Actually, they arrested him within hours of the bombing, but did not know exactly who he was so he was not charged until day three of his stint in jail on other unrelated charges

"Yeah, the paper first broke the story on Tuesday and it's caught fire with all of the news outlets since. I can't believe you haven't heard."

Stella was steadily cooing with Gabby while holding up her end of the conversation. When finished with my shoes, I returned to the living room where I found Stella making faces and doing her best to get Gabby to smile. She did not hear me return and when I spoke again it clearly startled her.

"So what are they saying about the suspect or person of interest or whatever they are calling him?" I asked.

"I forgot his name, but they're saying he was one of the security guards and he used to work at some college in North Georgia. According to the AJC, the president of the college reported him."

"Are they giving any reason as to why they think the guy's involved or what his motive might be?" I was so curious and I would have continued with Stella, but I really needed to get going. I took Gabby to kiss her goodbye before I left.

Stella stood up from where she was on the couch. "I'm sorry I don't remember more of the specifics. I should have just brought you the paper, not that you would have time to read it with all that you've got going on. Sorry."

"That's fine," I replied before handing Gabby back.

"Daddy loves you and will be back soon. Please be a good girl for Miss Stella." I kissed Gabby's forehead and as I was retreating, I swear she grinned at me. For the first time I noticed

143

that Gabby did not smile so much with her pouty little lips and mouth as she did with her eyes. She batted her long lashes at me and they became wide and bright.

I thought about a phrase my mother used to use when she reprimanded my sister and me. "Two wrongs don't make a right!" she would tell us. If she were here today and I could tell her everything about Beth and Dick and Gabby, I am sure she would know like I do that in this case, two wrongs made a right. Strictly speaking about the product and not the act or the resulting actions, two wrongs, Beth and Dick, made a right when they made Gabby.

***

Greensboro was at a point in the state where the radio stations from Augusta and Atlanta were fading in and out. The direction and strength of the wind seemed to be a factor in whether you could pick up the stations from the larger markets. Of course there were stations from areas that were a little more local: Athens and Milledgeville, and Dock 100 out of Greensboro, but their news broadcasts left a lot to be desired when you wanted to hear something beyond whose house was broken into, who got a DUI or whose cows got loose.

This morning, Stella had whet my appetite for news on the bombing. I was still fiddling with the radio dial when I got on I-20. Nothing was coming in clear from either direction. I even tried the AM stations, but did not get anything suitable until I was almost all the way to Madison.

The first station I found that came in clearly was a pop station out of Atlanta. They were playing music, "Killing Me Softly" by the Fugees. Although I was searching for news, I hung in there since it was nearly 7:30 a.m. and they would be doing the news on the half hour.

The usual morning DJs were pulling extra shifts like the rest of us due to the Olympics. After the listing of the latest in celebrity sightings around town came the news. The headline was, "Vehement denial by former security officer Richard Jewell."

144

The broadcaster continued on, "According to Jewell, he found the suspicious package, now known to have been an army issue type backpack, filled with a pipe bomb, shortly after midnight. Jewell claims to have alerted the GBI; after which, he joined other security officers in clearing the area."

As the coverage went on my blood boiled. "Initially credited as a hero for the discovery and evacuation, the FBI is now considering Jewell a suspect."

I was white knuckling the steering wheel as I found myself racing down the interstate. My fury at how someone could do such a thing, as what they were accusing Jewell, plant a bomb just so they could find it and then gain fame as a hero, distracted me and my speed reached 110 miles per hour before I realized it.

The news was over soon enough, but they reported on nothing else. Every story linked back to the bombing. Interviews with local politicians, athletes and spectators were still being interviewed as to how the bombing had affected the games. It had cast a shadow over the entire Olympics and I was just now coming to see the bigger picture. I had been in such a fog that I had not seen beyond the damage done to Amelia and to my little world.

CHAPTER 9

I entered Amelia's room at Grady expecting the same old same old, except that I was no longer public enemy numero uno. I took for granted that Amelia would still be lying there and I would be relieving Gayle. Other than the curtains being wide open and the sunniest day of the year seemed to be infecting what has been a stark hospital room, I did not even notice anything different as I entered the room.

"I swear the parking garage attendant has started to recognize me as one of the regulars. Amelia, you need to wake up before I have to put the attendant on the Christmas card list," I joked as I entered the room. I was carrying coffee for Gayle as I had done each morning. I now knew exactly how she took her coffee, more like a little coffee with her cream and sugar.

I had left all of the baggage from the news of the bombing in the car and in the deck with the attendant. I was determined that the good night I had last night was going to carry on through today and it did.

"If you would quit talking for a moment you might notice that I am awake." A familiar voice came from the direction of the bathroom door. The bathroom door was tucked behind the entryway to the room so when the door was open, the bathroom door was blocked. When I came in the room I had pushed the door to behind me and continued into the room.

I glanced at the hospital bed. Gayle was sitting in her usual spot so I had just assumed Amelia was lying there. No one was in the bed. It was just a pile of bunched up sheets and covers.

Gayle was smiling from ear to ear. I looked back to the direction of the voice. There in the bathroom door, stood the most beautiful girl I had ever seen. I struggled to catch my breath at the sight of her. I could not believe my eyes and I turned back to Gayle for confirmation. Was I truly seeing what I thought I was seeing or was I just exhausted to the point of delirium?

Gayle could tell I was in shock, "She woke up around 10:00 p.m. last night."

My head was spinning with excitement, relief and shock all at once. I turned back to Amelia and she chuckled. "You look as if you've seen a ghost, Mr. Hewitt."

There were no more tubes, no pole with bags attached to her, no drained pale look to her skin. She smiled at me; no make-up, but her cheeks were round and pink and her eyes were bright and squinted just a touch from smiling so big. She pressed her lips together to try to hide the enormity of the smile as if she was embarrassed for smiling so big. Amelia had never been more gorgeous to me than in that second, hospital gown be damned.

The shock was starting to wear away and all I could think about as I just looked at her was how badly I wanted to kiss her, to hold her, to promise that I would never let her go again, to make her promise that she would never leave me or scare me like this again. I wanted her to know how much she meant to me and how I would never be the same had I lost her, really lost her. I wanted her to know she was done waiting for me.

At one time this particular hospital room likely held two patients and evidence of this was left in the form of retractable privacy curtains. With her aunt still seated on the far side of the room by the bed, I grabbed the curtain and gave it a sling. As it slid through the tracks in the ceiling and divided the room leaving Gayle on one side and Amelia on the other it made an awful racket. It sounded as if I had snatched the whole ceiling down. Amelia giggled.

On one hand I would have done that a hundred times just to hear her laugh, but on the other, I meant business.

"Don't you laugh Miss Anderson," I said as I gently pulled her to me still aware of her injuries. She might have looked nearly back to normal, but she was not so far as what had gone on that the bandage wasn't still on the back of her head and the scabs from where tiny shards of shrapnel from the bomb showed on her arms. Also, she winced just a little when she moved. The pelvic injury was likely still a source of soreness.

I know the curtain did nothing to keep Gayle from hearing, but my eyes locked in Amelia's and I firmly explained, "This may not be on a beach or anywhere especially romantic and I am not going to ask permission, so you better brace yourself."

I could hear Gayle gasp as I spoke and Amelia only had a slight inclination of what was coming her way. I kissed her with all I had. I laid bare every emotion I had felt in the last week in the relief that she was awake and appeared to be fine. I kissed her for past, present and future. It was something the likes of which Burt Lancaster would have been proud. I meant for her knees to go weak and her heart to race as it did on the porch after the night at Cameron's and I could feel that I was succeeding. I meant for her to understand how much I loved her and could not live without her.

I could have gone on holding her and kissing her indefinitely, but Amelia eased her lips back and hung her head. Still holding her in my embrace, I dropped my head. I rested my forehead on top of her such that I could feel the bridge of my nose fit the curve of her forehead.

"Gabriel, I am pregnant," she whispered as if she were frightened to tell me.

I barely moved and as gently as she had delivered the news, I gave my response, "I know."

"Are you disappointed? I know we were careful. I am so sorry." It was as if she were asking for forgiveness, but there was nothing to forgive, and I recalled the one time we were not careful.

"Look at me." I lifted her chin so that she could see my face. "I have known since the very moment I first saw you that you were the mother of my children. So, please, don't ever say you are sorry. Not ever."

"You aren't mad with me?"

"Amelia Anderson, you silly girl, how could I ever be mad with you? This was always the plan for us, it's just a little sooner than expected that's all."

"What about..."

"What about what?"

"B...?"

"You let me worry about that. You worry about getting better and keeping Little One safe and healthy and I'll worry about everything else."

"Are you happy?"

"Now that I know you are alright, I am beyond happy."

"I meant, are you happy about the baby?"

"Amelia, seriously, you know me. I am ecstatic about the baby. I have been since the minute I found out. Are you happy about the baby?" There was the scary question. What if Amelia wasn't happy? I had not really thought about that.

I continued, "You aren't thinking about..."

She cut me off, "God, no!" Panic shot across her face before the giant smile returned. "I did not know what to think. I was so happy when they first told me, but then I thought about you and how you would take the news and I was terrified. I was terrified because I was so happy and what if you weren't. So much has gone on."

"None of that matters. Well, one thing about it matters, but we can talk about that later." I did my best to assure her and I did not want to fill her in on my plans for her involving Gabby right then.

From the other side of the curtain, Gayle finally spoke up. "There will be plenty of time for all of that later. The doctor is supposed to make his rounds at 8:30, so y'all need to wrap that up."

Easing my hand into hers and freeing her from my embrace, I stepped back. "Amelia, we will work everything out. Just trust me." I smiled at her, gave her a wink and nodded my head in the affirmative.

Amelia nodded and gave a subtle smile back, "Okay."

There had been times in the past when Amelia had taken care of me and now I needed to take care of her. There was balance

149

between us, a feeling that as long as we were together and stuck together then everything would be fine, just as I said it would.

The natural thing would have been for me to ease back the privacy curtain while Amelia returned to the bed, but I was reluctant to let even her hand go. I suppose she could feel that and therefore waited for me. Once finished with the curtain, I escorted her across the room and helped her back into bed. She walked with a slight limp favoring the side with the injury to her pelvis. It also crossed my mind to pick her up and carry her back to bed, but I knew how she liked to be self-sufficient.

"You know," Amelia started, "It was as if I could feel both of you here while I was out of it. I know," she turned to Gayle, "that you told me y'all took shifts staying with me, but it's like I remember each of you talking to me and telling me stories."

"We all talked to you. Me, Gabriel, Aunt Dot and the other visitors when they came, Jay and everyone else talked to you. Are you sure you aren't just remembering dreams?" Gayle asked her.

Gayle and I both had been informed of the drugs they had used to induce the coma so Gayle found it impossible to believe that Amelia could have actually remembered what all we had told her while she was under.

"I don't know. I feel like it was more than that." Amelia seemed confused trying to decipher whether what she was remembering were actual occurrences or dreams.

I pulled up a chair next to the bed and near Gayle. "While we wait on the doctor, why don't you tell us some of what you remember?" I was curious to know what she remembered of the bombing and if she really did remember and of the conversations. I wondered if she remembered me telling her what I did to my family.

Gayle also wondered what she remembered of the night of the bombing and asked her about that.

Amelia reached for my hand as she started to tell us about being at Centennial Olympic Park that night with Cara. "I don't remember anything after seeing a flash of blue light and feeling as

150

though I had been stung by an entire bee hive. Aunt Gayle said Cara did not get injured..."

Gayle stopped her to tell me that Amelia's first concern when she came to last night was of Cara. "Where's Cara and is she alright?" were her first words.

"Anyway, Aunt Gayle said it was only luck that I happened to be standing directly between Cara and the blast and thus shielded Cara. Aunt Gayle also explained how Cara and I got separated and that when Cara could not reach Jay she called you and that you came immediately. You searched with Cara and you found me. I need to thank Cara, but I want to thank you, too. She said you have been here every single day since you found me."

Amelia started to tear up, "Thank you so much for coming to find me. I thought you had moved on with..."

"No! That's not ever going to happen. I am never going to give up on you." I lifted her hand and kissed it. "I am sorry I let you think anything might be going on with..."

There was some force in the room determined that a certain name not to be spoken as we continually interrupted one another each time it came up. This time it was Gayle that shifted us away from speaking it.

"So you do remember right up until everything happened, but you have no idea how you managed to get to the hospital," Gayle observed.

"Right," Amelia began again. "We made it through the crowd, all the way to the stage. We were near this bench and were just about to sit down when a member of the security team came along and told us we had to move back. He and some other guys moved everyone back about fifteen yards. We protested because we had worked so hard to get that close to the stage."

Both Gayle and I gasped at the thought of what could have happened to them had they not been forced to move, but it was Gayle who voiced it out loud. "You could have been killed! The both of you could have been killed!"

I followed Gayle, "Amelia, you don't know how lucky you are. One woman was killed. I don't know about your aunt, but I was terrified when we first found out that you were there and you were lost. I was terrified that it was you that had been killed."

"I know, but I am fine now."

"We will let the doctor be the judge of that," Gayle was not taking any of this lightly. To hear the account of things from Amelia's point of view was obviously unnerving her.

No sooner had Gayle referenced the doctor than he appeared in the doorway of Amelia's room.

"Good morning. I hear Sleeping Beauty has awakened." It was Dr. Andrews and he was still fidgeting with his glasses. He had been the first doctor we saw when we found Amelia. There had been other doctors, various specialists in and out during the week, but he was my favorite. He was the most personable.

Dr. Andrews proceeded to Amelia's bed, the opposite side from where Gayle and I were seated even though we stood and moved back to allow him space. Before beginning any exam, he introduced himself. "I'm Dr. Andrews or Eric, whichever you prefer."

Again, he was very personable. What doctor asks patients to call them by their first name? Most that I have met act as if their first name is "doctor" as soon as they get that degree.

Dr. Andrews went on, "I was here the morning you were brought in and I must say you gave us all quite a scare."

"That she did," Gayle agreed.

"I am so sorry about all of that and thank you for all that you have done." Amelia was her usual charming, polite Southern self as she offered her hand to Dr. Andrews.

After shaking hands with her, the doctor turned to the sink and washed up while explaining what all he needed to do. "Now, it is up to you whether your mother and fiancé stay in the room during the exam."

As he continued, Amelia raised a curious eyebrow at both Gayle and I. I also looked to Gayle. I was not the only one who had allowed an assumption, or in my case, a flat out lie, to carry on all week. I could not believe that I had not realized that everyone had assumed Gayle was her mother. It was a natural assumption, but I thought I had told Dr. Andrews the morning I met him that the ladies with me were her aunts. Oh well, he had a lot of patients, so he could not be expected to remember every single patient's friends and family and how they were related.

Ultimately, Amelia made no protest to having Gayle and I remain in the room. Dr. Andrews ran a series of basic tests and asking her questions at the same time. I believe he was conducting a neurological exam while taking blood pressure and what not. He removed the dressing that covered the spot on the back of her head where they removed the piece of shrapnel.

"You know, we sent that piece of the screw to the crime lab. It could be your screw that identifies the Olympic Park Bomber. I am going to get the nurses to get you a new dressing for this. Does it hurt?"

Amelia glanced back at him, "It doesn't hurt until you touch it. Also, it's not my screw and before I get a new dressing, could I please wash my hair?"

"Sure," Dr. Andrew's voice was soft as he replied. He seemed to know exactly what she was getting at about the screw.

He moved her hair back around to cover the place where the stiches were before he spoke again. "I am going to open the back of your gown and have a look at the places on your back. We need to make sure they are healing properly."

After he was finished examining all of what Amelia had called bee stings and the incision where they removed the piece of metal from her pelvic bone, Dr. Andrews moved around to look her in the face. He then brought up the thing we all cared about the most. "I am guessing your aunt has already told you about your other condition."

Amelia acknowledged his comment sheepishly.

"I am no OB/GYN, but I am going to send one up to talk to you about the baby. It's not my specialty, but as I recall you are fourteen weeks along and at fourteen weeks we can tell what the sex of the baby is. So, if you want to know, and you ask nicely, we could probably arrange for a sonogram before you go home."

"OH MY GOD!!!" Amelia screamed with excitement. If the excitement was a speeding car, Amelia suddenly slammed on the brakes and the car came to a screeching halt. Tears started to well in her eyes. "You said I had been sedated to let the swelling go down on my brain. Would any of the drugs I was given affect the baby? Would any of the pain meds have affected it?"

I stood and took Amelia's hand. I was as interested in the answers to her questions as she was.

"I am sure the baby's fine, sweetie," Gayle said in an effort to comfort her. It was no comfort. Amelia gripped my hand tighter and tighter as the doctor began to answer.

"First of all, those really are questions for the OB, but I can tell you that you entered your second trimester after twelve weeks, so you are out of the most sensitive time for the development of the fetus. That means most medications are less likely to harm it. On top of that, we considered the baby and tailored your treatment to make sure no harm was done. Of course, there's always risk with taking almost any medication during pregnancy, but we did our best and I am sure the fetus is going to be fine. The specialist will be able to give you more information on that and more assurances."

The more he spoke and the more relaxed Amelia became, the more she eased her grip on my hand and circulation was allowed to return. Amelia tapered off with the questions as it seemed her fears had been settled.

"The CT scan they ran last night showed that the swelling subsided, so I am going to clear you for going home tomorrow. The OB/GYN will have to sign off as well as the attending tomorrow." I am sure I was not the only one that nearly jumped out of their skin at the idea of Amelia being released. Our cheering gained us a sharp look from the doctor as he tried to finish while Amelia hung on his every word.

"As I was saying, the stitches on the back of your head should dissolve on their own in a few more days and the same same goes for the incision on your abdomen." After he finished with the exam, Dr. Andrews was on his way.

The three of us talked about any and everything for another twenty minutes before Gayle got up and started to tidy up the room. "Gabriel, I know you have to run by Northside Hospital today so Aunt Dot agreed to come early. She should be here around 1:00 p.m. Now, if y'all don't mind, I am going to go ahead and get on the road."

I loved Gayle and all, but it was approaching 9:30 and I had wanted her up and out of there since I first saw Amelia standing in the bathroom doorway. I knew I was being selfish, but Gayle had had her to herself since she woke up the night before. I was desperate for my alone time with her.

I was a little afraid that Amelia might protest Gayle leaving, but she didn't. Instead Amelia asked her when she would return and thanked her profusely for never allowing her to be left alone in the hospital.

With purse and overnight bag in hand, Gayle leaned into Amelia. She wrapped her hand gently around Amelia's head and pulled her close and kissed the top of her head. "Millie, you are my girl and I would never leave you alone here. There's nothing more important than being with you this week."

In that moment, like several others I had witnessed between them, I could see why people would mistake Gayle for being her mother.

Gayle released Amelia and stood back up. She was clearly choking back tears and her tone changed. "I love you, but if you ever scare me like that again, I will never forgive you. I swear you took ten years off of my life. Do you see these gray hairs? I did not have these until last Sunday morning."

Gayle bent a little and pointed to the top of her head. I am sure she had been scared out of her wits over the course of the last week, so I kind of thought she was being serious until she started to laugh a little toward the end of her tirade about going gray.

Amelia quickly popped back at her, "About the gray hair, I've been meaning to say something..."

"What?!!!" Gayle acted shocked and offended. "Amelia Jane Anderson, did you just insinuate that I am getting old?"

"Well, you are going to be a grandmother soon," Amelia drew out her words for dramatic effect. The word "well" sounded as if it had five or six syllables.

I just watched the back and forth between the two of them. This was the way they always behaved with one another, teasing and picking at each other. Amelia had quoted her grandfather on many a topic, but one of my favorites was, "Granddaddy said if he didn't pick on you, you would think he didn't like you."

I think that was the motto the whole family lived by because they loved nothing better than picking at each other and Amelia and her aunts seemed to be the ring leaders.

Finally, they settled down, said their real goodbyes and Gayle was gone. I was standing at the door having just shut it after escorting Gayle out. I leaned back against the door. I could have stood there and looked at her indefinitely. Her hair was naturally straight and she rarely wore it like that. It was so long, longer than I remember it being. I could not help but stare at her as the smell of strawberries entered my mind like a reflex.

"I have missed you so much," Amelia calmly said and she patted the side of the bed inviting me to sit next to her.

I answered her request by proceeding over and easing onto the bed. The twin size hospital bed had not grown any since earlier in the week when I had sat next to her and begged her to come back to me. One of my legs hung over the edge then as it did now.

I extended my right arm to offer my chest to Amelia as a pillow. She raised up slightly and I reached around her as she laid her head against me.

"I have missed you, too. I thought I had lost you." The tears were coming again and I was thankful she could not see them. I did not want her to see me like that.

There was silence, but so much for us to talk about. I did not know where to begin. I would have been content just to cuddle up with her in the bed and lay there, but I felt as though I had not apologized enough to her for the last few months. I just wanted to tell her how much I loved her again and again. As I searched for the right words, Amelia dove right in.

"Aunt Gayle told me about Gabby. I don't mean to say I told you so, but..."

I threw myself on the sword, "You told me so. It's ok. I know. I am sorry; I just didn't know what to believe."

I paused for a moment to gather my nerve. This might be our biggest subject. "I suppose she told you that I want to keep Gabby?"

"She did."

"And how do you feel about that?" I said a little prayer as I asked. I did not know what I would do if she did not want to go along with me on this, but I asked the question anyway. I needed to know.

"Beth wanted her to be yours so badly, might as well make her yours." I was relieved by her response.

"And you are okay with that?" I looked down at Amelia and she turned her head up to me. I don't know how she knew, but I wanted to see her face when she answered.

"What's one more, right?" She patted her stomach and smiled and all of the little freckles on her face shone against her pale skin.

"Seriously," she continued, "boy or girl, which do you want?"

"I don't care as long as it's healthy..."

"That's a cop out answer."

The television had been on all morning, playing in the background. The picture was on, but the volume was muted. It was

157

mounted to the wall directly in front of the hospital bed. Suddenly something grabbed Amelia's attention as she was returning her head to my chest.

"Do you know where the remote is it? Can you turn that up? Quickly, please."

I found the remote buried beneath Gayle's stack of Enquirers and People magazines on the bedside table.

"Hurry! I want to hear what they are saying." Amelia sounded desperate.

"Okay, okay, I've got it." I hit the volume button multiple times and suddenly the room came alive with the sound of the news of the bombing.

The news anchor was talking about the bombing suspect. They flashed a picture of a hefty fellow with a mustache and stated, "Jewell used to work for Piedmont College in Demorest, Georgia. Initially hailed as the hero of the bombing..."

Amelia became agitated at the story and spoke as if she were arguing with the anchor, "He *IS* the hero!"

"Do you know him?" I had been shocked all along at what she had remembered of the night's events.

She turned from the television to me, "He saved us. He's the one that made us move from near the stage along with a ton of other people. They are saying he planted the bomb, but I know that's not true."

"They are saying he did it so he could be a hero," I explained to her what I had heard on the radio on the way in.

"That's not true! Who would do that? Plus, he hung around once the FBI and ATF and what not arrived. Why would he risk being killed by his own bomb? That makes no sense."

"I don't know, Amelia, but you should settle down. They know more about this than we do." She was becoming angrier and angrier at the TV and I could not imagine that was good for her considering all she had been through.

"Actually, I have two substantial wounds on me and three dozen smaller ones that say they don't know more about this than me. I am telling you, that man did not do this!" There was no sense debating with her on the subject and I certainly did not want to get her further upset.

They finally moved on to another headline, the end of the games. Now that was a story I could get behind. "I will be so glad when all of this is over."

"I am so sorry if I bit your head off a minute ago. I just know that Mr. Jewell did not have anything to do with this and I feel bad that he is being accused. Also, while they are focusing on him, they aren't looking for the person who's really behind this and that means they could strike again."

"Amelia, I want to talk to you about a million things. I could just sit here and listen to you talk, but I don't want you upset. In a couple of days, once you have improved a bit more, then we will call whomever we have to call and you can tell them all of what you witnessed. For now, please indulge me and let's relax a little."

The quiet lasted all of two minutes and in those two minutes I reveled in the fact that she was safe, awake, by all accounts going to be fine and in my arms. In those two minutes, I held her tight and closed my eyes. I relaxed for the first time in what seemed like forever. In those two minutes I was almost asleep when I felt her take a deep breath against me.

"You aren't wearing your usual cologne." Amelia aired her observance as she exhaled.

"I ran out and haven't had a chance to buy more." I shook my head. I could not believe she noticed. In all honesty, I ran out three months ago and cologne was among many items that no longer mattered to me in the grand scheme of things.

"Shame. I love that smell."

"Why?"

"It is the smell of you... and it has a hint of cedar, like the fresh cut Christmas trees my grandfather would go into the woods and cut down and bring home."

"I will make sure to swing by a mall and pick up more on my way home today. I don't want to deprive you of the smell of Christmas trees."

I could feel Amelia give a little laugh.

I leaned over and did the same type of deep breath into Amelia's hair. "While I am out, could I pick up some shampoo for you?"

She laughed again. "I love to hear you laugh."

"Aunt Gayle brought my shampoo and conditioner. I will need some help, but Dr. Andrews said I could wash my hair."

Perhaps I did not answer quickly enough. Amelia back tracked, "I could get Aunt Dot to help me once she gets here, if you..."

"Do you want a full shower or do you just want to do this in the sink?"

"I don't ever want to do it in the sink."

Was she suggesting what I think she suggesting? While I was analyzing her last statement, Amelia slid from the bed, careful and favoring her one side.

"Don't judge," she directed me as she walked with that slight limp toward the bathroom door slipping free of the hospital gown as she went.

I was getting out of the bed to follow her when she dropped the gown. The sight stopped me in my tracks, but not in the usual way looking at her stopped me. I had not seen the full extent of her injuries. It is one thing to have heard about them, one thing to have caught a glimpse through the gap in the back of the gown, but it was another to see them all at once.

Amelia had a ton of hair so even though they cut some of it to get to the spot where the screw was, she still had more than enough to cover and hide that wound. Her back and legs were covered with scabs and that was in addition to the stitching on her right hip. The stitches stretched about three inches and made a line beginning a couple of inches down and inside of the peak of her right hip.

I was frozen. Amelia looked back at me from the bathroom door. She noticed the look on my face and immediately bent down to scoop up the hospital gown and covered herself. I could tell bending down hurt her. She firmed her jaw and hardened her face to bear the pain in her hip. "Don't worry about it. Aunt Dot can help me."

I snapped out of it and wiped the tears off of my cheeks. I had embarrassed her. I met her on the floor squatting and reaching for it, but she already had it and was wrapping it around herself, wincing as she stood.

I stood only on my knees and wrapped my arms around her before she could move. "I am so sorry this happened to you. I don't know what I would have done if...I would take all of this for you if I could."

Amelia cradled my head against her as she spoke. "Gabriel, I would never want you to take this for me. I would never wish this on anyone. I know you are tired and that you are scared, but I am going to heal and this is not going to be what defines me. I can't have you feeling sorry for me, so I need you to get up and we are going to move on from this. We are going to wash my hair and do our best to get this hospital smell off of me."

Amelia was the bravest, strongest person I had ever met. From that moment on, I never heard her complain about the pain and I never saw her limp or wince again. I believe she toughed it out for my sake.

*** 

I stopped at Northside Hospital and even though it was the weekend, Gabby's medical records were ready and waiting on me. After the hospital, I proceeded to the nearest mall, Perimeter Mall, to

161

purchase more Christmas tree smelling cologne. I had been wearing the same cologne for years and had never noticed before that it smelled that strongly of cedar until the sales girl sprayed the tester on me. I too was suddenly overwhelmed with the smell of Christmas.

I had parked outside of one of the main mall entrances, so on the way back from Rich's, I passed by a jewelry shop. In a window cut out was a lone ring. It was stunning.

Talk about an impulse buy. I proceeded into the store and made the day of the first clerk that spoke to me. I did not necessarily ask to see the ring, so much as I asked to purchase it.

"At Bailey, Banks & Biddle, we pride ourselves on the finest in cut and clarity." The salesman went on and on about ratings for this and ratings for that.

I knew they were reputable as Beth's mother had purchased items for Beth from them in the past. Beth described a tennis bracelet from them as, "It's not Tiffany, but it will do." That was as good of a compliment as she could muster on any subject.

I studied the ring for just a moment as the clerk gave it the good old-fashioned pitch. I hardly heard a word he said. I was too busy looking at the ring and wondering if it was too much for Amelia's dainty hand.

The center diamond was one and a half carats and there was a half carat diamond on each side and outside of those were tiny diamonds that made up the band.

"Past, present and future," the clerk named each of the main diamonds in the ring.

I hardly heard a word he said before I threw out my credit card. The clerk was speechless. Despite the fact that I had always planned on giving my future wife my mother's rings, those rings had been stolen and likely tainted by Beth. When I saw this ring, I knew instantly it was made for Amelia. I had saved all my life for this moment.

\*\*\*

162

That night was the last night I had to serve the Olympians at the club. I did not think I could have been happier until I arrived home and the phone rang at quarter past eleven. It had been a long day, Gabby was asleep in her bed already, and hearing Amelia's voice on the other end of the line was just what I needed.

I was slipping off my shoes when I first picked up the phone. There was no greeting just her voice, "Aunt Gayle is sleeping like a rock and I feel as though I have jetlag. I can't sleep. I hope you don't mind me calling. I hope I did not wake the baby."

"You can call me anytime you know that. Other than not being able to sleep are you okay?"

"I'm fine. A little overwhelmed, but that will pass." Amelia had the most amazing outlook and her positivity was almost contagious.

"What's bothering you?"

"I did not know I was pregnant until what seems like five minutes ago and tomorrow I find out if it's a boy or a girl. And then there's Gabby..." Amelia stopped and I could feel she was trying to spare me. "I wish you were here. I sleep best when my head is on your chest."

I had managed to get my shirt and slacks off while she was talking and was changing into my pajamas when she mentioned sleeping. "I am just now getting into bed and was thinking the same thing. I sleep best when I am holding you. I have missing having you next to me."

"What's going to happen with Gabby?"

"Could we please talk about that tomorrow?"

"I suppose. You know, Aunt Gayle wants me to come back to Stillwater Plantation and recuperate there with her." I had not thought about where Amelia would go when she was released tomorrow.

163

"You don't want to go to her house?" I asked the question not knowing what her answer would be, but I would have given anything for her to have asked to come home with me.

"No. I think I want to go back to my house, but I..." She stopped and seemed to change course. "I start Mercer in Macon in a week. I have to go back to The Jefferson."

I glanced at the ring on the bedside table. I had propped open the box when I took it out of my pocket earlier so I could admire it. I did not think about all of the logistics of everything when I threw down my credit card earlier. Ring, plus wedding, plus baby, equaled happily ever after, that was the extent of my thought process. There was so much more to consider and I did not want to ask her to marry me over the phone just so we could figure out the details of our living arrangements right then.

Amelia was right. For her to drive to law school everyday living at The Jefferson did make the most sense. It also made financial sense for me to give up the house I was renting and for us to put the money I paid in rent somewhere else. I could commute to Port Honor to work if I stayed on there very much longer. I also did not want her to live in a house where she did not feel safe and I knew that since the night Beth had broken in there and then the incident before Christmas, Amelia had never felt safe there. I knew she would never agree to live here and in all honesty I did not want to live here anymore either.

I finally decided that I could get around asking her to marry me and still rectify the living arrangements for now. "Amelia, would you like for me to move into The Jefferson with you?"

"We could turn Emma's old room into a nursery for Gabby, but I can't put Jay out. I won't. I will have to check with him." That's the Amelia I knew and loved, always thinking of others before herself.

"We don't have to figure all of this out tonight," I tried to comfort her because I could hear the worry in her voice about Jay.

"Are you in bed?" Amelia changed the subject again.

"Yes, aren't you?"

"Yes."

"What are you wearing?" I knew what she was wearing, but I asked anyway.

"The sexiest hospital gown you have ever seen. And you?"

I lied, "The pirate pjs that you love." I was really wearing a run of the mill pair of boxers.

"Mr. Hewitt, are you trying to start something over the phone?"

"If I were trying to start anything I would describe to you how I was slipping my fingers under the hem of your panties and tracing the leg from the back around to your hip and with your aunt in the room..."

Amelia squealed and followed with giggling. I could then hear Gayle in the background, "Millie! Are you alright?"

"I love you and I've got to go." And the next thing I heard was her hanging up.

Like many nights before, I dreamed of her that night; kissing her and making love to her. I woke feeling spent as if it had not been a dream.

CHAPTER 10

I could tell it was going to be a good day from the way the sunlight lit up the room through the gap left between the curtain and the wall. Dr. Andrews had guaranteed that two things would happen today: finding out the sex of the child Amelia was carrying and releasing Amelia from the hospital. I was as excited about one as I was the other.

Mrs. Allen was able to keep Gabby for me today and it was a relief to have her back. Stella had been great, but I did not want to wear her out. I was already thinking ahead to what to do as far as Gabby's care if we moved to The Jefferson. It would be easy enough to drop Gabby off with Mrs. Allen at her home in Siloam on my way to work, but it would also be a great arrangement if we were able to have Stella on stand-by there in the building. The idea of moving to Millie's apartment was already shaping up to be a better idea for all of us.

This morning I grabbed not only the usual items for leaving the house; keys and wallet, but I also grabbed the box the ring was in. Today was the day I would ask her to marry me and I could hardly wait.

All these things rushed through my head as I made what I hoped would be my last trip to Grady Memorial Hospital.

\*\*\*

"You see right there? Looks like an equal sign?" The sonogram technician pointed to the screen. Amelia was laid back on the exam table and Gayle and I were on each side of her head. The three of us squinted a little and leaned toward the monitor for a closer look.

The technician continued, "That's your daughter's..."

"We get the picture," Gayle cut the woman off promptly before she said the medical term. Being the Southern lady, I am certain Gayle felt this was not a word that was spoken in mixed company.

"A GIRL!" Amelia screamed. "That's awesome! Now, can we wipe this slimy gel off of my stomach?"

The technician was a dark, heavy set woman of about fifty. Her ID badge said Quiona. She handed Amelia some tissue and Amelia began wiping feverishly.

"I've been here twenty years and you are the fastest one to wipe that stuff off," Quiona commented as she slid the monitor back. We had already heard the heartbeat, so finding out the sex was the last of the official business.

"Are you happy it's a girl?" I had to ask because I knew Amelia's happy voice and this was not it.

"Of course she's happy," Gayle answered for her, likely trying to save face for Amelia.

"We already have a girl so I just thought you might like..." Amelia's eyes began to fill with tears.

"Don't be ridiculous! I won't just like, I will love any child we have. Come here." I pulled her head into my chest and cradled her against me. "You have to stop worrying about what I might want. I already have more than I ever hoped for, I have you."

"If you folks will excuse me, I am going to go and get the printouts for you so that you will have pictures to show the rest of your families." The technician left the room.

Three floors down from the hospital room we had been camped out in all week was the radiology department and the room where we found out we were having another daughter. It was the room where Amelia first acknowledged that Gabby was ours and it was the room where I worked up the courage to ask Amelia Jane Anderson to marry me. I readily admit it was not the most ideal setting, but the ring really was burning a hole in my pocket.

"I have something for you and I don't know if there will ever be a perfect location or a perfect time or anything, but I want to give it to you now, in this moment. I am sorry if it's not the setting you might have always dreamed of, but this is my perfect moment." I explained as I reached in my pocket and took hold of the small Bailey, Banks & Biddle box.

Amelia did not know what to think, but Gayle did. I had not told a soul that I had purchased the ring. Gayle, Jay and I had talked about me asking Amelia to marry me days before, but I think they thought it was just in abstract terms. There was never anything abstract about it as far as I was concerned.

Amelia was still seated on the exam table and Gayle was holding her hand. Gayle's eyes became as big as saucers as I took Amelia's hand and dropped to one knee.

"Miss Anderson, I apologize for my timing, but would you do me the honor..."

I was not even finished with the question before she stopped me. "Please get up."

"Excuse me?"

"Get up."

"Did you ask Aunt Gayle's permission?"

I really had not thought of that. "Well, I would have, but I kind of thought that ship had sailed since..."

"Seriously? Ask her! It's tradition!"

All the while, Gayle was still in the room watching this banter back and forth between us. I turned to ask her when she finally spoke up, "Seriously Millie, cart before the horse. He's right."

"Granddaddy's not here so he needs to ask you," Amelia was quite insistent.

"Millie, you should thank your lucky stars that your granddaddy's not hear to witness this and I say again, cart before the horse." Gayle glanced in my direction, "Honestly, you would have been lucky to have gotten a shotgun wedding and not just the shotgun if he were here witnessing all of this."

"Fine," Amelia huffed. "I just wanted some tradition."

168

Gayle could not hold it in any longer and began to laugh. "Millie, he asked me days ago. Oh, and we are going to have some tradition," Gayle added. "The few who know have been sworn to secrecy about the pregnancy so if you want a big white wedding then you will have a big white wedding and no one will be the wiser as long as you wear an Empire waist dress."

Amelia was about to give us a good what for about messing with her, but I demanded their attention. "Ladies! Excuse me, but could we try this again?"

I dropped back to my knee and this time Amelia was speechless. She nodded her head in the affirmative, but no words were spoken.

"I had hoped to give you my mother's ring, but this will have to do," I explained as I took the ring from its cushioned spot in the box. I stood and slipped it on Amelia's finger. "We can have it sized."

"Will have to do? Are you joking? This is amazing!" Amelia admired the ring as all of the florescent lights in the room made it sparkle and reflect in every direction. "It is so..."

"Expensive looking," Gayle observed as Amelia held her hand out for her to see.

"So you like it?" I remembered our conversation from Cameron's very well and until that moment I had been afraid she would turn me down.

"I love it!" She sprang from her spot on the examination table. There was no hint of a limp or injury as she jumped into my arms. With caution to the wind, she kissed me passionately right there in front of her aunt. It was the type of kiss that could fog windows and make this grown man weak in the knees.

I finally pulled back from her as not to completely embarrass Gayle or ourselves for getting carried away. "You know, I had a whole speech prepared, but that 'Get up!' and 'tradition' lecture you just gave kind of put the kibosh on the moment."

"I don't need a speech." At first, Amelia addressed me, but then she turned her focus to her aunt. "And, I don't need a big wedding or an empire waist dress."

"So sorry about that..." Amelia was beginning to apologize when Quiona, the sonogram technician returned.

"Y'all are still here?" she asked and the look on her face conveyed that she was surprised to see us almost exactly where she had left us a few minutes ago.

We all glanced at one another curiously. Gayle voiced the thoughts that each of us was having. "We didn't realize you were finished."

"Oh yeah, we're all done here and your doctor is going to meet you in your room to go over everything. Good luck with baby girl. Feel free to name her after me. The world needs more Quionas," she laughed.

Again we all looked at one another with concern, each likely thinking the same thing, but only one of us speaking up. I beat Gayle to the punch this time. "I thought you said you were going to bring back sonogram photos of the baby for us?"

Quiona looked at me like I had two heads. "I sent them up to your room so the doctor could look over them," she responded as she held the door open signaling us to leave.

"Alright, well thanks for everything." Amelia said as she took both me and Gayle by the hand and pulled us along to the door.

*** 

We had not been long returned to Amelia's assigned room when an unfamiliar doctor entered. She introduced herself as Dr. Stephens. She appeared very young, too young to be a doctor, but nonetheless she was the OB/GYN on staff that Dr. Andrews had sent up.

"Miss Anderson, I have already taken a look at your radiology report and the sonogram photos from earlier. Looks like you are having a girl. Congratulations." The doctor approached Amelia and extended her hand.

"Thank you. We are very excited." Amelia's attitude toward having a girl seemed to be shifting.

"I am going to need to do an exam on you and I am going to ask that your mother and husband here to wait in the hall. This won't take more than about ten minutes." Dr. Stephens was young, but she exuded confidence in her voice. Perhaps, she just looked young.

I held the door for Gayle and the two of us proceeded to wait in the hallway. It really was about ten minutes before Dr. Stephens appeared and invited us back in.

No sooner had we reentered the room did Amelia announce, "Heart like a squirrel."

"What does that mean?" Clearly, she was referring to the baby.

Gayle responded, "The smaller the animal, the faster the heartbeat. Squirrels have fast heartbeats and a fetus has a fast heartbeat too. Gabe, it's a good thing."

"It means nothing about the bombing or my treatment thereafter hurt our little sunshine." I could hear the relief in Amelia's voice.

"Our little sunshine. I like it," I added.

Beth had never given Gabby a pet name beyond "it" the entire time she was pregnant. And, when Beth called the baby "it" she might as well have been calling her an alien. Even after she found out she was having a girl, it was still a bothersome creature to her and not a little, living person. I suppose that's what kept Gabby from being real to me until the first time I held her. This child was already real to me. I could just about see her even now; green eyes with gold flakes, the spitting image of Amelia.

True to Dr. Andrews' word, Amelia was released that afternoon. We were cautioned that there would still be some recovery for example, the wound to her hip would take a while to get over and she might have twinges of pain from time to time. It was not like a broken arm or anything that could be casted, so she would have to learn to live with the pain to some extent while moving. Also, a lingering effect from having had swelling on the brain might be headaches. We were warned that the headaches might be chronic or she might not have them at all. Follow-up with her primary care physician should take place within seven days. Otherwise, she was free to move on with her life.

Dr. Andrews congratulated us again on the pregnancy and reminded us just how lucky Amelia was to be alive. "She has an amazing will to live and she's a very lucky girl," he added.

Before leaving we all thanked Dr. Andrews profusely and I gave him my card. As I had done with Anthony the security guard who helped Cara and I that first morning at the Westin, I promised Dr. Andrews a free weekend at the inn. It was the least I could do for both of them.

***

Amelia had already started preparing Gayle that she was going back to The Jefferson, but it was obvious that Gayle had held out hope that Amelia would change her mind and return home with her. Amelia was firm in her decision and reminded Gayle that she would be starting law school at Mercer in two weeks, so it made the most sense that we live at the apartment in Milledgeville.

"We?" Gayle questioned.

"Gabriel, Gabby and I." Amelia followed with emphasis, "We will be living in my apartment."

This was not the discussion to have in the elevator of the hospital as she was being wheeled out, but that's where it took place. I guess I thought Amelia would have had that talk with Gayle before I arrived that morning, but she hadn't.

"I appreciate all that you have done, but I want to go home, my home," Amelia explained as if throwing herself on a sword to avoid hurting Gayle's feelings or perhaps she was seeking her approval, I was not sure. Gayle looked a little hurt by Amelia's decision.

I tried to aid the both of them. "It is going to take me a couple of days to move everything and for Amelia to sort things out with Jay."

I hated to continue, but I did not have much choice. I was no longer in a position just to pack a bag and run over to Milledgeville for the night. I had to think about what all Gabby needed and it was way more than just a bag. She needed a crib and what not just to be able to spend the night some place. So, as much as I wanted to spend every single night with Amelia, it just wasn't that simple anymore.

I continued, "Gayle, why don't you plan on staying over at Amelia's this week and helping with her recovery. I will go ahead and start moving things over and Gabby and I will be there officially by the weekend."

Amelia seemed slightly disappointed.

I tried to reassure Amelia and repeated myself, "Little One and I will be there by the weekend. In fact, why don't you ride home with me? You can meet Gabby and I will take you out to dinner? Gayle, would you be alright with meeting us at the apartment about the same time that you typically arrived here for overnight duty?"

Ultimately, Gayle was pacified. She agreed to everything, even agreed to wait with Amelia while I brought the car around.

Within a few moments, I was back with the car. As I made the approach, I could see Amelia standing on the corner. Her hair was blowing gently in the breeze and she appeared as though nothing had ever happened.

Gayle had bought her a new outfit for going home almost like one would for bringing home a baby. It was almost noon and the sun was shining right through the blue eyelet shirt that she had on. The street was busy with people passing by and each man, woman and child turned their head to look at Amelia. She was that pretty.

I was almost alongside of her at the curb when I noticed one of the last remaining news crews approach her. It was the guy from

WATL that had been camped out in front of the hospital all week. His camera man was in tow.

Gayle tried to drag Amelia along, but Amelia stayed. I parked in the loading lane and waited about five minutes before Amelia finished and made her way to the car.

"What was that about?" I asked as I got out and opened the car door for her.

"Apparently I am one of the last of the bombing victims to be released and he seemed to already know about me. He asked if he could interview me," Amelia answered as I helped her into the car.

"What did you tell him?" I asked once back in my seat.

"I told him that I had been injured and that I had also been saved by the heroics of Mr. Jewell and that I did not believe for one instance that Mr. Jewell was anything less than a hero."

"You were over there about five minutes. Did you tell him anything else?"

"I told him where I was from and how I came to be at the park that night. Why so many questions?" Amelia was becoming wary of my inquisition.

"Beth works for WATL," I answered cautiously.

"Not to worry, I did not say anything about you or Gabby." She buckled her seatbelt and leaned over for a kiss. "Take me home, Mr. Hewitt."

I was relieved, but neither of us took into account that the sizable engagement ring would be on full display for anyone tuning in to see, including Beth.

"Gladly soon-to-be Mrs. Hewitt," I replied with a smile that extended from one ear to the other. I liked the sound of it.

I put the car in gear and we pulled away, leaving Grady and all the chaos of that week behind.

174

About a mile down the road I broke the silence. "You feel like eating? You are probably dying for some real food, right?"

"I am. In fact, I would love a cheeseburger."

Out I-20 and a couple of lefts later down Memorial Drive, we came to Ann's Snack Bar. Miraculously, we were able to get spots at the counter. Miss Ann was known for the best burgers in the Metro area. I ordered the Ghetto burger and Amelia had the Hood burger.

As we waited, the sound system played a song by Brian McKnight, "Crazy Love." Amelia was listening to the chatter of the other patrons, but I could not help but listen to the words of the song. Cheesy as it was, it spoke to me. The lines of the song were true to the way I felt about her; the heavens opened every time she smiled and I did need her. Were we most anywhere else, I would have asked her to dance. Instead, I would have to settle for taking her hand and that wasn't settling at all.

"Listen to the song," I said to her as I gave her hand a gentle squeeze. It really was a crazy love that I had for her.

Amelia listened and before long we were both swaying with the rhythm. Back and forth we gently moved on our barstools. Swaying in my direction, Amelia whispered, "I would never have guessed you were an R&B fan."

She was right, R&B was not typically my thing, but neither was country music until I met her. "What, you think I am just into 80's hair bands or something?"

Amelia giggled, "Well..."

"You've seen my CD collection. I like to think I am well rounded."

"The Hollies and LL Cool J does not make one well-rounded." The song was ending when our conversation kicked in about my taste in music.

"Then you clearly did not notice the Twisted Sister CD, Ratt, Bon Jovi, Beastie Boys or Lita Ford."

"So you *are* an 80's hair band fan?"

"Hello, Beastie Boys?"

"That, LL Cool J and The Hollies, that's just for breaking the monotony."

Our burgers were finally ready and being placed in front of us when Amelia asked me what my favorite song was. "I don't know that I have just one favorite song. I like Stone Temple Pilots 'Interstate Love Song,' Bon Jovi's 'Wanted Dead or Alive,' and 'East Bound and Down.'"

"The theme from 'Smokey and the Bandit?'" Amelia asked before she picked up her Hood burger with both hands and took a bite.

"What boy from my generation would not pick that as one of his favorite songs? Honestly, Amelia, I thought you knew music. And just so you know, I would kill for that car, too."

Amelia chewed quickly and then catapulted us to the next subject, "Speaking of cars, I guess I will need a new one."

In between bites of my own burger, I asked, "Why would you need a new car?"

All of the particulars of our new life had not set in on me yet, but Amelia explained prior to taking another bite. "I can't put a baby, or two in our case, in my Corvette or the truck."

"Right, but you don't want to get rid of them do you?"

"God, no! I just might need something to drive that's more practical to my circumstances."

I was hesitant to offer the suggestion, but went for it anyway. "You could always take the Legend and I could drive one of yours."

Amelia glanced sideways at me, "That's not exactly what I had in mind."

"You want a new car?"

"I've never had one and the others are classics, so we should probably keep the miles off of them." I appreciated the way she used the word we.

We continued eating our burgers and discussing cars. Amelia was making a pretty good dent in her burger, but I finally had to ask, "Are you going to eat all of that?"

I had to ask because I was getting full and Amelia was yet to show any sign of slowing down. Each of our burgers took up the entire standard size Styrofoam plate on which they were served. My Ghetto burger consisted of two beef patties plus every topping known to man; lettuce, tomato, grilled onions, chili, bacon, mayo, ketchup and mustard. Amelia's Hood burger was equally impressive and differed from mine only by the addition of slaw.

"I am going to die trying. This is the best burger I have ever had! And, I *am* eating for two." There was noticeable emphasis when she said the word "am."

I had never seen her eat like that before. I had never seen any woman eat like that before. Perhaps she was eating for two or perhaps she was just starving from not having eaten much other than a couple of meals from the hospital in the last week. I felt bad for her and worried that she might make herself sick.

Amelia took a couple more bites and then backed off of the burger. We ended up leaving there with what appeared to be two tin foil bombs.

On the way to Greensboro we continued our discussions of any and everything and nothing at all. The ride was quick, but not because I was speeding or there was no traffic. It was quick because we talked and talked and talked some more.

We were turning onto Highway 44 when the stack of Gabby's medical records went sliding across the back seat. Amelia unhooked her seatbelt and picked them up. When she returned to her seat, she was still holding the stack of paper.

"Do you mind if I look over these?" Amelia asked before turning over the title page.

"What's mine is yours future Mrs. Hewitt."

"What exactly are you hoping to find in these?"

"I am not sure. Not that I wish this on Gabby, but the easiest thing would be for them to show that she had drugs in her system."

Amelia thumbed through the first couple of pages, "Patient info sheet says Gabby was born on July 1, 1996. Were you at the birth?"

"What? No, Beth's mother called me the following morning..."

"I heard she was born on July 3rd."

"Yeah, they called me the morning of the 4th. I had to work and Beth said she was going to her parents' house for the 4th. She left on the 1st. I was glad for her to go, so I did not think anything of it. Anyway, they said she had her at 11:08 pm July 3rd. I was upset that I was not there for the birth, but they told me it happened so quickly and there was no need in me getting on the road in the middle of the night, so they just waited to call me that morning. I had been so glad that Gabby was here that I had never bothered to question them further about not calling me when they were on their way to the hospital."

Amelia was thinking out loud as she read, "What would be the point in telling you she was born two days later than she actually was?"

My head was absolutely spinning. Amelia continued reading, "Do you know what NICU stands for?"

"No."

"Neonatal Intensive Care Unit. Gabby was sent to the NICU."

"For what?"

"She wasn't breathing and she only weighted four pounds, six ounces. How did you not know any of this?"

"I just thought she was tiny."

Amelia kept reading, flipping the pages as if she was looking for something. "Shit! Gabriel, she had cocaine in her system!"

I was stunned. I jerked the wheel of the car and the tires on the passenger side went off the road just barely. Amelia gasped and grabbed the dashboard. I got it back on the road, but not before giving us both a scare. I could not believe what she was telling me.

I knew Beth's taste for a little coke now and then and I knew what I said about the easiest thing, but I didn't really meant it. I did not want Gabby to suffer any, but I had seen plenty of 60 Minutes, 20/20 specials, Donahue, Montel Williams and Oprah episodes to know what to expect from children born on drugs. It's not like I purposely watched daytime television or news magazine shows, it's just that there was a time in the late 80's when shows dedicated to crack babies and those born addicted to drugs was a hot topic. My shock was steadily changing to rage.

"Jesus Christ! She's been a great baby, no withdrawal signs, nothing like you see on TV."

"No wonder Beth dumped the baby on you!" Amelia shook her head in disgust. "How did that happen anyway?"

"They were discharged on the sixth and I brought the car around. Mrs. Reed put Gabby in the car seat and Beth just sat there in the wheelchair. I did not even have a chance to ask Beth anything before her mother said to me, 'Elizabeth is going to be coming home with me to recuperate. She will call you in a few days.' I did not know what to think so I got in the car and drove away with Gabby sleeping in the back seat. You can imagine the thoughts that ran through my head on the way home."

"She was out of the NICU before they let you know she was born."

I did not know what to say. Amelia kept reading and finally, "Ah ha! Here, look at this," she said as she held a sheet of paper toward me.

The page was titled, "'Withdrawals: what to expect from your baby'. It looks like this is a copy of what was given to Beth for taking care of the baby." As soon as she thought I had had a chance to glance at it, Amelia took the page back and began reading aloud.

"Each baby is different. Blah blah blah. Your baby may not experience withdrawals immediately." She paused and read silently before picking back up, "Some babies do not experience withdrawals until they are approximately eight weeks old."

Amelia paused again from reading aloud and I spoke, "She's four weeks and she's perfect."

Amelia reached over and took my hand that had been resting on the gear column. Sometimes the spark when she touched me was electrifying and sometimes, like this one, it represented security and comfort. "I am sure she will be fine, but have you taken her to any pediatrician visits yet? Didn't anyone tell you?"

"No!"

"Gabriel, she should have gone to the pediatrician at least twice by now."

"I will take her tomorrow."

"I will call Jay's Aunt June and get her to recommend someone in Milledgeville. I will make an appointment and we will take her."

"You will do that?"

"It's what good mothers do. We'll do it together and we'll take these records with us. I could read and read, but I am no doctor so..."

It wasn't long before we were turning toward the gate of the club. We were flagged down by Ed as we approached the guard shack.

"Good afternoon." Ed waived as he approached the window that I had just let down on my side of the car. "Looks like you have Miss Millie with you."

Amelia leaned over and greeted him, "Hey, how have you been?"

"Fair to middlin, thank you for asking, but more importantly, how are you doing? I've been praying for you."

"Well, thank you for your prayers. Apparently the Lord was listening 'cause the doctors say I am going to be right as rain." It was as if they were speaking a language unto themselves with their Southern adjectives and similes.

"I won't keep y'all. I just wanted to see how you were doing." He then directed his attention to me, "You take care of our girl now." Ed then smiled, backed away from the car and waived us through. Both Amelia and I waived back as we passed.

We came to the turn off for my street. There was no stop sign. There was no traffic behind us so before making the left, I stopped the car.

Amelia turned toward me. "What's wrong?" she asked.

I unbuckled my seatbelt, "Come here."

Amelia unbuckled hers and leaned toward me. She was so pretty even when completely absent of make-up. The sun was still shining and the light caught in her hair and her eyes. She was beautiful and I wanted one more moment alone with her. I wanted to taste her on my lips and to revel in one last moment before we were both someone's parents. I did not know how that might change us, so I wanted one more moment to remember the way we were.

I reached my hand to her cheek and softly eased her hair from her face and tucked it behind her right ear. "You are the most beautiful woman I have ever seen."

Amelia blushed. I was taken aback that I could still make her blush after everything we had been through.

"May I?" I asked her. I wanted to kiss her, but more than anything I wanted her to let me know that she wanted me to kiss her. I still needed reassurance that she wanted our new life together after what she had just learned about Gabby.

"Please."

I did not know what I had done to deserve her. Her kiss was intoxicating and the spark was there and everything inside me ached for her. Were she not still recovering, I would have taken her there or at the very least thrown the car in gear and taken her in the garage of my house. I had never wanted her more.

I barely removed my lips from hers to utter the words, "I want you so badly."

She gripped my jeans at my thigh and pulled me toward her as much as she could. "Oh my God, Gabriel," she sighed.

The kiss was deep and I could feel her heart race through the pulse in her neck as I left a trail of kisses. Suddenly, she winced and the moment was over.

"I'm sorry. I'm sorry." I apologized. "I did not mean to get that carried away."

"Gabriel, I want you too and..."

"I am so relieved to hear you say that. I am scared that one more crazy detail and you are going to run."

I dropped my head, but Amelia held lifted my face and held it in her hands. "Look at me."

I raised my eyes to meet hers.

"Do you know what scared me most about the bombing?"

I shuddered to ask, but I did it anyway, "What?"

"As I fell that night, all I could think was what if I never saw you again. What if something happened to me and you never knew how I felt about you? What if you never knew that you were the light in the darkness that had been my life before we met? It's you and me."

She nodded her head in the affirmative as she repeated, "It's you and me. I won't run if you won't. Now let's go."

182

I had to ask one more thing. "I can't believe you are being so cool about Gabby. Why?"

"I want you and you want her so what choice do I have? And, beyond that, you have told me before that you don't want her growing up feeling like I did. How awful of a person would I be to not respect that?     How selfish would I be to try to prevent you from catching her when her mother has so clearly thrown her away? I know better than anyone about being thrown away and I would never do that to anyone."

"Most people would want me to give Gabby back to Beth and make her lie in the bed she made."

"I am not most people, now am I?" She was most definitely not most people and thank the Lord for it.

I put the car in drive and made the turn.

***

"Miss Millie!" Mrs. Allen screamed as she ran to Amelia when she saw her in the doorway. Mrs. Allen threw her arms around her and up on her toes Amelia went and into a big bear hug. "Miss Millie, don't you ever scare us like that again!"

"I am so sorry. I did not mean to scare anyone," Amelia apologized profusely as Mrs. Allen continued the hug. "Everything is set up for Rudy, so if anything had happened..."

"You shush child, no one cares about that!" Mrs. Allen dropped Amelia back to her feet. "Girl you nearly got killed and all you are thinking about is that Rudy might be out some money. You really did take a knock on the skull."

"Well I am fine now and I really do apologize for scaring you..."

Mrs. Allen cut her off at every turn. "Took ten years off my young life."

Amelia clearly did not know what else to say when Mrs. Allen started to giggle a little. "I suppose you would like to meet Little One," she added.

"If you wouldn't mind," Amelia replied.

"Mind, who am I to mind?" Mrs. Allen shrugged off Amelia.

Since Amelia had been injured, I finally broke down and confessed to Mrs. Allen that mine and Amelia's relationship was more than that of supervisor to employee. She is from another generation so I expected a bit of scolding over dipping my pen in the company ink, but she did nothing of the sort. She seemed pleased and congratulatory, even explained that she suspected something was up back when Amelia suggested she seek me out for a job. I was relieved. For whatever reason, Mrs. Allen was someone I felt the need not to disappoint.

While Amelia and Mrs. Allen had been chatting, I had picked Gabby up from the bassinette where she was sleeping. She hardly stirred in my arms as I gently moved her. I rocked her and hummed a little to try to insure she stayed asleep.

"Would you like to hold her?" I eased over to where Amelia was still standing near the couch.

Amelia turned toward me and her eyes filled with tears as she looked at me holding Sweet Pea. Could I be so lucky as it being love at first sight for Amelia? I had already asked for too much in just asking Amelia to take this on.

CHAPTER 11

It was nearly dusk. Mrs. Allen had gone home for the night and it was just the three of us, four if you believed that life started at conception. Amelia had been cradling Gabby in her arms for about fifteen minutes. She gently patted Little One on the bottom and bounced ever so slightly while seated on the couch. There was no television on, no other sounds in the room, but the faint sound Amelia's hand made when it made contact with the diaper.

I had taken a seat in the armchair at the end of the couch so I could take in the sight. I drank in the sight. I had not had a family in so many years and now this was my family. I had not known true peace until that moment.

Sitting there, watching them it suddenly occurred to me there was something I needed to rectify.

"Bring Gabby and come with me," I said as I stood. I could tell that Amelia would answer my request so I extended my hand to help her up while she held on to the still-sleeping baby.

"I am going to need your ring for a moment as well," I added as she got to her feet.

"Why?"

"Trust me, I will give it back."

With Gabby's little head tucked in the crook of her elbow on her left arm, Amelia secured her with her right. She held out her hand offering the ring. As gently as I possibly could, I slid the ring off and slipped it in my pocket.

"Follow me." I started for the front door and Amelia followed. I turned to her as I put my hand on the door knob. It dawned on me that there was no way Amelia was going to be able to make the walk and carry the little sack of potatoes at the same time, no matter how much pain meds she had taken. She had not shown any signs of limping all day and I did not want her to start now.

I offered my arms and made the offer, "Let me carry her."

185

Amelia obliged and we made the exchange.

Even while holding Little One, I managed to hold the door for Amelia. Once on the porch she allowed me to take the lead again and I started down through the yard.

"Gabriel?" she said my name.

"Are you okay?" I glanced back to make sure she had not fallen behind or fallen altogether. Perhaps this walk was too much for her this soon. I had not really considered that when the idea struck me.

"I am fine, but we are almost to the street. Where are we going?" Her answer and question were a relief.

"You will see. It's not that much farther."

I shifted Gabby to my left arm and offered my right to Amelia. When our hands locked the current of her touch ran through me. I could feel the vibration in every joint of my body. Gabby squirmed, lifted her little head and blinked ever so slightly at me and drifted back off to sleep. Had she actually felt that too? I had not had that deep of a tingling from her touch in a while. The sensation was always there, but it seemed stronger. I glanced at her, at myself and what I wanted to consider as our child. My God, I loved them.

I did not say anything. I just continued to lead through the yard of the neighbors across the street. We passed along the side of the house down a path lined with azaleas on one side and a privacy wall of cypress trees on the other. It was a narrow path and I took the lead pulling Amelia along just barely behind me by the hand.

Just past the corner of the stucco house, the path opened up onto an expansive backyard that sloped gently to the lake. There were few trees to obstruct the view of the lake and the grass was the same Zoysia that was planted on the greens and fairways of the course.

"Kick off your shoes," I directed.

As Amelia began to comply, she looked up at me. "Please tell me you know the people who live here."

"No one really lives here and I look after the place for the people who own it. It's okay." This was a second home to a family that rarely came up from Florida. Their property was lakefront and they had told me when I met them that I was always welcome to access the lake through their yard. Although I had only seen the yard and the lake once or twice, I had never taken them up on their offer until that moment.

We left our shoes by the edge of the yard and followed the path along the side of the house. We started through the grass and it was a familiar feeling. Amelia had insisted we walk barefoot on the green after her first shift at the club. It still felt like carpet as it gave under our steps just as it did now. I knew then that she was special.

There was a walkway of varying sized slabs of slate that cut the yard nearly in half and led from the back deck all the way down to the lake. We cut across the yard diagonally and picked up the slate path about halfway to the lake. I followed it and Amelia followed me.

At the end of the path was a dock. At first it was just a gangway and it extended into Lake Oconee one plank after another for about twenty-five feet until it opened up to a platform. The platform was about twelve feet by fifteen feet. It was a good size dock. When we were nearly center of the platform part of the dock, I knelt before her. "I was selfish earlier today and I want to rectify that."

Amelia's face was that of shock, again.

With Gabby still sleeping in one arm, I reached in my pocket with my other hand and pulled out the ring. "Amelia Jane Anderson, there is no one else that I would rather spend the rest of my life with than you. Would you please do me the honor of marrying me?"

For a moment she stood silent. She studied my face and the baby that was starting to waken in my arms. It was long enough for me to begin to wonder if she had changed her mind. She finally spoke.

"You mentioned before that it might not be what I dreamed of, but to tell you the truth I never dreamed of such things. I never dreamed of a proposal or getting married. I never dreamed of having children. My Grandparents were the only example of a marriage that I had and theirs was perfect. My parents were no example to me. There was nothing really to dream of until you came along."

Amelia paused and let out a huge breath. "I don't need marriage or a ring or a big wedding. I am content to just be near you, but every time I think I am settling in to being yours, something happens."

"Nothing is going to happen. It's just us now. The four of us and no one else." I did my best to assure her. I stood as this was not a conversation I wanted to have while squatting and distracted by the ache in my knee against the wood of the dock.

"I want to believe you and I think I want to marry you, but like you said, four, that's two more to protect than before and we could not seem to get that job done when it was just us."

The word "think" stung. With the exception of her little fit over tradition, she had seemed eager to accept when we were there in the hospital. Had it been a show for her Aunt? I did not think so. As much as I did not understand where things had taken a turn for her during the day, I completely understood where she was coming from. I did not know what else to do to convince her. I only knew that I could not live without her.

"I can't live without you. I won't live without you and I won't let anyone else get in the way of that ever again. I am so sorry that things have gone this way and it's been this hard for us. I don't know what the future holds, but I do know that nothing worth having is easy. I also know that we are worth having. The two of us, the four of us, we are in this together and we are worth having. So, please say you will marry me."

"Ask me again."

I dropped back to my knee and now Gabby was fully awake. As the sun set directly across the lake from the dock, the light rippled across the gentle waves of the lake and I asked Amelia to marry me, to marry us, for the third time in a day. This time she gave her consent readily and in the way of proposals it did not get much more romantic.

***

By the time we walked back to the house, it was getting on toward 9:00 p.m. Once back in the house, I mentioned that I needed to change Gabby's diaper and feed her.

"You get the bottle ready and I will change her," Amelia offered.

"Great idea. Thank you for helping me with her."

"Seriously, Gabriel? If you intend for me to be her mother, you don't have to thank me. I think this is how good parents are supposed to act." Amelia explained as she took Little One from me and started in the direction of the hallway leading to the bedrooms.

"Like partners?" I questioned as I took a few steps toward the kitchen.

Amelia looked back over her shoulder and confirmed we were on the same page. "Like partners."

Suddenly, I heard a muffled scream, "Gabriella Grace Hewitt!"

I knew full names were never good. I dropped the half prepared bottle in the sink and went running. I burst into the room to find Amelia changing a record breaker.

"There's poo on my shirt! I turned to get a diaper and when I turned back..." Amelia pressed her face into a hard, grin and bear it smile and squinched her eyes. I could tell she was trying not to gag.

The smell was ungodly. I gagged and Amelia could not hold it any longer. I finished changing Gabby while Amelia vomited and vomited and vomited some more into the tiny white wicker trash can.

189

"Still partners?" She sheepishly asked as she returned upright.

"Yeah, still partners," I shook my head and laughed all the while finishing up the diaper duty.

"I'm sorry."

"It's okay."

Amelia bent over to pick up the trash can and clean up her portion of the mess in the room. "You know, this is the saddest nursery I think I have ever seen."

"I did not know I was in need of a nursery until I was on the way home from the hospital with her and I did not know that this would be permanent."

"You have her sleeping in a play pen," Amelia pointed to what I thought was a crib.

"It's a crib."

"No, it's a play pen."

"It has a built in changing table."

"Gabriel, this is pitiful."

"I suppose it's a good thing we are moving." I smiled and winked at her. The play pen, as she called it, vomit and poop were not the only sad things in the room. I had not had a chance to paint it or put up anything that would indicate it was a nursery. What did I know about decorating a nursery? Nothing. I knew nothing and it showed in this room.

"Where did you get this and did anyone help you?"

"It was all they had in stock at the Wal-Mart in Madison and this nice high school girl helped me."

"How did she help you? Because she sure did not do Gabby any favors."

We just laughed and it was a relief to hear her laugh. I could not help commenting on it. "I have missed your laugh."

"I have missed everything about you," she responded. "Now, could I borrow a shirt because I don't want to kiss you with poop and vomit on me and I really want to kiss you now."

I sat the baby in the only other item of furniture in the room, her bouncy chair, and went to get Amelia a t-shirt. Amelia followed me into my bedroom.

"Mind if I go ahead and grab a shower?" she asked as she strode on into the bedroom pulling the blue eyelet shirt over her head as she went.

I don't know how I missed it, but she had not been wearing a bra. "Miss Anderson, aren't you missing an article of clothing?"

Her hair glided over her shoulder as she turned her head back to me and smiled. "You noticed."

I noticed now and unlike in the hospital room yesterday, the feeling I felt upon sight of her bare back was not pity or an aching to take the pain away from her. It had only been a day, but I swear there were less scabs than yesterday. She was nearly flawless.

Amelia kicked off the slip on tennis shoes she had been wearing and continued across the tile of the bathroom. She was down to her jeans and her engagement ring. The view was amazing, bare feet and bare back with her hair hanging down past where her bra strap would ordinarily be.

The jeans she was wearing were low cut and a little snug. The way they hugged her was the definition of a perfect fit. She often described herself as having the shape of a fifteen year old boy, lean and straight, but she was wrong. She was thin, but she had just the right balance of muscle and curves. From behind I could not tell she was pregnant at all.

She reached back and shook out her hair with her left hand. The light caught the ring and flashed rays around the room, but that was not what caught my eye. When her arm went up and she turned ever so slightly I could see the edge of her breast. Even from there I could tell they were a little fuller.

I could feel my pulse quicken. I wanted her.

It was as if everything was happening in slow motion as I watched her. Who would have thought seeing her turn on the shower would be such a show, but that's exactly what it was. She slid the door back and leaned in to cut the water on. I lingered in the doorway still watching and I should have been able to get a profile view of her, a better look at her breasts than the one I had just stolen when she shook out her hair. Instead, it was her hair that fell to block the view. It was still sexy as hell and I could not stand watching any longer.

"Do you mind if I join you?" I asked.

"Not at all, but what about Gabby?"

"I will check on her and be right back."

I did not just check on her. I brought the bouncy seat to the bathroom with me. I sat her on the floor in the doorway to the bathroom. I could see her, but she could not see us. Knowing Sweet Pea, she would be asleep again in a moment, so it's not like she would witness anything and she was too young for us to scar her. To aid her in getting back to sleep, I put on some music, a mix tape that Praise had given me for just this purpose.

"If you can't get her to sleep, put this on and rock her gently," Praise had told me when she handed me the tape. I had not needed it until then, so I really had no idea what was on there.

Once Gabby was settled in her bouncy seat on the floor, I found Amelia already in the shower. I eased out of my attire and into the shower with her as Anita Baker's "Sweet Love" serenaded our daughter.

While I was gone Amelia found a hair band and pulled up her hair. There was no more using it as a shield preventing me from seeing every beautiful inch of her. She stood with her back to the shower head allowing the water to run down her back. I moved around in front of her to the back of the shower stall.

192

The full view of her was breathtaking. Water rolled down her and glistened in the light. There was little evidence from the frontal view to indicate Amelia was with child. Had I not seen the sonogram today, I might not have believed she was as far along as she was. The only slightest of hints was that her breasts were fuller than I remembered.

The next song started to play as I reached for a washcloth. "You can reach me by railway..." a soulful female voice bellowed with little more than the accompaniment of a piano.

I was stopped in my tracks as Amelia touched my hand. "I need you closer," she said softly with the words of the song.

I obeyed and pulled her to me. There was nothing between us and for a moment we gently swayed with the music.

"I love this song," she whispered before picking back up singing along. She had doubted her voice in the past, but she was just as capable as this singer. ..."I need you closer."

"I would go anywhere, follow you anywhere," I said easing my hand behind her neck on her right side and I leaned down to her.

I stilled her mouth with mine. Her lips were soft and sweet and her tongue was magical to touch. Despite the steam and the heat of the water, there were chills down both of my legs. This was what my dreams had been made of for so long and now I wasn't dreaming.

Amelia was so tiny and petite next to me and still so fragile from the bombing. I could have spent an eternity kissing her, but I had to stop myself. It was too soon to go where this was heading. I wanted her, to be inside her, to have her know just how much I had missed her. I wanted her to know that I had missed us and I had not forgotten one single minute of our time together. I did my best to regain my senses and pull away from her. It was one of the hardest feats of my life.

"What's wrong?" she asked breathlessly, barely above a whisper and her body still pressed to mine and arms tangled around my neck.

Still holding her ever so tightly, I answered, "It's too soon. I don't want to hurt you."

Amelia lifted her head and looked up at me. Her green eyes were hooded and seductive. "I know you won't hurt me and, Gabriel, I know you want me and I need you."

I had never turned her down before and I was not sure I would succeed in my attempt, but I knew making love to her now was not the right decision. Shower sex was tricky enough, usually a quick act, but nothing about what I wanted to do to her would be quick. Most of all there was the injury to her hip to consider. She was just limping because of it yesterday so full enjoyment was not something to be had at this point.

I tried to divert the act with concern for the fetus. I slid a hand around from the small of her back to her stomach and inquired, "Aren't you nervous about Little One?"

I had never had sex or made love to a pregnant woman before. I had heard from several of my friends in the service that pregnant women were more horny than average and no one had ever mentioned that the unborn baby could be harmed, but no one had dispelled that either.

"No," Amelia kind of laughed. "You aren't going to thump her forehead or anything if that's what you are thinking."

"Apparently you know more about these things than I do."

"I seriously doubt that." Amelia was a touch snarky in her answer, but she quickly toned it down. There was disappointment in her voice. "Look, if you want to wait, that's fine, but don't think you are going to break me. I am fine."

"You are not fine and I won't risk losing you or harming you. Could I please just enjoy holding you?"

I barely had the words out of my mouth before she leaned into me, pressing her head against my chest. The next song came on and I gently swayed her to the music while the shower continued to run.

Three songs and fifteen minutes later, "I hate to say this, but perhaps we should get you home. I think your poor Aunt Gayle has worried about you enough for one lifetime." I truthfully did hate the thought of being without her for a single moment.

"As much as I don't like this house and I love my apartment, home is where you are." I could feel her lips move against my chest when she spoke. It sent the right combination of tickle and excitement coursing through me. My pecks tightened on reflex and, again, sent chill bumps down my legs.

It was almost a quarter to 10:00 by the time we got on the road to Milledgeville. Gabby was again asleep in her car seat in the back and Amelia and I hand-in-hand in the front. Her hands were so smooth and soft. I drove with my left and played with her engagement ring with my right.

"Do you like the ring?" I glanced at her in the darkness.

"I love it!"

"The sales clerk said the ring's three main stones represented past, present and future, but I say they represent those who will love you most: me, Gabby and ..."

"George-Anne Marie Hewitt." Amelia said quickly, giving our unborn daughter a name. "After my grandfather, George, my father, Andrew, and Aunt Gayle's middle name is Marie. And, her name starts with "G" for you."

"That's a lot of people, a lot of legacies to have to live up to. Don't you think?"

"You don't like it? Plus, it's not like Gabriella Grace doesn't have some living up to do too."

"Point well made, Mrs. Hewitt." I typically called her Miss Anderson, but I thought I would try her soon to be new name out on her.

Headlights flashed past us lighting up Amelia's face as I glanced at her to check her reaction.

She beamed, "Say it again."

"What?" I toyed with her.

"My name. Say my name." More headlights hit her face. Cutting her eyes at me, she bit her bottom lip in anticipation.

I pulled her hand up and kissed it. "I'm yours, Mrs. Hewitt."

"Mr. Hewitt, the things I would do to you if you would let me and if our daughter were not in the back seat." That was the most verbally forward Amelia had ever been with me. I liked it.

***

Entering the apartment at The Jefferson we were met by a full house, Jay, Cara, Stella, Travis and Aunt Gayle were all camped around the living room waiting to welcome Amelia home. Amelia cried upon sight of Cara.

"Thank you so much for all that you did to find me. Thank you for calling Gabriel and not giving up on me," Amelia said in between sobs as she held Cara.

"I am so sorry I left you," Cara cried as well.

"That wasn't your fault and you came back for me. That's what matters. You came back." They hugged and cried for nearly ten minutes and it was as if there was no one else in the room, but the two of them.

Finally Stella and Travis interrupted. Stella tapped Amelia on the shoulder. Amelia stepped back from Cara and Stella took over the hug.

"We hate to run, but Travis has got to get up early for work tomorrow," Stella explained. "We are so relieved to see that you are alright."

"Gabriel told me what all you did to help out with Gabby so he could look after me at the hospital. Thank you so much! You are the best!" Amelia wiped her eyes while she hugged Stella and thanked her.

Travis and I looked on as our counterparts gushed over each other. Travis finally nudged me. "I hear congratulations are in order," he said to me.

Travis extended his hand to me and as I took it, I thanked him. "I don't know what I would have done without Stella this last week. Thank you for the congratulations, but more importantly, thanks for loaning me your girlfriend. I really appreciate it man."

"No problem," Travis replied.

Within moments the room was nearly empty. All that was left was Gabby and I, Gayle, Jay and Amelia. As soon as the door closed behind the others, Jay took his turn hugging her.

"You made the Macon news," Jay said as he stepped to put his arms around Amelia.

"What?" Amelia was caught off guard.

"Yeah," Gayle chimed in, "they referenced their affiliate, the Fox Station out of Atlanta, with the story, but yeah, you were the star. I didn't realize you were with them for so long. You went on and on about how you did not believe the bomber was Richard Jewell and you barely mentioned your injuries."

"Let me get a look at that ring. I saw it sparkling all over the TV, so let me get a look at it in person," Jay said taking her hand and pulling it up for an inspection.

As Jay gave the ring a good looking over Gayle began to fret over Gabby as I sat her carrier down on the floor next to the couch where Gayle was seated. Gayle and I spoke for a moment, but not before Jay's attention was turned to me.

Amelia smiled with embarrassment as Jay gawked. "It's big. I like big," he continued as he turned his sights on me. "Good job."

"Thanks," I replied as I started to help Gayle take Gabby from her carrier.

"Let her sleep," Amelia directed us. All eyes had been on her since we arrived, but she never once did she forget that the baby and I were there.

Amelia moved toward me and continued, "I don't want to let you go, but I don't want you two on the road so late."

She looked back to Jay, "We have to discuss some things."

I had slept over before, but this was going to be different and Amelia wanted to talk to Jay about it. I know she did not want to put him out. She wanted him to be alright with all of us living there together for the foreseeable future.

"I know. I should have just packed up the play pen and brought it here. We could have stayed here." Amelia looked disappointed and that was heart wrenching. "I know, fine time for me to think of that now."

"It's okay, just plan on staying here tomorrow night," Amelia leaned down and kissed Gabby. "You take care of Daddy and I will see you tomorrow and I will have something special for you."

I looked on and enjoyed the sight of Amelia interacting with Little One. Soon enough she stood back up. I could tell the pain medication was beginning to wear off by the winced look on her face when she stood up from the squatting position next to Gabby.

"Are you alright?" I asked her.

"Oh, yeah, it's nothing a little ibuprofen can't handle." Thank goodness she was in her second trimester so she could take something for the pain.

"Promise you will take care of yourself and the precious cargo while I am away." I insisted as I pulled her into my arms.

"I promise, Mr. Hewitt."

"That's a good answer Mrs. Hewitt." Amelia snickered at the sound of her new name when I said it. In the car it had been sexy and now in front of her aunt and Jay, it had lost that effect on her.

Jay and Gayle made themselves scarce as Amelia and I said our brief goodbye. She walked me to the door. I had Gabby's carrier in hand and moved again to sit it down for one last kiss good night.

Before I could sit it down, Amelia placed her hand on mine as if she were helping to hold it. With her other hand, she caressed my cheek. Our eyes met as she began to speak, "I may be here and you two may be going back to Greensboro, but home is where you are."

That's exactly how I felt about her. Home was where she was and I was relieved to hear her say it.

I leaned into her hand and bent to her. I rested my nose and forehead on hers and lingered there for a moment before kissing her. With my free hand, I eased her into me. I whispered, "I love you, Mrs. Hewitt," before I touched my lips to hers.

I thought about that kiss all the way back to the gates of Port Honor. It was sweet and delicate and I could still taste her. I had hated to leave her.

Mixed with the thoughts of the kiss, I thought about the brief conversation Gayle and I had had before Amelia interrupted us. Gayle had reminded me of the scheme Jay had mentioned in the hospital for drawing Beth out. Amelia being on TV was not the plan, but it might work all the same in Jay's scheme.

"You know, it's possible Beth may have seen Millie and the ring on the news tonight," Gayle cautioned me.

I acknowledged that Gayle had a point and she continued, "You might want to prepare yourself for her to show up."

Gayle was right. If Beth did see the news and put two and two together and show up, it would be in my best interest to have people at the house to witness her behavior. Mrs. Allen was typically off on Mondays, but had already agreed to come back and watch Gabby for me while I started packing the house. I thought about calling Daniel as well. It was nearly midnight when I reached my house, but I called him anyway.

"Can you come by tomorrow?" I asked him. "I need help packing tomorrow and Tuesday."

Luckily, Daniel and Jerry were still up and Daniel was agreeable to my request. "Sure. What time do you have in mind?"

"How's 10:00 a.m.?" That might have been a little early for Daniel, but I wanted to get the jump on packing and get it over with.

"I will see you then. I will try to convince Jerry to come with me." Daniel was one of the few people I could count on and I was grateful to have him.

CHAPTER 12

Monday came and went. Daniel helped me pack while Mrs. Allen watched Gabby. Against Amelia's pleading, I chose to spend one last night at the house on Snug Harbor Drive with just Gabby and me. I hated being without her, but I felt I owed Gayle time alone with Amelia and she needed time to discuss our living arrangements with Jay.

...

Daniel and I had been in and out all Tuesday morning, throwing things out, packing boxes and taking things to the car.

"Hey, Gabriel, what became of those pearls you gave Amelia for her birthday?" Daniel called from my bedroom.

I was going back and forth between Gabby's room and the guest room when I heard Daniel. I yelled back to him, "Beth stole them and my mother's wedding set when she broke in here before Christmas."

Just the thought of how many times she had been in that house unwarranted made me glad to be getting us out of there.

Daniel called out to me again, "Are you sure she stole it and it didn't just fall behind the nightstand?"

"What?" I went running to the bedroom to find Daniel standing there with the strand of pearls hanging from one of his fingers. I had never been so glad to see jewelry in all my life. I hugged Daniel. He was a bit smaller than I was so I nearly lifted him off his feet with the hug.

"Hey there, I'm taken big fella," Daniel laughed.

"I thought these were lost forever! I can't thank you enough for finding them." The thing I really couldn't wait for was to give them back to Amelia.

I ended up putting the necklace in the pocket of my jeans where it remained the rest of the day while we continued packing.

201

Most of the furniture came with the rental of the house, but regardless of that it seemed like I might have been a pack rat with the volume of boxes Daniel and I packed and took out to the cars. Mrs. Allen even followed us in and out a few times carrying Gabby so she could see what was going on while she was awake. Every door in the house was unlocked and none of us really thought anything of it and we came and went through all of them as we took out mine and Gabby's belongings.

It was about 2:00 p.m. when I heard the front door. I was in my bedroom, Daniel was in the garage and Mrs. Allen was in the nursery changing a diaper. I shrugged it off at first thinking maybe Daniel had just come back in another direction or maybe Jerry had finally showed up.

For whatever reason, Gayle's warning popped in my head, Beth. I dropped what I was doing and started toward the living room.

Passing by Mrs. Allen in Gabby's room, I instructed her not to come out until I came back for her. She raised an eyebrow, but acknowledged she would do as I had asked. Like I had divulged my true relationship with Amelia, I also explained the circumstances with Gabby's mother to Mrs. Allen last week. She had the same look of disbelief on her face that most everyone got in response when they asked about Beth lately.

Daniel and I had been using the living room as a staging area, stacking boxes that I would have to come back for in there and loading smaller items in our cars. There were about four stacks plus random boxes scattered around the living room. As I made my way down the hallway, I could see Beth standing among the boxes. Looking at her, I was disgusted. I still could not fathom how Beth could have abandoned a newborn baby with me and just disappeared for a month. I could not get past what sort of mother or what sort of human being could just abandon their child. Second to that was my fury that she had nearly cost me Amelia and my own child.

It occurred to me as the sight of her became clearer and clearer that there were no explanations that she could give for where she had been and why she had done the things she had done that would matter at this point. In the past when I caught her in lies or half-truths or manipulations, I had allowed her to glaze over her behavior with excuses, gifts and more manipulation. This time, I only wanted her out of my living room, out of my house and out of my life.

Beth clearly did not see or hear my approach and called my name. She used that tone that had become like nails on a chalkboard to me. The tone of demanding she be catered to and it boomed through the house when she called my name, "GABE, where are you?" As if I had somehow put her out by not being at the front door ready to open it for her.

"What do you want?" I said as I stepped from the hall into the living room. I don't think she had ever heard true malice in my voice, but I did my best to match her tone and I felt I had succeeded.

Beth's back was to me when I entered and spoke. She quickly whipped her head around to face me. "What is the meaning of this?" She pointed to the boxes.

I just looked at her. I really did not feel I owed her an explanation. Her nostrils flared and she was clearly not happy with what she was seeing, but I really could have cared less.

"I believe I asked you a question," she all but repeated herself. Her tone was thick with distain as if she were talking to an unruly child and she turned up one side of her nose as she spoke.

I stood there, giving her nothing more than an eat-shit look.

"I saw your hayseed on television last night," was the way she referred to Amelia. Again, the tone in her voice was threatening and I did not like it one bit.

Beth continued, "I hope that's not your ring she's flashing all over the place."

I was boiling and could not hold my tongue any longer, "And what if it is?"

"I suggest you get it back." She gritted her teeth as she spoke. "I thought we had settled this. You are mine, sweetie."

I could not believe she had the audacity to call me hers. The one thing in the house that was hers she still had not asked about.

"Where have you been all these weeks?" I asked her as I clinched my fists.

"That does not matter. I am here now."

I took steps toward her, to get a better look. She seemed different. "I am going to ask you again. Where have you been?"

Her roots were showing, but other than that, not a hair was out of place. She appeared to have lost all of the baby weight and she was dressed to the nines as was her norm. She was pale and did not have her usual tan that she got from lounging around the pool all summer doing absolutely nothing. Something was off with her, but at this point I really did not care what it was.

Beth looked me up and down and rolled her eyes. I did not wait for her to say anything else before I snapped. I did not raise my voice and I typically did not curse at women, but this time was an exception. "Why don't you get out of my house?!"

"Excuse me?" Her eyes were wide with shock.

"You heard me. Get out of my fucking house!" I know I was cold. I meant to be.

All I could think about was that she was here trying to reclaim me and she had not once asked about her child. What sort of mother would do that? She was not concerned at all until she saw Amelia on television. I had never picked a fight with her. In fact, I had spent much of the time I knew her tiptoeing around her, doing my best to avoid her wrath. Perhaps it was time she incurred my wrath.

"What did you just say to me?" she screamed at me. I doubt anyone had ever dared speak to her like that before, apart from Amelia who always had her number.

"Are you deaf? You are not wanted here!" I screamed back.

"I don't think you realize who you are talking to..."

I cut her off, "I finally know exactly who you are after all these years and I know exactly who I am talking to, so I am going to tell you again. Get the fuck out!"

"How dare you talk to me..."

Again I was quick to cut her off. "How dare I? Did I just hear you right? How dare YOU! How dare you show your face here and not bother to ask about your child! How dare you! What sort of cold bitch are you?"

I could not remember the last time I had a full on screaming match with anyone. I felt I was holding my own fairly well until I played my hand too soon and let her know that my first thoughts if I were her, would have been of Gabby. I let her know I cared about the child and gave her leverage letting her know my weakness.

"Where is she?" Beth screamed. Now she was concerned with Gabby?

It crossed my mind to lie and say she was not there, but I did not have a chance to say anything. Beth started for the hall and I blocked her. I was careful not to lay hands on her, although I desperately wanted to, I simply grabbed each corner of the door frame to the hallway and blocked her.

"You will stay away from her! And, you will leave here right now!" I said as she pushed with her full weight behind her hands into my chest. She nearly bounced off.

"Let me pass, you bastard!" This time she came back kicking at me. Beyond blocking her knee to my groin with the twist of my hip, I did not budge.

Beth backed up and I really did not see it coming, but Jay had been right. My golf clubs were in their bag which was propped in the corner of the living room next to the door to the hall. Before I knew it, Beth had a club. I tried to duck, but she landed a blow. Luckily, it was a blind rage swing with no accuracy for its target which had likely been my head. Instead of a skull crushing blow, she landed a solid punch to my left shoulder with the sand wedge. It hurt like a motherfucker and I winced.

Quick behind the first, Beth swung again. Ducking once more, I grabbed for the club as it flew nearer to my head that time. I went into the door jam and down. The club struck the sheet rock of the living room wall and lodged there. Beth clearly was not expecting the club to get stuck and having swung with all of her might, it took her into the wall with it.

I was scrambling to get to my feet as she jerked the club free. Beth was in full attack mode and I was wondering where Daniel was, but I would not dare call for him as I did not want Mrs. Allen to come running with or without Gabby.

Beth managed to gain her footing before I did. Blood was seeping through my shirt from where the sand wedge had made contact with my shoulder and sliced it. It felt as if the whole shoulder was out of joint. Regardless, I recovered my footing and grabbed for the door jam again. "Get out of my house!" I screamed at her. This time I was louder and it sounded more like a roar.

She was taken aback only for a moment by the sound, but Beth was never one to know when to quit. In fact, she often bullied her way through most situations just by not taking no for an answer and acting entitled. I don't know that she had ever had to stoop to fighting like this before with anyone other than her older brother.

She came at me again with the club, but this time she drew over her head and slammed it into the overhead beam of the doorway. It rung her bell good, but she still did not give up. "Get the fuck out of my way Gabe or you will be sorry!"

"I am already sorry!" I screamed in her face, but I still refused to lay hands on her.

Daniel had been listening from the kitchen. He started in when he heard her demand to know Gabby's whereabouts. He had seen the whole thing from the kitchen door. Beth had jerked the club loose from the woodwork overhead and was drawing back to swing again when Daniel called her name. I was already ducking and it was as if he had not spoken at all. Beth was mid-swing when I heard the cocking of the gun. It came from behind me and I dropped to the floor.

"Missy, I suggest you put that club down," Mrs. Allen said calmly.

I uncovered my head enough to see Beth staring down the barrel of Mrs. Allen's .38 revolver.

Daniel took a couple of steps back toward the kitchen door. I could hear him gasp as he moved.

Fool that she was, Beth did not heed the warning. "And I suggest you put that gun down old lady before you get yourself into trouble."

Mrs. Allen stepped closer to Beth, still pointing the gun in her face, "I would just a soon drop your narrow ass where you stand, so twitch another eye, Missy, and see what happens to you."

Beth stepped back. For once Beth Reed might actually have been scared.

"Daniel," Mrs. Allen spoke softly, "would you mind dialing the sheriff?"

Mrs. Allen then turned her attention to me. I had started to get up when she asked if I was alright.

"I am fine, thank you, but where did you get that pistol?"

"My purse. Honey, I never leave home without it." She glanced back at Beth. "You best remember that, Missy. Now sit your ass on the floor over there and don't you move until your ride shows up."

Beth backed up to take a seat on the couch. "Uh uh," Mrs. Allen motioned with the gun letting Beth know the couch was off limits. "We don't allow trash on the furniture around here," Mrs. Allen added.

Beth rolled her eyes in response and took a seat on the floor. She then put on the syrupy sweet voice, "Gabe, are you going to let your Mammy talk to me like this?"

"What part of 'get the fuck out' was I unclear about?" I matched her eye rolling with my own. "As far as I'm concerned she can talk to you any way she sees fit."

It was a pretty solid cut to my left shoulder and blood was all the way down my arm by the time Daniel was off the phone with the Green County Sheriff's department. He described the incident as a domestic disturbance and asked them to send a car right away.

"They are on their way," Daniel said as he sat the cordless phone down. He then laughed, "The neighbors are going to be glad to see y'all go. No more police activity then."

Daniel had been a lot of things including an EMT for a while in Atlanta before he and Jerry made the move to Greensboro. I took a seat on the arm of the chair opposite from where Mrs. Allen made Beth sit on the floor and Daniel took a look at my shoulder. "It's definitely dislocated and you need stitches. From the volume of blood I suspected as much, so I told them to go ahead and send an ambulance."

"Thanks!" I replied. "It freakin' hurts!"

"I suspect it does. I'm sorry I did not get in here sooner," Daniel added. "I heard some noise, but thought you were just in here moving the boxes. I had no idea."

Mrs. Allen looked over to Beth, "Just so you know, your child is sleeping in the next room. And, just so you also know, I love her like one of my own, but you ever make a move toward Mr. Gabe like that again or lift a hand to that baby, we won't be waiting for the sheriff. You try me if you don't believe."

The whole time Mrs. Allen spoke she had a crook in her nose like she smelled something rank coming from Beth's direction.

Beth did her best to stare Mrs. Allen down and when that did not work she turned her head away and toward the window. I fully believed Mrs. Allen would have shot Beth and probably not lost a wink of sleep over it, too.

We all stayed in the living room waiting for the sheriff's deputies to arrive. I sat quietly. I had nothing more to say until the deputies arrived, but I could not say the same for Mrs. Allen.

"I heard Mr. Gabe ask you where you have been the last month. I think it's high time you answered him," Mrs. Allen instructed Beth.

Beth did not even turn her head.

"Girl, you better answer me!" Mrs. Allen demanded. "What was so important that you abandoned your child?"

Again, Beth did not so much as budge. She did give a bit of a huff and likely rolled her eyes, but I could not see since she was still facing the window.

Daniel answered for her. "My guess is she's been in rehab."

Daniel had glanced at Gabby's medical records from her birth at Northside this morning, but he had not said anything until now.

"I would be willing to bet that was a condition of Gabby's release from the hospital and that they would not release her to you." Daniel directed his words toward Beth.

Beth turned her head and glared at him. That was as goof of a confirmation that he was right as if she had spoken the words out loud. She did not have to say it. The look she gave him was more than enough.

"I can't look at her," I said as I stormed out of the room. I was absolutely disgusted with her.

Mrs. Allen took her eyes off of Beth only long enough for them to follow me out of the room.

My arm was still bleeding, but it wasn't gushing or anything. I so wished the sheriff's department would hurry up and get there. I went to check on Gabby and she was still sound asleep. How could she have possibly slept through all of that? I stood there watching her sleep and the more I watched, the madder I got. I did my best to stay there, but I wanted satisfaction from telling Beth exactly what I thought of her. I wanted her to know how she had wronged this child. She might not care and it might not affect her, but by God I was going to tell her.

As I left the nursery, it occurred to me, there would be no better time than now to serve her with my petition for custody. I left the room as quietly as I had entered so as not to disturb the baby or let anyone else in the house know what I was about to do. I went to my room and from there I phoned Attorney Ellis. I explained what was going on and offered to pay him double whatever his rate would be for preparing the document if he would have it at my house within two hours. I knew from last time that it would take the officers' time to get there and time to process what they called "the scene." Attorney Ellis sounded pleased with what had transpired and agreed to get the documents there as I had asked.

After hanging up the phone, I returned to the living room. Mrs. Allen and Daniel were shocked at my return. If there was such a thing as someone being in full concert for telling someone off, I was in it. I stooped down to the floor where Beth was sitting cross-legged. I wanted to see her face and I wanted her to see mine. I wanted to know that she heard me.

"Once upon a time I defended you to people. I told them, 'She's a good person deep down, you just have to be patient with her,' and I used to believe that about you. I told them you had had a rough childhood with your mother hiring one nanny after another for you. 'She's not that bad.' I was wrong. You are that bad. You treat people as if they were put on Earth just to serve you. You act as if you are better than everyone else. What makes you think you are so much better? All the qualities that make a person good and decent have been lost on you. You don't have them."

Beth tried to turn from me, but I just moved to corner her more and make her see me. "You look at me when I talk to you. You came here thinking you wanted me, well here I am. What did you think would happen here today? You have treated me like a light in a refrigerator for as long as I can remember, like I'm only supposed to be on when you open the door. Perhaps, I let you do it because I felt as if I had no one else for so long. Perhaps, I was foolish enough to believe that you loved me, in your own way, of course. I know now that you never loved me. You've never loved anyone. All of the ponies, all of the puppies, the cockatiel, your brothers, your parents, now Gabby, you love no one, but yourself."

I was hardly done, when tears started to stream down Beth's face. She still did not say a word and tried to look away. Her tears were lost on me and again I did not let her turn from me.

I continued, "Don't you dare cry! I'm serious, you dry that shit up right now! I don't know what makes you think you have the right to treat people the way you do, but your days of trying to control me are done. Aren't you the least bit afraid that one of these days when you call your daddy to bail you out of the local jail that he isn't going to come? What do you tell them when you make that call?" I asked before mocking her. "Do you say, 'Daddy I don't know what happened' and make something up or do you tell the truth? I just cannot imagine you telling your father, Mr. Navy himself, that you were coked out of your head chasing a man that was no longer interested in you."

I so desperately wanted to throw it in her face that I knew Gabby was not mine, but that's the one card I held.

Beth lifted a hand to wipe the tears. I could see her shift in posture, composing herself. She turned back to me and the superior tone was back. She looked me directly in the eye and it was scary how absolutely determined she was to regain control. "My dad knows all about you. What you did to your family and everything else. Including that you asked me to marry you."

I barely had the denial out of my mouth before Beth held out her left hand and there on her ring finger was my mother's wedding set. I had known it all along. I knew she had taken it. I knew it!

Suddenly Daniel was on me, pulling me back. I had never hit a woman before and it was all I could do not to hit her then. It crossed my mind to jerk away from Daniel. I could envision myself choking the life out of her with my bare hands. She knew what the few items that I had from my family meant to me, especially my mother's rings.

Daniel continued to tug me until we were nearly across the living room. He cautioned as we went, "If you lay a hand on her, she will ruin you. Go sit on the back porch. We'll wait here with her."

Still holding the revolver, Mrs. Allen walked past Daniel and me. I thought nothing of it until I heard the slap and the scream from Beth. Both Daniel and I turned to see what had transpired.

"It's not proper for a man to hit a woman, but I'm no man." Mrs. Allen smiled at me while Beth sat clutching the side of her face.

Finally, there was a knock at the door and the announcement, "Green County Sheriff's Department, we're coming in."

So much had gone on since Daniel had phoned them that it seemed like an eternity, but it had only been about fifteen minutes. One of the deputies was the same portly man that had responded to the call the night Beth broke into the house and scared Amelia and I half to death. The other was a deputy that I had not seen before, a young guy, maybe a trainee.

Once inside, both Daniel and Mrs. Allen gave an account of what had happened from their point of view. Each of them pointed out the holes in the sheetrock, the golf clubs and the end table and lamp that had been knocked over.

Twice Beth tried to interrupt. The second time she was more insistent. "That woman held me at gun point!"

"Miss Reed, we'll get to you in a moment. Now, sit back down and be quiet." The more long in the tooth deputy commanded. He really had no patience for her thanks to her actions and statements the night of the break-in.

The EMTs had entered the house only steps behind the deputies. They had taken me into the kitchen to look at my injuries, but I could hear everything that was going on in the living room.

Both of the ambulance personnel insisted that I go to the hospital. One of them was a student at Georgia College and was getting a degree in sports medicine. I agreed to go on to the hospital after everything was finished with the police and he agreed to go ahead and reset my shoulder. It took little to no effort for him to reset it, but it hurt like there was no tomorrow. I was doing my best to shake off the pain when the familiar deputy entered the kitchen.

"Mr. Hewitt, looks like Miss Reed has been up to her old tricks." The deputy scratched his head as he spoke. "I have checked the house and seen the damage. I am assuming you want to press charges."

"Yes, sir," I replied as respectfully as anyone could.

"She got you pretty good, huh?" He motioned toward my shoulder. "I will add assault to the list along with criminal trespass, destruction of property,..."

"And theft." I mentioned it and followed with an explanation. "When y'all were out here at Christmas, I did not notice at the time, but my mother's wedding rings were missing from the house. I called and added those to the list of items on the report. You will find Miss Reed is currently wearing the rings."

"And theft," he agreed.

"One more thing, please search Miss Reed's car for drugs, specifically, cocaine. Check the usual places, but don't just check under the seat on the floor board. Check the lining under the actual seat. She sometimes tucked it up under the driver's seat, in the seat itself. If you could do a blood test on her..."

"Well, the car is parked cock-eyed in the driveway. You know she's still got that pending DUI charge from the fall. If she gives me any trouble like that night, I will have them run the gamut on her as far as tests go."

I hung my head and I despised myself for what I was about to say, but I had to think about what was best for Gabby. The sooner we were all free of Beth, the better it would be for everyone especially Gabby. "Take the rings from her and she'll give you what you want in the way of excuses to run whatever tests you see fit."

Just as I finished my sentence, the deputy that had been interviewing Beth entered the room. "She says he hit her and refused to let her see her child."

Before they could ask me, I answered, "I never laid a hand on her, but no, I did not let her see the baby."

"So you fought over the baby?" the young deputy asked.

"No," I replied, "Ask the other two people that were in the house. They have already told you what happened. Ask them again if you don't believe me. When I would not allow her to see the baby she attacked me."

"What did you expect would happen when you tried to prevent a mother from seeing her child?" young Barney Fife questioned.

"Excuse me?" I said to him.

Thank goodness Mrs. Allen entered the room when she did and heard the last little back and forth between the deputy and myself. Mrs. Allen took over for me at that point. "I have been keeping that baby since the day after she came home from the hospital and today is the first time I have seen Miss Reed in all that time. If anyone is to blame for Miss Reed not seeing her child, it's Miss Reed. She has not bothered to call and check on the poor thing in all this time and then she picks today of all days to show up here demanding to see her child."

The older deputy interjected, "You will have to excuse Officer Trammell, he's new and he does not know the history of calls we have had to this house."

The young deputy, Officer Trammell, glanced back at the senior officer with surprise. "But, she said..."

"I am sure she did son," the other one cut him off.

Again Beth was handcuffed and carted off to be booked into the Green County jail, but not before another deputy showed up and served her with my petition for sole custody of Gabby as well as a restraining order. I had not asked for the restraining order, but it was a great touch. Attorney Ellis has earned his money this afternoon and likely called in a favor or two to have the restraining order signed by the judge in such a timely manner.

"What is the meaning of this?" Beth demanded as they led her away.

I did not respond; no one did. I figured she could read as well as the next person and since she was so superior she should have no trouble figuring it out.

Last time they took her away, I waited outside and watched until they drove away with her. I watched until she was out of sight, but not this time. This time I did not even exit the house and I had turned my back on her as they handed her the paperwork.

Despite what I told the EMTs, I did not follow through with the ride in the ambulance. My shoulder was back in place, the bleeding had stopped and they had bandaged the wound so there really wasn't the urgency that there had been before. They felt I still needed stitches so I agreed that I would get to the emergency room on my own. Reluctantly, the guys in the ambulance left me to my own devices.

I changed shirts and washed off the blood from my arm then Daniel and I quickly finished loading the vehicles, including putting Gabby in her seat. Mrs. Allen thanked us for an eventful afternoon and went on her way as we closed up the house and headed for Milledgeville. Both my car and Daniel's truck were filled to the gills and he followed me to The Jefferson.

As I retrieved Little One from the back seat, Daniel and I agreed that giving Amelia the play by play on the afternoon was not in her best interest. We agreed that telling her what all had gone on was fine, just not each and every gory detail.

"It's almost 5:00 p.m. I expected y'all an hour ago." Clearly, we had worried Amelia.

"We got hung up," Daniel apologized.

I figured it was better to go ahead and rip off the Band-Aid. "Beth came by and..."

215

"Oh my God, what's that on your arm?" Amelia noticed the bandage and the trickle of blood rolling down my arm from under the bandage.

"Dammit!" I glanced down at it. "I thought the bleeding had stopped."

"You need to go to the emergency room," Daniel again insisted.

"Daniel, can you watch Gabby?" Amelia asked.

"Wait, what? I don't need..."

She cut me off, "We are going to get whatever that is seen about."

"Yes," Daniel responded as he reached to take Gabby and her carrier from me. "We will be fine, just get stubborn ass here seen about."

"Come on, let's go," Amelia said as she grabbed her keys.

It took a bit of persuasion for Amelia to agree to let me drive, but I reminded her that working a stick with her hip injury might be a little painful. She then told me she was still taking the pain medication, so there was no pain. We went back and forth until it ended with me explaining that the doctors had forbid her to drive as long as she was taking the medication.

On the way to Oconee Regional, I gave Amelia an abbreviated version of the day's events ending with Beth once again being carried off to the Green County Detention Center. I specifically told her about the restraining order and having Beth served with my petition for sole custody. Amelia seemed both infuriated and pleased by the situation.

"I love you and I hate that she hurt you, but thank God you did not let her take Gabby. There's no telling what would happen to the poor thing in her care."

"I will protect this family at all costs, Amelia," I concluded.

216

I am sure I had the most serious expression on my face that I had likely ever had. The fact of the matter was that this slice to my shoulder was nothing compared to what I would endure to protect her and our children and I meant for her to understand that.

She seemed deep in thought the remainder of the ride there. We were on foot and entering the automatic doors of the medical center before Amelia spoke again.

"You say she comes from a prominent Atlanta family, how is it they tolerate her being in and out of jail like this. Doesn't that sort of sully the family name?" Amelia asked.

"It's not like where you are from Amelia. Back home, you're a big fish in a little pond. Atlanta's a big place. It's like an ocean and there are a lot of big fish, so not everyone knows everyone and with enough money everything can be explained away."

"Yeah, but who would want to throw good money after bad when they could just teach their child to do better and expect better from them?"

"Not everyone was raised with the same expectations as you were. Not everyone was raised to be accountable for their actions or to have to answer to anyone."

Amelia was quick with our banter back and forth and quick to add, "By God, any child of mine will be held accountable for their actions and if they can get themselves thrown in jail, then they can figure out how to get themselves out. Yes, I just channeled my grandfather in case you were wondering. I often wonder what he would have thought about all of this."

"From what you have told me about him, I doubt he would have thought much of it. He would likely have wanted to turn all of us across his knee." I may not have had the opportunity to know Amelia's grandfather, but I had known a few men like him in my life and I was pretty certain he would not have been happy about the Beth-situation or me getting his granddaughter pregnant out of wedlock.

We found the emergency room as we had the night she ran over my foot upon hearing of my indiscretion with one of the married

217

wives of a club member. I hated the smell of the place as much as I had that night so many months before. It smelled like every antiseptic cleaning product known to man, laced with mop water.

I checked in and was given the clipboard of paperwork to complete. As we waited for me to be called back to see the doctor, Amelia inquired as to what I ever saw in Beth. She was quick to correct herself.

"Alright, no need to explain what you first saw in her, but after you knew what kind of person she was, why did you stick around? Was she always so..."

"So self-centered and spoiled?"

"I was going to say 'Bitchy,' but close enough."

CHAPTER 13

Christmas 1992, I spent with the Reed family. Initially, I was going to stay on board the carrier and spend it like any other day, but three weeks before the holiday, Beth began to phone. The Reeds were hosting an engagement party on Christmas Eve for the younger of Beth's two brothers. According to Beth, she could not bear to go to it alone and insisted there was no one she would rather go with than me.

Beth phoned for days; begging, pleading, demanding and buying my plane ticket and over-nighting it to me before I had even agreed to go. She was persuasive and sometimes that was fun.

"It would be a huge favor to me and I would owe you big time," she begged.

Naturally, I gave in.

Christmas was on Friday that year and I flew in on Wednesday. Beth was supposed to pick me up at the airport. It was windy and cold and raining and I waited along the kiss ride curb for an hour. Finally, I schlepped my soaked ass to the Marta station and caught the train to the Lindberg station. From Lindberg, I caught a cab to Beth's parents' house off of West Paces Ferry Road. They lived within a stone's throw of the Governor's Mansion. I even met the governor once while I was walking Beth's dog and he was walking his.

When I finally arrived at the house, it was locked up tight as a drum, not even the maid was home. I had no place else to go so I waited. One hour turned to two, two to three, and at some point I fell asleep sitting there on the stoop propped against the side entry door to the garage. I had been there four hours when I awoke to the sound of a garage door opening. It was dark out and colder. I was still damp and chilled to the bone.

Headlights flashed across my face and I was temporarily blinded. I made my way to my feet as the car, Beth's mother's eight series BMW, rounded the driveway and pulled into the garage. Although my sight was returning quickly, I still had not made my way around the Leland Cypress at the corner of the house to see who was in the car, but I could hear Beth's voice. She was with her mother and they were giggling hysterically over something. They giggled as if they did not have a care in the world.

I was nearly frozen solid and the laughter infuriated me. I said nothing as the motion sensor lights popped on and cast my shadow into the garage when I stepped around behind the car. From the corner of her eye, Mrs. Reed caught sight of me and it startled her. She screamed and Beth jerked around to see what was the matter.

"Oh Mother, it's just Gabe," Beth said as she continued inside the house carrying a lone shopping bag from Neiman Marcus. She sounded so dismissive of her mother and that just added fuel to my flame. I had every intention of letting her know that I was fed up once and for all about how she treated me and most everyone else around her.

"I'm sorry dear, I did not realize we were expecting you," Mrs. Reed apologized for her reaction and invited me in.

Beth had assured me that her parents were aware that I was coming. She assured me that I was invited to the engagement party, but this was clearly the first her mother knew of any of this.

I stood in the threshold of the garage door clutching my military issued duffle bag for luggage as Mrs. Reed continued on through the hall toward the kitchen. I expected to find Beth waiting on me inside, but I could see no trace of her down the hallway leading from the garage.

Ellie Mae, Beth's little Bichon, came staggering to me as fast as three of her little legs would carry her. I noticed she was dragging one of her hind legs. I dropped my duffle bag and lifted a hand to pet her as she came nearer to me, but she cowered and backed away. It took a moment, but I coaxed Ellie Mae to me and finally, cautiously, she came. She whimpered and bit me when I stroked down her back. I suspected the dog had been beaten. I added that to my list of things I was going to address with Beth, a list that was becoming very long.

I let the dog down and looked again for Beth. I did not know what to think. Four days ago when I had last spoken to her, things were still a go for the holiday, but the events of today made me seriously doubt that.

"Gabe, come on in. Claudia will make up a room for you and show you where you will be sleeping." Mrs. Reed was very hospitable and she called for Claudia, their live-in housekeeper.

Despite my ringing and ringing of the doorbell, Claudia had not seen fit to answer it earlier, but she came at nearly a full sprint when Mrs. Reed summoned her.

"Claudia, please make up a room for Gabe. He's going to be staying with us through?" Her voice inflected at the end of the sentence asking me how long I would be staying with them. This was yet another sign that Mrs. Reed had no idea that Beth had sent for me.

"Don't worry about it," I began and both of their eyes grew wider as if they had not understood a word I had said. "I'm just going to go. Y'all have a Merry Christmas and I'm sorry about all of this. It's just been a big misunderstanding."

I was terribly embarrassed that I had come all that way and imposed on them, even though that's not at all what had happened.

"Well there you are," Beth announced as she bounced into the room. "I did not expect you until tomorrow."

Mrs. Reed was a kind woman who never spoke a cross word about anyone and I had entirely too much respect for her to make a scene. I did not know where I was going to go, but I wanted out of there. Despite the fact that Beth now appeared to be interested in me again, my bag and I took several steps back heading to the door from which I had not so long ago entered.

"Claudia, Gabe will shower and change in J.J.'s room while you make up the guest room," Beth said as she took me by the hand and began to lead. "Silly boys, they just don't listen. I swear I told you to be here tomorrow." She rolled her eyes as we cross the room in front of the two women and they laughed and rolled their eyes with her.

It was an easy lie to catch her in because she is the one that purchased the ticket for the flight from Osaka to Atlanta and shipped it to me. I fully intended to call her on it and stay mad at her for her thoughtlessness. I was sure we were out of earshot of her mother when we entered the formal living room. I pulled my hand from her and was about to say my peace and make my stand once and for all when the automatic timers kicked on a billion twinkling white Christmas lights including those covering a nearly twelve foot tree.

It was like something out of a movie and the only thing I had seen that came close to it was the way the Opryland Hotel had been decorated the year I worked there at Christmas. I had spent Christmases with the Reeds in the past, but they had always done a cruise or rented a beach house somewhere sunny and warm with no Christmas spirit. I had never seen the big house, as Beth's father called it, decorated for Christmas before. No expense had been spared and I was in awe.

I had worked in some capacity in restaurants since I was tall enough and old enough to wash dishes. I had seen it millions of times; parents would give their fussy children their keys to play with, to quiet them. When all of the sparkling lights cut on and the soft sound of Christmas music began to float through the room from the home's intercom system, it was as if I had been given a ring of keys. I was as distracted as any crying two year old and my fury escaped me. I was speechless and my train of thought for chewing Beth out about her lies and for jerking my chain all the time had been completely derailed.

"If you think this is something to see, then wait until you see the snow tomorrow," Beth nudged me as she noticed how I gawked at the tree in one corner, the wreath over the fireplace and the garland along the catwalk railing.

I was caught off guard. "Snow?" I questioned as I knew snow in Georgia before Christmas was extremely rare.

"Yeah, Daddy is having a snow blower brought in and it's going to be a white Christmas, well, a white Christmas Eve for Robert's engagement party." I know she was bragging about the extravagance, baiting me for she knew my upbringing and how all of this overwhelmed me.

222

"The entire front yard is going to be covered. Can you just imagine?" she added.

The front yard of the Reed estate was huge, a football field in length, sloping downward slightly until it reached the edge of West Paces Ferry Road. Year round the grass was green and landscaping was manicured to perfection. The home and grounds had been in Atlanta magazine more than once as far as I had been told.

Beth pranced from the room and I knew I had missed my moment as the stars from the extravagance left my eyes and I remembered how I had been forgotten for the day. I recalled how I had been made to sit in the cold for hours waiting for her as she went shopping. I was still chilled to the bone as I followed her from the room, but the chance to air my grievances had passed.

*** 

I showered in her older brother J.J.'s room. He was named after their father and their grandfather. J.J.'s given name was actually John Jackson Reed, III. He was the oldest and continually away serving in the Peace Corps. He was so very much the opposite of Beth. He used the family fortune to hand out mosquito netting to the children of the Ivory Coast and Beth used the family fortune to buy fish net stockings and serve herself. I was reminded of J.J.'s character as I dressed in his room and noticed all of the photos of him with children of all races and ages. He had a light in his eyes that was sheer happiness, a light that I had never seen in Beth's.

Dinner that night turned out to be a warm up act for the following night, sort of a party before the party. There were ten guests not including myself or the future Mrs. Reed, because we were continually referred to throughout the evening as family.

I leaned over to Beth at one point. "You have told them we are no longer dating, correct?" I whispered to her after the first reference to me as being "practically a member of the family".

"Of course, but you can't stop them from thinking of you like another son. This is your fourth Christmas with us." Beth dismissed my concerns as if I were just being ridiculous.

Nothing more was said on the matter, but I suspected she had down played our lack of involvement to her family. She likely told them we were only on a break while I was overseas when in all honesty I had given her a very clear "let's just be friends" talk before I left for Japan.

Various times throughout the evening I found Beth holding my hand and going above and beyond when laughing at my jokes. I could be funny, but I knew I was no Johnny Carson. I was determined to revisit the friend talk with her later. I did not know when, but I would definitely get this straightened out.

The house had ten bedrooms and that night I found myself in one of the six guest rooms. The room assigned to me was not even on the same wing of the house as Beth's. Mr. Reed had a thing about his children "shacking up" as he referred to it under his roof so I was put on the opposite end of the house from Beth. At this point, I figured he had nothing to worry about from me. I was still pissed with her from earlier and we were just friends, but little did I know.

My days and nights were mixed up from having lived on another continent for the last year and a half so at 2:00 a.m. I was still wide awake. I heard the turning of the door knob and the pitter patter of bare feet on the hardwood floor until they reached the area rug. The room was dark, but my eyes had adjusted. I rolled over to see who was in the room just in time to see Beth slip into bed with me.

"I bought a Christmas present for you. Actually, I bought two, a matching pair," Beth whispered as she climbed on top of me. She was wearing little more than what appeared to be a man's white dress shirt and it was thin.

I was stunned that she was in my room. Speechless.

"Let me help you unwrap what I bought for you."

The three buttons at the top of the white dress shirt were already unbuttoned and when she unbuttoned the fourth and fifth I knew exactly what she had bought and they were a matching pair. They were quite possibly the best money could buy.

"Wait a minute," Amelia interrupted. "I don't need to know the gory details. I don't want to ever know the gory details..."

"Fair enough," I replied. It's not like I was looking forward to or even going to tell her that both the snow and I got blown that night.

I continued, but made clear my point. "The point is she always knew how to work me, how to distract me and to get what she wanted. You asked me what I saw in her and how it went on for so long and I was telling you."

Amelia rolled her eyes.

"Don't roll your eyes. You have been begging me to tell you about myself and now I am doing that. Plus, I will turn you over my knee here in this waiting room."

"I don't need complete full disclosure of your love life with the crazy bitch." Amelia kept her voice low, but her tone emphasized her point and her body language signaled that she had heard enough. Amelia picked up one of the magazines from a table next to her and turned from me.

I reached and took the magazine from her hands to regain her attention. "You realize there was no love, no love life. I thought I loved her at one point. I thought she cared about me, but I was as much her charity case as those kids in Africa were to her brother. It was little more than sex and her having control over me. I was a glorified toy."

"Like a business transaction?"

"No, like a young boy coming of age. Amelia, I came from absolutely nothing. If it wasn't Beth it would have been someone else just like her. I saw what I wanted to see in her, a way out. I had a lot of growing up to do and granted, in a sick way, she helped with that. She helped me to understand that I wanted more than just a way out. I wanted to stand on my own two feet and I did not want to pay the price for someone else taking care of me any longer."

"So you used her?" I could tell the wheels were turning in Amelia's head as she asked the question. The look on her face gave her away. She was comparing herself to Beth and my intentions toward her were clearly in question.

"I know what you are thinking and stop it!" Still in the waiting room, I had to keep my voice low as well, but I took the same tone with her that she had taken with me only moments before. "The way I felt about Beth is nothing compared to the way I feel about you. I don't need or want you to take care of me beyond holding my hand here in the emergency room. And if you are thinking about your financial comparisons, don't. If you did not have a penny to your name, you would still be the one for me."

I could see Amelia's mood shift back to her normal light-heartedness. "But mine aren't the best money can buy."

I did not expect her to take the conversation in that direction and I laughed at the shock value of her statement. "No, Amelia, yours are the ones that those sort of women want their money to buy."

"Really?" she replied curiously. "You are lying!"

"I would never lie to you, Mrs. Hewitt. Yours are perfect."

Again with the curiosity. "Perfect?"

"Do you have the stomach for me to tell you why yours are perfect?"

Amelia's face went all skeptical so I clarified, "It means I will have to tell you a little about hers."

"Oh."

"It's not what you think. The first time Matt saw her, he made a comment about how his girlfriend could never have fake boobs because he would get too excited and pop them. Sure they look great, but these things were so hard and unnatural that it would have taken an ax to pop them. It was like dealing with two large, flesh covered cantaloupes."

Before I could speak further on hers, Amelia cut me off. "I always heard more than a mouthful was a waste."

226

The heavy set woman seated in front of us had been smacking her gum and listening to us for a while and when Amelia said what she did about more than a mouthful, the woman looked around and said, "Amen, girl." Poor thing, she was no small woman, so she would have been one to know.

Amelia was petrified that anyone had heard the conversation. She had a way of talking about any and everything with Jay, but typically went all red in the face whenever situations like this were aired in public. Sometimes I liked to mess with her just to see her turn all red and get embarrassed.

Amelia changed the subject again, "I wonder when they are going to call you back? We have been here almost an hour and thirty minutes."

"Yeah, thank goodness Daniel taped this up," I said glancing at my shoulder. It still hurt, but nothing that wasn't manageable with a handful of ibuprofen. I wanted to leave, but Amelia insisted on staying.

\*\*\*

As it turned out I needed eight stitches to seal the wound. The club had left a cut three inches long and a quarter inch deep on my shoulder. The doctor was impressed with the job that Daniel had done in taping it up and trying to stop the bleeding.

"He's going to need a copy of his medical records from this incident as well," Amelia advised the nurse as I was being discharged from the emergency room.

I cut my eyes toward her not understanding why she wanted the records. Amelia gave me a look to indicate she would clue me in later just before she continued with her conversation with the nurse.

"The records will show his blood type correct?" Amelia inquired.

"They should," the nurse responded.

"And may I pick them up tomorrow morning? And one more thing, which pediatrician around town would you recommend?"

"Tomorrow morning," the nurse agreed, "And Dr. Roberts is the best in town. He's located across the street in the medical complex."

"Excellent! Thanks so much!"

Once in the hallway, Amelia shared with me her train of thought. "We need your medical records on the assault to give to your attorney. Plus, you need your blood type to match against Gabby. I know you think it's in our best interest not to disclose that you know you are not the father, but you never know. Now that you have had her served with the papers for custody of Gabby, it's going to be game on. You will need to turn over everything you have on her and all of this is just more nails in her coffin."

Amelia paused only long enough to catch her breath as we made our way through the halls of the hospital and back to the exit. "We also need to find a pediatrician and have her seen about as quickly as possible. I will call Dr. Roberts's office and make an appointment tomorrow. It would be great if I could get her in tomorrow as well, but we'll have to wait and see."

We had just found the car when Amelia finished explaining and I was in awe of her. She had thought of everything, but most importantly, Amelia was thinking about what was in the best interest of Gabby. I admired her already as a mother.

We had taken the Corvette to the emergency room since my car was still packed. I opened the passenger side door for her, but before I allowed her to take her seat I leaned into her.

"Wait a moment," I said.

Amelia turned back to me.

"Remember the night in the door of the car after the Delta Digital party?" That night was the culmination of what seemed like a lifetime of foreplay between us.

"Of course," she answered and the question had the effect on her that I had hoped. She was wearing a button up shirt with the sleeves rolled up and the top three buttons undone. Under the button up shirt was a pink tank top and I could see that her skin had broken out in hives and the skin on her chest was the color of the tank top. Amelia was flushed just thinking about the night we first made love.

"Me, too, and I can hardly wait to have a million other moments like that with you." I finished my statement and leaned into her pushing her into the frame of the car.

"You know that's not my favorite, right?" she asked while holding me at bay.

A storm had been building in the distance when we first entered the hospital that afternoon, but now it was upon us. Though I would have loved to have stayed in the moment and continued our discussion then and there, a flash burst across Amelia's face as thunder boomed all around us.

Amelia screamed and hid her face in my chest. My arms went instinctively around her with no concern for how the movement would affect my newly stitched up wound.

Immediately, Amelia gave a muffled apology, "I'm so sorry. I did not mean to scream in your face. I think I just had a..."

"A flashback from the bombing?"

"I suppose."

I gave her a peck on the top of her head and clutched her tightly as lightening crashed and thunder boomed for a second time. I could feel her flinch in my arms. "Let's get you home."

Amelia nodded her head against me in response.

The drive from Oconee Regional to The Jefferson was relatively short, but it took nearly thirty minutes due to the flash flood that followed the thunder and lightning. I turned on the radio to try to distract Amelia. It was quite the distraction. Billy Idol's "Rebel Yell" was coming in loud and clear over the stereo in the Corvette. Usually it was Amelia that sang along, but this time it was me. I did my best to entertain her to keep her from dwelling on the storm.

My best performance was the next song and it made her laugh out loud as I sang along with Brett Michaels to Poison's "Talk Dirty To Me." I will be the first to admit I am no singer so I turned up the volume even more so that Brett's voice covered mine. I was in full concert. I sang and Amelia squealed with delight, egging me on.

It poured buckets and there were times when I could hardly see the hood of the car, but the songs kept coming and I kept singing along. I don't think she knew I had it in me to sing at all, but I sang along to all of them. I sang to her and she was distracted from any flashbacks of the bombing that the storm might have caused.

The one that entertained her the most was "Bed of Roses" by Bon Jovi. It's funny that song conveys exactly what I was feeling in the months that we were apart. We spoke on the phone a few times, but all I could think about was getting back to her. There were things going on with Beth and everything that tried to keep my mind off of her, but none of it worked. I just wanted to hear her voice, for her to know that I was always thinking about her.

Before we knew it, the thirty minutes trapped in the car on what should have been a five to ten minute ride was over.

We had just pulled up in front of The Jefferson. I managed to get one of the few spaces for parallel parking along the front of the building. I shut off the car and reached for the door knob to get out when Amelia reached over and touched me, grabbing my attention and stopping me.

"Are we going to be good parents?" Amelia asked.

I knew exactly what she was getting at, neither of us had our own parents as examples to go by. "You will be a great mother," I tried to assure her and I said nothing of myself. I was as unsure as she was about what sort of parent I would make.

"How can you be so sure?"

"Because you already take care of everyone you know and I cannot imagine you doing less for our children."

"Oh," she said with a sigh.

We sat in silence with the rain beating down on the roof of the car for a moment before Amelia spoke again. "Do you ever miss your parents?"

"I miss them every hour of every day even though I often think now that I only miss the idea of them. Do you miss yours?" I knew the answer regarding her mother, but we had never spoken much of her father.

"How can you miss something you never had."

"You know, I am counting on you to help me instill that way of thinking in Gabby about Beth."

Amelia let out a huff and shook her head. She did that shake she does when she is disgusted.

I turned in my seat to face her as best I could in the cramped interior of the Corvette. I did not want to ask her, but I felt that this talk of our parents begged the asking, "You mentioned that you thought you heard us telling you stories while you were in the hospital. Do you recall what I told you?"

"Yes, about how your parents' died."

"Right, and I want to let you know one more reason why I stuck it out with Beth as long as I did," I began to explain. "I felt that I did not deserve any better than Beth. I believed this was God's punishment for me for what I had done to my parents and my sister. I had no right to true happiness or love and there were times where I resigned myself to that being my lot in life. For the longest time, I allowed myself to believe that I was not worthy of anything else."

Amelia gasped, "No! No! Gabriel, that's not how God works!"

I hung my head. There's no way a few words from her could undo a lifetime of belief that I was being punished for my deeds. "I have spent the better part of my life trying to make up for what I did, but I don't deserve you." I muttered.

Amelia lifted my head. "Jesus, Gabriel, if God gave people what they deserved, half of us would be wiped off the face of the

231

earth on even days and the other half on odd days. Don't you think that if God gave my mother what she deserved, she would be living under a bridge off of I-20 somewhere? Instead, last I heard, she was living in the lap of luxury in a beach front mansion near Tampa. If Dr. Cannon got what he deserved; he'd be castrated and wiping Saddam Hussein's ass for a living. And, if my Aunt Gayle got what she deserved, she would not have to have witnessed my grandfather suffocate from lung cancer. Aunt Gayle has never done one single thing to be punished like that and neither have I. God does not give people what they deserve; he gives us free will, forgiveness and chances to do better."

"I don't know, Amelia."

"Well, I do and you are just going to have to trust me on it. You are also going to have to forgive yourself for what happened twenty years ago. I know it's hard, but you need to stop living in the past. If you don't, you let people like Beth win."

Amelia was a powerful force of positivity. She had been since I met her. It always appeared as if she did not worry about what she could not change and refused to let what had gone on with her mother define her or drag her down. She was the definition of rising above.

The rain had slacked off and it was little more than a drizzle. "Come on. Let's get inside while we can," I told her in an attempt to change the subject. "Wait here. I will get the car door for you."

I had hoped to pick up where we left off before the first flashes of lightening, but once inside the apartment, we found nearly every tenant in the building waiting for us, plus Daniel. Both Amelia and I looked puzzled to see the entire clan.

Something smelled wonderful and just as I began to recall what night it was, Stella greeted us with Gabby. "It's Tuesday night, family dinner time," she said as Amelia reached out her arms to take Gabby.

"Hi, baby," Amelia whispered sweetly as she began to rock back and forth while patting her bottom. "I have something for you and I will show you in just a little while. I think you are going to like it. I hope you like it. I got it just for you my sweet, sweet girl."

Stella and I looked on, but Amelia spoke to Gabby as if they were the only two people in the room. The baby was not old enough to wonder what the surprise might be, but I was and I wondered.

Thoughts entered my head, the ones Amelia had tried to push away with our conversation in the car. As I watched them, I could not help reminding myself that I did not deserve either of them or Sweet Pea that would be joining us in a few months, but I would spend my life trying to deserve them.

Stella's words snapped me back to reality, "Dinner's almost ready if y'all want to wash up."

"I cooked!" Jay yelled from the kitchen as he spotted us.

"And we helped," Cara added while gesturing to everyone else in the room.

"Not to worry, they only allowed me to pick up sugar for the sweet tea," Travis leaned back from his spot at the end of the couch and commented as we passed him on the way to the bathroom.

"That's probably for the best, Banana Brick," I laughed while giving him a pat on the back.

Amelia did her best not to laugh, but failed. One of the last few times I attended family dinner, Stella had to work so Travis came alone. He did not want to show up empty-handed so tried to make his mother's recipe for banana bread. It came out more like something you could use to lay a foundation. Since then, his nickname had been Banana Brick.

We continued on from Travis across the living room to the door to the room that had been Emma's. From the moment Amelia opened the door, it was as if we had stepped into the showroom of the finest children's boutique around. Everything was pink and white stripes and polka dots, eyelet lace ruffles and bows galore.

There were two white cribs and a large bunny that sat in each. One bunny was white with a bow around his neck that matched the pink and white stripes of the bedding and the other bunny was pink with the same bow around his neck. The letters of Gabby's name were cut from wood and painted pink with white dots and hung above the crib that Amelia had clearly assigned to her. The wall above the other crib was blank. I suppose Amelia had not settled on a name for number two after all.

There wasn't an inch of that room that had not been touched and retouched in preparation for Gabby and the arrival of her sister. It was nearly overwhelming to think that Amelia had done all of this in only two days.

Amelia had not said a word since opening the door. She just let me take it all in. I could feel the rest of the room looking on from behind us. They had likely seen it already, but were anxiously awaiting my reaction.

I put my arm around Amelia as she cradled what was so clearly our daughter in her arms. I pulled her to me in a bit of a side arm hug and I said, "You have been a very busy girl."

"Do you like it?" I could not believe she would even ask such a question.

"Do I like it? I love it! Did you do all of this yourself?"

"Oh, no, I had help. Aunt Gayle, Aunt Dot and Jay's Aunt June plus Jay and everyone else here, they all helped."

"I may not be able to bake, but I can hang curtains like nobody's business," Travis added from his spot on the couch.

I was nearly speechless as it occurred to me this was the closest to a real family I had had in all my life. For once, I was the one holding back tears and I was hoping no one would notice. The fact that everyone pitched in and made this room perfect, all over something I wanted, a child that they had no real attachment to, was quite possibly one of the nicest things anyone had ever done for me.

I turned to face everyone that was in the room. "I don't know how to thank you all and I don't know how I will ever repay you for all of the kindness you have shown me this last year. I don't know if Amelia has told y'all about my family and my background, but the short story is that I haven't had much, if anything, in the way of family since I was a small child. That being said, I am sincerely grateful to have each of you in my life. Y'all are the closest thing I have had to family in a very long time. I am sure Gabby will feel the same way."

By the time I finished, there was hardly a dry eye in the house. One by one they all approached and hugged Amelia and me. After all of the hugs and thank you's, Jay again invited us to the dining room for dinner.

As we took our seats at the table, Jay insisted that I sit at the head. "It's your house now," he said. There was a bit of sadness in his voice acknowledging the end of an era for him. I felt a little bad for him.

Once in her seat, Amelia leaned into me and whispered, "I talked to Jay. He and Cara had already sorted out that he would be moving in with her."

"What about Megan?" I asked.

"She was already set to move in with her boyfriend when they returned to school next semester. Cara was going to have to find a new roommate anyway, so this worked out well for them. He did not want to stay on here and feel like a third wheel."

"Are you okay with him going?"

"He will only be downstairs. If he were going across town, I would feel worse, but I am good with this."

"Can you imagine, I start law school tomorrow?" Amelia asked me as she rolled over in bed to face me.

"Do you still want to go?" I propped myself up on my elbow so I could see her better.

"I made a deal with Aunt Gayle and I have to honor it," she replied. I would not have blamed her if her tone had been that of exasperation, but it wasn't.

"You have so much on your plate, but you seem completely fine with everything. You make it a little hard to keep up with you."

The ten o'clock news played on the television giving background noise to our conversation and the only light to the room. It had been two weeks since the bombing at Centennial Olympic Park. They were still talking about it and Richard Jewell on the news. Aside of a few storms that unnerved her and an occasional headache, Amelia was doing remarkably well. The tiny wounds on her back had all healed and only a few left slight scars. The scab covering the wound on her hip would likely be gone at any moment and the place on the back of her head was well covered by her hair.

It had been a week since Amelia came home from the hospital and not quite a week since we had moved in together. She had once voiced concern when we first started dating that we might be too domesticated. I laughed it off at the time because being domesticated with her was like a dream and now I was living the dream.

In the days since Gabby and I had moved in, a lot had happened. Amelia had taken Gabby to her first appointment with Dr. Roberts. He came highly recommended from the desk nurse at the Oconee Regional Medical Center's emergency room, as well as from Jay's Aunt June. In fact, his aunt had accompanied Amelia to the appointment. I would have gone with them, but the only space he had available on his calendar was the day and time I was scheduled to meet with Attorney Ellis.

Jay's Aunt June not only attended church with Dr. Roberts, but he had also treated her children and grandchildren. According to Amelia, it took some persuasion or gentle threatening by Aunt June for Dr. Roberts to agree to talk to her about Gabby considering she was not a relative or legal guardian of the child. Amelia relayed their conversation to me and how she had blushed when June referred to her as Christian-like when it was becoming obvious that she was also pregnant and without a wedding ring.

Amelia said that Jay's Aunt June told the doctor, "Now, Tom, I have known you for years and years and we both know that all of these HIPAA regulations are just hogwash. This girl's Christian-like enough to take this child in as her own, we should be Christian like enough to help her. Also, it wouldn't do for it to get out among our Baptist brothers and sisters that your car was seen at Hooters in Macon recently."

The doctor was as shocked by June as if he did not know she had it in her to threaten him and his response shocked Amelia. The doctor told June, "You know I was there with your husband, so how would that look?"

"Yes, but everyone knows that Lloyd is a known philanderer and they have the best wings in town." Amelia had not known until that moment that Uncle Lloyd was a known philanderer and she was quick to make that point when recounting the doctor's visit.

"You can imagine how my mouth fell open at the shock. It's not every day that you hear someone admit that their husband is known for running around on them." Even then Amelia covered her mouth when she told me.

The doctor did agree to see Gabby at which time Amelia presented him with copies of her birth records from Northside Hospital. Amelia said she realized it was quite a volume of records so she gave the doctor a summary of their contents, boiling it down to the fact that Little One had been exposed to cocaine use by her mother.

Dr. Roberts examined Gabby as he explained to Amelia that not all babies show signs of withdrawals or any affects from the drug use. He cautioned that the number of children that do not show signs are very slim. He found Gabby to be in the eightieth percentile for both head circumference and length, but only in the fiftieth percentile for weight. Dr. Roberts advised that we begin supplementing Gabby's formula with rice cereal to try to get her weight up. Ultimately, Amelia reported back that he felt her weight had been affected by Beth's drug use, but that was not something that could not be easily corrected.

Amelia was given a wealth of pamphlets regarding drugs and children. Specifically, she was given everything Dr. Roberts could find, including a couple of medical journals, regarding the effects of intrauterine drug use on babies. She said the doctor told her as he handed her a grocery bag to hold everything, "By the time you finish reading all of this, you'll feel like an expert in the field."

I saw the bag of pamphlets and it was a lot. Amelia came back with a world of reading to do and I left my attorney's office having given him a world of reading. Although I summarized the contents of the medical record copies, Attorney Ellis swore he would read them all for himself. I shuddered to think how much of his time that would take and how much that would cost me, but Amelia had told me to feel free to tell him, "Money was no object."

It was the first time I had ever used that phrase. I held back saying it until the end of my meeting with him. I did not feel comfortable saying it because we were headed into a gray area of what was mine and what was Amelia's. She had assured me that what was hers was mine, but it did not lessen the tug in my gut that I did not want to spend what I had not earned. I did not want anyone taking care of me. I told Amelia that much when she gave me the go ahead and she said she wasn't taking care of me. She was taking care of Gabby and our family. That softened my opinion only slightly.

When Mr. Ellis went on explaining his hourly rate time and time again, I felt compelled to ease his mind about my ability to pay him. I said the phrase. I said it having convinced myself that I would spend my salary to free Gabby from Beth. I only had to pay one more month of rent on the house on Snug Harbor and there was no rent at The Jefferson so that would free up money. Amelia already purchased the groceries for the apartment and I would supplement with meals from the club as I had always done. I rationalized that I had cut my monthly expenses, so I would be able to use my income to pay attorney's fees. As long as I stayed at the club, my financial pride would remain intact.

***

"You know, I don't expect you to keep up with me," Amelia replied.

"What do you expect?" I asked as I brushed back the few strands of hair that had fallen across her face.

"Well, I am not very tired," Amelia said while running her hand down my bare chest. "And I have waited patiently..."

"Patiently? Mrs. Hewitt, you have propositioned me nearly every night for the last week." I stilled her hand on my chest, covering hers with mine. I was so relieved to know she still wanted me, but it had been all I could do to deny her. She was still so fresh out of the hospital, fresh from a coma.

"So you know, I know your concerns and I am telling you again, I'm fine." Amelia shifted her shoulder in such a manner that the spaghetti strap of her nighty fell.

Although she was still barely showing in her belly, her breasts were becoming fuller and with the strap having fallen, this was painfully obvious. The way it draped left little more than the nipple of her left breast covered.

"You are so hard to resist," I mumbled.

"Then stop resisting, Mr. Hewitt," Amelia whispered as she eased from her side and rolled over on top of me. She sat up and straddled me. "I will do all of the work."

Amelia had never spoken to me like that before. It was a nice change, a very nice change.

She continued as she started to move on top of me, "If it hurts me, I promise I will stop."

"How can I say no to you?" I reached my hands to grip her, one cheek per hand. In taking hold of her, I still had not decided

239

whether I was going to lift her off of me or steady her and aid her in her task. I could feel the lines of her panties through the satin of the nightgown. It was short, but fell just around me so I could not see my own boxers any longer.

"I don't think you can." Amelia lowered her weight onto me and widened her stride atop me. She grinded just enough, gave me a devilish smile with a little bite to her lower lip, letting me know she could feel that I did not particularly want to resist her.

The strap of her nighty dipped lower as she moved and nothing was left to my imagination and she did not bother to cover herself. I could feel the heat coming off of myself. Fighting her was useless. I wanted her so badly I ached inside.

The television cut off and all that was left lighting the room was the street lights that shined through the French doors. I looked to the doors. "We forgot to close the curtains," I said to her.

Amelia shifted her shoulders and torso again and braced her hands against my chest. The other strap fell as she whispered, "Do you think anyone can see us?"

There was a hint in her voice as if she did not care if anyone saw as she did not care that one breast was completely exposed and the other was barely covered.

"Amelia," I sighed.

The next thing I knew her lips were on mine and her hand had found my penis through the top of my boxers at the same time. In the past I had been the one directing our activities, teaching her as we went, but this was not a lesson I had given her. This was a new twist in our relationship and it was exquisite. The only thing that had come close was the night we conceived on my birthday.

"I want you, Gabriel. I want you so much, so badly," she panted.

I sighed her name again, "Oh my God, Amelia. I'm yours."

Within moments we were moving in unison. Her hands locked in mine just above my head and everything of the last two weeks escaped my mind as we made love. There was a freedom in this exchange. I had never experienced anything like this with anyone before, the way our bodies communicated with one another. There was an unspoken release; more than just that of orgasm. It was a release of everything that had weighed on us lately and an assurance that everything was going to be okay.

I could feel her unlock her fingers from mine and lifted up. I felt the material of the nighty slide across my skin and I opened my eyes just in time to see Amelia. She was sitting upright. She arched her back slightly and eased up on me as she pulled the nightgown over her head. The rest of the room was dark, but the light from the doors cast directly on her. She tossed the nighty to the floor as she eased back down me. Just watching her as she moved was titillating. She was beautiful and hadn't a care in the world beyond us.

Morning arrived before I knew it. I was still naked from the night before. This was the first night I had slept all the way through since I brought Gabby home from the hospital.

Panic set in at once. Amelia was not in the bed beside me. Gabby had not awakened me in the night. Where was Amelia? Why had the baby not cried or had she and I did not hear her? Panic was solidified when I remembered the pamphlet Amelia had shown me about SIDS, Sudden Infant Death Syndrome.

I had barely wiped the sleep from my eyes when I bound through the door to Gabby's new nursery. I stopped only long enough to pull on my boxers which I found still on the floor from where Amelia had thrown them last night.

"Did we wake you?" Amelia asked softly as she rocked Gabby in her arms.

"No," I replied barely above a whisper. I felt a little ashamed that I did not wake to feed her, but I did not want to disturb them only to have my own guilt eased.

Amelia went back to singing gently the tune to Patsy Cline's "Walking After Midnight" as she rocked. They were a vision considering what had just run through my mind. Thanks to Beth's recreational drug use during pregnancy, Gabby's chances for SIDS were dramatically increased. Her chances for having Attention Deficit Hyperactivity Disorder (ADHD), were also greater than the average child whose mother took care of herself and them. So far, Gabby showed no signs of ADHD and she certainly was not showing them then as I stood in the doorway and watched. She was completely focused and at ease as she sucked on the bottle that Amelia held for her.

When the bottle was finished, Gabby went safely to sleep. No sooner had the nipple of the bottle left her mouth, than her little thumb entered it.

Amelia began to stand with Gabby still in her arms. From our activities last night, I knew she was not as fragile as I had made her out to be over the last week. Regardless of her lack of fragility, I made my way to her and offer to take Gabby.

"I have her," Amelia responded. "Isn't she so pretty?"

We both gazed at her admirably and I replied, "I know. How could I have ever thought she was mine, right?"

Amelia laughed at my response, but not too loudly. Neither of us wanted to wake Little One. Amelia laid her in her crib and we both lingered. We leaned on the crib and my arm went instinctively around Amelia. When I touched Amelia, even in this tender moment, I could not deny that the electricity between us was still there.

"I am one lucky man, Mrs. Hewitt."

"About that," Amelia began to speak, but her eyes stayed focused on Gabby.

I could hear in her voice that she did not want to ask me and I was certain I knew what she was concerned about, so I stopped her. "I want to make it official. What do you say to Labor Day weekend?"

"I was just going to say that I wanted to keep my maiden name."

"You what?" I was shocked. "I thought you liked me calling you, Mrs. Hewitt. I thought you wanted..."

Amelia backed away from the crib and I paused. She turned toward the door and I followed. Amelia pulled the door to behind me and once in the living room, the conversation resumed.

"I love it, and short of a healthy baby and nothing being wrong with Gabby, there's nothing I want more." Amelia continued on into the kitchen.

"Then what?" I asked. I followed her, but stopped across the bar from her and did not go all the way into the kitchen.

"I just thought for law school and my degree I would leave my name the same."

"Why?"

"Because once I finish school, I plan to practice law back home and everyone knows me as Millie Anderson. It would make getting business easier."

"Don't you just have everything planned out?" I rubbed my eyes still trying to get the sleep out of them.

As she opened the refrigerator door, she looked back over her shoulder at me, "Let's face it, I am only Amelia Hewitt to you and me.

Amelia turned back around with the milk jug in hand. I raised an eyebrow at her. That was the first time we had said the name I had given her together and without any sport in it. Just the sound of the name and I wanted to kiss her.

"Say it again."

She knew what I wanted her to say and she fulfilled the request as I moved around the bar to close the distance between us. "Amelia Hewitt."

The verbalizing of the name I had given her was like an aphrodisiac to me. "Say it again." I commanded as I took hold of the lapel of her robe and pulled her to me. She wasn't exactly expecting my pull and the jug of milk she was holding slipped from her grasp and landed on the floor. There was a bit of a thud and then the cold liquid sprayed us. Amelia squealed at the chill of the milk splattered against her bare legs.

"If you think for one moment we are cleaning that up right now, you are mistaken." I licked my lips and then hers.

Without breaking the connection of my mouth against hers, I let go of her robe only to take hold of her just below the cheeks of her ass. I lifted her to a seated position on top of the counter. Weight-wise, I could not tell she had gained an ounce with the pregnancy yet. She was as light as ever.

As I had lifted her, her legs went open and then around my waist. I pulled her into me, closer. I braced myself with one hand flat against the counter. The other hand was in her hair pulling her head back as my mouth left hers and traveled down her neck.

"Amelia Hewitt," she whispered with her first free breath.

We had christened just about every room in the house I rented at the club, but this was our first time outside of the bedroom at The Jefferson. That, too, was an inspiration to my performance, as if I needed anything other than Amelia.

The milk was still dripping down my leg when I slid my boxers down, but I hardly noticed. There was nothing distracting me as she said her name again when I pushed into her.

With a gasp she said it, "Amelia Hewitt."

One might think having their partner say their own name during sex would be a turn off, but not like this. It was just plain hot. It was as if she were begging me to take her.

I could feel her breath against me. "You can call me anything, Gabriel." With those words I held her tighter to me and we continued. I could feel she was near climax as she arched her back. "You say it," she pleaded.

I buried my face in her breast and I could have stayed with her like this forever or again and again. This was my heaven on earth. I picked up my pace as I answered her, "Amelia Hewitt...Mrs. Gabriel Hewitt! Haaahhh..."

My knees trembled. I was spent. My back stung a little and I knew there were likely scratches from Amelia's nails, but that was not the half of what I was feeling.

In all my life I had never... not even close. I mean, this sort of experience was a myth as far as I was concerned. At the same time, that's just things guys tell to brag to one another. I did not even realize it could happen. Seriously, I really thought it was a fantasy until that moment. I had not even really been trying for the same time as her, but it happened and it was mind blowing.

***

I had Gabby ready and in the car seat and waiting in the living room and I was going over the kitchen floor one last time to make sure I had gotten all of the milk up from earlier.

Amelia was due in class in Macon at 10:00 a.m. It was 9:00 and we needed to get going. As far as I knew she was almost done drying her hair. All of a sudden, I heard her scream from the master bathroom, "GABRIEL!!!"

I went running as fast as I could. "Give me your hand!" Amelia insisted as I burst through the bathroom door expecting any number of tragedies. Amelia appeared fine with dryer still in one hand as she extended the other to me.

"Give me your hand!" She demanded again.

I did as I was told and she put my hand across her belly. "I swear she moved. Just wait for her."

"She moved? You felt it?"

"Yes, I thought I had felt it once before, but wasn't sure. This time I know it was her. Just wait."

I stood there looking at my hand on her belly. I had never felt Gabby move inside Beth. I had always felt I missed out on that experience, but since everything was back on track with Amelia those thoughts had faded. Here I was having the experience as I was intended, with the person with whom I knew I was meant to have all of those life experiences.

I fell to my knees and waited with my hand still in place on her stomach. Amelia ran her hands through my hair. "Don't move. Surely she will do it again," Amelia was hopeful, but I was beginning to think the moment passed.

I glanced up at Amelia and as my eyes met hers I felt it. "Was that..."

"Yes." Her eyes danced with excitement.

There was a slight thump beneath my middle finger. It was higher up Amelia's mid-drift than I had expected it to be. Instantly, I moved the palm of my hand over the spot and again I waited. It was amazing and I was dying to feel her again.

We must have waited there five minutes before Amelia spoke. "You know, we need to get going. Don't be disappointed; I only felt it the once myself. She'll do it again."

*** 

Amelia's first day at Mercer was a breeze. The first week was a breeze. She had to take a one week introduction course on The Study of Law and she loved it. She also began Torts, Contracts, Civil Litigation and Family Law. In addition to the pregnancy and everything going on with Gabby, I had worried it would be too much for Amelia, but she seemed fine. She was well on her way to getting back to her old self.

"I thought all I wanted to do was restore Seven Springs and now, I don't know. I like this, Gabriel. I really like it, but if you tell Aunt Gayle, I will be cross with you forever," Amelia explained in between bites of her chicken wings at the Brick. She ate with one hand and rocked Gabby in her carrier with the other.

"I won't tell Aunt Gayle, but speaking of Seven Springs. I saw Jay today." I took a swig of my Coke with one hand and helped myself to one of her wings with the other.

"What did he say? I feel terrible. I have not seen him since Tuesday and its Friday. Is he doing alright?"

"Don't worry about him. He's doing fine. He said that he was down at the springs yesterday and your cousin Dixon has done some amazing work around the place."

"Dixon's still working?" Amelia asked in disbelieve.

"That's what you wanted right?"

"I have not been there since before, well you know, and I guess I never told him to stop, so he just kept working." Amelia scrunched her nose as if something was out of sorts.

"Jay said it looked great. He said something about the pagoda being finished and the vine was already starting to take off around it. He said that Dixon had cleaned off the banks around the creek and planted some wild ferns around it. According to Jay, the property had really taken shape."

"I feel awful. I did not mean for Dixon to have to do all of that by himself." Amelia shook her head as if she was disappointed in herself.

"The doctor said that you could start driving at the two week mark. Tomorrow makes two weeks. Why don't you take Gabby tomorrow and go to your Aunt Gayle's. I have to work all day and I could just come there after work. You could go over to the springs and have a look at everything."

Amelia's face lit up at my suggestion. "I guess I could call and ask her if we could come."

"While I am at work tonight, why don't you go downstairs and ask Jay if he wants to come with you?"

Her smile got bigger. "Mr. Hewitt, you always know just what to say."

After we finished lunch I dropped Amelia and Gabby back at the house before I headed off to work. I ran in only long enough to change from my jeans and t-shirt to my chef's attire and kiss the two of them goodbye. No matter how well the air conditioner in the car worked, summers in Georgia were entirely too hot to put on my jacket until I got to work. I also took an extra undershirt with me because the walk to and from the car alone was enough to make me break a sweat. This particular Friday was no different. It was sweltering.

While I changed, Amelia checked the messages on the answering machine. I was in the middle of pulling up my pants when Amelia appeared in the doorway of the bedroom.

"Gabriel, Attorney Ellis was on the machine. He said you need to call him and that it's pretty urgent." The look on her face was of concern as she gave me the message.

"I'm sure it's nothing to worry about. I'll call him as soon as I finish here."

Amelia handed me the cordless before heading back into the living room. As soon as I got my pants pulled up, I dialed the number to the law office.

\*\*\*

"Gabriel, what is it?" Amelia stood up from the couch when she saw me.

I am certain she noticed the heat coming off of me and the veins in my head were likely showing. I was pissed.

"I can't talk right now. I have to go."

"Wait a minute. What did he say? What happened?" Amelia followed me down the stairs.

I went out the door and continued to the car. Amelia did her best to keep up. "Gabriel, I can't follow you any further, I have to go back to see about the baby."

I knew this was not fair to her. I knew she would worry until I gave her an explanation, but I was too mad to even discuss it. I needed a chance to calm down. I could hardly see straight and I needed to clear my head.

I turned back to her, "Don't worry. I will call you when I get to the club. I just need a few minutes to calm down. Everything's going to be alright." I lied. I wasn't sure if anything was going to be alright.

I kissed Amelia on the forehead and did my best to convince her that I was just mad. I did not want her to ever see me scared. Amelia seemed to accept what I told her, but I could tell her mind was racing and I had worried her.

"Call me," she nodded in agreement and added, "as soon as you get there."

The truth was, Beth was out of jail. She had been bailed out, probably by her father or Dick. I wasn't sure, but that wasn't the worst. She had an attorney and they had filed a counter-suit for custody of Gabby. The restraining order had not stuck and she had accused me of having a history of violence.

I replayed the conversation with Attorney Ellis in my head as I made the drive to Greensboro. He had first told me that she counter-sued and saved the kicker for last. "She said you have a history of violence and that you served time in a youth detention center. Is there any truth to this? She said you hit her. She's also pressed charges against your maid for kidnapping and assaulting her. She's also threatened to press charges against you if you did not turn the child over."

My first response had been, "I don't have a maid," and as soon as the words escaped my lips I realized they were talking about Mrs. Allen. "She filed charges against Mrs. Allen? That's the nanny for the baby. The woman that's been raising her child while she was doing God only knows what."

"She's listed the two deputies that arrived at the house as witnesses for the nanny holding her at gun point."

"Mrs. Allen would never have taken out the gun had Beth not attacked me in my home."

"Ah, and that's another thing, she said it's her home and that you pushed her down when she requested to see her infant daughter."

"That's not true!" I remember I had tried to keep my voice down because I did not want to get Amelia upset or disturb Gabby.

"Here's the bottom line, son, you are going to have to put up a real fight with this one and if you have any skeletons in your closet you need to let me know. I can't help you if you aren't honest with me. What's this about YDC?"

"It's true, but those records are sealed."

"Sealed or not, she knows about them and couple that with the bruises she has in the photos, well, I'm not going to sugar coat it. It ain't lookin' good." I could tell he was losing faith in our case and that scared me. It also added fuel to my fire of hate for Beth.

"What bruises and what photos?" I had no idea what he was talking about.

"She's presented photos and said last week wasn't the first time you had been physical with her."

"What?!!" I gasped. "I have never!"

"Never?" he questioned me.

"I swear to God, if I did not love that childlike she was my own, I would pack her stuff and send her back to Beth right now. I don't need this shit! I want her out of my life, but I will be damned if she will raise another human being to be just like her!"

"What do you mean, 'like she was your own?'" Now Attorney Ellis was the one gasping.

"That's right, the child isn't even mine, but she has no one else."

"So, you are fighting for custody of a child that was dumped on you and going through all of this and..."

"Look in the medical records. She's not mine. And, yes, I spent time in YDC and I would rather not discuss that and I was holding on to the fact that the child's not mine to spare everyone."

I paused for a moment to try to calm down. "I will come talk to you on Monday, but for the time being, what do I need to do to get things sorted out for Mrs. Allen. Can you take care of those charges?"

"I think we can get Miss Reed to drop the charges, but you will likely have to give something in return."

"Tell her I will let her have supervised visitation with Gabby, but the one doing the supervision is either a court appointed person and that could take months or she can get her brother, J.J., here to supervise. Those are my terms. And I need you to do whatever you have to do to keep my adolescent records sealed."

Attorney Ellis was right about fighting and if she was going to fight and use my past, then I would do the same. She and her brother, J.J., were about as bitter toward one another as my sister and I had been. For a long time, I did not understand why he hated her so much, but now I completely understood. I hated her, too.

Sealed or not, I had to tell Amelia about my past now. I could not chance her finding out from anyone else. I had hated telling her about my parents, but I hated telling her about this even more. I was such a fool thinking I would be able to keep it to myself forever, thinking that she would never find out.

Before I knew it, I found myself being waived through the gate at the club. I needed to snap out of it and get a hold of myself. I made the turn to head toward the club and as I passed the Inn I could see down the hill; Joan's car was still in the lot. I remembered the warning Dick had given me while Amelia was still in the hospital about my priorities. If ever I had my priorities in order it was now and since his pet was hell bent on hitting me where I lived, perhaps it was time I hit them where they lived.

I gathered my nerve for what I was about to do as I parked the car. At this point, I really felt it necessary. I hated to hurt Joan, after all she had been the driving force behind hiring Amelia and had she not done that, where would I be now? I was certain that Joan did not know about Beth and her husband that far back. She probably did not even know about them at the time of the dinner at the Von Bremen's in Atlanta, but I was confident she knew about them now.

I was equally confident that she knew about Gabby and who the father actually was. Things had been too awkward around Joan lately for her not to know.

Typically, I entered the clubhouse through the door to the kitchen on the loading dock, but not today. Today I entered through the front door right next to Joan's desk. She was gathering her things and preparing to leave for the day. I could tell by the look on her face that she was shocked to see me. It had been a few weeks since we had laid eyes on one another.

"Good afternoon," she greeted me and I could hear the discomfort in her voice. She was too polite not to speak.

"Joan," I replied.

I lingered near her desk and she became more fidgety. "Dick would not happen to be in would he?"

"No, he's gone for the day."

"Do you think I could find him on the course or perhaps at Beth Reed's house? Beth and I are no longer an item, you know."

Joan almost shrieked. "I really wouldn't know what you are talking about," she protested.

"Really? The way I figure it, you know all about the shit I am in and I am about tired of being in it alone." I looked around to make sure none of the spying eyes were lurking before I continued. "Here's the thing, I have been sued for custody of Beth's baby and I think you and I both know I'm no more the father than the man in the moon. I'll be damned if I will turn over this poor child to Beth, but I have always thought you were a decent person, Joan. So, here's what I propose: when I get off of work tonight, I am going to go home and pack up all of the baby stuff and then I am going to be on your doorstep to drop off your husband's child. You might want to leave the light on because it's going to be about 2:00 a.m. before I can get back out here."

I was totally bluffing of course. I had no intention of giving Gabby to them, but Joan did not have to know that. I hated threatening her and I hated seeing the tears in her eyes. This whole ordeal had to be killing her, but if anyone could help me, it might be Joan.

I shook off the feelings of guilt and I continued. Beth had once told Amelia that this was war and she was right. I had to think of this as just another battle, a battle I intended to win.

"By the way, I will do you the courtesy of telling you that Beth used cocaine while pregnant so we don't know how that's going to affect Gabby yet. I will bring all of the paperwork and reading material the doctor gave us with her other things. I'll also bring her medical records so you can see. I am sure your children are going to be thrilled to have a little sister. Your youngest is what, thirteen now?"

Joan wiped away the tears and finally cut me off, "What do you want?"

"I can't have what I want, but I will settle for you getting your husband to sign over his rights to me. I will keep that document and never release it to anyone, not even Gabby, in exchange for me raising the child and not screaming from the rooftop of every business in Green County that your husband is a cheating asshole and has an illegitimate child. I will also tell every church lady, hairdresser and tennis pro around that you knew about it and put me through all of this."

I paused only to take a breath, but I was not done with her. "I will also expect you to testify at any hearings or trial over custody regarding my character. As far as you are concerned, I am the nicest guy you ever met and you will need to really sell it. You will also need to convince everyone that will listen to you that Beth Reed is nothing but compost in pretty packaging, I don't think you will have a problem convincing folks of how you feel about her."

"Gabe, you don't understand what it's like for me with Richard." At that point, I hate to say, but I did not care how it was for her with him. I wanted her to confront him and I wanted him to feel some of the fallout from the predicament Beth had put me in.

Joan wiped her eyes and continued, "You think I have some power to make him do something..."

"Joan, I hear you, but what I am telling you is that you better figure it out. I am not bluffing. You will end up raising this child or I will. Now you need to decide how much you are willing to put up with and are you willing to have his mistress' child living in the house with you?"

Joan had tried to get around me and get to the door twice during our conversation. Each time I had blocked her. The conversation was finished as far as I was concerned, so the third time she tried, I let her pass. I watched her as she fled to her car in tears. I genuinely felt horrible and I did not want to be in her shoes when she addressed all of this with her husband.

I had known women who suffered at the hands of men before. Of course, there's more to it, but that sort of situation is how I ended up in YDC when I was thirteen years old. I knew I had put Joan in a bad spot, but if ever she needed to stand and fight, this was the time. I needed her to stand and fight for herself, and in turn, fight for me.

I was certain that Dick would never allow his mistress' child inside his house. I was counting on that. How would that look to the club members? How would that affect his standing in the community? If I knew nothing else about Dick, it was that he was all about his image. He needed to keep this as quiet as possible, but I needed him to understand that the more Beth pushed me, the more I would push him. It was a vicious circle and if he thought he was getting out of the circle unscathed, he was mistaken.

Once downstairs, I called Amelia as I told her I would. I dialed the number and the phone rang once before she snatched it up. I could hear Gabby scream in the background as Amelia answered, "Gabriel, this better be you."

"It is," I replied with little zest. "I'm so sorry, Amelia. I just needed a moment to process the conversation with Attorney Ellis."

"Do you want to talk about it now?"

"Not really. You know I want to tell you everything, but I don't want to upset you. I don't want any more of this nonsense affecting you or our children, including the one you are carrying." I tried to explain and pacify her curiosity as to what might have made me so mad.

I could tell by her hesitation that she did not believe me. On one hand, Amelia knew me; she had a way of knowing when I was not telling the complete truth. On the other hand, as evidenced by my current fear of her finding out about my stint in the Marion Juvenile Detention Center in Ocala, Florida, she might not know me at all. Although I had just implemented a plan to shut Beth up by blackmailing Joan, I had to tell Amelia. The more I thought about it, the more I knew I had to tell her myself and I was not about to tell her over the phone now.

CHAPTER 15

I arrived home from work around midnight. There wasn't a light on in the place, but moonlight shown through the windows in the dining room and kitchen and lit the entire area.

I found my way to the nursery and looked in on Gabby. She was fast asleep in her crib. I watched her sleep for a few minutes. She sucked her thumb with such vigor that her whole head bobbed with each suck. I reached over the side of the crib and caressed her head. Her hair was coming in more. She was so pretty.

My mind ran away with me as I watched her sleep. I wondered what I would do if I had to turn her over to Beth. The thought broke my heart to the extent that I could no longer stand there and watch her. I turned to leave the nursery and found Amelia in the doorway.

"How long have you been standing there?" I asked her.

"Ever since I heard the front door open and came to find you." Amelia smiled at me. She was wearing a white nightgown and what little light there was caused it to appear sheer. I was distracted by the sight of her. Usually, I was distracted by how beautiful I thought she was, but this time it was more than that. This time I was distracted by the fact that I had not noticed until that moment that she was showing.

I walked toward her and she opened her arms to me. "I don't know what Attorney Ellis said to you..."

I buried my face in her hair and cut her off. I thought I was going to rip off the Band-Aid and just tell her. "He said Beth had filed an answer to my petition for custody and she had counter-sued me. She wants full custody."

"I'm sure it will be alright..."

I pulled back from Amelia and as I led her to our bedroom, I began. "That's not the half of it."

I went on to explain everything to Amelia. While the conversation progressed, I showered and changed into my pajamas. Amelia sat on the toilet and listened to me as I showered. Naturally, Amelia was beyond pissed.

Peeking around the shower curtain, I begged her, "Amelia, you promised not to get upset. It's not good for you or the baby if you get worked up over all of this and if you continue to get this upset, I will have no choice but to stop telling you. I won't have this nonsense jeopardize your health or that of our child. Do I make myself clear?"

"Crystal," she huffed back. "Oh, if I could get my hands on her, Gabriel. Just five minutes. That's all I'd need."

"Amelia..." I cautioned her as I stepped from the shower and she handed me a towel.

"Honestly, I just can't believe the nerve of her, and accusing Mrs. Allen like that. Seriously, there are swamps in Georgia where no one would ever find her."

I shook my head. "I need you to calm down and never say anything like that in public."

The conversation continued in our bed. Before I could get to the part about the threat Beth made about my past or talking to Joan, Amelia drifted off to sleep. It was like she could not help herself. It had been a long day for her and she likely wore herself out by getting worked up.

***

"Gabriel! Gabriel!" Amelia nudged me.

I came to, but it was pitch black in there. I had managed to close the blinds and curtains over the French doors and not a trace of moonlight was in the room. Memories of the night Beth broke into the house flooded my mind as Amelia nudged me again. It also occurred to me that Attorney Ellis had told me that Beth had been bailed out of the Green County Detention Center and I did not know where she was.

"Gabriel, she's moving. Give me your hand," Amelia demanded.

I was relieved and rolled over toward her.

"Give me your hand," she repeated as I searched the dark and found her hand.

Amelia was lying flat of her back and she placed my hand across the newly formed baby bump. Unlike the last time Amelia had me feel her stomach, this time I did not have to wait to feel the baby move.

"Feel it?" Amelia asked.

"Yes!" I was so excited. This was different from the thump, thump that I had felt days before.

"It's as if she's rolling over," Amelia described. "I bet if we cut the lamp on we could probably see her move."

"I don't want to move my hand. I am afraid she will stop."

"You may be right. She's been at it for ten minutes now. Surely she will get tired any minute."

Within a few seconds of voicing that she might stop moving, the baby stopped and became still. I could no longer feel her, but that had been the best feeling. Again, I decided to try to tell Amelia about Beth's threat and I cut the moment short. "Amelia, you know I love you and I want to marry you..."

It turned into a bit of a banter, which is not what I intended, but Amelia cut me off. "I want to marry you too and I don't want to be that pregnant girl in a white wedding dress."

My eyes had adjusted to the darkness a bit and I could see that she rubbed over the area where the baby had just been moving moments before.

"I completely understand, but there's something I have to tell you."

I did not bother to cut the light on. I did not want her to see my face as I told her the rest of the details of the phone call from Mr. Ellis and the story that went with it.

"That sounds very serious, Gabriel." I could feel Amelia roll over to face me.

I propped myself up on my elbow. Over Amelia's shoulder, I could see the alarm clock on the bedside table behind her. It was 3:00 a.m. If I wanted to ruin the moment, I would have told her all about my childhood. In a split second, I imagined the conversation going something like this:

"I don't want you to get upset, but I have to tell you that Mrs. Allen was not the only one Beth threatened and made accusations against."

"What do you mean?" Amelia squirmed to get comfortable and pulled the covers up.

"I mean she accused me of having a history of violence and she filed a restraining order against me as well. She said that I pushed her down when she tried to see Gabby and that's what started everything the other day. She claims that she was just defending herself when she hit me with the golf club and that she did not know what I was capable of." This time I could feel Amelia sit up in the bed as I spoke. I sat up as well.

"A history of violence?" Amelia questioned. "What's that supposed to mean? What's she talking about? And, you stopped her from seeing Gabby because she's crazy. She completely abandoned her with you."

"First of all, she knows about what happened to my parents and my sister. You know I have never been able to get over that. I will go to my grave blaming myself for what happened to them, but that's not all."

"What else is there?"

Before continuing, I took Amelia's hands in mine. "Amelia, I told you that I was shipped from relative to relative after my parents died."

"Right, I remember," Amelia said as she took one hand from mine and brushed the hair back out of her face. Once finished with her hair, she returned her hand to mine.

"You probably remember that I don't like to talk about anything from my childhood."

"I remember."

"I know I have hurt your feelings on a number of occasions by not telling you. I know you feel that I have not let you in and I am sorry. I made a mistake once of telling someone..."

"Beth." Amelia let out her name with a huff of disappointment.

"Yes, and I've regretted it ever since. Before today I regretted it because I was ashamed, but today I came to regret it because she is attempting to use it against me."

I think it took a lot for Amelia to ask, but she asked, "Why would you tell her and not tell me?"

"Because I did not love her. I never really cared if she left and I would be devastated if you left. I would never be the same. I was foolish to think that I could get through our lives without letting you know everything about me. I was stupid to think that you could love me when you hardly know me."

"Gabriel!" Amelia demanded. "I know you plenty enough to know I love you."

"Amelia, just let me get this out. From the time I was seven until I was ten, I was shipped between no less than five different relatives. It was a miserable time. Just before my tenth birthday, I was sent to live with my Aunt Mary. Well, I called her Aunt Mary, but she was really my mother's first cousin. She was wonderful. She looked enough like my mother and that it helped solidify my mother's image in my mind when I was starting to forget her. Sometimes I even slipped up and called her mother. Unlike the other relatives I had lived with before her, she did not have children of her own, so there was no one else compelling her to correct me when I called her 'Mommy,' no one to remind me that she was their mother and not mine."

"Aunt Mary was kind to me in so many ways. For about a year and a half, it was just Aunt Mary and me. I was fed regularly. I had clean clothes regularly and I was told that I was loved. She threw me the first birthday party I had had in three years. She even enrolled me in baseball and football. Everything was going great and I was finally starting to adjust from losing my parents. Mary did her best to help me get back to being a normal kid."

I let go of Amelia's hands just long enough to shift my position in the bed before retaking them. I continued, "We lived in a small house outside of Chiefland, Florida, about fifteen minutes from where we were living when my parents got killed. Anyway, Aunt Mary was single. Occasionally, when she went out, she sent me to stay with my grandparents in Gainesville."

"Now, you may recall, my grandmother blamed me for her only child's death, my mother. My grandfather wasn't so bad and not nearly as hard on me as my grandmother. On weekends, Mary sent me to stay with my grandparents. While at my grandparents', some of the neighborhood kids invited me out to play. My grandmother was all too eager to let me go. She did not bother to ask where I was going or if there would be any adult supervision. She was just happy to have me out of the house."

"There were about six boys, ranging in age from eight to fourteen, and one little girl. I thought I was just going out to play baseball or something. I was excited to get out of the house and have something to do. I would have followed those kids anywhere and I just about did."

"I followed them and we went two streets over behind my grandparents' house. Finally we came to a path that led into the woods and not too far into the woods was a set of railroad tracks. They started down the tracks and I kept up. We didn't go to see a dead body or anything like in 'Stand By Me,' but it was an adventure of just walking on the train tracks. We came to a trestle over a river and we all took turns jumping off of the trestle into the water."

"I had the best day of just being a kid that day. When I got back to my grandparents, I was still soaking wet. My grandmother was furious. I had tracked up her house and got mud on the carpet. She beat me on sight. It wasn't the first beating I had taken at her hands. As usual, she whaled on me until she wore herself out."

"While she rested, my grandfather gathered me up quietly and sat me at the kitchen table. He opened a can of Chef Boyardee Beefaroni and gave it to me. I was starving and exhausted from my day and from the trauma just inflicted. It was never just a beating about what I had done in that moment, but a payback of sorts for killing her daughter."

"I sat sniffling and eating at the kitchen table when she returned. I was twelve and a little big for my age, but the chair flew out from under me all the same when she kicked it. I went flying and the red sauce from the Beffaroni went flying like a bloody massacre."

"In that moment, I decided she was not going to lay another hand on me. I was as big as she was, if not bigger, and my grandfather was a tiny man. I had barely hit the floor and had time to slide in the sauce when I was back on my feet. As my grandmother drew back at me, I caught her forearm in my hand and took her to her knees. She screamed when she hit the floor. I had not meant to hurt her, but only to stop her from continuing to take out her frustrations on me. I still don't know if she landed wrong or if I took her down with too much force, regardless, her hip was broken. My grandfather did not have to pull me off of her, I had let go as soon as she was down."

"'You are the devil!'" she screamed at me. She called me that so often that it was like a pet name."

"My grandfather tried to talk her out of it, but she insisted on phoning the police after the ambulance was called. When the police arrived, she had me charged with assault and taken away. Back then it was her word against mine and she was all too eager to explain how I had killed my parents. At the hearing my grandfather admitted that my grandmother treated me poorly and Aunt Mary vouched for the fact that I had never been in trouble before. I could have done a year, but got off with only two weeks in YDC. It gave me a juvenile record, but that's supposed to be sealed."

"A couple of years later, Mary dated a guy that laid hands on her. At first, I only threatened him, but I was fourteen and almost the size I am now so that did not fare well. I threatened him with a bat and that was after I cracked the windshield of his car with it. He let that slide, but two weeks later he tried his luck with Mary again and I did not just threaten him. She ended up with a black eye. He ended up with a broken nose, two black eyes, a busted eye socket, two cracked ribs, and a bruised lung. I ended up in the Ocala Youth Detention Center for the second time. It was said that I beat him within an inch of his life. I served a year at Ocala, went to eighth grade there."

"For my own good, Aunt Mary tracked down my father's sister in Tennessee and sent me there for a fresh start when I was released. That was the best thing that could have ever happened to me."

***

I could not tell Amelia all of that, all of the details of my youth in that moment. I wanted to, but as badly as I wanted everything off of my chest once and for all, I chose to keep my mouth shut about it. If and when I told her anything else about my past, it would be on my own terms and not because I was pushed into it. Most of all, I did not tell her because I did not want to clear my conscience at the expense of her joy or at the risk of her pregnancy. That's what I told myself at the time, but perhaps it was just that I was scared that she would lose faith in me getting custody and ask me to give up.

Amelia was so proud to feel the baby move. For the longest time, we just laid there with her head on my chest. I had one arm around her and the other across her. My hand was on one side of her belly and hers was on the other. The baby would roll from one side to the other, from her hand to mine and back again. We laid there in the quiet of the night talking barely above a whisper about wedding plans.

"I know you said that you intended to restore Seven Springs and hold weddings there. I haven't seen it since y'all started work on it, but do you want to try to have our wedding there? I mean, if it is even possible?" I asked her. I did not care where we had the wedding

263

as long as she was officially mine, but I wanted her to have the wedding she wanted.

I could feel Amelia take a deep breath against me before she answered. "I don't know. I've always pictured other people getting married there, but I never pictured getting married there myself."

"Why not? Is there somewhere else you have in mind?"

"To be honest, I never pictured myself getting married at all."

"Really, not even after…"

Amelia cut me off and cut to the chase, "Well, I tried not to let myself think that far ahead as not to jinx things any more than they have already been jinxed by Beth. Let's face it, there's been a lot of back and forth with us and we are both so young."

"What about in the last few weeks?"

"You mean, since you gave me the ring?" She held her hand up and what little light there was in the room caught the diamond and it sparkled. I could tell she was admiring it.

"Yeah, that didn't set your imagination in motion?"

"I don't mean to discount it or anything, I love it and I love you, but we have had a lot going on: you and the custody battle, your move here, Jay moving out, me starting Mercer and studying and still recovering from the bombing at the park, doctor appointments for me and Gabby. When have I had a chance to imagine anything?"

"I see your point, but you do trust me that we are going to get married, right?" The baby had settled down and it had been a few minutes since she had last moved, so I removed my hand and rolled over on my side to face Amelia. I wanted to see her expression as best I could in the dark.

Amelia also rolled over to face me. "I believe you," she started, "but I just don't think either of us has been able to make it a priority lately."

She had a point and I let her know that and that we needed to make it a priority. We agreed to do our best to make the wedding happen over Labor Day weekend.

***

The next morning, I awoke to find Amelia missing from the bed. I wiped the sleep from my eyes and went to find her and to check on Gabby. Again, I found Amelia in the rocking chair in the nursery. I stood in the doorway and watched her with Gabby as they played together.

Feeding time was over and the empty bottle sat on the floor by the side of the rocker. Amelia had her feet propped on the foot stool and Gabby lying on her legs. Gabby was getting bigger and she stretched comfortably from Amelia's knees down her thighs to where her bottom rested against Amelia's stomach. Everything about Gabby still seemed to be normal and each day that passed, we were thankful that she had showed no signs of withdrawals.

Between Amelia, her Aunt Gayle, Aunt Dot and Jay's Aunt June, Gabby had gained an entire new wardrobe since we moved to The Jefferson. This morning, Amelia had already changed her from her pajamas and dressed her in a white jumper with yellow daisies. She even had on a matching head band which looked like a ring of tiny yellow daisies.

It appeared that Amelia had gotten distracted while trying to put Gabby's socks on and was now using the tiny socks as puppets. The puppets were busy pointing out which little piggy went to market and which little piggy stayed home. With each piggy, Amelia made a different funny voice and Gabby, as small as she was, squealed with delight and batted her little hands. It was the first time I had seen Gabby laugh like this.

As I watched, I thought about the phone call from the day before. I also thought about the threat I had made to Joan. Looking at Amelia and how she was with Gabby, I could not imagine taking that from her. There was no way I was turning over Gabby to anyone without one hell of a fight.

I was snapped back to reality when Amelia noticed me. "Good morning, sleepy head," she said in the voice that she had been using for one of the piggies.

"Good morning, Mrs. Hewitt. You are up awful early and seem to have made a bit of progress with Little One."

"Oh, you mean the change of clothes?" Amelia looked back to Gabby's outfit and over to the changing table and little knotted bag lying on the floor next to it. "She had an award winner this morning."

"What?" I did not understand what she was getting at.

Amelia spelled it out for me, "Gabby, would you like to tell Daddy how you won the shit of the year award?"

"She what?" That was a little crass for referencing a baby. "Did you just say she won 'shit of the year'?"

"Yes."

"I did not know there was an award for such things."

"If there isn't, there should be. It was so bad that I had to throw out the pajamas and use the sprayer from the sink on her. It was too much for the diaper and went all the way up her back. I am surprised we did not wake you during the commotion, between my gagging and her laughing at me. Not to mention, the ruckus of the sink and the whole process. Honestly, Gabriel, if she was a little boy, this would be something to brag about." Amelia gagged a little more while telling the story and revisiting the image in her head.

"She seems happy now."

"I reckon so, I would be happy if I lost two pounds that easily," Amelia laughed and Gabby laughed with her.

"I guess this can be the topic of family night dinner one night," I suggested.

"That's a good idea. I will have to remember this," Amelia seemed almost excited to have a story to tell the others.

There was a running competition at family night dinner as to who could tell the grossest story. Cara had made what Amelia called a "spirit stick" as a prize and each week it was passed from the winner the week before to the new winner. As best I knew, Amelia had won three times, but Travis held the record for most wins at four.

Amelia got up out of the rocking chair and carried Gabby toward me. I met her halfway and gave them each a good morning kiss.

"Would you mind trading cars with me today?" Amelia asked as she passed Gabby to me. "I can't fit the car seat in either of mine."

"Right, I totally forgot about that," I replied. "I guess we should revisit the subject of a new car for you."

"We should, but I am not getting rid of either of my current cars."

"Of course, not." There was no way I would have her get rid of the Corvette. I loved that car as much as she did.

Driving the Corvette was fun, but to Amelia it represented her father. To me, it was a vital piece of the background in one of the first memories I have of her. I would never forget the way she looked the day of her interview, the way she looked back at me when she was leaving and walking to the car. She was still just as beautiful.

I also could not imagine getting rid of the truck either. I may not have had much of a father figure growing up to teach me father-son type things like the value of having a truck, but I always knew having a truck was handy.

While Amelia got dressed, I hung out with Gabby. I introduced her to Saturday morning cartoons. We were barely into the Smurfs when she drifted off. I returned her to her crib and joined Amelia in the bathroom.

I planned to slip out of my pajamas and join her in the shower when she heard me.

"Would you mind handing me a towel?" Amelia asked. I suppose she was finished with her shower. I was slightly disappointed as I thought I had missed my opportunity with her.

I handed her the towel and then took a seat on the toilet to wait for her. Within a moment, she stepped from the shower with it wrapped around her. Her hair was pinned back and there were beads of water still on her shoulders. Her skin glistened.

"Do you remember the night we conceived?" Amelia asked as she continued to secure the towel.

This was the first time we had discussed this. Of course I remembered it and I answered as such while the memories of that weekend started to flood my mind. "Of course, it was my birthday."

"I was completely shocked when you showed up that Friday afternoon. I had not seen you in weeks and I did not know when I might see you again or if I would see you again. Plus, you worked on Friday nights. I was completely caught off guard when I saw you sitting on the steps outside." Amelia reached back and removed the pins that held up the bulk of her hair while she began to reminisce.

"I figured you would be and I was surprised when you agreed to come with me," I admitted.

"You said it was your birthday and you wanted to spend it with me. You begged and little did you know I would follow you anywhere." As the conversation continued, Amelia took a seat, straddling me and placing her arms loosely around my neck.

"Anywhere?" I asked.

"Anywhere," she confirmed while adjusting her position on top of me.

"Are you trying to give me a lap dance, Mrs. Hewitt?" Amelia threw her head back and laughed at my question.

"No," she laughed, "I'm trying to have a serious conversation with you."

"Do go on," I insisted.

"I don't want to get married at Seven Springs," Amelia bit her hip and hesitated before she continued. "I want to get married at the inn where we had dinner that Friday night."

"You want to get married at Glen Ella Springs?" She might have thought I would have forgotten the name of the place, but I remembered every detail of that weekend.

"Yes! I want to rent out the entire place and have our friends and family stay there. I want it to be one big party weekend for all of us. What do you think of that?"

"I think it's a great idea, but I'm sure they will be booked for Labor Day weekend. Oh, and I had almost forgot, I have a wedding to work at Port Honor that weekend. The usual: rehearsal dinner Friday night and reception Saturday afternoon, so maybe our plan should not be that weekend after all."

"I will call Glen Ella later on and find out if they have anything the rest of the month." Amelia kissed me once more and then left me sitting there to finish getting dressed.

\*\*\*

We went our separate ways that morning. We traded cars and Amelia took Gabby and went to her Aunt Gayle's house in Avera. I left shortly after them and headed to work. The sun was shining and, with the exception of being away from them, everything should have been right with the world, but the events of the day before still weighed on me.

All the way to the club I dreaded seeing Dick or Joan. I even dreaded seeing their son, Jason, who worked as a cart boy for the pro-shop. He was always out zipping around delivering carts to the golfers all day on Saturdays. He was a nice enough boy, but I dreaded seeing him about as much as I dreaded seeing his parents. I hated the role I might have in busting up his family if it came to that.

I regretted bullying Joan the day before and threatening her. I did not like treating people poorly and I had treated her very poorly and that ate at me. It wasn't her fault that her husband could not keep his pants up and it had resulted in an illegitimate child. I acted in haste yesterday and aside from hurting Joan, I wondered what

269

other repercussions that might have. My intention was not to hurt Joan, but I had used her as a means to get at Dick for Beth's actions. I meant for Dick and Beth to get the horns for messing with me, but I regretted involving Joan. For all I knew, she was just as much a victim in all of this as Gabby and I were.

I managed to avoid Jason until he came in to get a sandwich at lunchtime. I was at the bar when he came in. I did not mean to eavesdrop, but I overheard him explain to another of the cart boys that he could not go out that night because he was staying over with his brother.

Jason continued, after he ordered his sandwich and Coke, "I don't know what's up, but my mother left for a vacation with one of her friends last night. She never does that, but while she's gone I have to stay at my brother's place."

I could not make out what the other kid said, but Jason answered him, "Oh, my dad is fit to be tied, so I'm fine with not being home. Mom called me this morning and was a little weird. She mentioned getting me a puppy. Dad would never allow us to have a dog, so I am not sure what she was talking about."

Again, the other boy asked something, but I was making a drink for Mr. Baker and missed what he said. I was also trying not to get caught eavesdropping on them. I did hear Jason's answer.

"If she was leaving him, I would not blame her. She thinks we don't know how he is, but she's wrong. Dad tries to make out around here like he's the big man, so nice to the members and all, but he's not like that at home. He's a real miserable asshole at home and Mom's the main one he takes out his frustrations on. I feel sorry for her."

I had to leave the bar at that point. I felt terrible. Joan's own children felt sorry for her. I never knew. I did not know until recently that Dick ran around on her. They always appeared to be the perfect couple. I clearly remembered him doting on her the night we all went to the Von Bremens', but I guess that was all a show. Now I really regretted what all I had said to her yesterday and I knew that no matter how much I threatened her, it meant nothing. Joan had no power over Dick so she would be no help in my battle for Gabby. I had hurt her for no reason.

***

Glen Ella Springs was available for the weekend of September 20, through September 22, 1996 and Amelia booked it as soon as she found out. That's the news I received when she greeted me on her Aunt Gayle's porch. I had gotten off work at 9:00 p.m. and driven straight to Avera. I was so happy to see her, just looking at her made me feel better.

# CHAPTER 16

In the weeks between being attacked by Beth and having her served with my petition for sole custody of Gabby and the wedding, so many things happened. First of all, I learned that Beth was counter-suing me and threatening to expose more of my past that I particularly did not want to revisit. Secondly, Amelia had been visited by the FBI regarding what she might have witnessed at Centennial Olympic Park the night of the bombing. That was not as concerning as the issue with Beth and the fact that Gabby started showing signs that we were told to look for when it came to her having residual effects from the drugs Beth had used while pregnant. Lastly, there was planning for the wedding, which I mostly left to Amelia and her aunts.

There were other things that went on as well, but nothing as significant as watching the sweet baby that Amelia and I had come to love become inconsolable at times and for no apparent reason. At five weeks old, it was as if a light switch of pain was turned on for Gabby. We tried everything to calm and comfort Gabby, but the only thing that seemed to calm her was being held by one or the other of us. While holding her, standing and pacing was the only thing that seemed to help. If we sat down she knew it and we had to start all over with the pacing. She cried and cried and screamed and cried and screamed some more. She often appeared terrorized by something and could hardly stand for us to put her down.

Finally, Amelia made another appointment for Gabby with Dr. Roberts. He had cautioned us in the beginning that Gabby may not develop any adverse effects from Beth's drug use and, as it turned out, Gabby was very lucky in that regard. According to Dr. Roberts, Gabby was perfectly fine and only suffering from a case of the colic. One can imagine how relieved we were to get a clean bill of health on our child and especially relieved that there was an end in sight. Dr. Roberts advised that most babies outgrew colic around twelve to sixteen weeks old. Until then, he recommended we give her Mylicon drops and Amelia bought enough of those to keep the company in business for a few weeks. She went a little overboard and put a bottle of the drops in every room of the apartment at The Jefferson, plus in each of the cars and the truck.

The Thursday before Labor Day, Amelia had just left her contracts class at Mercer and was walking to her next class when two FBI agents approached her. They asked to speak with her about the bombing and the events of the night before it went off. They asked her if she saw anything out of the ordinary. She replied to them that she was a small town girl and everything about the whole day was out of the ordinary to her.

Amelia went on to explain to them that she did not believe for one instance that the person they were targeting as a suspect, Richard Jewell, had anything at all to do with the bomb. She said that she was adamant that Mr. Jewell had only tried to be helpful in the situation and was doing his job when he asked her and Cara to move away from the stage after he discovered the backpack under the bench.

Amelia was forced to admit that she did not personally know Mr. Jewell and could not speak for his character, but could not imagine the man who was responsible for saving her life was also the man responsible for everything. She could not reconcile the two acts coming from the same person. It just did not make sense that anyone would plant the bomb just so they could find it and try to gain notoriety for saving people.

By the time the FBI agents were done with her, they had thanked her for her time, but Amelia felt she had done little to convince them that they were barking up the wrong tree when it came to Mr. Jewell. She believed they just listened to her for more than two minutes as a courtesy since she was one of the more injured of the victims. She may have been right since the news continued to report on Richard Jewell's every move, potential motive and every ounce of his past.

Every time Amelia saw Richard Jewell on the news, she turned the channel. It absolutely disgusted her that no one seemed to be looking for any other suspects. It also solidified her decision to go along with her aunt's plan for her to become a lawyer.

According to Amelia, "What is being done to this man is a travesty of justice. It is as if they are trying him through the media

273

and they have already convicted him. It is as though our legal system has been made into a sport for the entertainment of the masses. They don't know any more than I do as to whether this man is guilty, but they have stolen every right he has for a fair trial. I just don't like it."

I thought she was taking it too personally and when I shared that belief, I was promptly corrected. "This is personal for me and I have the scars to prove it."

I may not have completely agreed with her, but I could certainly respect her convictions. I also admired her willingness to fight for her beliefs. It was yet another quality I found attractive in her.

***

The day I first spoke to Attorney Ellis regarding Beth's threats about my past, he suggested that I give her something as a peace offering. Against my better judgment, I offered her visitation with Gabby. My condition for her visitation was that it was supervised by her brother, J.J., or someone appointed by the court. In the weeks since that offer, Attorney Ellis heard nothing from Beth or her attorney in an effort to take us up on the offer. He did not even get a counter demand for unsupervised visitation. The only response that came was that of a motion to transfer the venue of the case to Fulton County.

Attorney Ellis responded to Beth's request for change of venue to Fulton County by asking for an oral hearing before the judge currently assigned to the case in Green County. Since the case was about custody, he asked to be placed on the first available calendar and was seen within two weeks of his request. At the hearing, Mr. Ellis submitted several items to the court indicating Beth's address in Green County. The first article was Beth's change of address form to the United States Postal Service. The second item was the raffle ticket she submitted at the club on New Year's Eve where she registered to win tickets for the 1997 Master's tournament and even then she listed the address of her parents' lake house. Thirdly, he submitted her patient information sheet from where she entered Northside Hospital to give birth to Gabby. The patient information sheet listed my address again as hers. The fourth piece of evidence he submitted to the court was the registration for Beth's BMW, which she had tagged in Green County.

At the hearing, Mr. Ellis not only quashed the change of venue, but he also laid the ground work for proving Beth was a liar. Beth's attorney provided affidavits from Beth and her parents stating that she was a resident of Fulton County and had been all her life. He questioned at what point was Beth lying. Was she lying when filling out the forms or was she lying now on the affidavits? He argued that she could not live in both counties, one had to be her primary residence and at the time of the birth of the child in question she resided at the Snug Harbor address and she admitted it in her own handwriting with the change of address form.

Attorney Ellis further argued to the judge, "Miss. Reed seems to reside in Green County when it is convenient for her such as when it comes time to save money on her tag bill. She likes to reap the benefits of our lower tax rates as opposed to paying the higher rates in Fulton County."

It was also argued that the issue of custody pertained to the time at which Gabby was born and covered the span for when Beth had abandoned Gabby with me. Attorney Ellis had specifically used the term "abandoned" in his argument and began laying that foundation as well.

The judge ultimately ruled in our favor and the affidavits from Beth and her parents were set aside. The judge gave more weight to the tag bill and Beth's own handwriting on the change of address form than anything else. It was a major win for us, but Attorney Ellis warned that Beth's attorney would likely be better prepared the next time around.

■■■■■■■■■■■■■■■■■■■■■■■■■■■■■■■■■■■■■■■■■■■■■■■■■■■■■

In the weeks since I had threatened Joan, I had not seen her at the club. I heard rumors through some of the members that there was trouble in paradise, but nothing specific. I tried not to appear as though I was interested and only let the members tell me. I never asked questions, but those who talked were always eager to talk without being probed.

One member was all too eager to tell me that Joan had moved out of the house and another insisted that the youngest child

275

had been sent to boarding school. The most credible information came from Mrs. Baker who let slip that Joan had found out about Dick's latest mistress and how she was fed up. Mrs. Baker and Joan often played tennis together and were good friends. She felt sorry for Joan and claimed to know that Dick was in deep with this particular mistress, a girl who he could not control as he had Joan for so many years, and now he was likely to pay the price.

"Dick and Joan both liked to think that no one knew about Dick's wandering eye, but everyone knew," Mrs. Baker insisted. "The only thing we did not know is why Joan stayed with the jerk."

Also, on the rare occasion that I saw Dick, it was always while other members of the staff were present. Our usual meetings for budget and what not regarding the food and beverage operation were reduced to memos sent back and forth through his secretary. I believed both he and Joan were avoiding me and, for the time being, I was fine with that.

***

As for the wedding, I was looking forward to the day Amelia would officially be mine and time seemed to stand still in the days leading up to it. I am not sure how she did it, but Amelia and her aunts went to Glen Ella twice in the weeks leading up to the wedding just to finalize details. I offered time and again to help her with planning, but she refused.

Over dinner one night there was quite the discussion as to the invitations to the wedding. My only chore for the wedding had been to give her the name and address of any of my family members that I wished to invite, but I had not given her anything. Amelia was adamant that she meet someone from my family and that they couldn't all be bad.

"Seriously, Gabriel, if we were having the wedding at a church, the building would tip over and land on its side due to all of the guests sitting on my side," Amelia teased as she set the table for the two of us.

"Mrs. Hewitt, will it not be enough just to have me there?" I questioned while I returned the lasagna to the oven for the cheese on top to melt.

"Of course, but surely you have someone from your family that you would like to invite. There's got to be someone that you would like to celebrate your accomplishments with." Amelia was very persuasive as she came back to the kitchen and put her arms around me. "Surely you want to show off your new family."

"I would rather just forget most everything until I met you. The past is the past, Amelia."

Amelia was not giving up and she put up a good argument, "But, it's our pasts that make us who we are and you have said yourself that there were good times. You mentioned having an Aunt Mary. What about inviting her?"

"I have not seen her since I was fourteen or fifteen. I think it would be weird." I tried to convince Amelia that I was fine with it just being my new friends and family.

"Why would it be weird to let someone know that you remembered their kindness toward you and invite them to your wedding? I think there's no time like the present to mend fences." Amelia kissed me down my neck as she attempted to persuade me.

I backed away and grabbed the oven mitts. "Can't we just let this go?"

"No."

I might as well have given in when she first mentioned it, but I didn't and now she was not letting go. She put the subject on hold long enough for us to have dinner and put Gabby down for the night, but picked it back up when she joined me in the shower.

"You know, we still have rooms available at the Inn. There are sixteen rooms and I have not assigned three of them so we have room for your Aunt Mary to come from Florida and your aunt and uncle from Nashville. Nashville's not that far."

My response was a roll of my eyes.

277

"I saw that," she quipped as she eased around me to get under the water.

"I meant for you to."

"You are horrible, Mr. Hewitt."

"And you are perfect, Mrs. Hewitt."

I thought she had given up on the conversation, but I should have known better. Amelia had only paused the subject long enough to dry her hair before meeting me in bed and continuing. She used all of her new found persuasive skills, teasing me and withholding sex until I relented.

"You are shameless," I commented on how she had brought me to the brink of ecstasy and then backed off until I agreed to provide names and addresses for the invitations.

"I learned from the master," she replied as I rolled her over and lifted the hem of her nightgown.

"The master, huh?" I smiled down at her while I tried to control the moment. "I like it."

The following morning, I left the address that I had for my Aunt Mary on the counter in the kitchen along with the address for Aunt Anne and Uncle Dave.

"I don't know if these are any good, but this is what I have for them," I said as I finished writing.

Amelia was busying herself with making Gabby a bottle and packing her things for class as we spoke. "Thanks," she replied, "but would you like to try calling them before just sending them invitations? I mean, since you have not spoken to any of them in..."

I cut Amelia off, "I haven't spoken to them in ten years and I don't particularly want to call them."

"Could I ask why?"

I could tell she was getting agitated, but she did not raise her voice or change her tone as she picked up Gabby from her bouncy chair. It really was a fair question and if I were in Amelia's shoes, I would want to know all about her as well. I thought about it for a moment and it occurred to me that this could be the right moment for me to tell her everything. Of course, I chickened out.

"I would just rather leave that part of my life in the past."

"I just don't understand what was so bad that you cannot even talk about it with me."

"I don't want to discuss this with you about to run off to school this morning and then I will be rushing off to work when you get home. It's just not the right time."

"It's two weeks before our wedding, Gabriel, do you think you could squeeze in a talk with me about your life story sometime before then?" Again, she did not raise her voice, but her tone was definitely different. She was pissed with me. Her patience with me was wearing thin and with Beth's threat, I really had everything to lose by not confiding in Amelia.

Amelia took a breath before continuing, "I know folks might think the ship has sailed on me marrying you considering my condition and the fact that we are already living together, but don't be fooled. I am not about to marry someone that I don't know."

That hurt. Was she seriously thinking about calling off the wedding? Was she really threatening me?

"You are not serious." I tried not to raise my voice, but I was shocked by her words.

"I am serious," she responded while passing Gabby to me.

Before I knew it, she picked up her books and keys and headed for the door. She glanced back at me before starting down the stairs, "I am not giving you an ultimatum. I'm not fond of those. I am just saying, I don't think starting a marriage with secrets is a good idea and it's not for me. If we can't come to some sort of understanding, then I will call and cancel the inn. Let me know what I need to do."

I did not have time to respond before she was down the stairs and gone. My head was spinning. She had never spoken to me like that and it frightened me. Could I really lose her? I could not bear the thought of being without her. I could hardly stand to be away from her while she was at school and I was at work.

I had always thought that I ran the risk of losing Amelia by telling her what all had gone on with me as a child and during my teen years. I never wanted her to look at me as if I was damaged or broken. I also never wanted her to feel sorry for me. What woman wants a man they have to feel sorry for? I did not want that and I did not want to lose the way she looked at me or kill the light that was in her eyes for me. What was I to do, but tell her and risk it?

When she arrived home from school, I did my best to get her to talk to me, but she refused. Amelia was really serious. She barely allowed me to kiss her goodbye before I left for work.

"It's Friday, so I may take Gabby and go to Aunt Gayle's for the weekend. I don't know yet," Amelia said as she shrugged off my advance and carried on toward the bathroom.

I followed her. "Are you really that mad with me?" I asked only to have the door shut in my face.

Through the door I could hear her, "If you don't want to talk, then neither do I."

I started to speak again, but was cut off by the sound of the flushing toilet. I stood at the door and waited for her. It was getting on toward 3:45 p.m. and I had to leave for work soon, but I did not want to leave with things the way they were. Amelia was not running this time as she had in the past when we fought, but the silent treatment that she was giving me wasn't much better.

I knew I was likely going to be late for work, but I just could not bring myself to leave with things like this. It was nearly ten minutes before she came out of the bathroom. I had backed up to the edge of the bed and taken a seat facing the bathroom door and waited on her.

I stood as Amelia opened the door. "I am not leaving for work until we work this out."

280

She rolled her eyes and headed for the bedroom door.

Again I followed her. I let her get all the way to the kitchen before I broke. "Alright. I give in. I will tell you everything when I get home from work tonight. I promise."

Amelia turned from the refrigerator and raised an eyebrow at me. The look on her face conveyed that she was skeptical.

"I promise. I will tell you things that I never dared to tell anyone, not even Beth."

Amelia gave a little smile, but still did not say anything.

"Come on. I can't take the silent treatment." I ran my hands through my hair in exasperation as I spoke. I ended up propped on the bar top with my head in my hands.

"You better get on the road or you are going to be really late," was all she said, but her face softened and her posture relaxed.

"Yeah, I should have left fifteen minutes ago, but I..." As I was speaking, she made her way around the counter that had separated us.

"I know, Gabriel," Amelia reached out her arms to me. "I know, there are things that you are not comfortable talking about, but there's nothing you could tell me that would change anything." Amelia shook her head in the negative and shrugged her shoulders as she assured me that giving in was the right thing to do for both of us.

I held her for a moment and buried myself in her hair. As always, it smelled of strawberries. We both checked on Gabby and I kissed her goodbye as she slept. We crept out of the room and I grabbed my jacket for work. Amelia went as far as the car with me.

"I will wait up for you, no matter how late," she said before closing the car door for me and backing away.

As I backed down the driveway, I rolled down the window and called out to her. "Mrs. Hewitt, I love you and I am so glad you found me."

Amelia smiled and threw a kiss to me. I was well down Jefferson Street when I glanced in the rearview mirror. I could still see her standing there watching as I drove away. She had worn her hair down and it was blowing gently in the breeze. One hand was in her hair pulling it back from her face and the other was across her abdomen as if she were comforting the fetus or talking to it. Even from that distance, nearly a quarter mile away, I could tell that she was with child. Not only was her shape changing with every passing day, there was a glow about her, a glow that she had shut down earlier in the day, but it was back now.

All the way to work, I thought about her. I loved everything about Amelia and the thought of ever losing her was too much. I would give her anything and all she had been asking for was words. It seemed like such an easy thing to give, but I had held back all that time. I think we both knew it was more than words. It was a piece of myself that I had been holding back from her.

I was a little late for work, but it seemed to go unnoticed. There was no note from Dick this time and no sign of him or Joan. Alvin was in and he was his usual cheerful, helpful self. I enjoyed working with him. Cara, Daniel, Jerry and Andy were all on shift that night as well.

Throughout the dinner shift, I found it hard to focus. I played and replayed the conversation I was going to have with Amelia when I got home. I knew she was not lying about waiting up on me. She typically tried to wait up on me. Sometimes she failed in her efforts and other times she took naps in the evening so she could wait up. While I was at work, she typically busied herself studying for law school along with playing with and taking care of Gabby. I don't know how she fit in the nap, but she often did. I knew on this particular occasion she would definitely squeeze in a nap as to insure she would be up when I got home.

It was a busy night, but it went by quickly. Cara and Matt were an on again/off again item and they seemed to be back on that night. The most eventful thing of the night was catching them making out in the corridor behind the fireplace as I headed out for the night. They looked like giddy children when I caught them. I did not bother to scold them for their antics while on the job because once Amelia and I had been in that same predicament in that same spot.

On the ride home, I thought about the night behind the fireplace. That was just the beginning that night and it was the night of the Delta Digital Christmas party. Amelia had worn the dress that I bought her to wear the night we went to the dinner at the Von Bremens' at the Georgian Terrace. It was a long black dress that was slit nearly to her hip on her left side. Amelia was not that tall, but with the silver, stiletto sandals that Joan had picked out to go with the dress, it made Amelia's legs look as if they went on for days.

The first time she had worn the dress I could not take my eyes off of her. I shifted at every glance to keep from becoming noticeably aroused at the sight of her. The dress cinched around her neck and around her waist and gathered in the front. There was no back to the dress and Amelia could not wear a bra with it. She was very conscious of being without her bra, but that aspect of the dress hardly registered with me. It was the peek that high up her hip that did it for me. It was as if I was seeing something that I wasn't supposed to see and that was a definite turn on.

I requested she wear the dress the night of the Delta Digital party and she did. As soon as I saw her, the feeling of the night at The Georgian Terrace returned. Unlike the night of the dinner with the board members, I did not fight the urge to kiss her. That desire to possess her is what led to our session behind the fireplace.

I had yet to fully have Amelia and I knew she was a virgin, so I was always careful in not taking things too far with her. Had those not been the circumstances, I might have thrown caution to the wind and taken her quickly in the corridor, especially if I had taken the time to send the other staff members on various errands to occupy them and insure a moment alone with her. That was not the case, so I settled for more foreplay with her.

As I made the drive on autopilot, I continued to replay the scene behind the fireplace. I remembered pulling her back there and how hot she was. I could hardly think beyond seeing her ankle bare to her hip that night and how she might taste were I to run my tongue from one extreme to the other. Instead, I would have to settle for using my hand.

I pressed her back against the wall that backed the fireplace. I held her by the waist and pulled her toward me. Her back arched as I kissed her and I pulled her tighter into me. I reached a hand into the slit of the dress and found that she was wearing lace panties. I could not see them, but they were likely black like the dress. It was never enough for me just to feel her panties. I always wanted to feel more.

I slipped a finger between her skin and the hem of the leg of her underpants and left a trail around the hem. I knew she was inexperienced so I was never sure if she knew what she was doing or was she just acting on instinct. Either way, when I ran my finger from her hip around the back of her ass, Amelia widened her stance and lifted her left leg. Her bare knee slid up and came to rest next to the opening of the front pocket of my dress slacks. I could also feel her pull me closer. It was as if she were encouraging me to continue. I could feel her tilt her pelvis into me and chills run down her legs from my touch.

I remembered wondering how much longer I would be able to resist her and knowing that a lesser man would have at least copped more of a feel right then, but I refrained. I am not sure if she would have protested, but I didn't want her like that. I wanted her on my terms and those terms included respecting her and there would have been nothing respectful about toying with her behind the fireplace where anyone might see.

I replayed every detail of that entire night all the way home. I could nearly feel her beneath me as I thought about how later that night we made love for the first time. Thinking of her all the way home, I had worked myself into an arousal. I know I had promised to talk to her and I had planned how that would go all night, but now I was nearly home and all I wanted to do was feel her skin on mine.

It was nearly eleven when I pulled into the driveway of The Jefferson. As I parked the car, I glanced up to see the light above the sink in the kitchen was still on. I knew Amelia would have kept her word and I was sure to find her waiting on me. I grabbed the to-go box filled with Alvin's strawberry cheesecake from the passenger seat and I headed inside. I could hardly wait to see her.

I opened the door to what was now our apartment and I continued up the stairs. I stepped into the living room to find the only light in there was that of the television and that lone light in the kitchen. Amelia had heard me coming up the stairs and sat up from the couch.

"I tried to wait up," she said as she rubbed her eyes and stretched. The eleven o'clock news played barely above a whisper on the television and Amelia had spoken just loud enough for me to hear her over the weatherman.

"I brought you something, but it will keep until tomorrow." My intention was to put the cheesecake in the refrigerator, but Amelia reached out a hand to me as I passed.

"Is it cheesecake?" She perked up. "Tell me it's cheesecake. I have been craving strawberry cheesecake."

I handed her the box. "I'll get a fork for you."

Amelia twisted on the couch toward me as I went into the galley kitchen to get a fork from the drawer. "Mr. Hewitt, you take care of me so well. I am sorry I threatened you earlier."

I returned to the couch and took a seat opposite her. I brought a fork for myself as well. "Mrs. Hewitt, I'm sorry I made you feel as though you had to threaten me. If you are up for it, I will tell you everything."

I still wanted her. I could smell the scent of Coast soap still on her skin mixed with the strawberry shampoo and I could see that the ends of her hair were still wet. Amelia was freshly showered and in a new pink tank top and matching pajama shorts. She looked so young and that glow was all about her even though I could tell she was tired. It took some effort, but I squashed my desire for her and settled into the couch with her.

I gave her the first bite as I worked up the courage to begin the conversation. I had rehearsed it in my head all the while plating up orders at work earlier and now here I was. First, I asked about Gabby and after we talked about how their night went, I started.

285

"It goes without saying that I don't like to talk about my upbringing. I think I have mentioned to you before that I don't want you to look at me any differently. I love what we have together and I don't want that to change."

Amelia quickly swallowed what she had in her mouth and added to what I was saying, "Gabriel, things change. That's just the nature of people. Nothing ever stays the same, but it does not mean that all change is for the worse."

"I know, but this is the best I have ever had things and I don't want that to change in the slightest. I know it's unrealistic, but it does not mean I don't want it. So, I like that you know me for the man I am now and I don't want to do anything to tarnish the image you have of me."

I paused long enough to eat what I had scooped onto my fork. Amelia waited patiently for me to continue. As we alternated taking bites of the cake, I explained to her again all that I remembered of the night my parents were killed. This time she was awake and assured me that it was not my fault.

"You were only a little boy." Amelia wiped tears from her eyes and sat the to-go box on the coffee table.

"If I had not been a spiteful child and had to get even with my sister, the events of that night would have never been set in motion."

We were still facing one another on the couch. Amelia's feet were over mine and our knees pressed against one another. I was still in my jacket and pants from work, but I had slipped my shoes off when I first came in. Amelia reached over to unbutton the jacket, but I placed my hands on hers to stop her. "You can't do that or I won't be able to focus and finish the conversation."

I released my grip on her hands and Amelia pulled back uttering the word, "Oh," and gave a slight smile, biting her lower lip. She knew exactly what I was getting at.

I finished the buttons and took the jacket off. I laid it across the back of the couch and continued my story.

"My mother was an only child and all of her family lived in the vicinity of Gainesville, Florida. My father's family was flung all around the country. No one really bothered to check with any of my father's side to see if they could take me, but there was sort of a straw drawing cession that resulted in me going to live with one of my mother's cousins. You have heard me talk about my Aunt Mary. Mary had a sister that was older, Maggie. Maggie was married to Dwight and they had three children. Dwight was eager to take me because he figured my parents had a life insurance policy and he would get his hands on it. I was to be the salvation of all of their financial woes.

It took Dwight six months before he accepted that I wasn't worth anything. My parents had a life insurance policy on each of them, but my grandmother was the trustee. My grandmother was what one might call a 'shrewd broad' and she was letting neither Dwight nor the murderer of her only child collect on a windfall."

Amelia's eyes grew big at my description of myself as being the "murderer" of my grandmother's only child, so I felt forced to explain further. "From the morning my grandmother learned of the circumstances surrounding my parents' death, I was no longer her grandchild. I was at best 'that boy'."

Amelia shook her head in disbelief and disgust. She also inched closer to me, closing the gap between us just a little. Amelia reached for my hands, which were propped on my knees. She locked her fingers in mine as if she were pulling me back to her from the dark place the conversation was taking us.

"All the while I lived with Dwight and Maggie, I was reminded of how they struggled daily and how I had not made things any easier. When the day came that I was shipped off to Maggie and Mary's brother, I was glad to go. Little did I know, life at Marty's wasn't going to be any easier."

Amelia gripped my hands tighter. I am sure she wondered what horror I was going to tell her next as if a child that was unwanted wasn't bad enough.

"Marty was a man's man. He was married with two daughters and I was to be the son he never had. He immediately enrolled me in any sport he could think of and he volunteered to coach. I was eight by this time so imagine an eight year old boy who believes he has killed his family and that no one wants him. Do you think I had any athletic ability at that time?"

Amelia shook her head slightly in the negative.

"Exactly, I was about as athletic as a dead fish. Now, compound that with the disappointment from Marty thrown on top and add a helping of embarrassment to him and that was our relationship. He was disappointed and I embarrassed him at every opportunity. How did it look to the guys when the coach's kid was the number one bench warmer? What he failed to understand was that it took every ounce of spirit I had to get out of bed in the mornings, so there was nothing left over for swinging a bat or throwing a ball."

Amelia went on shaking her head the entire time I spoke of Marty.

"One day, he had sent me out in the yard with some of the neighborhood kids to practice throwing the ball. All of the kids were bigger than me, but there was this one kid that kept hitting me with the ball, just beaning the shit out of me. Finally, I had enough and I went crying inside to Marty's wife, Carmen. She was nice enough to me and was icing the bruises when Marty came back in from smoking on the back porch."

"'What's goin' on here?' he demanded as he gave me a good looking over."

"Carmen stepped back as she cowered at the tone Marty took. 'That Tyson boy hit Gabe with the ball,' she said with her voice full of caution and concern."

"'Did he now?'"

"The next thing I knew, Marty had me by the arm and was dragging me down the street to the Tyson's house. I thought maybe he was going to have a word with Greg Tyson's father about his twelve year old son picking on the smaller kids like me, but that was not the case. At Marty's request, Greg Tyson's father sent him into the yard with his ball and glove."

288

"'Throw the ball at him again!' Marty ordered the kid who stood there bewildered."

"'Throw it!' Marty nearly screamed at Greg as tears were already starting to stream down my face."

"'He is going to throw this ball at you until you learn how to catch it!'"

"Greg Tyson threw two balls at me. One hit me in the chest, but not for my lack of trying to catch it. The wind was knocked out of me and as tears ran down my face, Marty demanded that I 'suck it up and be a man' and that Greg throw another one."

"The next one Greg threw was wild and he missed me by about six feet to my left. As soon as he let fly of the second ball he went running inside. I supposed he told his father what was going on."

"'You disgust me!' were the words coming out of Marty's mouth when Greg Tyson's father came out into the yard. Marty had snatched me up by my collar and was holding me about a foot off the ground. He had a fist drawn back at me when Mr. Tyson spoke.

"'Marty Mason, I am only going to ask you once to take your hands off of that boy." Mr. Tyson was a big man and Marty barely came to his chest. He had a deep voice and he was the type that smart folks tended to listen to when he spoke.

"Marty wasn't that smart. Before he could complete the question, "Or what?" Mr. Tyson had popped him in the nose once and in the jaw once. Marty let go of me, but where was I to go? When he picked himself up, all bloody, from the yard of the Tysons he screamed at me that I was no longer welcome at his house."

"'You were just one more mouth to feed anyway!' he shouted back as he staggered down the street."

"Mr. Tyson took me inside and had Mrs. Tyson clean me up. They cleaned me up and gave me some of Greg's hand me downs to wear and they kept me for six months. I was starting to feel like I had a family again when Mr. Tyson found out he was being transferred with his job. He worked for the power company and they were building a new nuclear power plant near Waynesboro, Georgia, and he was being transferred there. They tried to take me with them, but I wasn't theirs and they were not my guardians. Anyway, they tried. They spoke with my Grandparents about adopting me, but my grandmother figured I had not suffered enough so she refused and they had to leave me. I loved living with the Tysons. For a while, I had a brother, a real sibling, nothing like my sister and I, but someone to play with and look after me."

Amelia finally interrupted me, "Whatever happened to the Tysons?"

"I don't know. They moved to Waynesboro or somewhere near there."

"Do you know where Waynesboro is?" Amelia inched closer to me as she asked.

"No, just somewhere in Georgia."

"Gabriel, it's twenty miles from Avera, on the other side of Wrens. We could try to find out if they are still there. I have family down that way. They might know them." Amelia was excited.

"It's been a long time. They probably don't even remember." I tried to settle her down.

"But you remember them and that's what matters."

I managed to get Amelia refocused so I could finish. While I had my momentum of disclosure up, I did not want to get off track. I had resolved to get all of it out in the open with her once and for all.

I proceeded to tell her all about a couple of other relatives I was shipped to before going to live with Aunt Mary and the incident with my grandmother and Mary's boyfriend. I told her about going to YDC and she was mortified.

"Everything that you had gone through had to manifest somehow," Amelia slid closer to me and reached her arms around to comfort me. "You needed some sort of therapy for everything and you got nothing but more shit dumped on you. You were just a little boy."

290

"Mary did what she could for me, but you are right about my grandmother. The best thing that ever happened to me was Mary tracking down my dad's sister and sending me to Tennessee. Other than Mary and the Tysons, they were the driving force in me making something of myself."

"It's a wonder you have turned out the way you have. It would not do for me to ever meet that grandmother of yours." Amelia's pity for me soon turned to anger toward my grandmother. "With relatives like that, one does not need enemies."

"Well, you don't have to worry about ever meeting her. She died about six years ago."

"I am surprised. Folks like her usually live forever because the devil is afraid they would take over." I think Amelia was almost disappointed in my grandmother being deceased because it prevented her from being able to tell her what she thought of her one day.

Amelia rearranged herself on the couch and backed up to me. She sat in between my legs and pulled my arms around her. She leaned her head back and rested it against my shoulder. I could smell her hair and for a moment, I was completely distracted.

I regained my senses and started again. "Things got better for me when I moved to Nashville. My record was sealed and I had a new start. Life was good. My uncle was a recruiter for the Navy and he convinced me that it might be a good option for me. I agreed and I signed up after my junior year of high school. It was like joining the reserves. The first summer I went to basic training with a group of other boys my age that were in the same program. Then during my senior year, I went one weekend a month. I also had a banner year in football and my uncle made sure the Navy guys took notice. My grades were good and my self-esteem was on the rise. Midway through the year, I found out that I had been offered a spot on the football team at the Naval Academy. Everyone on my dad's side of the family wrote letters to me congratulating me on my acceptance. It was a huge deal and I still have those letters."

Amelia turned her head toward me and I could feel her squeeze my hand. "That was awesome, Gabriel! I am so proud of you! You have accomplished so much despite everything. I can't understand why you don't want to contact anyone from your family."

"Because it is still hard for me not to think of myself as that boy who killed his parents and keeping my distance from them keeps that boy away from the man I have become."

Again, all Amelia could manage to say was, "Oh." There's no way she could have known and I could sense in her voice, from just that little word, that she felt sorry for me and I did not want that.

I brushed my cheek against her hair and whispered, begging her, "Please, don't feel sorry for me. I don't want to be that boy in your eyes."

I wanted to be her protector and the one that took care of her. I never wanted her to think of me as less than who I was, although I knew there were times in our past where she had already taken care of me.

We sat in silence for a while with Amelia's head against my chest. Our only movement was that she took my hand and placed it across her belly so I could fell the movement of the baby. Finally, Amelia spoke, but did not move a muscle to look back at me. "Beth has threatened to expose all of this about you hasn't she? She's using the stays in the youth detention center against you to try to get Gabby."

"Yes." I let my face drop and rest with a kiss on her shoulder.

Amelia leaned up and turned to face me. She took my face in her hands and directed my eyes to hers. "I don't know why you are hanging your head. You have overcome so much more than this and I am proud of you for it. It's okay to be scared for Gabby, but don't you dare let her make you feel ashamed."

Amelia sealed her words with a kiss and then I carried her to bed. It was after 1:00 a.m., but for a while, we forgot about all what we were facing from Beth, my past, wedding plans and any other worries we had.

CHAPTER 17

It was three days before we were to leave for the wedding and Amelia was already packed for the trip. Everyone she had invited had returned their R.S.V.P. cards, except the few that went out late. Those few were to my family. All of our friends and her family were coming, including Mr. Graham, Amelia's Aunt Gayle's boyfriend, and his mother. The only unknowns would be whether my Aunt Mary made it up from Florida and whether my Aunt Ella and Uncle Mike could make it from Nashville, and that's if they still lived in Nashville and received the invitation.

That afternoon, I was in the bedroom packing and getting ready for work when I heard a knock at the front door. I was expecting Amelia home from class at any moment. Other than Amelia, I was not expecting anyone, but it was not unusual for Cara, Jay or Stella to drop by unannounced. I went to the door thinking it would be one of them, but instead I was greeted by a social worker.

"Hi, I am Ms. McGuire," the woman with the clipboard and briefcase in the doorway said as she extended her free hand. "I have been appointed by the Green County Court System as Guardian Ad Litem for the minor child, Gabriella Grace Hewitt. May I come in?"

"Certainly," I said the word, but I am sure I conveyed hesitation in my voice. I led her up the stairs anyway. "Right this way."

"Thank you," she huffed after climbing the first few stairs. She was a woman of about fifty, about five foot five inches tall and probably weighed close to three hundred pounds.

I made it to the top of the stairs only to look back and find Ms. McGuire resting about halfway up. I did not know whether to offer to help her or call 911. She had already broken out in a sweat and her chest was heaving as she tried to breathe.

When she finally made it up, I offered her something to drink. "We are preparing to go out of town for the weekend, so we haven't had a chance to do much grocery shopping, but we have milk, orange juice or water."

"Ice water will be fine, thank you. May I have a seat?"

"Of course," I replied and she took a seat in the armchair to the left of the couch.

While I fixed the glass of water, Ms. McGuire took in all of the sights of the apartment. From that particular chair, she could see through the entire living room, kitchen and dining room as well as through the doorway to Gabby's nursery and our bedroom since both doors were open.

"Is the child home now?" she asked as I handed her the glass of water.

"Yes, she is sleeping." I motioned toward her room with my hand and the woman's eyes followed as if she had not already looked as much as she could through the door.

Just as Ms. McGuire started to ask if she could see Gabby, I heard the key in the door downstairs. It was Amelia.

"If you could give me just a moment, that's my fiancé coming up the stairs now," I moved from where I was standing back to the top of the staircase.

I did not wait for Amelia to reach the top before I greeted her and explained about our guest. "The Guardian Ad Litem from the court is here, Ms. McGuire."

Immediately, Amelia looked puzzled. She sat her bag down just inside the living room door and gave Ms. McGuire a good looking over as she asked me, "Did you have an appointment with her that you forgot to tell me about?"

I leaned into Amelia so as to be discrete in my response, "No, she just showed up about ten minutes ago."

"And your attorney did not make you aware that she was coming?"

"Nooooo," I drew out the word wondering what Amelia was getting at.

Amelia was polite, but firm in ending the meeting. "Ma'am, I hate that your time has been wasted, but we really cannot meet with you without our attorney present. If you would like to schedule an appointment through his office, we would be more than happy to accommodate you, but meetings in this manner are improper since we are represented by counsel. I really am sorry for your trouble. Gabe will see you to your car."

As I watched and listened, my eyes grew wide with surprise and so did those of Ms. McGuire as Amelia politely told her to get out. I was impressed with Amelia and admired that she did it with such legal ease. She hardly batted an eye.

Ms. McGuire gathered her things and I escorted her down the stairs. This time they proved to be far less challenging for her than the trip up had been.

As soon as she was on her way, I returned upstairs to find Amelia fuming. She was coming out of Gabby's room from checking on her when I exited the stairwell.

"Did she show you any credentials?" Amelia demanded.

"No, she just told me who she was and..."

"They don't just show up like that, Gabriel. They make appointments with your attorney and you meet them at his office. This isn't passing the smell test, Gabriel. You need to call Attorney Ellis right now and let him know about this."

I did as Amelia asked and dialed the number to my attorney's office. His assistant answered and got him on the phone straight away once I told her why I was calling.

"Gabe, now tell me what just went on," Attorney Ellis was definitely interested in what I had to say. "Someone claiming to be a Guardian Ad Litem stopped by?"

"Yes, a Ms. McGuire from the Green County Courts, that's how she identified herself," I explained.

"Gabriel, there's been no one appointed at this time and any meeting would be set up through my office. There's not even been

295

mention that your case might warrant such an appointment." I could hear shuffling of papers on his desk as he spoke.

"Then who was this?" My thoughts started to race and what I thought came out of my mouth, "I let this woman in my home. She asked to see Gabby, but luckily Amelia came home. Oh my God, I was about to..."

"Just calm down now, I don't know who she was, but I will see what I can find out. Maybe there's something I don't know. I will call the judge's office and see what I can find out."

"Okay. Okay," I repeated myself, trying to calm down.

All I could think was, what if Amelia had not come home? At this point, I did not know what Beth was capable of and what if she hired someone to take Gabby? I was a mix of emotions: fear and infuriation all at once. I paced while I was on the phone and Amelia listened in the background. My tone had awakened Gabby and Amelia tended to her so that I could focus on the phone and try to calm down.

"By the way, while I've got you on the phone, I looked into that other matter you asked me about last week, the matter of the insurance," Attorney Ellis' voice changed and it was lighter as he reminded me of the other task I had given him.

After my full disclosure to Amelia regarding my childhood, it occurred to me that I never knew what my grandmother did with the insurance money from my parents' death. For all I knew, she spent it, but according to Amelia she could not have spent it because she was only the trustee and I was likely the beneficiary. As it turned out, Amelia was learning a great deal in her first semester of law school and what she was not already being taught in her classes she never hesitated to ask her professors and then report back. Amelia was proving to be quite the asset in more ways than one.

"And what did you find out?" I was curious, but also knew that despite the law, it was very likely that my grandmother squandered the money.

"I called the county in Florida where your grandmother was a resident when she died. I found the name and number of the

296

attorney who probated her will and called him. I had him fax copies of your grandmother's will and all of the estate documents to me."

"I knew she had died, but..."

"You didn't think about what that really meant to you?" Attorney Ellis was quite excited about what he found and had cut me off. "I know, you told me your mother was an only child and therefore you would take the place of your mother as her heir. For your grandmother's estate to have been properly disposed, you would have had to have been listed as an heir. You would have had to have been contacted and made to sign off on the documents."

"Even if I was left out of the will?" I asked. None of this was making much sense to me. I had put the phone on speaker so Amelia could listen and she was nodding her head in the affirmative.

"Yes, they have to list all heirs whether or not they are to inherit anything or not. In this case, the only heir listed is your grandfather."

"Is he still alive?"

Attorney Ellis was sidetracked by my question, but answered and then continued, "Yes, but the thing is, you have a case to reopen your grandmother's estate."

For some strange reason a feeling of relief came over me at the thought of my grandfather still being alive. I had not thought of him much in years, but I always remembered him being kind to me. The only thing I ever faulted him with was not being a stronger man and standing up to my grandmother. He treated her like a queen and she treated him like dirt beneath her feet. I think I always saw a kindred spirit in him.

"I don't want anything from him. There is no case." I was firm in my response and Amelia's eyes grew big. "I just want what's mine, if there's anything left."

"Well, the attorney for the estate put me in touch with your grandfather. He wants to see you. He wants to give you what's left of the money in person."

"What?" That was not what I was expecting to hear.

"Yes, apparently your Aunt Mary received an invitation and he wants to attend your wedding as her guest, but would not come until he received word from you that you wanted to see him."

Amelia had been sitting in the armchair holding Gabby in her arms and I was on the couch with the phone in my hands. Amelia shifted Gabby to one arm and leaned and took my hand. She squeezed my hand and pulled my gaze from the phone to her, "It's your choice. If you want to put this off until after the wedding, that's fine or if you want to have him come, that's up to you."

I redirected my attention to the phone and Attorney Ellis on the other end of the line. "May I call you back in just a few minutes and let you know my decision?"

"Of course," he replied and then we said our goodbyes.

The receiver was barely down when Amelia asked, "What are you going to do?"

"It is your wedding too, what do you want to do?"

"Oh no, I am not making this decision for you."

"I don't know what I want to do. You know, it was a big step in just letting you send the invitations to my aunts. I kind of thought they would get lost in the mail or have bad addresses and then we could just move on with our lives. Now, here we are within days of the wedding..."

"Gabriel, what does your gut tell you?"

"Right now it's telling me I better get dressed for work and get on the road." I changed the subject and left the room to think about what to do.

I had no gut feeling one way or the other, which in itself was strange. My first instinct was usually to avoid the topic of my family altogether, but for once the prospect of seeing my grandfather gave me pause. This was a new feeling for me.

I quickly changed from my jeans and t-shirt into my work attire all the while not knowing what to do; extend an invitation to my grandfather or not. I had not seen him in almost fifteen years. Amelia had already told me she wasn't going to make the decision for me, but I did think about what she would do if she were in this situation. One of the things I admired about Amelia was that she was always willing to meet a problem head on no matter what the outcome might be. I decided I would try living by her example.

As soon as I finished dressing, I returned to the living room. I stood and took Gabby from Amelia and paced with her while working up the courage to commit to what I was thinking. It took me a moment, but I finally came out with it, "What's your saying about 'the more the merrier'? But, let me assure you, Mrs. Hewitt, this day is about me and you and that's it. Satan himself could show up and I promise I will not let anything ruin our day."

"Then that's settled," Amelia sighed as she handed me the phone to dial Attorney Ellis again.

About twenty minutes had passed between hanging up with Attorney Ellis and calling him back. I handed Gabby back to Amelia as I dialed the numbers. The phone rang twice before his assistant answered and put me through to him.

Before I could get the words out of my mouth, Attorney Ellis began apologizing, "Gabe, it appears there has been a bit of a mix up. There has been a guardian ad litem appointed in your custody case. I called the judge's office and found out that an order had been issued. I am not sure why I did not receive notice, but setting that aside, Ms. McGuire is new to her post. She came to us from the Department of Family and Children Services. I have spoken to her and she has apologized profusely for overstepping, but in her last post, it was common practice to show up at the residence of the child unannounced. I have explained to her that that is not how things are conducted in legal matters such as this. She sends her apologies and she also mentioned that in the brief time she was in your home, she could not find anything amiss with the child's living conditions."

"I guess that's good to hear," I replied and Amelia looked on. I shrugged my shoulders at her and gave her the indication that I would explain what he had said as soon as I was off the phone. This time, I had not thought to put the phone on speaker.

"Yes, it's good. Even though things did not start off in the typical manner, you made a first impression on Ms. McGuire and it was a good impression, so yes, that's good," Mr. Ellis congratulated me.

"I was also calling to let you know that I am fine with you extending the invitation to my grandfather." The words left my mouth and again it was strange that they did not taste like vinegar as they rolled off my tongue.

I glanced at Amelia and she gave a nod. It was about the equivalent of a pat on the back without her raising a hand. I winked back at her.

"I will make the call as soon as we hang up." I could tell from the spring in his voice that Mr. Ellis was likely pleased with my decision as well.

Once off the phone, I kissed Amelia and Gabby goodbye and started down the stairs. I had to get on the road or I really was going to be late. Halfway down the stairs, I turned back. I ran back up and found Amelia putting Gabby in her crib. There was surprise on her face when she turned back to me.

"Did you forget something?" she asked.

I whirled her around and pulled her into my arms. Amelia let out a bit of a laugh.

"I did. I forgot to tell you just how much I love you, Mrs. Hewitt, and I could not face any of this without you. Three more days until you are officially mine and I can hardly wait! I just wanted you to know that." I kissed her again and that time, I really left for work.

...

Two days later we were on our way back up Highway 441 toward Glenn Ella Springs. There was an entire caravan of us traveling one car behind the other from Milledgeville. Amelia, Gabby

300

and I were in my car in front followed by Jay, his sister and Cara in another car and behind them were Travis and Stella. The last car held Jay's Aunt June and Uncle Dwight until Daniel and Jerry fell in behind us as we passed through Eatonton.

There was another caravan coming out of Jefferson County and headed up through Thomson and to Athens the same as us. Amelia's Aunt Gayle was riding with Mr. Graham and his mother. They were followed by Aunt Dot and Uncle Jim. Jay's parents joined that caravan as they passed through Thomson.

Alvin was handling the club that night and he was going to drive up after he finished. Matt was going to ride with him. The plan was for Alvin to prep sandwiches and everything for the day shift and Andy would handle everything from the bar. Andy also agreed to work a double on Saturday so everyone else could attend the wedding. Kelly also stayed behind to wait tables. We had held on to the new sous chef at the club even after the Olympics and he was getting his first chance to run the kitchen alone on Saturday and Sunday.

At first, we thought that Jerry was going to have to stay behind to wait tables, but at the very last minute, Joan showed up and volunteered to help out. She also offered the services of her son, Jason, as well. I had not heard from her since the night I threatened to drop Gabby on her doorstep, but on Wednesday night she showed up in the kitchen.

"Gabriel, may I have a word with you?" I recognized her voice even though I was facing the stove and had my back turned to the prep line. I turned around to find Joan standing on the other side of the stainless steel shelves that made up the line.

"Sure, just give me one moment," I said as I handed the whisk to Alvin and explained to him what I had been doing. I was prepping a port wine reduction sauce to top the beef tenderloin that we were offering as one of the night's specials.

I took off my apron as I headed down the line. Joan followed on the opposite side until we turned and I led her to the back loading dock.

As soon as the kitchen door closed behind us, Joan began to apologize, "I know the trouble my husband has caused you and I'm so terribly sorry. I cannot guarantee you anything, but I am working on what you asked me to, to get him to sign over his rights. Anyway, I heard about the wedding and I wanted to wish you the best of luck."

Joan paused to take a breath and I could see tears building in her eyes. She really was a good person and I had felt badly ever since I had been such an asshole to her. She did not deserve what she got from Dick and I'm sure I only compounded her problems by rubbing her face in his infidelity.

"I know the club is going to be short-handed because of the wedding and Dick is counting on that, so he can fire you when you get back." Joan sniffled to suck back the tears.

"What? The club's going to be fine. I have..."

I could feel my face getting hot when Joan interrupted me, "I know it's going to be fine. I'm going to wait tables for you and my son Jason's going to help. We'll pick up whatever slack there is to pick up and your job will be safe when you return. Although at this point, I don't know why you'd still want it."

As I continued to lead the caravan up the road toward Glen Ella, Amelia and I discussed my conversation with Joan. I told Amelia about Joan volunteering her and her son to pick up the slack while everyone was away. In that conversation, I told Amelia how I had threatened Joan. Amelia was not happy that I would ever threaten to give Gabby up and I had some explaining to do.

"What would you have done if she had told you to bring Gabby on over that night?" Amelia gasped as I finished telling her about the conversation with Joan the day I found out Beth was counter-suing me and had claimed that I had a history of violence.

"I guess I did not think it through. All I could think about that day was strangling everyone but you and sticking it to Dick was the next best thing. Admittedly, I did not go about it the right way."

"My granddaddy always said, 'Two wrongs don't make a right.'"

"In case I have not told you before, your granddaddy was a wise man." Keeping one hand on the steering wheel, I pulled her hand to my lips and kissed it after I paid my compliment. I knew she and her grandfather were right and I had known all along that lashing out at Joan to get at Dick was despicable.

The drive was passing by quickly even though we had ridden in silence all the way from Athens to Commerce. I kept coming back to what Joan said about if I still wanted the job. I was working up the words to talk to Amelia about it when she broke the silence.

"What are you thinking about?" Amelia asked.

"Joan said the reason she was going to help out this weekend was because Dick was going to use anything that went wrong as an excuse to fire me when we got back from the wedding. She assured me things would be fine and my job would be safe and then commented, 'Even though I don't know why you would still want it at this point.'"

"Do you want to stay on there?" Amelia turned in her seat to get a better view of me as we talked.

I glanced back at her, "I don't know. I love the members and my friends are the staff, but I resent that Dick and Beth have almost tainted it for me. I despise that man and my skin crawls every time I am reminded that he is my boss."

"Do you want to start looking for something else?" Amelia inquired.

"I don't mind the work and I don't want to let them run me off. I feel like I'm caught. I don't know what to do."

"Maybe the right thing to do is stay the course so you can keep track of him, at least as long as the custody is in dispute? I know what Joan said, but don't you think after all this time that he's a little more scared of you than you are of being fired?"

"I suppose you have a point." I paused for a moment before asking a question of my own. "Amelia, how did you get so smart?"

The question came from her always knowing the right thing to say. Amelia was wise beyond her years. Whenever I had a problem, she always knew just what to do and ninety-nine percent of the time she was right. I'm not saying I let her make my decisions for me, but if ever I needed advice, Amelia's was always spot on.

Amelia gave an answer. It was a simple, "I don't know."

In thinking all of this about her, I reminded myself again just how young she was. At twenty-one years old, I was still in the Naval Academy. I didn't have a care in the world. I didn't even give a thought to the fact that I was about to enter the full blown Navy and it certainly did not register that they were going to ship me to an aircraft carrier in Japan.

I looked over at Amelia and she was just staring out at the road ahead. She had rolled her hair that day and it hung in soft curls around her face and down her back. Her make-up was subtle like usual and I could see the dimples in her cheeks when she smiled. She was five months pregnant and although she wasn't huge, there was no mistaking it in the shorts and T-shirt she had on. Amelia was a mother to a three month old daughter, pregnant with another daughter, a college graduate, a law school student, the owner of an apartment building, a millionaire and this was the day before she was to get married. She looked so fresh and young. At twenty-one her life was so full compared to how mine had been. I am not sure how anyone would not be amazed by her.

Amelia cut her eyes at me and caught me looking. "What are you looking at?"

"You," I answered.

Amelia blushed and gave a slight smile and changed the subject by looking to the back seat. She commented on Gabby, "I can't believe she is going to sleep the entire way there."

"I can. She sleeps all the time," I looked in the rearview mirror, but I could only see the top of the carrier.

"I wonder if Beth misses her." Amelia turned back to me and there was a look of sad curiosity on her face. She rubbed her hand across her stomach. "I couldn't imagine giving birth and never getting to see her or hold her."

"Are you feeling sorry for Beth?" Now that was something I was curious about, but not the least bit sad over.

"No, just wondering how she could let you drive away from the hospital that day with her baby."

"Does this have anything to do with your mother letting you go?"

Amelia took a moment to think before answering. "I could see how you might think that, but no, I know my mother's motive. I wonder what Beth's is."

"I don't know and I don't really care," I am certain I sounded heartless, but I really didn't care. "As far as I am concerned, Gabby is ours now."

Amelia's face lit up at my statement. "She's ours," she repeated.

"Yep, unless or until the Green County Judge tells us otherwise."

"I am learning a lot at school, like nothing is certain in the law. They call it 'the practice of law' for a reason. So, as much as I know Beth should never end up with Gabby, I just wonder what the odds are of her being able to take Gabby back at some point."

I had let go of Amelia's hand at one of the last turns, but I reached over and took it back. I could tell this was something that worried her. I held her hand close to my chest in a gesture to assure her, "I won't let that happen."

"Sometimes things are out of your control, Gabriel. Most of the time, even bad mothers are awarded their children."

I had once worried about Amelia accepting Gabby, but it turned out that I had worried for nothing. Amelia had the biggest heart of anyone I knew and now there was a glimpse of how her heart would be broken if we lost Gabby. In all honesty, we would both be broken hearted.

"I am telling you Amelia, I won't let anyone take her away from us. Now, let's put all of that out of our heads for the remainder of the weekend. We will have plenty of time to discuss all of this once we are back home after the wedding. I don't want one more mention of Beth Reed. Do I make myself clear?"

"Yes, sir, Mr. Hewitt." Amelia pressed her lips together and gave me another smile, a reluctant smile.

The radio had been on the entire trip, but it was turned down low for background noise. As we continued along in silence, Amelia reached over and turned up the radio.

"I like this song," she said as she adjusted the dial to try to make it come in clearer.

We were headed into the foothills and the stations from Atlanta faded in and out a bit. In and out came the words of John Mellencamp's "Key West Intermezzo." Amelia sang along and when the station cut out, she filled in the gaps. I joined in on the chorus and we danced in our seats. Amelia kept up with the rhythm and pointed to me here and there as if she were singing to me and acting out the song. The feeling and the spirit inside the car at that moment was the way I wanted the whole weekend to be.

When the song finished, Amelia mentioned that John Mellencamp was one of her favorite singers.

"Remember when he first came out, he called himself John Cougar?" I was older than she was so she may not have been old enough to remember.

"Oh, I remember. I never did understand what the deal was that made him change. I don't care what his name is, I like his music."

"You like 'Pink Houses'?"

"Yeah, but I wouldn't want to live in one," Amelia laughed. "I like 'Wild Nights' better."

"Do you now?"

I had nearly forgotten how well versed in music Amelia was. Between all that she had going on with school and Gabby and planning for the wedding, she had hardly played anything since she came home from the hospital after the bombing. Although I waited a moment, I felt it was a good time to ask her about it. I wanted to make sure that her lack of playing really was due to her time constraints and nothing else.

"And I want to go to Key West. What about you?"

"Sure. We could do that. Maybe a honeymoon there."

Amelia rubbed her belly, "We'll have to get a sitter."

I glanced to the back seat, "Or take them with us."

"On a honeymoon?"

This time I reached over and placed my hand on the little baby bump. "By the time you are free from school and in any condition to take a honeymoon, it won't exactly be a honeymoon anymore."

Amelia laughed and I changed the subject.

"You have not been playing much lately. Why is that?" I asked her.

Amelia shrugged her shoulders. "I really haven't had the time."

"And, you swear that's all it is?" If she had answered honestly, I was relieved, but there was something nagging at me. It sounded like a cop out.

"That's all there is," she paused, giving herself away.

"There's more to it."

"I have to feel like playing or there's no use. Aunt Gayle says I have an artist temperament."

307

"What does that mean?"

"It means, I have to be in the mood and I haven't been in the mood lately."

"Why not?"

"Your guess is as good as mine."

My guess was that there was too much going on for her and she was likely stressed. Any normal person would be. "Perhaps things will slow down for you after the wedding and maybe you will get your mojo back when it comes to your music."

"My mojo?" Amelia questioned my use of the word 'mojo' with a laugh.

It wasn't long before we were at the turn off from Historic 441 onto the road that would take us toward Bear Gap and on to Glen Ella Springs. I forgot the turn because I wasn't familiar with the area and had only been there once. Amelia forgot the turn because we were talking and singing along with the radio at the same time. This was not the first time she had forgotten to remind me of a turn, but it was the first time that I was nearly rear-ended by three car loads of people we knew when I came to a screeching halt and slid into the turn at the last minute.

"Jesus, Amelia! A little more notice next time! Jay nearly hit us and Travis nearly hit him and your Aunt Gayle just fishtailed it to avoid Travis and the ditch."

"Sorry."

Just a few more minutes and then we turned in at the inn. This time I saw the building coming, so there was no missing the turn. There was an elderly man standing outside next to the wishing well at the inn. He had a cane and that hat that he always wore. It had been so many years that it stood to reason that I would not have recognized him, but I did. It wasn't the worn brown fedora or the mustache that gave him away. It was the overall picture. He looked almost exactly the same as the last time I saw him. The only difference was that his hair had turned white over the years and he appeared far more frail than I would have imagined he could ever be. It was my grandfather and I knew him as soon as I laid eyes on him.

He squinted his eyes beneath his glasses to try to get a better look at us. Amelia was only steps behind me and I had my hands full with a few pieces of our luggage. I paused in my tracks for a second when I first rounded the path from the parking lot and saw him up close. Aside from the recognition of him, I did not know what to think. I know I had agreed to him coming, but there he was in the flesh. I could not say that I had completely thought it through. I was quick to gather my thoughts and keep moving forward before Amelia ran into the back of me.

"Gabriel Hewitt?" the elderly man questioned. I had recognized him, but he was not sure about me.

"Yes, sir," I answered as I approached him.

I know I had a look of skepticism on my face. I sat our bags down and dropped my hand back to catch Amelia's. As sure as I was that the old man was likely harmless, I was sure that I needed her support in this moment. Amelia did exactly as I had hoped she would. She sat Gabby's carrier down on the sidewalk. She took my hand and stepped close enough to me that I could feel her body brushing against my arm. She did not say a word, she just stood there observing and Gabby was again asleep in her carrier.

"Is that really you?" He sought confirmation.

I nodded my head.

He looked me up and down as he spoke, "You probably don't remember me, but I'm your grandfather."

"I remember you," I acknowledged. I still could not bring myself to start a full-on conversation with him. This was just too surreal for me.

"I remember you too and you sure are taller than the last time I saw you." He took off his hat and rubbed his head before patting down what little white hair he had left.

He was right, I was quite a bit taller. I had last seen him when I was thirteen and was sent away to the youth detention center my first time. I did not remember my father as a tall man, but looking at him, I knew my height must have come from my father's side of the family. This man, my mother's father, was hardly taller than Amelia.

My grandfather continued to take in the sight of me, but finally he took notice of Amelia and I felt obligated to introduce the two of them. "This is my fiancé, Amelia Anderson."

Amelia extended her hand to him. "You can call me Millie." She glanced up at me, "Everyone else does except Gabriel."

He shook her hand, but turned his attention back to me. I don't believe he was trying to be rude to her. I just think he could not help himself.

"You go by Gabriel now?"

"No," I looked to her and smiled, "She just calls me that."

"Ah," he sighed. "And who is that?" He pointed to Gabby who was starting to stir in her seat.

"That's our daughter," Amelia said as she turned a little toward her. She also gave away her condition.

"So, I have a great-granddaughter and..." He paused, looking curiously at Amelia's protruding belly.

"It's a long story," I interjected.

There was someone else coming up the walkway and that was enough of a distraction to keep me from having to explain further or ask him if I may explain later. Surely his wheels were turning. Gabby was obviously only a few months old and there was my finance already pregnant again. I could see how that would make one take pause.

"This is my Aunt Gayle and Aunt Dot," Amelia gestured to her aunts who were being followed by her Uncle Jim and their luggage.

310

While my grandfather explained his relation, Aunt Mary emerged from the front door of the inn. Before she realized we were all standing out there with him, she announced to him, "Uncle Martin, our rooms are ready."

Amelia was still making the introductions and Mary soon realized she was speaking over everyone. From the moment I first heard the door open and saw her, I could not take my eyes off of her. I am not sure if she looked exactly like my mother or if I had confused the memory of the two.

"Gabe, is that you?!!" She screamed as soon as she saw me. She ran to me, cutting between Amelia and my grandfather, and threw her arms around my neck. Her weight fully went on to me and I took a couple of steps back to regain my balance.

"Let me look at you," she said ecstatically as she released me. Tears filled her eyes as she looked at me. "There's not a day that goes by that I have not thought of you."

Everyone just stood watching us. I could feel tears coming to my own eyes. I did not know what to say. I could not tell her that I had tried not to think of her or them or anyone related to me for that matter. I had tried to forget my childhood and everyone in it.

As much as Mary looked me over, I did the same in return. It appeared the years had been kind to her. She was four years younger than my mother and my mother was thirty two when she died. Mary would have been twenty-eight when Mother died and that would make her fifty-nine now. She looked younger than that. As far as I could remember, her hair color was the same, likely dyed this color at this stage in her life. She was a couple of inches taller than my grandfather and was thin. She was not one of those women who gained ten pounds every ten years.

I guess Amelia could tell I was stuck in the moment so she stepped forward and introduced herself. "You must be Gabriel's Aunt Mary."

Amelia had hardly finished her statement before the two women were hugging. I probably was not supposed to hear, but

Amelia whispered to Mary, "He was lucky to have you and he may not show it, but he thought of you, too."

"Aren't you the sweetest thing?" Mary gushed over Amelia.

"Thank you, ma'am," Amelia graciously accepted the compliment.

After all of the introductions were made, Amelia and her family excused themselves.

"We are just going to go and get checked in and give y'all a little chance to catch up." She bent down and picked up Gabby and her carrier. "I'll take her with me if you will bring the luggage when you come."

"I can come with you," I tried to offer, but she would have none of it.

"Gabriel, see to your guests." I did not realize it at the time, but her point was for me to get all of my business with them out of the way before the rehearsal dinner and the wedding.

Amelia was soon in the door of the inn with her aunts and her uncle. The rest of the caravan had passed us and were already checked in by the time she went inside.

"We still have to take our luggage to our rooms and I'm sure you probably feel compelled to do the same, so why don't we take care of that and then meet back up on the porch?" Mary asked.

"That sounds like a fine idea. It looks like the porch wraps around both levels and there are rocking chairs out in front of the rooms," my grandfather added.

"I could meet y'all in front of your rooms in about fifteen minutes, if that's enough time for you?" I asked.

"That would be wonderful. I have already forgotten the room number, but it's the first room on the back side on the first floor. Your grandfather is next door to me."

"Alright, I will come around to find y'all in about fifteen minutes or do you need help bringing your things in from the car?"

"Oh, no, we don't have much and I can get it. It was very nice of you to offer and I just cannot get over how tall and handsome you are; that you've grown up so much." Mary shook her head in disbelief.

I was in a bit of disbelief myself. I just could not believe they were here.

I quickly found Amelia as she was on her way to one of the penthouse rooms. Her room was on the third floor. I took Gabby from her and left our suitcases by the base of the stairs. We talked as we climbed the stairs.

"Do you mind terribly if I hang out with them for a little while?" I asked her.

"Do I mind? I wish you would. I could use a little nap."

"Are you trying to get rid of me already, Mrs. Hewitt?"

"You are probably going to think that when I show you to your room," she laughed.

I stopped at the base of the next flight of stairs. "What do you mean?"

"Gabby and I are bunking with Aunt Gayle and you are bunking in a room on the second floor."

"What?" We had hardly been apart a night since she came home from the bombing and I had not considered that we would not be in the same room that night.

"I just thought, before the wedding and all..."

I shot a look to her stomach, "You are kidding right?"

"No, but I get what you are implying and that's very judgmental of you." Amelia caught her breath from the climb of the first flight and started up the second. "You will sleep downstairs and then tomorrow night you will come to my room. Aunt Gayle will go

313

into the other penthouse with Mr. Graham and his mother will go to your room. It's all settled."

"All settled?"

"Yes, all settled."

"Like musical beds."

"Say what you will, but we have enough bad luck without you seeing me before the wedding."

"You mean I don't get to see you at all tomorrow? The wedding does not start until 5:00 p.m."

Our feet hit the landing at the top at the same time and Amelia let out a huff. "I know and you'll live."

Of the two doors on the third floor, Amelia unlocked the one on the left and I followed her inside. As soon as I was inside, I sat Gabby down in the carrier. "There's something I need to get me through this or I cannot agree."

Amelia was nearly to the bed when she turned back to me, "And what's that?"

I made my way across the room to her. "May I?" I had not asked permission in a while, but the way she answered always turned me on. It was just one word, but I wanted to hear her say it.

"Please."

CHAPTER 18

It was quarter 'til five, September 21, 1996.

Behind the Glen Ella Springs Inn was a meadow and under the shade of an oak tree were six rows of white chairs, divided down the middle by a single aisle. There were stakes in the ground shooting up four feet in the air with bouquets of green hydrangeas and white daisies atop them. The flowers matched the green of the grass in the meadow perfectly. Each pole of flowers was linked by a drape of white toile, roping off the center aisle and reserving it for the feet of Amelia and her bridal party only.

The wedding march had yet to begin, but soft music from a lone piano floated through the air. Most everyone was in their seats and my groomsmen were behind me. The wedding party was stacked in Amelia's favor as she had Jay as her maid of honor, and Cara and her cousin Dixie as her bridesmaids. I only had my grandfather and Daniel.

Surprisingly enough, I asked my grandfather to be my best man. Initially, Daniel was to be my best man, but after the events and conversations of the day before, he had been demoted. Daniel did not seem to mind and, in fact, both he and Amelia were quite surprised and pleased with the turn of events.

There was nothing to do as I stood there, other than take it all in. My knees were starting to shake a little, not from nervousness, but from anticipation. I was ringing wet with sweat for the same reason.

That morning it had rained and Amelia had sent me a note that read, "It's supposed to be good luck if it rains on your wedding day and I wish you all the luck in the world. I hope it pours!" By noon, the rain had cleared up and it was sunny the rest of the day. It was not hot out and by this time of the day, the sun had already started to set behind the mountains that surrounded the inn. There was a breeze blowing across my face and through my hair and I could see it shifting the leaves in the trees and the hem of Cara's dress.

Jay, Cara and Dixie were waiting across the meadow to lead the way for Amelia to come down the aisle. I could see them clearly from the distance, but I could not see hide nor hair of Amelia and her aunt.

Ordinarily, I would not notice every detail of a day, but this day was the culmination of my life thus far and I was certain to remember absolutely everything. It was as if my senses were on hyper-drive and every moment sparked the birth of a new memory and the recollection of an old one.

I knew there were only minutes left before I would see her. I was anxious to get a glimpse of her. There was no question in my mind that Amelia would be the most beautiful bride, the most beautiful woman I had ever seen. I knew this because she had been since the moment I first saw her last September. As I waited and looked for her across the field from the inn, I thought about all the moments we had shared in this last year and all that we had been through. I thought about all of that including the rehearsal dinner and the time we spent alone after it.

As I waited my mind slipped away to memories of the night before. Amelia had rented out the entire inn as she said she would and the place was alive with all of our friends and family.

At the insistence of Amelia's Aunt Gayle, each guest took a turn speaking about us and giving a toast at dinner. Gayle led with the first toast, "To my beautiful girl, I have loved you all your life and from what I have learned of Gabe, he has loved you all of his. I think he loved you even before he met you."

"I knew from the first time you said his name, that you had found what you thought was a prize and when I saw you together at Thanksgiving, it was confirmed. I knew he was the one and that was concerning for me because you have always been my prize. Then, the things y'all went through and your heart was shattered." Gayle paused and shook her head and wiped away tears.

"We won't talk about that. Then, there were those days in the hospital. Those days were awful for all of us, but maybe for him most of all. I have never seen a man more broken-hearted. I think he might have died right along with you. There wasn't a soul that saw the two of you that week that wasn't broken hearted for him as he worried about you. If Gabby had had anyone else, he would have never left your side. We all knew it."

Amelia gripped my hand and looked away to hide her own tears as Gayle spoke.

"Anyway," her aunt went on, "there's not many people that can say they are loved like that, but I am so proud of the two of you and so happy that you are those people."

Gayle stopped again and everyone raised their glasses thinking she was finished, but she cleared her throat and added a little something more. "Gabriel, as proud as I am of you and as happy as I am to have you join our family, just know, if you ever hurt or disappoint Millie again, in the immortal words of Dolly Parton in '9 to 5', 'I'm gonna get that gun in my purse and change you from a rooster to a hen in one shot and don't think I can't do it!'"

I shifted in my seat and crossed my legs for comedic effect as the whole room broke up in laughter. Amelia rolled her eyes and laughed right along with them while Gayle returned to her chair.

The next up was Jay, then Cara, and so on. There was no particular order to who spoke when, but finally Amelia's cousin Dixie stood up. She introduced herself and Amelia glanced back to me. I am sure I had a distracted look on my face because I could never get past how opposite in the looks department she was from Amelia. I could not fathom that those two were swimming anywhere near the same gene pool.

"I'm Millie's cousin, Dixie. We grew up together and somewhere along the way we developed this fierce competition. I don't know why it started, but I did my level best to keep up with her. If she did it, I felt the need to do it bigger and better. I know I was the family's running joke for a while over my efforts to play the cello. Seriously, Millie took up the fiddle and she could play it like a house on fire. I picked up the cello and strained to even carry it let alone make it carry a tune. There were more instances than one like that and one day my daddy had a talk with me and explained poker. I did not particularly get it at the time, but he said, 'Darlin' sometimes you knowin' when yer beat is as important as winnin.' Not long after that

I accepted that Millie had beat me, but when she showed up to Thanksgiving with *him*. Oh my God! Let's just say I hated her because I wanted to be her."

The whole room gasped at that inappropriate speech. I think my gasp might have been heard the loudest. The only one who did not gasp was Jerry and he laughed openly. I could see him elbow punch Daniel in the side and snicker, "As if she was in the ballpark. Ha!"

Before the poor girl could embarrass herself further, Stella leapt to her feet and started her toast. She went on and on about what great parents we were to Gabby and just wonderful friends to have. "Millie would come get you off the side of the road in the middle of the night even if you called her from a roadside in California. She would come, that's just the type of friend she is. And, Gabe, I have no doubt would do the same. They are the definition of 'good people' and I'm lucky to know y'all. Here's to Millie and Gabe!"

The speeches went on until my grandfather stood up. I was nervous about what he might say. The afternoon had gone so well, but a lifetime of distance and resentment was a lot to expect anyone to get past in one afternoon and I was not sure if I could do it.

Like everyone else, he began by introducing himself, "You all don't know me, but I'm Martin Verde, Gabe's grandfather and I would like to thank Gabe for growing up to be a man that his mother would have been proud of. It takes a lot for me to say this because it makes me admit my own shortcomings, but the man you see before you, Gabe Hewitt, is a good man despite me and my family. I am ashamed of the way we treated him and I'm so very thankful that he has found love. If anyone deserves it, my grandson does. I'm also thankful to Amelia for helping to bring him back to me and thankful to all of you good folks for listening to this old man tonight. I have no right to ask and I certainly have no right to ask right now, but no one is ever promised tomorrow, so I am asking right here in front of you all..."

He stopped and hung his head and the tears that had gathered in his eyes rolled down his cheeks. He took a handkerchief from his pocket and wiped his face before continuing. "In front of

318

you all, I ask my grandson to forgive me. The depths of my sorrow for how we neglected him after his parents died knows no bounds. I know these words cannot undo anything, but I would like the chance to get to know the man you all know."

I gripped Amelia's hand the entire time he spoke and turned away several times to discretely wipe away my own tears. He had already apologized to me earlier in the afternoon and I shrugged him off. "All of that is water under the bridge," I had told him dismissively when he admitted that letting my grandmother control the situation with me was the worst mistake of his life. Now, as I did earlier, I could tell this was something that had eaten at him for a very long time.

As my grandfather neared the closing of his speech, Amelia reached her free arm around me and laid her head against my shoulder. She whispered to me, "No one will think any less of you if you cry or if you get up and hug him."

When he finished, I left Amelia and went to him. I gathered the old man in my arms and held him. "It's okay," I told him and he sobbed.

"I know I have been a failure to you and to your mother and you will never know how truly sorry I am. Thank you for inviting me today and I'm sorry if I've made a spectacle of myself in front of your friends." He continued to cry.

I just shook my head, "No spectacle," I said and before I knew it the words escaped my lips, "I love you, Granddad. Please don't cry for me. I have turned out fine and I am happy."

Finally, Aunt Mary joined us and the three of us managed to agree to put the past behind us. It was as if a great weight had been lifted off of me and I needed to tell Amelia. I needed to thank her for pushing me into this.

Once we had all calmed down, I asked Aunt Mary if she and Granddad were up to it and if they wouldn't mind looking after Gabby for me for a little while. Both of them were overjoyed that I would ask.

"I am a great-grandfather now," he aired his observation. "I suppose there's no time like the present to start spoiling her."

"Uncle Martin, you be careful, maybe Gabe doesn't want her spoiled," Aunt Mary cautioned him with a bit of teasing.

"You bring me that baby," he insisted. For a man of his age, he was quite spry.

I found Amelia and took Gabby from her. "Wait right here, I'll be back."

The dessert plates were being cleared when I returned and offered Amelia my hand. "Come with me," I instructed her.

Amelia smiled that high wattage smile of hers and took my hand and we slipped away. Out a side door I led her and down the steps to the meadow behind the inn. "I want a few minutes alone with you, Miss Anderson."

"What became of Mrs. Hewitt?" she asked as she followed.

"She will be back tomorrow."

We continued to walk until we came to the beginnings of what would become our wedding site tomorrow. The chairs were already out in rows, but little else had been done that night. I stopped just shy of the oak tree at the head of the aisle where the alter would be.

"You know, the groom's family was supposed to pay for the rehearsal dinner." I gave Amelia a subtle chastising because when I went to pay the bill, it had already been paid.

I towered over her and propped my hand against the tree above her head. Amelia leaned against the tree and peered up at me, "I *am* your family."

"Not until tomorrow, so you should not have paid for tonight."

"You know I've been yours since the day I first saw you." Amelia batted her eyelashes at me.

"Have you?"

"Like you didn't know," Amelia said softly as she bit the left side of her bottom lip.

I leaned into the tree and into her. As if I had not had enough tears for the night already, I felt them coming again. This was not me. I wasn't a crier, but that didn't matter. "I love you," I whispered to her as I rested my forehead against hers.

Something caught her eye back toward the inn and Amelia turned her head for a better look. She quickly turned back and buried her face in my chest and clutched fists full of my shirt around my back. "They are all watching us."

I looked toward the inn and she was right. Everyone from the rehearsal dinner had made their way to the balcony and they were watching us.

I lifted her chin. "Then we should give them a show."

While we were discussing it, a collective chant came from the inn, "Kiss her! Kiss her! Kiss her!"

I obliged. Amelia had the faint taste of the chocolate cake that had been served for dessert. We kissed every single day, but nothing like this. This was the equivalent of the kiss underneath the streetlight on the walk back from The Brick the night of our first date. This was the kiss that did not need to lead to anything else; it was long and wet and could stand alone when it came to communication and satisfaction. I could tell Amelia a thousand times verbally that I loved her, but this type of kiss only took once to let her know exactly what I was thinking.

When she finally eased back from me, I confessed, "I can hardly wait until tomorrow."

The way she looked at me is the way men long for a woman to look at them. She smiled at me so genuinely and shook her head as if in disbelief, but no, she corrected my thoughts. "Tomorrow's just a formality, just a big show for everyone else. No ceremony or pronunciation can define what we have."

I cupped my hand behind her neck and brought her to me again. "I love you more than you could know."

This time she stood on her toes and wrapped her arms around my neck and kissed me. Her lips were so soft and the kiss was light. It was a half dozen tiny little kisses, but each one more sensual than the last and her hands moved along with her mouth. A finger from each hand twirled in the back of my hair for a moment. Then, she circled my neck leaving a trail with her touch. She took my collar in her hands and pulled me closer in and the kiss went deeper.

I would never tire of her or the sting of electricity that still coursed through me each time we touched. I first thought that might one day wear off. I feared that day and prayed it would never come. I reveled in that charge. It was a reminder that I was alive and tied to her by something beyond any explanation I could ever give.

...

I was suddenly snapped back to reality of the wedding with the pounding out of the first few notes of the wedding march. I was not entirely sure how they made it happen, perhaps I was just distracted with my own thoughts, but suddenly Amelia appeared at the start of the aisle. She was more stunning than I had imagined she would be.

Her Aunt Gayle was by her side to give her away in the absence of her grandfather and any other father figure. Even though she had called it a formality for our friends and family the night before, Amelia wanted the tradition of a wedding, but broke with typical traditions of the ceremony at every turn. Having her aunt, a female relative, walk her down the aisle was just one of her broken traditions and having a gay man as her maid of honor was another.

I could not begin to tell you what Gayle was wearing. I recall it was black and Amelia had picked it out, but other than that, it could have been a man's tuxedo for all I noticed. I was too star struck with Amelia to notice much of anything once I laid eyes on her.

Another break with tradition was that Amelia wore white even though most everyone there knew she was already pregnant. I had not been allowed to see the dress before that moment, but Amelia had told me of the discussion she had had with her aunt the day she purchased the dress. Gayle warned her that wearing white would be inappropriate in her condition and people would talk. Amelia's opinion was that they were already talking, "So what the hell?" Those were her words and I did not disagree. As much as she said this was a show for everyone else, this was her day as far as I was concerned.

Aside of being white, the gown was made of a thick, lace overlay and the lace looked like roses. The dress had a halter top to it which gathered below her breasts to make an empire waist. There was a row of pearls that separated the top from the bottom. The skirt had just enough flare to hide the pregnancy, but by no means was it a maternity dress. As she took strides toward the make-shift alter, the dress hardly appeared to move other than the train that drug behind her. I was not sure if she had it made to fit her, but it appeared as though she had.

As I watched her come down the aisle, I could not take my eyes off of her. She was exquisite. I could not squelch the screams of my inner child. "She's mine!" the boy inside me screamed in delight over and over. I am certain I had a giddy smile on my face that likely stretched from ear to ear and everyone in the audience knew what I was thinking. Our eyes met and Amelia smiled and looked down bashfully. She knew what was going on in my head as well.

The time it took her to make it down the aisle and join me seemed like an eternity. At the rehearsal, the minister had said something about, "Who gives this woman?" and Gayle had answered, "Myself and her family." Who knew what words they exchanged today. Once Amelia arrived next to me, I really could not think.

Even though the boy inside had gone silent, my head was spinning. For one split second, I felt the presence of my parents standing with me. It might have been my imagination, but I could have sworn I felt a pat on my back and the phrase "atta-boy," whispered in my ear. On any other day, I might have turned to try to get a look at them, but I could not stop looking at my bride.

I was pulled back from the thoughts within my head by Gayle passing Amelia's hand to mine. I fumbled for a moment in taking her hand and everyone seemed to notice. Everyone could see I was every bit the kid in the candy store who had just been offered a five pound bag of M&Ms. There was a collective snicker that came from our little crowd of spectators. I distinctively heard Jay, but that could have been because he was closest to me and just behind Amelia. I did not hear my grandfather behind me, but I think that's only because he did not have a good vantage point of seeing me miss taking her hand when her aunt offered it.

I had been distracted with her eyes, her hair, her make-up, the dress, the entire picture before me. With that in mind, once I firmly had a grip on her hand, I leaned in to Amelia and kissed her cheek. As I withdrew from the kiss I whispered to her, "I will never know what I did to deserve you."

Tears filled Amelia's eyes, but they were not tears of sadness. The tears were accompanied by a giant smile equal to that on my own face and it was the raising of her cheeks from the smile that pushed the tears from her eyes. Had she not smiled so big, she would have been able to hold them back.

The minister allowed us to have that moment before he started the ceremony. We had chosen the traditional wedding vows. I had heard the ceremony a few dozen times in hosting weddings at the club so I knew the words by heart. The fact was that I wasn't really giving my full attention to what Pastor Jack, the minister from the nearest mountain church that typically officiated weddings at Glen Ella, had to say. Despite that, I managed to get the vows out correctly anyway.

While the minister read his portions of the ceremony, I studied Amelia. Her hair was parted to the side and pulled back at the base of her skull in a bun. In the bun were pearl pins that matched the pearls around the bodice of the dress. It was elegant, but different from any way I had ever seen her wear her hair before. She wore the pearl necklace that I had given her. The strand of pearls had belonged to my mother and it touched me profoundly that Amelia had thought to include her in our day if by nothing else, then wearing her pearls.

I looked Amelia over and over as the ceremony continued. I wanted to remember her in this very moment with crystal clarity. I did not want to ever have to rely on the wedding photos to refresh my memory. I wanted the image of her from this moment burned in my mind forever.

Despite being utterly distracted by her presence, I answered each of my "I do's" with enthusiasm. I did not doubt that she was as happy as I was, but her answers were more demure. She kept her excitement to a pressed smile and the squint of her nose as if she was holding back.

When the minister finally pronounced us man and wife and granted me permission to kiss the bride, I reached for her face and gently lifted her chin. In that moment Amelia let go of the high wattage smile that she had been stifling the entire ceremony. It stretched from ear to ear and sparkled in her eyes. She tried to bite her lip to call back the smile, but it was of no use.

I leaned down to her, but before taking her lips to mine, I informed her, "If I die today, I will die a very happy, happy man."

I almost forgot our audience as all I thought about was how she was officially mine. I could have gone on kissing her forever and it felt as if she might let me until we heard Gabby make her presence known. There was a squeal that came from the child that echoed off of the mountain. It was as if she had been tickled.

Amelia eased back from me, cut her eyes to Gabby, who was sitting in her Aunt Dot's arms. She cut back to me and again with that huge smile of hers said, "That's our girl."

"Yes, she is, Mrs. Hewitt," I replied.

Pastor Jack then cut us off and announced to the crowd, "I am pleased to present, Mr. and Mrs. Gabriel Hewitt."

The piano struck up again. Everyone stood from their seats and clapped. I escorted Amelia back down the aisle and she reached for Gabby as we passed her. Then, the three of us continued down the aisle. All eyes were on us when we made it past the last row. I pulled the both of them to me. I kissed Gabby on the forehead and gave Amelia another on the lips. This time the kiss I delivered to Amelia was more of the sort that I should have given her at the altar, instead of the grand gesture that I had planted on her.

When I released her, Amelia looked to me and then Gabby, "I love our little family, Mr. Hewitt, and this is the most wonderful day."

She had confirmed her sentiments several times during the ceremony with the smile on her face and the way her eyes lit up, but this was the first Amelia had verbalized it. Although I had not doubted her, I was thrilled to hear her say it. It also solidified the fact that today wasn't just about the two of us. It was about Little One and her sister as well. Now, the four of us were as official as we could be with the custody battle still raging on and until Amelia gave birth.

The reception...

Our first dance was to the song "At Last" by Etta James, but on this day, it was sung by Amelia's Aunt Gayle. Her vocal cords never ceased to amaze me, but it was Amelia that captivated me. Before the dance, and before she ate one bite of food at the reception, she greeted each and every guest personally and thanked them for making the trip.

I held her hand and followed her example as we approached each person. Amelia did the bulk of the talking, but I made sure I thanked everyone as well.

To Mrs. Allen and Rudy, Amelia made sure to ask how Rudy was doing at college. She continued, "How are your studies coming? Are you finding enough time to visit your grandmother?"

"Yes, ma'am," Rudy replied respectfully even though Amelia was barely three years older than he was. "I try to get home every other weekend."

"Have you given any thought to trying out for the track team at college next semester?" Amelia asked.

Rudy shook his head, "No, ma'am. I am just trying to focus on my grades and make you proud."

"Oh, don't worry about making me proud. You make yourself proud and that will be good enough for all of us." Amelia seemed puzzled that he would want to make her proud.

Mrs. Allen noticed the look of wonder on Amelia's face and added, "He just wants to make sure he doesn't waste your money."

Amelia was quick to correct her, "It's his money now. He earned it as far as I am concerned." Amelia released my hand long enough to pat Rudy on the back as she spoke.

It was only a moment more before Amelia's attention was directed elsewhere. "Again, thank y'all for making the trip up here for us today. I am so glad you are a part of our family." It was then Mrs. Allen and Rudy that were left with wonder at Amelia's words. I think they were stuck on the phrase about being a part of our family. I thanked them as well and shook each of their hands before following Amelia.

Amelia's attention had been caught by Jay's parents and his sister. They were seated at a table all by themselves so Amelia led us over to them. She pulled out a chair for herself and took a seat there with them.

"Are you all enjoying the food?" she asked them.

"Well, we've never had chicken like this before," Mrs. McDonald replied. I could tell from her tone that the real answer to Amelia's question was "no."

Their food had only just arrived right before Amelia sat down and Mrs. McDonald had only taken one bite. She was turning up her nose and pushing it to the side as she answered, but Mr. McDonald and Jolene, Jay's sister, were getting the jump on cleaning their plates.

"Oh, Mama, behave. Amelia, the chicken is fine," Mr. McDonald corrected his wife.

"Not to worry, I know how you like fried chicken, so I have requested a special plate for you, Mama," Amelia responded and she was being sincere. She really had requested a special meal for Mrs. McDonald's entree and it was being delivered at that very moment. Mrs. McDonald's eyes grew wide with delight over the plate of piping hot fried chicken. Amelia had explained earlier that Mrs. McDonald only ate two forms of meat, well done steak and fried chicken.

Amelia did not want anyone at the table to feel slighted for her attention, so she turned toward Jay's sister, whom I had met once at family dinner night at The Jefferson. "It was very kind of you to come all this way to the wedding. I'm sure it had more to do with seeing your brother in a tux, but I'm glad you came no matter what your reasons." Amelia gave her a devilish smile and the two of them giggled over the fact that Jay was not one to get dressed up or take off his Doc Martin shoes for just any occasion.

Amelia was not done making nice with the McDonalds before something caught her eye. It was Aunt Dot and she was letting Gabby taste the wedding cake off of her finger. "Aunt Dot! You can't give Gabby sugar like that!" Amelia shouted across two tables.

Every eye in the pavilion turned to Amelia as she marched over and took Gabby from her aunt. Gabby was still licking at her lips when Amelia pulled her away. At the same time Amelia was making a scene, the DJ from the inn asked, "Will the Bride and Groom please take the floor for the first dance?"

Amelia was befuddled at his timing and reluctantly passed Gabby back to Aunt Dot, but not before giving her a look that spoke volumes. The volumes included an assortment of warnings about how she better not give Gabby frosting again or it would end badly for Aunt Dot.

As soon as Amelia's hands were free again, I offered her mine to lead her to the dance floor. As her aunt sang, so did Amelia, but not so loudly that anyone but me could hear her. Their voices blended beautifully and they were as meant for this song as anyone else who had ever sung it.

It wasn't the first time I had heard this song at a wedding, but this was the first time I listened to the words. I could understand now why every single wedding played this song especially if every groom felt about their bride the way I felt about Amelia. For so many years, it was as if I lived in the dark and then she came along and smiled at me. She smiled and the spell was cast on me and as of today she really was mine. Just thinking about it again, I felt as if my heart was going to jump out of my chest, take on a life of its own and do a dance right in front of everyone.

When the song finished, I assumed all of our guests stood and clapped. I was oblivious as I was in heaven just kissing Amelia again.

The DJ thumped the microphone three times to get our attention and I reluctantly released her. Amelia giggled as if she might have been a little embarrassed that we had forgotten ourselves in front of everyone.

Once he had everyone's attention, the announcer began to speak. "The next song is for Gabriel's Aunt Mary."

"You must ask her to dance," Amelia instructed me.

I did not know what song was on tap, but I quickly found Aunt Mary bashfully heading toward me. I extended my hand to her as the music began. The song we danced to was Elvis' "Always on My Mind". The last time I had heard that song was at the Delta Digital Christmas party, but I knew exactly what it was within the first few notes.

I thought for a second as I listened to the words, that I was going to choke Amelia for this. The words pulled at my heart and I understood everything Amelia had been trying to tell me about getting in touch with my family. That being said, I did not want to be seen at my wedding crying as I danced with the woman who had been my substitute mother and I had written out of my life.

"I know you did your best with me and I am sorry I haven't been in touch," I whispered to her as I tried to think of things beyond what I was saying. I needed my mind to wander so I could hold back the tears. After my conversations with her and my grandfather today and the day before, I understood how wrong I had been to cut Mary out of my life. If ever anyone had been there for me, it was her. I had not realized that her heart had been broken by having to send me to Tennessee, but she knew it was the right thing to do for me.

"It's okay, Gabe. I know things were hard on you and I am really sorry about all of that. If I ever made you feel like I didn't want you, I'm so, so sorry." Despite her words, I managed to keep my emotions in check.

"I have lived the last decade thinking that I never wanted to see anyone from my family again and I was so wrong. Thank you so much for coming today and for bringing Granddad. You really did make a difference in my life and I know I would not have made it as far as I have without your influence," I explained all the while continuing with the dance.

"You don't have to apologize to me for anything. No one would have blamed you if you wanted to forget your childhood all together, least of all me."

I pulled Mary into a hug and I hid my face in the top of her hair. She held on to me as tightly as I held on to her. I was strong and kept hold of myself. I could not say the same for Aunt Mary. I could feel her sniffle against me.

The next round of music began, but this time there was no announcement. I think Amelia did that so there would be no further pointing out that she did not have a father present. I don't really know how I missed it, but Amelia had returned to the dance floor with my grandfather.

The song was Sarah McLachlan's "I Will Remember You." Although she did not say so, I think she picked the song as a tribute to her grandfather and used mine as a stand in for hers. From the way he kept her engaged in conversation through the song, my grandfather knew what was up and kept her talking so she would not dwell on who she was missing. I saw the tears building in her eyes, but they never fell.

As I watched them, I just could not believe the turn of events and the change of heart I had had about my family. I started to remember more things about my childhood. Good memories started to creep from spaces in my mind that had long since been covered by the bad. I remembered watching the Mandrell Sisters' show with my grandfather and how he enjoyed it. It was during that show that he tried to explain the birds and the bees with me one night while Grandmother was in the bath. Ultimately, I told him that I already knew about such things even though I didn't. The conversation ended with Grandmother returning and putting the kibosh on any fun I might have been having.

Standing there thinking of those times, I thought it might be interesting to let him know that I remembered. I slipped over to the DJ. I knew it was a long shot, but I asked anyway. "You would not happen to have anything by Barbara Mandrell, would you? She was my grandfather's favorite singer."

It took him a few minutes of digging through his CDs, but then he popped back up with, "It's not exactly wedding appropriate, but I have "I Was Country When Country Wasn't Cool."

"That is perfect. Would you play that next?"

The DJ shook his head, "That's not on Mrs. Millie's playlist..."

"But you will play it, right."

"Yes, sir," he replied and he started setting up the disc.

"Please announce this one and say it's for Granddad from Gabriel," I slipped him an extra twenty from my pocket and thanked him.

When the music stopped from their dance, Amelia thanked my grandfather and started to make her exit when the DJ quickly made the announcement as I asked. Both Amelia and Granddad turned to look at me. I motioned for them to continue and she took his hand again for the second dance. I could see the gesture made his night. He smiled from ear to ear.

Amelia could also tell that he liked the song, so she sang along to him and he laughed at every word. The version of the song that was being played was the version where George Jones joined in. When George Jones' voice came on, my grandfather was quick to sing back to Amelia. She threw her head back and laughed as he carried on.

The night went on with the cake cutting and toasts much like the ones from the night before. First to toast us was Jay.

"Everyone knows Millie is like another sister to me. That being said, of the three of us she's the first to go to grad school. The first to buy a house. The first of us to get married. She'll be the first

331

to give our parents grandchildren." He winked at Amelia as he said that part, but did not miss a beat in his speech. "She sets the bar kind of high for the rest of the McDonald children, but that's okay because for all of her overachieving, she overachieves the most at letting us all know how much she loves us. She has given me so much and today she's given me my first brother-in-law and I just want him to know how lucky he is to have joined the ranks of those loved by Millie. I hope he knows that he got the pick of our litter."

Amelia beamed as Jay lifted his glass. "To my little sister, she's five days younger than me, just so you know. May you and Gabriel have an amazing life together."

Amelia laughed that Jay pointed out that she was five days younger than he was and lifted her glass toward him.

Jay was hardly back in his seat when my grandfather stood. He introduced himself as some of the guests, like Amelia's friends from Young Harris, had not been there the night before when his initial introduction was made. "Now that's a hard act to follow," he continued and tipped his head to Jay. Jay grinned back with pride.

Granddad went on addressing the entire crowd of guests, "There's this song from my generation that talks about if you wanna be happy for the rest of your life, never make a pretty woman your wife. You may have heard of it. The singer goes on to tell that a pretty woman will break her husband's heart and so forth and if you want to be happy then you are to get yourself and ugly wife."

Snickers were beginning to pop up from members of his audience especially from Amelia's older relatives who clearly knew the song. One glance at Amelia's Aunt Gayle and I could tell she was wondering where this was going. She was not one of the ones laughing.

Granddad then turned his attention to me, "Son, it's too late to get yourself an ugly wife so it's a good thing Millie here is the exception to the rule because I hate to break it to you but, you've got yourself one heck of a pretty wife. So, here's to you, may you never wish you had gotten yourself an ugly wife."

The whole room erupted in laughter at his speech. I am sure those who had missed his speech the night before thought he might have been crazy, but this really was the best. When he was finished he shook my hand and genuinely congratulated me. He then kissed Amelia on the cheek, hugged her and welcomed her to his family.

Our last dance of the night was to "Unforgettable" by Nat King Cole. Almost everyone joined us on the dance floor, but again, it was as if Amelia and I were alone. I held her close and pressed my cheek to her forehead. This time I sang along to the song. Midway through the song, I thanked her for all she had done to make the night unforgettable.

Amelia lifted her face to me. "You've had a good time?" she asked.

"Of course," I replied as I continued to lead her in our dance.

"I am so glad," she pressed her lips together and batted her eyes at me. She shook her head affirming that she was pleased at my response and happy for me.

"Are you about ready to get out of here?"

"I thought you would never ask," she ruffled her nose and nodded.

"We have some business to attend to," I said as I took her hand and began to lead her from the dance floor.

The music was winding down and Amelia signaled to the DJ that we were ready to leave and he quickly announced our departure. Our remaining guests lined up to throw bird seed at us and by the time we made it through all of them, I thought I was going to have to shower just to get all of the seeds off of me before we could take care of what we had just referred to as "business."

Although most everyone who was still at the reception when we left were staying on at the Glen Ella that night, they had the good graces to stay put while Amelia and I made our way to the penthouse room. Amelia had stayed in the room the night before with Gayle and Gabby, but Gayle had taken Gabby back to the other room that shared the third floor of the inn. That night we had a room to ourselves with no worry about getting up to feed Gabby in the middle of the night or waking early with her in the morning. Gabby was spending the night with Gayle and Mr. Graham.

Out from under the pavilion, the night air was cool. I had not had it on all night and I had only put it on for the pictures that were being taken of our departure, so giving my jacket to Amelia was of little consequence to me. I did not even offer it to her; I just took it off and draped it around her shoulders. Amelia glanced at me and her smile was enough of a thank you for me. I enjoyed taking care of her and now I got to do just that for the rest of my life.

We proceeded on across the meadow toward the inn with my jacket around her shoulders and her hand in mine. Half way across the meadow, Amelia pulled at my hand to stop me. I looked down to her and she was already smiling up at me. I could see her dimples in her smile.

"I think I need you to pinch me," she said and her smile got wider. As usual she tried to hold it back by biting her lip, but there was no use. I could see everything about her face lit up in the moonlight and her eyes sparkled in it.

"Pinch you?" I asked with a curious look.

"To make sure I'm not dreaming," she explained.

"Oh," and I reached around and gave her a slight pinch to her behind.

"Ouch!" she laughed.

"Not dreaming, Mrs. Hewitt."

"I like the sound of that, Mr. Hewitt."

"Mrs. Hewitt," I said it again just to get her reaction and again she appeared delighted at the sound. "Mrs. Hewitt, may I show you to your room?"

In a sly voice, different from the playful laugh that accompanied the "Ouch!" just before, Amelia answered my question, "Yes, you may, Mr. Hewitt."

We reached the stairs of the inn and I backed off to allow her to go first. It was the gentlemanly thing to do and being a gentleman to her wasn't about to stop just because we were now married. I didn't want a thing to change about us or between us like married couples usually did. I was determined we would carry on as we always had and I would start that night making sure that did not happen with us.

On our way to the top floor, Amelia stopped at the landing of the second. She turned back and I was still two steps behind her. We were eye to eye then and she reached out to me. She hooked her index finger of her right hand around my tie and pulled me toward her.

"I'm not going to kiss you here, Mr. Hewitt." Amelia cocked an eyebrow at me and untied my tie.

I remembered a time when I had made a similar statement to her and I suppose she remembered it as well since she continued to use my words on me. I just watched Amelia as she continued. Amelia licked her top lip as she pulled me closer with the loosened tie.

"I am not going to kiss you because if I did, I wouldn't stop." She unbuttoned the top few buttons of my shirt as she spoke.

I was unbelievably aroused and we were still another flight of stairs away from our room.

Amelia continued with the seduction, "I want you, Mr. Hewitt. I want you very badly, but there are a lot of buttons to the back of this dress and I am not sure..."

I jerked her to me with one hand and with the other, I inched up the hem of her wedding gown. "I don't think the dress will be much of a problem, Mrs. Hewitt. You have a very, very resourceful husband," I explained all the while pulling the hem up and reaching under her dress. Up her leg, my fingers walked and she lifted her knee, sliding it up my leg. That was one of her signature moves and it always got my attention, but what really got my attention was finding the garter belt.

"A garter belt?!" I was stunned. This was my version of the night JFK eased his hand up Marilynn Monroe's thigh under the table to find she wasn't wearing panties at all. There was nothing more seductive in the world than a garter belt.

"Sweet Jesus, Mrs. Hewitt," I sighed as I ran my finger under it.

"If you would like to see it, then you are going to have to help me get out of this dress," she whispered, then she slipped away from me, grabbed up handfuls of the skirt of the gown and darted up the last flight of stairs.

I reached for her, nearly catching the material of the wedding gown, but it slipped through my fingers. Amelia giggled and I gave chase. In her condition, I suppose that wasn't the wisest idea for us to run up the stairs. Luckily, nothing happened.

Amelia sprinted through the door and I was hot on her heels. I stopped just inside the door and closed it behind me. "Come here," I said to her in a low commanding voice.

Amelia had made it as far as the edge of the bed, but stopped in her tracks at the sound of my voice. She looked back over her shoulder at me, pressed her lips and smiled while tossing the jacket to the bed post.

"Back up," I addressed her again. She obliged and I took two steps forward to meet her.

Before starting on the buttons down the back of her dress, I slipped the pins out of her hair that had been holding the bun. Even on this day, Amelia had not bothered to use hair spray and her hair was as soft and inviting to my touch as it ever was. I ran my fingers through it from the base of her skull all the way to the end. Amelia cocked her head and leaned into my touch. When my fingers made their way to the end, I inhaled deeply. As always, her hair smelled of strawberries and it was both a comfort and a turn on to smell it as it fell down her back in soft curls and waves from being pinned up all day.

"You always smell so good," I exhaled into her neck. My breath caused chill bumps on her. The chill bumps begged to be kissed and I could not deny them. I ran my tongue from just below her earlobe down her neck and across her shoulder, lifting my tongue only to skip over the strap of her dress.

"Thank you," she replied. I could feel her hands against my suit pants. She took hold of fists full and pulled me closer into her.

I moved her hair over to one shoulder so I could have a better view of the buttons on the back of her dress. "Wow! You weren't lying about their being a lot of buttons."

I could not hear her, but I could see by the jiggle of her back that Amelia snickered at my observation. "It took Aunt Gayle twenty minutes just to button them all this afternoon."

There must have been forty little buttons stacked one on top of the other, I made it through five of them before asking, "How partial are you to these buttons?"

"Why?" Amelia was clearly surprised by my question, but she was more surprised by what I did next.

I took out my pocket knife, the one that had been my dad's. I never used it, but mostly kept it on me at all times as a reminder of him. This particular night, I put it to good use and I cut the loops that held buttons.

"Did you just cut my dress?!"

"Sure did, but I will take it to the dry cleaners and have it cleaned and fixed in case one of our daughters want to use it one day."

"You have cut my dress and now you are talking about marrying off our daughters, Mr. Hewitt, are you trying to kill the mood?"

Before she could ask any other foolish questions I whirled Amelia around, stripped that dress off of her and found a white bustier, matching lace panties and satin garter belts holding up thigh-high stockings. I looked her up and down and the pregnancy bump did not even register with me. "Mrs. Hewitt, wow."

She appeared pleased with herself and my reaction when she asked, "You like?"

"Oh, yeah." I mean, what was there not to like?

I had seen her in satin nightgowns, in only my under shirt, in my dress shirt and in nothing at all, but I had never seen her like this before. I had never seen her as being anything close to a Victoria's Secret model, but she looked every bit the part.

The first time we ever made love was a combination of the need to possess her and to know what it was like to have someone like her. There were other times where a carnal lust for her had taken over, but this particular night I could not explain. With the way she looked, it would have been easy to understand if it were lust that fueled my passion for her that night, but it wasn't. I think what fueled me was the idea that this sweet, beautiful woman before me was mine forever.

I pulled Amelia up with one scoop and carried her to the king size bed that took up the far side of the room. She kissed my neck as I carried her. On the way there, I used the remote to cut on the gas fireplace. I laid her gently down, cross ways on the bed and reached over and cut off the lamp. The only light left in the room was that from the fireplace.

I held open my hand for her right foot and she complied. I lifted her leg and planted deep kisses behind her knee through the stocking. The kisses sent chill bumps all over her leg and she squirmed a little with pleasure. I continued the process down to her ankle and again gave her kisses and chill bumps to her left leg.

Amelia did not take her eyes off of me, watching me the whole time. I loved the way she looked at me. Sometimes she did that thing where she bit the left side of her bottom lip and it always made me want to bite it too, but in a whole other way. It was sweet and sexy and I interpreted that look as her wanting me as badly as I wanted her. It was a look that sometimes made me wonder if she was going to take me instead of the other way around. Tonight when she did it, I commented, "Patience, my dear," and she blushed as if she had been caught thinking dirty thoughts.

Finally, I released her leg and started to unbutton my dress shirt. Amelia scrambled to her knees. "Let me do that for you."

I smiled at her and gave my consent without saying a word.

Amelia pulled me closer to her, but I remained standing. Even on her knees and on the bed, she still wasn't tall enough to be eye to eye with me, so she pulled me down to her.

"I can multitask," she said in a breathless whisper before she pulled my mouth to hers. She kissed me as if that was her single focus, but all the while she was moving steadily from one button to the next down my shirt. There was even a bonus in the kiss of her sucking my tongue, which was a new technique for her and I liked it.

When she completed the last button, she ran her hands over the top of my undershirt back to the collar and eased the shirt off of my shoulders and down my arms. Never once did she break the connection of our kiss or imply that she had anything other than kissing me going on.

Once my arms were free from the long sleeves, Amelia moved her hand to the bottom hem of my undershirt. She slipped her hands under and ran them up my chest using only the backs of them to pull the t-shirt up. Her finger tips were so light against my skin that it tickled and it was me that felt the chill bumps and they were all the way down each of my legs.

Amelia came to a point where we had to break the connection of the kiss for her to get the undershirt over my head. When her mouth left mine and she began to raise the shirt, she dropped down and kissed my chest. I had been turned on by her plenty of times in the past, but nothing like this. It was as if the entire day had been foreplay.

Within seconds, my t-shirt was tossed away and the lace of her white bustier was pressed against the bare skin of my chest. There was a soft, yet scratchy feel to it and I could feel her heart beat through it. As I planted kisses around her neck and across what was uncovered of her chest, Amelia unhooked my belt and tossed it to the same spot in the floor where my shirts had landed moments before.

Again, I cradled Amelia against me and lifted her with one arm to lay her across the bed. This time I hovered over her as we went down and her legs went around my waist. Her legs were so soft and smooth against my skin. They were like ribbons of silk gliding around me.

Both my slacks and her panties were still on as I pressed into her. I could feel her rise to meet me. We moved in unison, simulating the act that was soon to come. Finally, Amelia whispered, "I need the real thing, Mr. Hewitt. I am begging you."

I managed to remove her panties and my slacks with little to no effort, but left the bustier, garter belt and stockings. The bustier barely covered her and her breasts heaved as if she was going to bust loose. I buried my face in her cleavage and ran my tongue along the top line of the bustier. I could taste the hint of salt on her skin and still smelled the lingering scent of perfume that she had dabbed on her chest when she got dressed earlier. Amelia shivered as I ran my tongue just under the top line of material and across each breast.

She arched her back and begged with her body. I could torture neither of us any longer and Amelia held her breath as I pushed into her. She was tiny and I always feared I would hurt her, but she never let on that I brought anything other than pleasure to her. Each time I returned to her, she met me and pulled me closer. The rhythm was slow and steady.

"I like it best like this," she sighed. "Please don't stop."

At some point, the bustier slipped down and I could feel more of her skin on mine. There was warm friction as my chest slid up and down hers. I had taken her hands, locked her fingers in mine and pinned them over her head.

I could feel her quiver around me. I had been thinking of everything I could to hold off my orgasm for quite a while by the time the signs of hers started to materialize. I let go of my wandering thoughts and came back to the moment. I embraced the feeling of having her and the thrill of the day and allowed us both to have satisfaction.

Amelia cried out my name as she climaxed, "Gabriel!" and I answered her with a breathless, "I love you so much, Mrs. Hewitt."

I fell asleep that night entwined with my wife around 4:00 a.m. after making love to her three times over. The last thing I remembered of that day was kissing each of the tiny scars on her back that remained from the bombing and then saying a prayer. I prayed and thanked God for giving her to me, because although I had made amends with my grandfather, there were still lingering doubts as to whether I really deserved Amelia.

CHAPTER 19

"You know, it's funny how things work out sometimes," I said as I cut the television off and glanced over at Amelia.

"What do you mean?" She had been studying all night and this was the first time she looked up from the text book since she kissed Gabby good night.

"Do you know what today is?" I pulled her feet into my lap and began to massage them.

"No, am I supposed to know?"

"We met one year ago today."

"Oh," I could tell by the look on Amelia's face that she had completely forgotten. She closed the book on contract law and leaned over and set it on the coffee table.

"Did you ever think back then that this is how we would end up?" I asked her as I inched up the couch closer to her.

Amelia rubbed her belly and glanced to the door to the nursery, "Not in a million years. How about you?"

"I wanted you from the moment I saw you, but did I think this much would change in a year? Never, but it's a good change. I have a family now."

We continued to talk about how much things had changed. We were married and expecting our first child together. In addition, we were already raising a child together. I was back in touch with my grandfather and my aunt and everything was going well.

"Despite the custody battle, I have never been happier and I just wanted you to know that," I told her.

"I'm so glad. I've never been happier either, but speaking of custody battle, I need to get back to studying. I'm working on something that might...

I cut her off. While on the phone with Attorney Ellis the day before, he had a talk with me about Amelia's participation in the case. His opinion was that nothing good would come of her involvement. He was quite stern in letting me know that I needed to make her stop interfering.

"About that, Attorney Ellis wants you to back off."

Amelia did not take that kindly and snatched her feet from my lap and stormed to the kitchen. "Back off?" she repeated in a demanding way, snatching open the refrigerator door.

"Amelia, he did not mean to hurt your feelings. Let's face it, he has thirty years of experience and you aren't even finished with your first year of law school. You have to see it from his point of view. You keep trying to tell him how to do his job."

Again she protested, "If he were doing his job, this might be over already. We have given him enough on Beth to have her parental rights revoked for being a horrible mother. You can't even call her a mother!"

"Right, but please understand, he's told you before, the court's opinion is that children need their mothers and even a bad mother is better than no mother."

"Well, it's his job to make them see differently!" Amelia glanced at the pitcher of tea in her hand, "I don't even want this now!" She slung it back in the refrigerator and slammed the door.

During her tantrum, I approached her. I put my arms around her and rubbed her ever increasing belly. I could feel the baby move beneath my touch. Amelia laid her head back against me.

"I know you don't want to lose Gabby, but you need to calm down," I said quietly.

Under my hand, I felt a tightening and Amelia winced and nearly doubled over. I reacted with questions and moved so that I could see her face. "What was that? Are you alright?"

"I'm not sure, but it hurt!"

343

"You don't think...maybe we should call the doctor."

"The doctor's office isn't open at ten o'clock at night, Gabriel."

"Well, if it happens again, we are going to the ER!"

"I'm sure it's nothing."

Amelia tried to assure me as she slipped away from me and headed back into the living room. She continued on toward the bedroom, but I could tell that it hit her again just as she reached the doorway. Amelia grabbed the door molding with one hand and her stomach with the other and she doubled completely over that time. I rushed to her side to make sure she did not go all the way to the floor.

Just as I caught her, she looked back at me, with tears in her eyes. She pressed her lips and tried not to let on that she was scared. I don't think I had ever seen Amelia scared before, but this was what it looked like and it was mixed with pain. This could not be real labor because it was way too early.

"Gabriel, please dial Aunt Gayle for me," she asked as silent tears ran down her face.

"Of course." I helped her back to the couch and then found the phone on the far end where I had set it after I finished speaking with my grandfather earlier. I dialed the numbers and handed Amelia the phone.

"I'll go get changed in case we need to take you to the hospital. Don't move, I'll be right back," I told her while the phone was ringing.

I returned to the living room pulling my shirt over my head with every intention of finding my keys and then taking her to Oconee Regional. I found Amelia sitting with her feet up on the couch, watch in hand and staring at it.

"I'll bring the car around," I mentioned while I began looking for my keys. I typically sat my keys in the same spot every time I came in, but I was a little panicked and I could not think for the life of me where that spot was.

"Just hold on there. Aunt Gayle said it's probably just false contractions. She told me to time them. If they were coming at a rate of one every five minutes and increasing in pain, she said we were to go to the hospital immediately."

"So you are timing them? I'll keep looking for my keys just in case." I was spinning around the room searching here, there and everywhere; under the couch pillows, behind the lamps on the end tables, on the coffee table and so on.

"Looking for your keys? They're right behind you by the door where you always hang them." Amelia nearly laughed at me, but just as soon as the smile started to sprout another round of pain hit her. She took a deep breath, holding it until the pain subsided.

She exhaled, "Seven minutes between the last two, but that one was stronger."

"Are you okay? We can go to the hospital now if you want to."

"What about Gabby?" Amelia asked as she glanced up from the second hand on her watch.

"I'll go downstairs and get Stella or Jay to come up and stay with her." Honestly, I had momentarily forgotten Gabby. I felt terrible, but I was a little terrified that Amelia might be losing the baby.

"Gabriel, come sit with me." Amelia patted the seat on the couch as she took her feet down to allow me room. "Now you are the one that needs to calm down. Take a deep breath. I'm sure it's just Braxton Hicks contractions. Aunt Gayle said it's the body's way of practicing for the real thing."

I rolled my eyes and continued to pace, "Calm down? What does she know, she's a vet?"

"Being snide and pacing isn't helping! Sit! Please."

345

I sat for fear of making her more agitated. Amelia timed the contraction and the next one came at the five minute mark. I started to stand and she placed her hand on my knee. "It's okay. That one wasn't as strong as the last one. Just wait. She said we should worry if they got steadily stronger."

I put my hand on hers. I leaned my head over to hers. "I don't know what I would do if anything happened to you and the baby."

Amelia tilted her head to mine and whispered calmly, "Nothing is going to happen to us and you can't think like that. If something happened, then you would be all Gabby had and you can't forget her. She's just as important as anyone else in this family."

My stomach churned at the thought of carrying on without her, of fighting for Gabby without her, but perhaps this was tonight's lesson. Hopefully, this was just false labor and another way of us being told that I did need to fight for Gabby without Amelia. Attorney Ellis had told me to sever Amelia's involvement and now our unborn child was telling me also.

We sat in silence as I refrained from verbalizing my concerns for her further involvement in the case. I did not want to upset her again, so I held my tongue. Five minutes passed and another contraction hit her.

"Put your hand here and you can feel it tighten," she said as she first felt it coming on.

Amelia winced a little and I could feel it tighten as she had described. "It feels like a basketball," I observed.

"Yeah, it seems to start in my back and come around, full circle. I am not going to lie, it hurts, but it's not unbearable."

Amelia called out the time again and the clock started over. Another five minutes passed and it hit her again. "That wasn't nearly as bad as the last. I think Aunt Gayle's right. These aren't consistent and they certainly aren't coming harder each time."

"But what about the rate of time at which they are coming?"

346

"I think we just have to wait for them to stop right now."

Amelia and her aunt were right. By 11:30, the contractions had stopped and we went to bed. I hardly slept, but Amelia slept like the dead. I just kept waking up with a feeling of dread. The contractions had scared both of us, but they had really freaked me out. I did not know if that was what was wrong with me or what.

Two days later, the feeling of dread was still with me. Perhaps I felt the pending storm, I'm not sure. It was around 2:00 p.m. I had just put Gabby down for a nap when the phone rang. Amelia was not home from class yet and I am glad she wasn't. I rushed to get the phone and found my attorney on the other end of the line. He had bad news.

"I'm sorry, Gabe. Keep in mind, it's just a temporary thing and we'll get it reversed," Attorney Ellis began after identifying himself.

"What's going on? What are you talking about?" I did not understand a thing he was saying. I think he was trying to prepare me for the real news.

"The Judge issued an Order granting Beth visitation."

I had walked to the dining room area of the apartment to keep my conversation from waking Gabby. It was when Attorney Ellis revealed the ruling that I punched a hole in the dining room wall. I was furious and cut him off, "What do you mean granted her visitation?"

"I know that's not what you wanted, but he did deny her Petition for Summary Judgment throwing out your case, so we are still going to trial on this and you will have your day in court."

"How long before that happens?' I just can't believe this."

"I am trying to get us on the judge's calendar for December. That's the soonest they have available."

Before I realized what I was saying, I verbalized my frustration, "Are you fucking kidding me? December? That's two months from now and..."

347

"And the child's mother gets to see her every other weekend for the whole weekend until then."

"For the love of God, please tell me it's supervised visitation. Were you able to get her brother J.J. to supervise? Tell me my daughter is not going to be left alone with this woman."

"It would serve you well to remember this woman is the child's mother in the eyes of the court."

"That's a load of shit. She's no more of a mother to the child than the damn barking dog I can hear in the distance." I was livid. "It is supervised visitation, right?"

"Yes, but it's by her mother."

"That's just great! That's the equivalent of no supervision at all." I paused only to regain my composure and not spew every curse word I knew. "Is there anything that you can do about this? Did they take into account any of her arrests or anything?"

"That hasn't come out yet."

Attorney Ellis went on to explain the legal process to me again. This time he was more detailed in his explanation. He also explained the terms of the visitation. Beth and her mother were to pick Gabby up the coming Saturday at 9:00 a.m. and have her until Sunday afternoon when they were to return her at 4:00 p.m.

None of that mattered. The only thing that mattered was that Gabby was going to be left alone with Beth. Her mother did not raise her own children and look at how Beth turned out. The woman saw no fault whatsoever in her children and she turned a blind eye to any indiscretion they had committed. Beth often laughed at her mother's willingness to believe whatever story she gave to get herself out of trouble. When she was fourteen and kicked out of cotillion, Beth told her mother that she chose to quit because the other girls were picking on her. The real story was that Beth slipped off her panties and told one of the boys whose parents were newly rich, "Here wear these. It's the only way you'll ever get into anyone here's panties."

If all of that wasn't bad enough, I would have to tell Amelia about the visitation ruling when she got home from school. When I was off the phone, I tried to think of ways around telling Amelia, but I didn't know which was worse, telling her or not telling her and having her find out from someone else. I sat in the silence of the apartment. The only sound in the place was coming from Gabby's room. It was the sound of her sucking her thumb and I knew that sound without having to lay eyes on her.

I walked to the edge of her crib and watched her as she slept. I thought about how there was no one who knew her better than me, not even Amelia. I knew the sound of her cry when she was hungry, when she was angry and when she was hurt. Each cry was distinctive and I knew them all. How could I ever turn her over to someone who not only did not know these things about her, but who cared no more for her than to abandon her when she was less than a week old. I felt more helpless in this moment than in any of the moments of my own childhood. According to Attorney Ellis, there was nothing I could do about it.

I picked up the phone and I dialed the number to my grandfather's house. The phone rang a few times before he answered, "Hello?"

I still felt the need to identify myself because I was not to the point where I took for granted that he recognized my voice. "Granddad, it's me, Gabe."

"Good afternoon, my boy," he replied and I liked the way he called me "my boy."

"I hope I'm not bothering you. I need some advice and I was hoping I could talk to you about what's going on."

I paced with the phone as he gave me the go ahead. "Lay it on me. I'll do what I can."

I knew I had to make it quick because Amelia would be home any minute. I did not bother retelling him my history with Beth, but simply reminded him of what I had told him while we were together the weekend of the wedding. "You remember what I told you about Gabby's biological mother?"

"Yes, of course, the tart that left her with you."

"Right and I told you about the custody battle. I just found out this afternoon that the court has awarded her visitation with Gabby. I just don't know if I can do it. I don't know if I can turn her over to Beth. I fear what would happen and how can I tell Amelia? Just last night we had a scare with premature labor for her. We had a disagreement and it sent her into false labor. It turned out it was just what she called Braxton Hicks contractions, but still. I don't want her upset in her condition. I just don't know what to do. I feel like I can't tell Amelia, but I can't not tell her either."

I could hear my grandfather clear his throat, before he spoke. "I know I am just a foolish old man and you can take this for what it's worth. I hear your concerns, but it's been my experience that nothing good comes from hiding the truth. I know that's not what you wanted to hear. I'm sorry."

He was right, that's not what I wanted to hear, but I knew he was right. I knew that was the answer before I even called and asked the question. I had one more question and I didn't already know the answer to that one. "Do you think I am fighting a losing battle? I've told you she's not even my child."

"Do you believe you are doing the right thing by fighting for her?" he asked.

"I do." I hung my head in my hand as I answered.

"Then how dare you think of quitting. Don't be like me. Don't you quit on that child. I promise you, you will regret it the rest of your life."

Granddad had a point. I would regret letting her go and there was no way I could ask Amelia to let her go either. If I were going to give Gabby back, I should have done it before I made Amelia her mother. Nothing about this was fair to anyone, least of all Gabby.

I did not linger on the phone with my grandfather. I knew what I had to do and he confirmed it for me. I had to tell Amelia. There was no way around it.

I was still stewing over everything and Gabby was still napping when I heard the door to the apartment opening at the bottom of the stairs. Amelia was home and although it was time for me to face the music, I still had not decided how. I just could not figure out the softest way to tell her that Beth had been granted visitation.

I could hear her footsteps approaching the top of the stairs. I stood up from the couch as she yelled from the bottom of the stairs with her usual greeting, "Honey, I'm home!" I could hardly see the top of her head as she made her announcement.

She was barely through the front door and setting her backpack down when Amelia noticed my face. She knew instantly that something was wrong.

"Are you alright?" she asked.

"Not really," I replied somberly, knowing I had failed her and Gabby and now I had to confess it.

"What is it?" Her voice was becoming more urgent with each question. It was obvious that the look on my face alone had concerned her. "What? Is something wrong with your grandfather?"

"Granddad is fine. This has nothing to do with him." I had forgotten that I mentioned to Amelia that he was not doing well the last time I spoke to him.

"Then what's the matter?" She moved closer to me and finished her usual greeting by kissing me and adding the touch of her hand along my cheek. It served as comfort as she had intended.

I hated that she had not come to the conclusion on her own. I think the blow would have been easier on her if she had guessed it herself. At least having been able to guess it would show that she already knew Beth's gaining visitation was a possibility, instead of something coming at her from left field.

"Please have a seat." I motioned to the couch.

"Really, is it that bad?" she asked as I leaned into her touch.

"I think it is."

Amelia took a seat on the couch and I began to tell her about the phone call from my attorney. "He said he received an Order from the court today granting Beth visitation with Gabby. It's supervised visitation but..."

I really should not have bothered asking Amelia to sit since she sprang to her feet in a fury over my first sentence. She cut me off, "But it's visitation none the less. And who's supervising?"

I grabbed Amelia's hands in an effort to try to calm her. She snatched her hands back as I answered her question. "Beth's mother has been assigned as the supervisor. Mr. Ellis said the bright spot was that they were not allowed to leave the county with her, so we will know where Gabby is. The Order provides for the visitation to take place at her parents' house on Lake Oconee."

"Is he fighting this? When is it supposed to start? You just told me last night that I had to back off and let him handle this. Well damn, Gabriel, I may only be a first year law student, but I could have done this much!"

Where I had held my tongue on the use of explicatives, Amelia did not. She was pissed and that was what I was afraid of. It showed not only in her language, but in the way she stormed around the living room. Amelia had a thing about cleaning when she was mad and she was already straightening the books on the bookcase.

"Amelia, you need to calm down. This isn't good for you or the baby."

"You're right! It isn't good for me, the baby inside me or the one in there!" She said rubbing her stomach with one hand and pointing to the nursery with the other. "Jesus, Gabriel! And there's nothing we can do?"

Amelia stormed to the bedroom and I followed. "How long do we have before we have to hand her over? And I don't want Beth or her mother or anyone involved with them coming here! Do I make myself clear? I don't want them knowing where we live!"

"Crystal!" I replied, gritting my teeth with restraint. I understood she was angry, but she was real close to taking it out on me. "You know I did not do this. This wasn't my idea or anything."

Amelia looked back to me from where she had begun making the bed. She took a calmer tone. "Of course I know that, but I am just so pissed, I can hardly see straight. Did he at least tell you that he would request a hearing on the matter to argue against it?"

I moved toward her and wrapped my arms around her. I had been hesitant, uncertain as to whether she would even let me touch her in that moment.

"He told me there was no need. He said the trial was set for December and it was all he could do to get us on that calendar. He also mentioned taking our depositions in late October. Apparently, her attorney is demanding to depose you as well. Mr. Ellis said he would see what he could do to refuse to allow you to be deposed. He said something about a Protective Order, but I'm not sure what that means."

"It means, he will try to block their efforts to get to me. At least he is doing something, I suppose." Amelia held my arms around her and leaned back against me. "We can't lose her, Gabriel. We just can't."

I did not want to promise her anything, but the words escaped my lips before I realized. "We won't. This is just another bump in the road."

I'm not sure who I was trying to convince, Amelia or myself.

*** 

Amelia and I muddled through the next few days. Thursday night I arrived home after work at almost 10:30 p.m. and Amelia greeted me in the doorway at the top of the stairs. She planted a kiss on me and I immediately knew she was in better spirits.

As soon as my eyes reopened from the kiss, I saw everyone living in the building was waiting on me.

"What's going on?" I asked as I acknowledged them.

353

"I had to do something. I can't just let Gabby go, so we came up with a plan," Amelia began to explain before being interrupted by Jay.

Jay stepped to Amelia's side. "We are going to do a full court press on Beth," he started.

"That's a basketball term, right?" I questioned. I knew it was a basketball term, but I wasn't sure he knew. I never figured Jay for the basketball playing type.

I made my way past him to the kitchen to put down the leftovers I had brought home from the club. Jay and Amelia followed and Jay began to explain his meaning. "We are going to follow her everywhere. As long as she has Gabby, she's got one of us watching her."

"We have divided the days into shifts," Cara added.

Amelia continued, "She does not know any of them," and she gestured to our friends, "so she won't recognize their cars."

There were a few problems with their plan and I began to point them out. "You know Beth's parents' house is in the most secure club on the lake. Do y'all plan to just drive up to the gate and ask to be let in? How do you think that will work out?"

"I have that covered." I could tell by Amelia's voice that she was impressed with herself and she thought she had solved that problem. "I rented the house two doors down for the weekend. And, don't worry, I rented it in Jay's sister's name. In fact, Jolene will be vacationing in the house and watching Beth's comings and goings. Plus, I have all of these folks on the list for access to the house."

"You rented a house? That's stalking," I pointed out.

"I would have rented it for the rest of the year, but they would only rent it to me by the weekend," Amelia remarked off-handedly and ignored my comment about stalking.

Stella was quick to answer for Amelia and almost talked over her, "Yes, Millie is quite aware of what stalking is. I believe she learned it first hand from Beth."

Travis grabbed Stella's hand to silence her, but she snatched it away. "I figure what's good for the goose is good for the gander," she said in conclusion.

"I agree," Cara said, patting Stella on the back. Amelia gave a wink of approval as well.

Amelia piped up again, "I bought cell phones for everyone so we could pass off shifts and be more effective at spying." Amelia tossed a phone to each one of them.

"I taped the numbers on the back of each of them and the girl at the store programmed all of them. Aren't these awesome?"

Amelia was pleased with her purchases, but I thought she had gone overboard with the phones and the rental house. She had never been one to throw away money, but it seems she was going wild.

"Is there any arguing with you?" I looked from my new phone back to Amelia and she had a look of the cat that ate the canary and I had a feeling she intended Beth to be the canary. "Don't you think this is throwing away money?"

I think everyone in the room saw her face turn red and feared Amelia was about to snap at me. She took a moment before speaking and no one said a word. I could almost hear her grit her teeth as she spoke. "You mean throwing good money after bad like with the attorney we have? We see where that got us. Just to be clear, I will spend any amount of money I see fit to protect our children."

I think she tried to refrain from embarrassing us by not screaming at me in front of everyone, but I was a bit embarrassed nonetheless. I had never been corrected by her in such a manner and in front of everyone like that before.

Travis saw the look on my face and chimed in. He tried to defuse the situation. "I'm against this, but they have made up their minds. They've even recruited Daniel to help."

"You always say, 'You mess with the bull, you'll get the horns.' I think it's about time she got the horns even if she gets them from me." Amelia smiled.

As proud of her as I was for taking the initiative to solve the problem, I was not impressed with Amelia thinking she was the bull. Even more than that, I did not like her reprimanding me in front of our friends. I was well aware that she wore the financial pants in our relationship, but I never needed to be reminded of that and especially not in front of other people.

After everyone else left for the evening, Amelia and I were getting ready for bed when she mentioned the second part of her plan. "We need to hit her where she lives. I think we need to make her as uncomfortable as she has made us. Give her a reason to stop this that she will understand."

I finished brushing my teeth before I responded to her. "What do you have in mind?"

"We need to request child support."

"You know, not everything is about money and you know she won't be the one paying it."

"That's not the point." Amelia threw back the covers to the bed and we got in.

I eased in to my side of the bed and rolled over facing her. "Do you miss how things used to be?"

"What do you mean?" Amelia asked.

"I mean, I miss just going to bed and thinking about nothing but the way your hair felt across my chest. Do you miss those times?"

"What's this about?"

"I feel like we are being consumed by this and I don't know how to stop it. You should not have to orchestrate our friends to follow Beth or rent a weekend house for someone to spy on her. I don't like this and this is not who you are."

Amelia sat up in bed and eased over on top of me. "Let me explain to you who I am so you will fully understand. I am your wife and the mother of your children and you are my family and I will fight for my family."

Amelia placed my hand across her belly as she spoke and I could feel Sweet Pea moving in her as she did every night when we settled into bed. Amelia continued as I ran my hand across her stomach feeling the baby roll inside of her, "I will spend every dime I have to fight for you. Don't ever mistake this for being about money, because the money means nothing without the three of you."

When she was finished speaking, Amelia took my hands in hers and pinned them over my head. She leaned over and kissed me. She did her best to remind me that my worries were unfounded. "The best is yet to come," she whispered to me as she eased back from the kiss.

Despite her condition, I rolled Amelia over and pinned her. "You mentioned something about being the bull this afternoon and I think I am going to have to remind you who the bull is Mrs. Hewitt."

Amelia giggled and I knew she was right. What we had was worth all of the money in the world. She was so smart and wise beyond her years and I just had to be reminded sometimes that she really was mine and she wasn't going anywhere.

The next morning, I did as she suggested about the child support. The legal fees surrounding the custody were mounting and although we had the money, this would help. I called Attorney Ellis as soon as I thought he was in the office. He agreed to file the motion for temporary child support to be paid to me by Beth by the end of the day. The last Beth had mentioned, she was making around $45,000 working for the television station, so we asked for the maximum amount typically awarded in Georgia. We asked for twenty-three percent which amounted to roughly $862 per month.

\*\*\*

I don't know what I was thinking going along with Amelia's plan for our friends to follow Beth as long as she had Gabby. Of course, I wanted to be a fly on the wall, but I was scared of the repercussions with the court if we got caught. Would this hurt our chances of being free of Beth? I feared, if caught, we would appear no better than what we wanted the court to believe Beth was.

I thought of all of these things as I made the drive back to the clubhouse at Port Honor that Saturday morning. Evidently at some point, Amelia told Cara about our pasts. I thought about the argument Cara made in favor of us spying on Beth.

"You all did not have a traditional upbringing, so let me tell you about one of my mother's rules for her children," Cara began to educate us on her mother's version of a responsible parent. "Her rule was that neither my brother nor I was allowed to go anywhere or with anyone other than daycare unaccompanied by her or my father until we were old enough to communicate and report back. The reason for this was so that she would know if we were mistreated and even then there were only a small handful of very trusted people that she allowed to take us anywhere. I was seven before I spent the night away from home for the first time without her."

Stella had a similar story and concluded hers with, "Good parents don't want to be away from their children, but when they are they want the person the child is with to care for the child as they would."

I passed through the gate at Port Honor, waving at the guard, at around 9:00 a.m. I had dropped Gabby off with Attorney Ellis' secretary, Joyce, and she was to make the exchange with Beth. It had only been about fifteen minutes since I had handed Gabby over to Mrs. Joyce, but she was on the phone as soon as I stepped through the kitchen door. Mrs. Joyce didn't give any details. She just said the child was picked up. If knowing that she no longer had Gabby was supposed to make me feel better, it didn't. She shouldn't have wasted the call. I had been hoping all morning that Beth would flake out and not show up.

I did not typically get to work so early on Saturday, but I figured I would hang around the area in the hopes that taking care of a baby would prove too much for Beth. I prayed she would call me to come and get Gabby and this would be the end of it. Unfortunately, those hopes were dashed.

I proceeded to get the jump on dinner preparations while Alvin did his usual Saturday morning thing. He had quite the routine down and I got the feeling that I was cramping his style and I tried to stay out of his way. I was so preoccupied with my worries for Gabby, it didn't take much effort to forget Alvin was even around.

"Hey, man!" Alvin snapped his fingers to really get my attention. "Are you going to stop stirring that? It's been done for twenty minutes."

"Oh, I'm sorry," I said, blinking my eyes back to reality.

"I got this. Why don't you go hang out in the bar, schmooze with the members and watch the Georgia game with them," Alvin insisted. He had an idea of what was wrong with me today since I had told him about the visitation ruling while we were passing the time on Thursday night.

"There's a game today?" I asked absentmindedly.

"Yes. It starts at noon. You've got five minutes to get out there and get a seat. Go."

I went to my office at the back of the kitchen to put my apron down. The desk phone was ringing off the hook when I walked in. I snatched it up, hoping it was Beth. It wasn't Beth. It was Amelia and I had never been disappointed to hear her voice until that moment.

"Any word?" Amelia was clearly on edge about this.

"No," I replied in a deflated tone.

"Jay called. He said Beth didn't pick up Gabby. Said she wasn't even in the car."

"What?! You've got to be kidding me..." I was livid. Beth didn't even have the decency to pick Gabby up herself. Needless to say, Mrs. Joyce from Attorney Ellis' office did not tell me that part, but Amelia was quick to cut me off and inform me.

"It was a woman in an 8 series BMW. Gabriel, this isn't completely bad. At least we know Beth wasn't driving and that's a good thing considering her record."

"I guess you have a point," I sighed as I took a seat in my office chair and hung my head in my hands. "You know, it was probably Beth's mother. Jay wasn't spotted was he?"

"No, he said he stayed a couple of cars in back of her even when he went through the gate at their club."

I let out a long exhale of relief, but reminded her what could happen if they got caught.

"We won't get caught. If she can manage to break in your house and steal your mother's wedding ring set without getting caught, then surely we can follow her a little while."

"Amelia, I am being serious. We can't get caught."

"We won't. I promise." Amelia tried to assure me, but I just wanted all of this to be over for Gabby's sake.

We sat there in silence just breathing over the phone to each other for a few minutes. Amelia was the first one to break the silence.

"I know you have to go," Amelia admitted barely above a whisper. "I love you and I love Gabby. I know she's not really mine, but ever since you put her in my arms at Grady that day..."

Amelia paused and took a breath. I think she was crying. Before I could question her, she started again, "I've wished she was. I couldn't love her more. I don't know why. I can't explain it. I feel like my heart is breaking."

"I'm not sorry that we have Gabby, but I am so sorry that I brought this on you. I'm so sorry, Amelia. If I knew how to stop it, I would. If I knew how to make Beth go away for good, I would."

I hated to hear Amelia cry and I could hear her sniffles through the phone. She was trying to hide it, but I could hear her. I wished I was there with her, to hold her and tell her in person that everything was going to work out somehow although I did not know exactly how. I just knew things had to work out for us, for Gabby.

CHAPTER 20

The Order had provided that Beth would return Gabby at 4:00 p.m. on Sunday afternoon. She was to drop Gabby off back where she picked her up at Attorney Ellis' office. I typically left Port Honor after the brunch shift around 2:00 p.m. On this particular Sunday, I hung around so I could go straight to his office in downtown Greensboro.

As much as I did not want to see Beth, I could not help but arrive early to pick up Gabby. I was anxious to see her and make sure she was alright. Also, I did not want Gabby to wait one more minute longer than she had to before she was back into the arms of someone who truly loved her. Both Amelia and I had endured the entire weekend wondering if Gabby was safe and looked after. I would have given anything to know what Gabby must have been thinking and wondering about us.

When I turned the corner at the light onto Broad Street, I could see the driveway in front of the Victorian house that held Attorney Ellis' office. There were no cars parked outside. It was five minutes until four. Beth still had five minute to spare and I had five minutes to wait. I still did not care what anyone said, I knew Gabby was not biologically mine, but she had been mine in every other meaning of the word since the day Beth's mother called me to the hospital after her birth.

I had barely pulled into a space when Joyce, Attorney Ellis' secretary pulled up along beside me. She drove an older Oldsmobile and it suited her. I dare say the brown paint of her car was the same color her hair was dyed. She was a woman in her fifties and from the times I had met her before, I could tell she was not the type of woman to be out on a Sunday afternoon for no good reason.

Joyce began to roll down her window and I followed suit, thinking she wanted to say something to me. I was wrong. She was merely cracking her window for the smoke from her cigarette to escape. I could hear the voice of the announcer from the Falcons' game floating through her cracked window and I could smell the cigarette smoke. I thought about rolling my window back up, but did not want to offend her. I also rationalized that I only had to smell the smoke for a few minutes and I did not mind listening to the game.

I glanced at my watch every couple of minutes. It was a long five minutes, but it came and went. Another five minutes passed and there was still no sign of Beth, her mother or anyone else returning Gabby. The cell phone rang in the cup holder. I glanced to Joyce as I snatched up the phone. She kind of smiled a pursed, put out smile at me. She was probably feeling a tenth of what I was and what I was feeling was frustrated and pissed and I now had to answer a call that I knew was from Amelia.

"Hello?" I answered. I tried to keep the frustration from my voice. I did not want to get Amelia riled up for nothing. Although I did not like it one bit, it was typical of Beth to be late to everything.

"Do you have Gabby? Are you on your way home?" Amelia was quick with her words and anxious for an answer.

I had never lied to her before, but I really wanted to tell what I hoped would be a white lie then. I refrained and told the truth. "No, but I am sure they will be here any moment. I've told you before, Beth's late to everything and I am sure she's just messing with me. This is the only bit of control she has over me now, so I'm sure she's just flexing that muscle. We'll be home soon."

"I know you're probably right, but what if she doesn't bring her back? What will we do? What can be done? Jolene called and said they left their lake house with Gabby right after lunch and they haven't come back. Where do you think they went?" Amelia was not satisfied with my response. I could hear her pacing through the poor connection of the cell phone.

"I don't know Amelia. Right now, I feel like I just have to have faith that she's only running late. I will call you back when I have Gabby." I did not want to get Amelia more worked up by going back and forth about what ifs. That did not do her any good and I did not want her getting more upset than she already was.

It was nearly 4:20 p.m. when Joyce rolled her window down and motioned to get my attention. "How long do you want to wait before we call the sheriff?"

I am sure I had a puzzled look on my face. "Call the sheriff?" I sighed. Were we really going to have Beth locked up again?

"You will need to file kidnapping charges at some point. Do you want to do it now or wait until I have missed the entire second half of the game?" Joyce was very matter of fact in her demeanor as she lit another cigarette.

"Isn't there a certain amount of time I have to wait before I ..."

"You could have called them when she was five minutes late. She's twenty minutes late now. It's your call. I will open the office for you and we will get Mr. Ellis up here if you like."

What bothered me the most is that Joyce said all of this like it was common practice. I guess she had seen it all in the years she had been a legal secretary, but this was my first trip to the show and kidnapping was a big word for me. My mind circled and circled with the word and I felt nauseous. The word kidnapping wasn't just someone running late. It meant they weren't coming back.

I opened the car door and I suppose Joyce took that as a sign that I wanted to go into the office and call Mr. Ellis. She exited her car as well and started around, but that wasn't it. I needed air, clean air, not the stuff that had been drifting through from her cigs. In the car I was being suffocated by my thoughts and her Lucky Strikes. I stood and grabbed my breath. Was this what hyperventilating felt like?

Maybe I looked a little green, I'm not sure, but Joyce could tell I was not taking this well. She rushed around her car. "Are you alright, Mr. Hewitt?"

"I'm not alright!" I was fucking pissed and scared. Scared of what would happen to Gabby if left with Beth and scared of whether I could get her back or not.

"Come, let's go inside," Joyce patted me on the shoulder and started to lead.

Just as we headed toward the front porch of the old house, a car turned into the driveway. It was a silver 8 series BMW. I recognized the car. It was Beth's mom's and it pulled up on the other side of Joyce's.

The color had drained from my face when Joyce had mentioned kidnapping, but I could feel it returning as the BMW rolled to a stop.

"Wait here," Joyce told me before she approached the car. I stayed by my car as she instructed.

The windows were slightly tinted, but I could make out Beth in the driver's seat. Her mother exited the front passenger's door and glared at me. In that moment, I knew who Gabby looked like. I had known for weeks that there were hints of Dick in her, but Gabby was nearly the spitting image of Beth's mother. Unlike Beth, Mrs. Reed had never dyed her hair. She wore it natural and at nearly sixty, it had held most of its color. The shape of their faces, the dark hair, they were definitely related. My heart sank at the glimpse into Gabby's future and for just a moment I wasn't furious.

Mrs. Reed opened the back passenger's side door and started to unbuckle Gabby from the car seat. The fury returned as I watched and wondered what the point in all of this was. Joyce held her arms open to take Gabby when Mrs. Reed stood up with her, but she was passed by as if Mrs. Reed did not see her at all. Mrs. Reed carried Gabby straight to me.

"I know you are a good man, Gabriel, and you can stop this nonsense and let her go," Mrs. Reed said as she reluctantly handed Little One back to me. "You know she belongs with Beth."

I could not resist. "If she belonged with Beth, then why did you ever give her to me that day at the hospital? And, where was Beth all of that time?"

Mrs. Reed tried to kiss Gabby on the forehead and I did not prevent her, but Gabby did. Sometimes even babies know wrong from right and I suppose this was one of those moments for my daughter. She knew she was back with Daddy and she nuzzled into my neck and away from her grandmother.

Mrs. Reed never responded to my question, but she addressed Gabby, "Remember, Grand-mommy loves you."

When Gabby refused her, I could not help myself. I was not ready to play my hand as to Gabby's paternity, but I wasn't above taking a jab. I backed away from Mrs. Reed and gave her a message to give to Beth.

"Please tell your daughter that some people say blood is thicker than water, but I'm not so sure about that." I looked her square in the eye when I said it and the look on my face was daring her to respond.

Mrs. Reed did little more than raise an eyebrow, but I knew it was something for her to think about. All she said in return was a very stern, "Goodbye, Gabe."

No sooner had she spoken the words then she turned her back and returned to her car. Joyce called after her, "You will need to be on time from now on."

Mrs. Reed simply waived a dismissive hand and got back in the car. I'm certain she thought I was referring to Amelia's relationship with Gabby and not my own when it came to blood versus water. She probably did not think anything more of it than me calling her daughter a horrible mother when really I was calling her a whore. I still wasn't certain that I did not sleep with her the night we left the club drunk and I woke up in her bed. The one thing I was certain of is that if I had slept with her, I wasn't the only one that was with her about the time she conceived.

Beth jerked the car in gear and whipped it around to exit the driveway. As soon as she had it straight, she squalled the tires. Joyce was in the middle of telling me that she would report to Mr. Ellis regarding the events of the drop off first thing tomorrow when Beth let off of the brake and slammed the gas. Beth peeled out of the driveway throwing gravel and dirt at all three of us. I heard the tires and turned just quick enough to shield Gabby. I was fortunate that nothing significant hit me above my jeans, but Joyce was not so fortunate. She took a piece of gravel to the side of her neck. Joyce's hand immediately shot to her neck.

"Are you alright?" I gasped.

"I'm sure it's just a scratch, but she could have hit the baby." Joyce was clearly put out and injured. She rubbed at the place on her neck and there was blood.

"Do you need me to get you home or call someone?"

"Oh, it will take more than that to put this old bird down," Joyce responded. "Why don't you go ahead and get on the road. I'm gonna run by Jack's house and let him know how this afternoon went. I was going to wait until tomorrow, but we'll just get some photos of my neck and add this to our list of careless acts by Miss Reed."

I had not even thought of that. I guess Joyce just took one for the team and I thanked her before loading Gabby and heading to Milledgeville. Gabby was asleep in her car seat before I made the turn back onto Main Street. Main Street became Highway 44 toward Eatonton right outside of the city limits. Just past the city limits sign exiting Greensboro, I called Amelia to let her know we were on our way. She wanted to know what the hold-up had been and I told her that I would tell her all about it as soon as we got home.

I spent half of the drive looking back at Gabby. Sometimes I looked using the rearview mirror and the mirror that was mounted to the headrest in the back seat. Other times I turned my face from the road and looked back at her. A fair portion of the ride I drove with one hand and had the other resting on the top of her head.

I stroked my hand lightly across her head and she did not stir at all. Her hair was getting thicker and filling in. It was so soft and fine. I made all sorts of observations of her as she slept and I drove, but the biggest wasn't about her hair or that she was getting bigger by the day. The most important observation was that I would have to endure weekends without her. I would have to endure every other weekend without her for the foreseeable future with this visitation arrangement being what it was. Unlike my other observations, this one absolutely disgusted me.

Forty-five minutes later, we pulled up at The Jefferson. Pulling into the driveway, I hit that gutter spot, that dip, that separated the street from the tracks of the driveway and still Gabby did not budge. That jarring of the car was the familiar signal that I was home and I let out a sigh of relief. I was so glad to be home and even more glad for Little One to be back home.

Amelia must have been watching for us because I was barely parked in my spot in the carport before she was opening the back door and getting Gabby out.

"Come here, sweet baby," Amelia cooed at Gabby as she pulled her from the car seat and into her arms. "Mommy has missed you so much."

Amelia hugged and hugged and planted kisses all over Gabby's little face. I proceeded to get out of the car, but Amelia hardly noticed. She only had eyes for that baby. "I have missed you! Missed you! Missed you!" she said in between each of the kisses she planted on Gabby's cheeks and forehead.

"You are going to chap her face if you keep that up," I cautioned as I followed Amelia.

Once inside, Amelia did not bother to inquire further as to the details of why it took us so long to get home. "I have a surprise for you," she told Gabby as she sat her in her bouncy seat. "Mommy will be right back."

Amelia left the room and returned with her violin. She proceeded to serenade Gabby with the song, "Baby of Mine." She said it was from the movie Dumbo. It was beautiful and if she was trying to put Gabby to sleep she succeeded admirably.

***

Two weeks later, we repeated the same visitation arrangement. Everything was exactly the same right down to Amelia renting the house, Jay and Jolene having a little covert vacation and Gabby being returned late. This time it was 4:30 when Beth and her mother showed up. The only difference was that this time Joyce and I were prepared for the flying gravel and so was Mr. Ellis who was photographing everything from the front window of his office. I managed to get Gabby in the car before Beth spun the tires and kicked up the gravel, but it still wasn't in time to keep the gravel from pelting me. I was not injured and neither was Joyce this time, but there were some significant dings to my car.

Mr. Ellis was pleased. He said this showed blatant disregard for the safety of the child. I wasn't so pleased. Despite this, it was just another piece to a puzzle and it did nothing to keep me from having to abide by the visitation order until we went to trial about the whole situation.

***

Two days later the visitation was repeated. The only difference was that this time, I made Amelia give up the rental house and spying. She reluctantly agreed, but the persuasion came in the form of one of her classes at law school that dealt with ethics. I had not used the word unethical, but apparently one of her professors did when she gave the scenario as an example in class. The professor was quite blunt with the advice to stop it because if caught, it would prevent her from attaining her license to practice law.

The other difference in this weekend was that I wasn't the only one at the club schmoozing with the members and watching the game. This time Dick was there too.

Again, Alvin had encouraged me to watch the game with the members and as soon as I went through the swinging door, I noticed him sitting there. I returned to the kitchen without having been noticed.

"Ugh!" I grunted as I stormed back down the corridor by the walk-in cooler where the beer was kept.

"What's the problem?" Alvin called to me from the dish pit area.

"Dick's here! Game day is ruined!" I stopped shy of chasing Alvin around the kitchen and just stood on the server side of the serving line. Surely Alvin was going to return to the items he left on the stove and there was no need for me to follow him around just to see him while we spoke.

"Yeah, and if you don't get back out there it will be ruined for all of the members too. Remember if they don't have a good time during the day, they won't come back here for dinner tonight." Alvin had a point.

"I can't stand him!" I groaned, drawing out every word.

Alvin returned to the line. He looked at me with his big green eyes and he was serious. "Stop your whining. Be a man. Get back out there. You know the thing that gets at Dick the most is when he is not the center of attention when it comes to the members. He loves to be seen as the big man. Get back out there and be yourself. The members will do the rest and he can eat his heart out."

I was out there and things were going as Alvin suggested they would. Dick was a Florida fan and I am not sure what he was thinking. Of all the days he decided to come to the bar for a game was the day that Georgia played Florida. All of the members that came to the bar on Saturdays were die-hard UGA fans. Any idiot could tell that he was really chapping their asses cheering for Florida, but it was as if he was clueless. To make matters worse, Florida was winning and it was painful to watch.

Alvin had indicated that I should kill Dick with kindness and further endear myself to the members simply by being myself. With or without my kindness, Dick did not need any aid in killing himself. His incessant cheering for Florida was his own suicide. Mr. Martin tried to caution Dick to settle down, but he didn't listen.

Matt was at the bar and was catching everything. He regularly shook his head in disbelief. While I was picking up drinks for a couple of the men sitting at the table with me, Matt whispered, "I don't know who's putting on more of a show, the television or our fearless leader. It's like watching a train wreck."

I just nodded in agreement. He was right, it was awful to watch, but no one could make him stop.

The third quarter had just begun when I heard the swinging of the kitchen door. I looked back thinking it was Matt, but it was Alvin and he was motioning for me.

"You gents excuse me." I eased from my chair. "I am needed in the kitchen."

I made my way to the kitchen door and found Alvin waiting for me on the other side. It was as if he was standing guard to make sure no one else came with me. As soon as I was inside, Alvin reached and stopped the door from swinging behind me. It was all so odd.

"Come with me. There's someone who wants to speak with you." Alvin led me to the back door.

Alvin held the door for me and outside waiting on me was Joan. She was standing there, looking around as if she was making sure no one was watching. She was fidgeting while holding a rather substantial stack of papers.

"I can only stay for a minute. I can't be seen, but I wanted to give this to you," Joan said, handing me the stack of papers that she had been holding.

I took the stack and looked back to Alvin. "Please go and make sure no one comes out here."

Alvin left as I had asked.

Quickly, Joan began to explain, "I got everything I could."

I held the pile as she flipped through and continued. I watched as she went on.

"This binder holds our home telephone records. I highlighted the calls made from Beth to the house in pink and the ones Dick made to her in blue."

Joan flipped to the next clipped stack. "These are the records from Dick's cell phone. I used the same color code." Joan pointed to a line in pink. "Recognize the number?"

"Yeah," I answered. I was too shocked at what she was providing to get excited right then.

"This next stack," Joan flipped the two other bound stacks to the side and pointed, "this is Dick's credit card purchases for the last year and a half. It lists the stores and their locations. If you start matching the phone calls and the purchases, you can tell when they were meeting up."

"Oh my God, Joan. Thank you!"

"I'm not done." Joan flipped to the next stack. "This is Beth's family's membership records from their club." She must have known what I was thinking by the look on my face. "Don't ask. I have a friend that works over there so let's leave it at that. Anyway, you can tell when she was in town by her purchases at the clubhouse. You can also tell when she stayed at their inn. Match the phone calls with the dates she stayed there and I think you will figure out when and where your daughter was conceived."

"Joan, I am so sorry about all of this, but thank you so much!"

"I'm still not done." She flipped to the last stack and clipped to it was an envelope. "The envelope contains all of the hair from Dick's hair brush in case you would like to have a DNA test performed to make sure. I have also included his last physical with his blood type on it."

"Joan, does he know you have all of this?" I gasped as I flipped through the documents.

Joan glanced around again to make sure no one was watching. "I know he's here watching the game, so I felt I was safe to give these to you now, but he has no idea about any of it. I need to keep it that way for a little while longer."

"May I give these to my attorney or what do you expect me to do with them?" I did not want to do anything to make her life more difficult, but I needed to know if I could use them if needed.

"Of course you can give them to your attorney, but don't make them public knowledge yet."

I reached out and patted her on the back, "I appreciate this more than you know and I am so sorry you are in this spot with us. My attorney says he does not think we will go to trial on this until December, so I know nothing will come of this information until at least then."

Joan seemed satisfied with the time frame I gave her.

"Well, I better get going. If someone sees me and reports back..."

"I know. You don't have to tell me how he is." I was certain that the way he was to work for was only magnified at home. He only did one kind thing a year and he had probably spent that kindness on Beth for all I knew.

Florida might have beat Georgia that day, but that night after I got home from work, Amelia and I celebrated what we saw as a small win of our own. If nothing else, we felt sure we could now prove that Beth and Dick had been having an affair.

Amelia and I laid all of the paperwork that Joan had given us out on the coffee table and started matching phone calls and credit card charges. From what we could tell, the affair really heated up two months before Gabby was probably conceived.

Amelia reached over and picked up one of the pages from Dick's cell phone bill. She brought it to her face for a closer look. She did not take her eyes off of the ledger as she asked, "Do you remember the date of the night that Beth broke in the house? The night that she got arrested for DUI?"

"Not right off," I answered, "but hold on."

I went to the room that used to be Jay's. I still had not unpacked everything from my house and I had some boxes stored in there. I dug through three boxes before I came across what I was looking for, the police report from the night she broke in. I grabbed it and returned to the living room.

"It was Sunday, November 19th," I said, pointing to the date on the report as I handed it to Amelia.

"Right. Look at this," Amelia handed the list of phone calls that she had been studying to me. "See right here? On November 18th, she started calling him at 9:15 p.m. Each call is logged as one minute and they are back to back to back. I bet he wasn't picking up."

I glanced down to see what she was showing me. I counted silently and got all the way to fifteen calls back to back before I stopped counting. "There must be forty calls here and that's definitely her number."

"Notice at 1:45 a.m. on the 19th, he finally picked up." Amelia pointed to the line showing the call at that time. "It lasted four minutes and then twenty minutes later she was at your house."

"Yeah." I didn't know what else to say.

"I would be willing to bet she told him she was pregnant that night and he told her to get lost."

I flopped down on the couch next to Amelia and ran my hands through my hair. "That would make so much sense."

"I bet that's what happened. By the look of these phone calls, she went crazy. I also bet that she panicked and came to your house that night to tell you the baby was yours."

"Thank God you were there that night or who knows how that would have gone."

Amelia reached over and patted me on the back as I held my head in my hands. I lifted my head enough to look back to her. "I think we already know the answer, but I think we should have the DNA test done on Gabby. It won't change how I feel about her. She's mine as far as I am concerned, but in case we need to play that card in court, we need something to back it up."

She leaned against me and sighed as I returned my head to my hands. "I know I should not say it, but I want to know that I am the one and only mother of your children."

From the corner of my eye, I could see Amelia rub her stomach.

I sat up right and turned to her. "Amelia, I understand what you're saying, but you are the mother of my children, including Gabby. It takes more than giving birth to be a mother and you of all people should know that."

The next afternoon I arrived at Attorney Ellis' office at five minutes until four. I sat there in the parking lot alone until nearly 4:20 p.m. Amelia called around 4:15 and kept me company until Mrs. Joyce arrived.

"I guess everyone's given up on being on time today," I uttered a slight complaint just before Mrs. Joyce pulled in.

Joyce pulled up beside me and rolled down her window. The past few times I had instinctively rolled down mine thinking she wanted to speak to me. Each time I had been wrong as she only wanted to let her cigarette smoke escape the car. This time I just sat there with every intention of continuing my conversation with Amelia until I saw Joyce motioning for me to let my window down.

"Jesus, I can't win for losing," I griped.

"What is it?" Amelia was quick to question.

"Oh, nothing. I'll tell you later. I have to go." Cell phone minutes were more expensive than even the regular MCI or AT&T long distance, so I refrained from wasting them on my petty grievance.

"Alright. I'll see you when you get home." Amelia then parted with, "Goodbye. Love you," and I replied the same.

I had already started rolling down the window while hanging up with Amelia. Once Joyce could tell I was off the phone, she stated her excuse for being late.

"Sorry. The Falcons' game ran a little long." She pointed to the window off their office. "Look, Jack beat me here too, but I guess Miss Reed is exhibiting her usual disregard for punctuality."

"Appears that way," I shrugged.

"I'm going to say something to them about peeling out of here and throwing rocks today." Joyce flicked her cigarette out of the window before she revealed her true feelings. "I'm too old for this childish shit and it's just plain dangerous."

"I know," I added as I tried not to inhale too much of the smoke that was floating my way. "Unfortunately, all of this is pretty typical Beth behavior."

Again Joyce was blunt, "Then how on Earth did she ever get her hooks in you?"

374

I'm sure my face turned a little red with embarrassment. "I was young and stupid, I suppose." It was a much longer story than that, but that about summed it up.

"Typical man, huh?" She lit another cigarette and was flicking ash out of the window again.

"Yeah, I like to think I'm smarter now."

Joyce just shook her head and took another drag off of the cigarette. She did not speak again until around 4:45. She sat there smoking her cigs and I leaned my head against my headrest and listened to the music from the radio.

"Later than usual today," Joyce observed. "How much longer do you want to give her?"

"Might as well give her 'til 5:00. I mean, we've waited this long." In all honesty, I was certain Beth and her mother would drive up as soon as we called the police. Then we would just waste more time on the report. I didn't think it was worth it yet.

Joyce looked disgusted with my answer and she lit another cigarette. I think that was her fourth one, not counting the one she was smoking when she first drove up. "It's your decision."

In that moment, I was regretting that I made Amelia discontinue renting the house near Beth's parents' on the lake. I would have killed to know if Beth or her mother had even left to bring Gabby back yet. Renting the house seemed like a waste of money four weeks ago, but now it did not seem like such a waste. I would have given most anything to have been able to pick up the phone and find out Beth's whereabouts with Gabby.

I was lost in my thoughts of regret when I heard the tires on the gravel driveway. I lifted my head slightly from the headrest and looked to the rearview mirror. Pulling up behind me was Beth's white 3 series BMW. The car was going relatively slow, but it kept coming.

It wasn't a long stretch from the road to where we were parked, but it was long enough for me to realize she wasn't stopping. I wasn't sure what to do; sit there and pray she did not hit me, pray

375

that Gabby wasn't in the car with her and that she did hit me, or just jump out of my car and run in case she really did hit me.

At the last possible moment, I scrambled out of my car. I did a Dukes of Hazard power slide across the hood of Joyce's car and cleared the vehicles as Beth's BMW slammed into the back of my car. The next thing I knew, I landed on my feet on the front driver's side of Joyce's car. I turned back to find Beth's car still resting on the rear of mine, but occupying the parking space where mine had been. Upon impact, my car had been knocked over the railroad tie that separated the parking spaces from the grass. Now, all four of my tires were sitting in the grass, but Beth's were stopped against the railroad tie.

Both Joyce and I rushed to the doors of Beth's car. I snatched open the passenger's side and Joyce did the same to the driver's side. I nearly tore the front seat out of the car moving it so I could get to Gabby. I was terrified and Gabby was screaming such that I wasn't sure if she was hurt or scared. Amelia recognized all of her cries. She said there was a separate one for hungry, scared, hurt, sleepy and so forth. She was right. I could tell the difference, but she could tell the difference way better than I ever could.

Even though my focus was getting Gabby from the backseat, I could hear Beth arguing with Mrs. Joyce. I reached to unbuckle Gabby only to find that she was not strapped into the car seat at all. In fact, she was just lying on top of the straps. Whoever had put her in the seat, had not buckled her in and had only thrown a blanket over the top of her.

"Come here, baby," I said softly to try to calm her, but she just screamed and real tears ran down her little face.

"Daddy's got you," I continued as I slipped my hands under her and lifted. "Shhhh, shhhh. It's okay now. Daddy's got you."

As I stood from the car, I found Mr. Ellis behind me. "I called the ambulance so we could have her checked out." He was calm as he spoke. "I got it all on camera."

"Let go of me!" Beth screamed at the top of her lungs as she snatched her car door shut.

I looked and saw Ms. Joyce struggling to catch hold of the car door. It was barely a sideways glance, but my attention was immediately called back to Gabby as she responded to Beth with a blood curdling scream of her own.

Within a second, Beth was spinning her tires out of the driveway. We all rushed to take cover from the flying rocks.

"Gabe, where's that cell phone of yours?" Joyce was already on the move before I answered. Clearly she did not want to waste the time it would take for her to run inside and use the office phone.

"It was in the front seat of my car." I stood from where I had crouched to shield Gabby from any gravel that might have been slung up when Beth swung her car around and threw it in gear.

I continued to try to settle Gabby and Joyce had her hands on the phone in my car before she fully asked to borrow it. I thought she was dialing 911, but apparently she had more of a straight shot.

"This is Joyce ... Yeah, I know it's Sunday afternoon, but could you put Bobby on the phone?"

Joyce just looked at us as she waited. Mr. Ellis had walked down to the street to see which way Beth turned at the light downtown and I paced back and forth with Gabby. I just could not get her to calm down and I was concerned that she wasn't just scared, but perhaps she was hurt.

"Bobby, sorry about the interruption, but I need you to send one of the deputies out." There was fluctuation in her voice as Joyce looked to Mr. Ellis for the answer of which way Beth had gone.

"Highway 44 toward Eatonton," Mr. Ellis shouted back.

Joyce continued, "There's a white BMW headed toward Eatonton, she's probably made it to the city limits sign by now. It's got significant frontend damage and she just left the scene of an accident. I need you all to get her."

Joyce was right about the frontend damage. I only got a glance at it for everything else that happened, but I was surprised the car was drivable, mine certainly wasn't.

I could only hear Joyce's side of the conversation and I could only make out about half of that over Gabby's crying. It appeared Joyce might have been on the phone with the sheriff himself. As Joyce went on, Mr. Ellis walked back toward us.

"Yeah, she had an infant in the car with her and I think the child may be hurt... Yes, the ambulance is on its way... Alright. Thank you....Okay, no, I don't think it's necessary that you come down here... Yes, bye now."

It really was as if she was struggling to get off of the phone with him, but as soon as she hung up, she began to explain that the sheriff of Green County was her brother. I hardly heard her for my own inner struggle of what to do to calm Gabby and wondering when the ambulance was going to get there. In trying to calm her, it occurred to me to think like Amelia. What would Amelia do in this situation? She was a born mother and I was all thumbs.

"Ah!" It came to me and I announced as such. "Joyce, would you crank my car just enough to cut the radio on and put in the Patsy Cline CD and hand me the blue bunny from the passenger's seat?"

Mrs. Joyce was quick to fulfill my request and within seconds, Walking After Midnight was bellowing through the yard. I swayed back and forth with Gabby and her favorite stuffed animal.

Amelia had decorated the nursery with everything pink right down to two pink bunnies for the girls. Gabby wanted nothing to do with her pink bunny, but she could not get enough of the blue bunny that Jay won at the college fair.

Patsy Cline and Blue Bunny seemed to be working until the ambulance came blaring its siren down the street and into the driveway. All of the commotion just jump-started the crying and wailing again. The fact that she had calmed down a little provided a little assurance that maybe she was not hurt, maybe she really was just frightened after all.

Gabby settled down again as soon as the siren was cut off. The EMTs looked her over and could not find anything wrong with her.

378

The female member of the ambulance patted Gabby on the head. "It might make you feel better to have her checked out, but she's fine. Babies are tougher than we give them credit for and she was probably just scared out of her pretty little head with all of the ruckus." She spoke her peace in a very thick Southern accent of baby talk. If it had been under different circumstances, I would have probably laughed at the way the woman sounded.

While the EMTs were packing to leave, Green County's finest arrived. I could see the two deputies shaking their heads, but I did not find out what they were disgusted about until after the EMTs left.

I carried Gabby over to where they were all standing with Joyce and Mr. Ellis at the front of my car. One was already writing up a report and the other was assessing the damage to the car.

"Mr. Hewitt, this here's your car?" The stout one asked me.

"Yes, sir," I answered as I extended a free hand to greet him. I continued to snuggle Gabby and Blue Bunny against my shoulder with the other hand.

"You may want to call someone to come get you. Looks like the ball joint on this front tire here is shot," he explained as he pointed to the front passenger side tire. "Probably knocked it loose when it went over the railroad tie."

"That took some force," the other deputy added.

Before calling Amelia or anyone to come get us and having to explain why, I wanted to know if they caught Beth, so I asked, "Not to change the subject, but where is Miss Reed?"

"Well your guess is as good as ours," the younger deputy who was writing the report looked up and said.

"Y'all have not caught her?" Panic set in. They did not know where she was. I did not know where she was and clearly she was in one of her crazy states of mind. All I knew was that Amelia was home alone.

"Joyce, where's that cell phone?"

"Here," she offered. I handed her Gabby as she handed me the phone.

"Excuse me." I told them and I stepped away to dial Jay's number. Luckily, I had bothered to memorize it just in case I ever needed him.

Cara answered. Before she could finish her greeting, I interrupted, "Cara, is Jay home?"

"No, he went to his parents' house for the weekend. I don't expect him back until later tonight."

"Shit!" I shouted before I realized it.

"Gabe, what's wrong? Is it Millie?"

"I need you to do me a favor."

"Sure, anything." Cara had cheer in her voice and I was about to squash that.

"Can you come get me and Gabby? We are fine, but my car has been in a wreck. Also, if you could go and get Amelia to come with you, but do it without worrying her, I would appreciate it."

"Okay." The cheer had turned to concerned.

"Please make sure you tell Amelia that we are fine. I am fine and Gabby is fine. As soon as I hang up with you, I will call and tell Amelia what's going on."

"Alright." Again, skepticism was in her voice and even though she knew there was more to the story, but thankfully she did not question me.

They didn't find Beth that day. There was a part of me that wanted to find Beth myself, not to bring her back into our lives, but to hurt her. I wanted her to pay. When I was in the moment that day I last saw her, all I could think about was Gabby and making sure she was alright. On the ride home that day, I could hardly contain myself. I just wanted to hurt her. I wanted to wrap my hands around her neck and squeeze until there was no more air.

380

I did not want to hurt her because of my own fury. I wanted to hurt Beth because she had so little regard for Gabby. I wanted to hurt her because we did end up at the emergency room that night. Cara brought Amelia to get us like I asked and she agreed to take us to the emergency room to have Gabby checked out. Amelia saw my car and the damage. I tried to soften the blow and not give her the play-by-play, but I did not have to, Joyce did all the work for me.

I was nervous to let her drift off, but we were barely down the road toward Eatonton and Gabby was fast asleep in the car seat that I had transferred from my car to Cara's. Amelia insisted on sitting in the back seat with Gabby, but she was fuming. She had said her peace four times over about what she would do to Beth when she got her hands on her.

"Amelia," I looked back over the front seat to caution her. She had a hand caressing Gabby's head as she slept, but she was turned away from the child. Amelia was staring out the window deep in her vengeance. She did not even turn to look at me when I said her name.

"Amelia," I repeated, "You need to let this roll off. I will handle it."

"Let it roll off? She could have killed the both of you!" Amelia huffed. "I am so tired of all of this!"

"Millie, you need to calm down and consider the baby," Cara added, straightening the rearview mirror so she could keep an eye on the road and Amelia.

Amelia glanced back at me and seethed, "What's your famous phrase? Mess with the bull and get the horns? Isn't that it? Where's the bull now? When is she going to get the horns, Gabriel?"

Before I could answer, Amelia doubled over and I could hear her gasp.

"Are you okay?"

"NO!" There were tears of pain in her voice and the word was more of a muffled whine than her normal speaking tone.

Cara looked to the rearview mirror, "Millie, what is it?"

Her reply was a full on cry, "I don't know, the baby."

I unbuckled my seatbelt and turned around to Amelia to find her clutching her stomach. She took a deep breath in and followed by little huffs out as if it hurt just to exhale.

"Take my hand," I insisted. "Squeeze it with the pain and hold on."

This was not typical Braxton Hicks. She did not have to tell us when the contractions were coming. Cara and I could both tell by the change in her breathing and I could tell by the force she applied when squeezing my hand. I thought she had broken it during one contraction. Amelia huffed and huffed and Cara stepped on the gas.

Once we reached the hospital, the three of us were all terrified that Amelia had gone into full blown labor. We still had to get Gabby checked out and I hated having to choose, but I had to take Gabby because it had to be a parent or guardian with her and Cara was neither. Cara had to go with Amelia and I had to go with Gabby and I just added this to the list of things that made me hate Beth Reed. I hated that her actions had caused Gabby to have to be checked out for injuries from a car wreck and I hated her because she might have driven my wife to lose our child, and if she miscarried, I would not be the one holding her hand. I might not be the one telling her it was going to be alright and there would be other children in that moment. I hated Beth Reed and I knew exactly where the bull was.

The bright spot of that day, if there was one, was that Amelia did not lose the baby. Also, Beth's actions enabled Attorney Ellis to call an emergency hearing with the judge that week and have the visitation order overturned.

The miracle workers at Oconee Regional stopped Amelia's contractions and she continued to get bigger with every passing day, but the fact that Beth was essentially missing again did not make the passing weeks of her pregnancy joyful for me. I continued to receive correspondence regarding how the case was progressing, but none of that really mattered. Amelia and I argued as my opinion was that the battle was over. Beth played her hand and everyone saw. Amelia agreed that we had won a battle, but as always, the war wasn't over. It was her opinion that the war with Beth would never be over.

I had just locked the door behind me. I had Gabby in the car carrier and she wasn't as light as she once was. I exhaled a long breath as I stopped at the front door of The Jefferson. I had a hand on the door knob as I listened to the phone ring for the third time. I could hear it all the way down the stairs from our apartment. It crossed my mind to keep going, but the thought that always made me go back was, "What if it was Amelia calling?"

"Shit!" I said under my breath before apologizing to Gabby for my language. "I know, like you even understand."

I looked down at Little One and her eyes lit up and she giggled at me. I just shook my head and turned back to unlock the door.

I had three more rings of the phone before the answering machine kicked on, so I sat Gabby down at the landing at the bottom of the stairs. Sitting her down allowed me to sprint up the steps and make it to the phone.

"Daddy will be right back," I assured her before I took the steps two at a time on my way up.

I caught hold of the handset of the phone just as the machine answered. I tried to cut the machine off, but it wasn't cooperating.

"Hold on," I spoke over the greeting.

The caller waited until after the beep and then identified himself, "Gabe, it's Jack. I'm glad I caught you."

It was Attorney Ellis and he barely caught me. I was on my way to drop Gabby off with Mrs. Allen and then on to work. Amelia had a study group at Mercer that night, so we could not do our usual trade off. We still used Mrs. Allen during the week when I went in to work during the day.

"I hated making this call, but I received notice that Ms. Reed has a new attorney and a copy of the petition that he filed with the court yesterday. He's asking the court to continue the trial." I could hear the exasperation in his voice. Attorney Ellis was about as tired of this case and all of the nonsense that went with it as I was.

"What does that mean, to continue the trial?" Amelia would have known just what that meant, but I had no idea. With all of this, I was getting an education, but not the same as her.

"It means he wants to remove the case from the December calendar," he answered.

I wiped my brow and ran a hand through my hair, a habit of mine when I was the least bit frustrated.

He went on, "He's included an exhibit to his petition stating that Beth is under medical care and is in no condition to attend the trial."

"Medical care?"

"I find it all odd since her last attorney told me that they couldn't find her. I think she's in rehab or something and they're throwing themselves on their sword and trying to gain understanding for her actions. Paint a picture that she's trying to get help."

I let out a huff of air. I was disgusted. "And what do you think will happen?"

"I am going to counter with a Motion for Summary Judgment. Admitting she's in rehab is an admission that she has a problem with drugs, an admission of being unfit. I'm going to ask the court to rule in your favor and deny her custody once and for all."

The whole conversation had only taken a few minutes and the whole time I had been watching Gabby from the top of the stairs. I could see she was starting to get a little fussy and I still had to keep her in the carrier for the drive to Siloam, which was about thirty minutes from Milledgeville. Poor baby's good nature had an expiration when it came to being in the carrier. I had to wind the conversation with Mr. Ellis down if I expected to make it to Mrs. Allen's house with our nerves intact.

"I really appreciate you calling and please do all that you can to get this over with, but I have to get to work. I'm sorry and..."

He cut me short, "No, it's fine. I just wanted you to know what was going on and I did not want you to hear about this in a letter."

"Thanks again."

"I'll let you know as soon as I get an answer. Bye, now."

CHAPTER 21

November 6, 1996, was quiet compared to that of 1995. We were exhausted, but it was still Amelia's birthday and I was not about to let it pass as just another day. It fell on a Wednesday and although Amelia could not get out of class, I was able to get off work for the occasion.

I had been asking her for weeks what she wanted for her birthday and where she wanted to go to dinner, but the only thing Amelia wanted was peace and quiet. Well, she wasn't about to get that.

Jay agreed to drop by as soon as she got home from class and insist that she allow him to take her out shopping. Amelia initially refused him, but he reminded her how much fun they used to have just shopping together and how they had not done it in so long. He laid on the guilt pretty heavily and Amelia caved. One of the things he said to get her to go along was that they would only run out to the Milledgeville Mall for a little while, but he and I agreed that he would whisk her away to the Macon Mall and they would not return until at least 6:00 p.m.

I also made arrangements with Cara to pick up a cake, but she decided to make one instead. I was nervous about that until she showed up at 5:00 p.m. with a chocolate cake that looked like Abe Lincoln's top hat. It was tall and very store-bought looking.

"I made it myself! Don't look at me like that. I did make it myself, frosting and all." Cara swore as she put it on the bar in the kitchen.

Stella was in on the night's events as well. She was pivotal in keeping Gabby occupied while I cooked dinner. She also allowed me to keep all of the ingredients for dinner in her refrigerator so Amelia would not notice anything. On the menu tonight was filet mignon with gorgonzola cream sauce, roasted rosemary potatoes, grilled Roma tomatoes topped with melted parmesan cheese and Caesar salad. It was one of the specials that I made at the club regularly and the first thing I made that Amelia tasted. I have often wondered if the way to her heart was through her stomach because she had a standing order every time it was on the menu.

"Don't come home without it," she told me one night and that was well before the pregnancy cravings could have started.

Unlike last year, the guest list did not include everyone she knew. This year I kept it to the usual crew from family night dinners, which included Daniel and Jerry even though they did not live in The Jefferson. I also invited Gayle, but she was on call for the birth of a colt at one of her client's farms. I came close to inviting Mrs. Allen, but I knew she had to take care of her grandchildren, so I glazed over the fact that we were having an actual party and promised to send her a piece of birthday cake. I still felt a little guilty not inviting her since she had been so important to us and so great with Gabby.

By 5:30 everyone was there, but Amelia and Jay. Cara put the final touches on decorating. Daniel acted as my sous chef. Jerry set the table with the fine china that Gayle had given Amelia as our wedding present. It had belonged to her mother, Amelia's grandmother, and this was the first opportunity for us to use it. Everyone had a job and I appreciated all of their help. It seemed I could manage a whole clubhouse, but I could not put on a small birthday party without the help of every friend I had.

At 6:05 we heard the key in the lock downstairs and everyone scurried like mice to hide. Most of them ducked behind the counter in the kitchen, but Jerry got stuck hiding behind the dining room table. I grabbed Gabby and flopped down on the couch. I snuggled Gabby to my chest and cut the TV on. I tried to look casual as if Little One and I were just having some daddy/daughter time.

We were all still going with the element of surprise for the party although that was ridiculous since the leaf was clearly in the dining room table and there were more chairs, the presents were sitting on the bar and what few decorations there were would surely give it away.

I had been afraid Jay would let the cat out of the bag or Amelia would figure it out while they were shopping, but clearly that was not the case. Amelia was oblivious to everything.

"I am so exhausted. He parked at the far end of the mall and then wanted to go to JC Penney's. Why he couldn't just park at Penney's I don't know." Amelia kicked off her shoes and started around the couch. "I am so glad we aren't having a party this year."

I did not know what to say, but Jerry did. He sprang from the back side of the dining room table. "Did someone say something about a party?" he flounced.

Amelia barely moved her head to look my way. "You didn't," she sighed.

Everyone else jumped up from behind the kitchen counter and the bar and all at once they said, "Oh, yes, he did."

Jay also popped up from the stairwell and Amelia just looked back at him and laughed. "You knew about this all along?"

"Yep. Sure did."

"If I weren't so tired, I swear..."

Cara chimed in, "You would hug each and every one of us."

Stella came forward and took Gabby from me. I stood up from the couch and asked, "Are you all ready for some dinner?"

"Oh, yeah," Daniel and Jay said in unison. Jerry cut an eye of jealousy at Daniel as if he had spoken out of turn. The look spoke volumes and most everyone caught it loud and clear. It was awkward and everyone, including Daniel, ignored him.

I nominated Jay to say the blessing as we all gathered at the table. Despite what some might think due to his orientation and activities, I had found him to be more religious than the rest of us. In fact, he could bless a meal better than most men of my grandfather's generation.

Jay always asked us all to join hands before he began and this reminded me of Thanksgiving and Christmas at Aunt Dot's house. Even though Daniel had not acknowledged Jerry's scathing look moments before, he knew where his bread was buttered and he took a seat on the opposite side of the table and opposite end from

Jay. He picked the seat next to Cara and Jerry quickly scooted into the chair next to him. Now there was no chance of him having to hold hands with Jay, not even for the prayer.

"Let us bow our heads," Jay started and everyone dropped their heads, except Gabby in her highchair, who was still taking it all in.

"Dear Lord, we ask you to bless this food before us and the hands that prepared it. I ask that you bless our friend, Millie, for whom we have gathered here tonight. Your scripture tells us, Lord, that if two or more of us gather, you are among us. There are nine of us and we ask that you join us in honoring her birthday. We ask that in her twenty-second year, peace be returned to her life. Lord, we thank you for all you do, for all of the blessings you bestow upon us. In Jesus' name we pray. Amen."

Amelia squeezed my hand several times during Jay's words. He did not need to elaborate in his words to God and, when he said "Amen," the whole lot of us concurred. All of us knew what needed to happen this year for peace to be returned to Amelia. I needed to win the case for custody of Gabby and free our lives of Beth once and for all. We also needed to have a healthy birth of our own baby.

The food was laid out family style and everyone began passing dishes toward Amelia, but she was always so gracious. "No, y'all go ahead and serve yourselves."

As everyone filled their plates, Travis suggested the topic of the night. There was always a topic of discussion at the table on family dinner night, a tradition Amelia started when she first bought The Jefferson. Tonight's topic was "Best and worst birthday." We were to tell about either our best or our worst birthday or birthday party.

"I'll start." Cara passed the salad to Daniel and began her story. "I was just about to turn eight. All of the kids were having skating parties and I wanted a skating party so badly. I wanted to go to Redwing Skating Rink just like all of my friends."

"Back then I did not know how poor we were." Cara shrugged her shoulders and we all listened a little closer as we continued to make our plates. "Between my grandmother buying me a pair of the right Nikes for school and my mother buying me a Members Only jacket, I managed to fly under the radar so the other kids did not know either. I knew the kids who were poor. They were made fun of and I was lucky not to be one of them. As an adult, I know there's nothing wrong with being poor. I'm still poor, but kids can be mean."

"Anyway, my mother agreed to throw me a skating party. I was over the moon. She made out these cute little invitations with Strawberry Shortcake on them. They were scented. I can still smell them now. I handed them out to everyone in my third grade class. They said the party was going to be at my grandmother's house, but I did not pay a bit of attention to that. I thought everyone was going to meet there and then we would caravan to the skating rink that was in the next town over. Boy, was I wrong, when we got there my mother promptly backed out Granny's car so we could all skate under the carport. I was crushed and mortified. Everyone was going to find out that we could not afford to go to the skating rink."

"I prayed for anything to save me from what was about to happen. I was about to be found out and at my birthday party no less. Luckily, it started raining. Not just raining, flooding. Kids showed up with skates and sheets of rain came in droves. I told everyone that my mother was afraid to drive in the rain so we could not go to the skating rink and no one was the wiser. It was a bad birthday, but it could have been worse."

When Cara was finished she looked to Daniel to tell his birthday story and Daniel passed to Jerry.

"I dropped out of high school in the eleventh grade. Broke my mother's heart, but California was calling me. I was going to be a model. I was going to be a star. I managed to get cast as an extra in this movie called 'Pretty Maids All in a Row.' Rock Hudson was in it and I had heard the rumors."

Jerry glanced to Daniel, "Ear muffs, dear."

Daniel acted as if he was going to put his hands over his ears for a moment before giving a little quip of his own, "Oh, Hell, I've heard the story a hundred times. Go on."

Jerry puffed out his chest with pride and finished his story. "On my eighteenth birthday I unwrapped Rock Hudson. Best birthday ever! Top that, bitches!"

"Rock Hudson? No, way!" Jay challenged.

Everyone was initially laughing at Jerry's story, but suddenly we were all silent.

The silence was broken when Amelia asked, "Travis, can I get you some more tea?" She glanced around the table and Travis was the only one who had even halfway emptied his glass.

Stella responded before Travis had a chance to, "He would love more tea, Millie. Thank you so much!"

I thought about telling my birthday story about when my Aunt Mary took me in after my parents died, but before I could Travis began his.

"Mine is my best and worst all in one. I don't know if you all know, but I have a step-sister that is a day younger than I am. When our parents married, it was the beginning of combined birthday parties. We too were not well off so one birthday party instead of two made more sense. I hated her and the feeling was mutual. Anyway, my parents saved and rented out the Shriner's club and hosted a dance for us. As if it wasn't bad enough that I was sharing a birthday with someone who's death I plotted regularly, I came down with mono the Monday before the party which was scheduled for Friday."

"That's terrible!" Amelia choked over her steak.

"I know," Travis responded, "I looked and felt like death warmed over all week and there was no cancelling the party. The money was spent and there was no getting it back. On top of that, 'It wouldn't be fair to Heather'."

Stella added to the story, "Can you still hear the distain in his voice. The only reason there's a truce between them now is because she attends college in California and never comes home."

Travis continued, "We were fourteen when our parents got married. As if puberty wasn't awkward enough, for me it came with

391

a new sister that looked like Phoebe Cates in "Fast Times at Ridgemont High." She stole every friend I had. All of my friends got to second base with her and half of them got a homerun and that was just during that first year!"

Again, Stella added off-handed commentary, "Heather was the sex education department of our school."

"So, there I was the night of our party, looking half dead and there was Heather dancing with all of my friends. She pranced around like she was the belle of the ball..."

Jerry pounced on the opportunity to correct Travis. "She was the belle of the ball." As always, cattiness dripped from his words.

"Anyway, this night was a little different for me, not just because of the party, but because I wanted to kill her more than usual. Instead, I remembered what my mama always said about killing folks with kindness. When it came time to cut our birthday cake, before she blew out the candles, I shocked everyone by apologizing to Heather for being a horrible brother, but it was only because I secretly loved her. After my speech, I kissed her. They don't say mono is the kissing disease for nothing. Oh, yeah, I put it on her real good and then she blew out the candles. That skanky sister of mine plus every guy at the party got mono and so did their girlfriends. It ended up being a happy birthday for me after all."

The stories went on and the prize slice of birthday cake was about to be passed to the winner, Travis, for his birthday story, when Jay challenged.

"Wait, wait, I have a story." Jay reached out and took the slice of cake. "Best birthday: I was ten and my Noni was in the hospital. In all honesty, the whole family forgot my birthday. Noni was my mother's mother and she had fought a long battle with cancer and everyone thought she was nearing the end. Aunts, uncles, cousins that were old enough, and my parents, everyone was taking shifts at the hospital to be there when she passed."

"Millie and I took piano lessons from the same teacher. I was always dropped off early and her Aunt Gayle was almost always running late to pick her up. Anyway, we ended up waiting in Mrs.

392

Kelley's living room together and that's how we became friends. That year the only cake I got on my birthday was the cupcake that Millie brought me. She even put a candle in it. It wasn't lit, of course, but as I went to take a bite of the cupcake, Millie asked me, 'Aren't you going to blow out the candle and make a wish?' So I pretended to blow out the candle and I made a wish."

"I wished for my Noni to be okay. I never told anyone that before. I wished so hard that it might have been more of a prayer than a wish. I don't know if that wish did the trick, I just know that I have had an extra eleven years with my Noni. I still talk to her every day. I just know there was something special about that wish, the cupcake and Millie."

I glanced to Amelia as Jay spoke and her eyes were full of tears. I reached under the table and took her hand.

Jay also looked at Amelia when he spoke. "See, I never cared about getting a cake or everyone else forgetting my birthday. I really just cared about my Noni because she's one of two people that ever really made a fuss over me. Most everyone's always been able to tell how I am and a lot of people back home go the other direction when they see me coming, but not her and not Millie. I could be purple and inside out and they wouldn't care. Everyone forgetting my birthday is nothing compared to the thought of losing either of them."

"Millie, I love you to the moon and back," Jay shrugged as he concluded.

Amelia did not say a word at first. She stood from her chair and went around to Jay. She threw her arms around him and cried. "I never knew and I love you no matter what. You are perfect just the way you are."

Within a couple of minutes, Amelia composed herself enough to reach to the middle of the table and take the prize slice of cake and pass it to Jay. No one said it, but we all agreed that he won.

The moment passed and the conversation shifted. It became lighter and there were jokes and laughter and the meaning of friendship filled the room. I looked around the room and thought about Amelia's birthday this year compared to last. I noticed Gabby. She was happy and oblivious to everything as she played with her spoon as if it was a drum stick and the tray of her high chair the drum. Although I did not want to think of Little One as a grown girl, I could not help but make my own birthday wish for her. I wished for Gabby to find a boy that would feel the love for her that I felt when I kissed Amelia for the first time on her birthday last year. I also wished that she would find friends like the ones that surrounded Amelia in our dining room tonight. I wished the same thing for our unborn daughter as well.

Stella put Gabby to bed for us around 8:00 and we had not heard a peep out of her despite the noise of laughter that filled the apartment until the party wound down around 11:00. Jay was the last to leave and it seemed like mere minutes before Amelia and I were in bed too.

I snuggled up behind Amelia in the spooning position and whispered to her. "Did you have a good birthday?"

"It was the best," she replied.

"You aren't just saying that so you can win another piece of cake are you?"

I could feel her move as she giggled.

I knew Amelia better than to think that she would ever acknowledge I had not given her anything, but I had not given her the present I had for her yet. "I hope you didn't think I forgot."

"Forgot? Forgot what?"

"A present for you." I had the tiny box in my hand all the while I had my arms around her, but she did not notice until I gave it to her. It was a small box and this year I wrapped it myself. I left my bedside lamp on so she could see it when I gave it to her.

Amelia sat up in the bed to unwrap it. "Oh, my God, Gabriel! It's beautiful!"

"Do you like it? I can get you something else if you..."

Amelia stopped my words with a kiss. She leaned back. "I love it. This is the prettiest; I mean, it is amazing. I can put Gabby's picture in one side and George-Anne's in the other. I have always wanted a locket."

"I feel like I am always giving you hand-me-down gifts." I apologized again despite her sheer joy over it. "My grandfather sent me a box of things that were my mother's last week and this was in there. I thought you might... Well, I wanted to get you a new car, but that's a big decision to make for someone. What if I bought you something you didn't like to drive. Anyway, I'm going to get you a car, but I hope this will do for now..."

"You don't have to buy me a car and this will do forever. I love it! I can put a picture of you in here too. You on one side and the girls on the other. Yes, that's what I'll do." Amelia continued to turn it over and look inside and out of the locket. "I can buy a car myself, but this type of gift, well, I would never buy myself something like this. One has to be given something like this. Who gave it to your mother? Did your grandfather tell you?" Amelia seemed fascinated with the locket.

"It was given to her by her grandfather. Apparently they were very close. There's an inscription," I pointed to the back.

Amelia read, "You are my sunshine. Awe, Gabriel. Are you sure you don't want to save this and give it to Gabby or George-Anne?"

"Are you really going with the name George-Anne? Isn't that a mouthful for a little girl?" She had not been referring to the one on the way by an actual name so I had nearly forgotten about the name she had picked out.

"I like the name, but that's beside the point. Are you sure you don't want to pass it to one of them?"

"Amelia, it's yours until you want to pass it to them. We will go and pick out a car for you this week. Start thinking about what you might like and I will start thinking about alternative names for our sweet little girl, because 'George-Anne' does not scream sweet girl to me. I get your intentions, but come on."

"I would argue with you about the name, but I love this locket too much to argue in front of it." Amelia pretended to shield the locket as if it had ears. She was capable of putting up a fight for things she believed in, but she was also capable of deflecting with humor to get her way by the back door sometimes, too.

Amelia put the locket back in its box and sat it on the night stand. Ideally, we would have made love, but the pregnancy was taking a toll on her back. Now that her waistline was expanding and her weight was increasing it was wreaking havoc on her small frame. She had been putting on a good front, but her back was giving her a good bit of pain and that night I settled for rubbing it until she fell asleep.

***

Two days later, I was headed out the door again and again I had to go back for the ringing phone. It was Attorney Ellis. He had a knack for calling at 3:30 p.m.

"Good news!" His words nearly jumped through the phone. "The judge refused the continuance requested by Ms. Reed's attorney!"

"So, all of this could be over in two weeks?" I could not believe my ears.

"More like three weeks. Trial starts on Monday, December 16th. I anticipate it will take three days, but one can never be one hundred percent sure."

I did not know what to say. I stood at the top of the stairs and watched Gabby bat at the toys that hung from the arm of her car carrier. I did not really like babies until I met her and I never thought about being a father until she came along. Gabby, the new baby and Amelia were my sun, my moon and my stars. I was completely distracted with thoughts that she could finally and officially be mine. Still not biologically, but legally, Gabby would be my daughter.

Attorney Ellis changed the subject. "We will need to meet the Friday afternoon before for trial prep. We can discuss more then, but we already know they are going to try to paint you as someone who is out of control. They have also called witnesses from the club to say that Amelia was in an altercation in which she assaulted two elderly gentlemen from the club..."

"What?!" I said in a voice demanding enough that it upset Gabby and she started to cry.

I carried the phone down the stairs and gently rocked the carrier while Attorney Ellis began to explain.

"I received the pre-trial report today with a list of their witnesses. Two former club members have accused Amelia of assaulting them on the course and then you had their membership revoked."

"That's not what happened." I was fuming at the thought that Beth would again try to use this incident against Amelia, but here we were. I tried to keep my temper in check in an effort to keep Gabby settled.

"Do you know of anyone that saw the incident? I understand that she was alone on the course with them."

"I don't, but I can try to get information on the girls that the men tried to assault on the other courses around the lake."

"Alright. I have not turned in my portion of the pre-trial order, so I can add more witnesses if needed. Do you think the other girls will testify?"

"It certainly won't hurt to ask."

I don't know what made me think of it, but suddenly it occurred to me that two could play this game with Beth. She had more dirty laundry than the dry cleaners so perhaps more of hers needed to be added.

"Can you request records from the vet's office that Beth uses for her pets?"

"Sure, but we are cutting it close."

"Get the records on any and all of her pets from Dr. Vivaldi in Atlanta. The records might not specifically say that she abused three of her dogs, two of which were puppies, but anyone in their right mind would know that's what was going on. One was so badly injured that it had to be put down."

I could hear Attorney Ellis gasp, "What? Why are you just now telling me about this?"

"Sorry. I just now thought of it."

"Okay, I have to go and get on this right now. I will go ahead and list Dr. Vivaldi as a witness that we plan to call to trial, just in case we need him."

"Thanks, and again, I am sorry about that. I can't believe I did not think of it sooner."

We said our goodbyes and I was off to work.

*** 

Visitation was suspended for the time being thanks to Beth's recent actions. Thank goodness it was suspended for so many reasons, but also because November 28, 1996 was Thanksgiving and I had been looking forward to that day since last Thanksgiving. Last year was the first time I had met all of Amelia's family and this year they were mine and Gabby's family too.

I had to work the lunch shift, same as last year, but this year Amelia wasn't there to make it go faster. I dare say the morning drug by and the buffet crowd seemed to go on forever. I didn't think they were going to stop coming. I thought about Amelia and Gabby already being at her Aunt Gayle's and what fun they were having without me. I imagined what all they were doing. Everyone was probably fussing over Amelia and her condition and passing Gabby from one relative to the next. I'm sure everyone had to hold her and kiss her. I'm sure Aunt Dot was the ring leader in spoiling Gabby. I was not jealous, I just missed them and wanted to be with them.

It was around 2:30 p.m. when I finally got out of the club and on the road to Avera. I made it to Aunt Dot's just in time for dinner. Everyone from last year was still there. The men folk were in the yard kicking tires and shooting the breeze when I pulled into the driveway. Dixon was the first one to make it to the car and I barely had the car in park before he opened the door for me.

"Gabe, it's 'bout time you decided to show up," Dixon said as if I had just been late for the sake of being late. I always had to keep in mind what Amelia said about him and not hang on his every word.

"You know how it goes, just can't get off work sometimes," I explained to him while shaking his hand.

Uncle Jim was right behind Dixon to offer a greeting. "Gabe," he said offering his hand.

"Uncle Jim," I replied. "Amelia said you were writing to Congress to try to get your Purple Heart metal. How's that coming?"

He dropped his head and shook it in the negative, "It's not. You'd think they'd be eager to replace the metal, but it's like they don't believe me. I got these scars on my back for my service and I don't regret a one and I'm not complainin', but I'm sure disappointed in our government right now."

I put my arm around him and we started toward the house. "I'm sure it's just a misunderstanding and you'll get it worked out. You might try having Amelia write a letter for you. She's pretty good at putting up an argument and you might as well get everyone's money's worth from sending her to law school. I'm sure she'd be glad to do it for you."

"That's mighty kind of you to offer. I'll think on taking you up on it."

Uncle Jim and I walked on toward the house with Dixon following close behind. A few of the men folk spoke to me as we passed, but continued to linger and shoot the breeze in the yard.

Amelia and I had given into Gayle's request and agreed to spend the night. I was carrying our luggage in one hand and as we neared the house I let my arm drop from Uncle Jim. Both he and Dixon offered to help me with the bags, but I declined. Dixon got the door for me and no sooner had he done so did I feel the tug of another hand on the handle of my duffle bag.

399

Although I told him it really wasn't necessary, Dixon insisted, "I'll take this over to the barn for you." Dixon then took his leave and headed off to the apartment in the barn across the road at Gayle's house.

We entered Uncle Jim and Aunt Dot's house from the carport. The room was filled to capacity with all of the women folk reheating everything that was left from lunch and getting ready to put it out for dinner. The fact that they served two meals was yet another aspect of Thanksgiving that I appreciated about Amelia's family. They ate once at noon and again at 5:30 p.m. It helped out folks like me that had to work during lunch and folks like Amelia's cousin, Bonnie, and her section of the family who had to go to her in-laws for lunch. It gave me the opportunity to have a Thanksgiving meal that was not at a restaurant. For folks like Bonnie, it allowed her to fulfill her commitments to her husband's family and still spend time with her own.

I stood in the doorway taking in the sights and smells for a moment. Amelia was in the thick of everyone. She was stirring a pot of something on one of the left eyes of the stove. Her cousin, Dixie, was tending the pots on the right side. Aunt Dot was adding sugar to a pitcher of tea near the sink. Amelia's Aunt Gayle was cutting cakes and pies to put out and Bonnie was chasing her children, trying to herd them out of the kitchen. I looked around to find her, but I did not see Gabby anywhere.

Finally, Uncle Jim announced my presence, "Look what we found milling around outside."

All eyes suddenly turned toward the door. Amelia's face lit up at the sight of me and she smiled that infectious smile of hers. I could not help but smile back. She left the stove and made her way to me. Although everyone spoke, they immediately went back to their jobs. For a second it was as if we were alone in the room full of her relatives.

It seemed strange that we had only been apart since that morning and I had missed her as much as I had. Working at the club on this particular day without her had been torture. Last year we had worked together and then made the trip down here. It was the first time I met her entire family and the whole day had left a lasting impression. I had never known what family was until last Thanksgiving.

It wasn't a huge kitchen, but the stove was clear across the room from the door to the carport, so it took Amelia a few steps to reach me. She was almost to me when I started toward her. I had this uncontrollable need to hug her and I reached out to her. I was not one to make a show of public displays of affection, so I left it to just a hug, but she didn't.

Amelia eased up on her toes and kissed me. It was nothing over the top, but I could hear the room go silent as everyone stopped what they were doing to watch. As soon as she was finished, she whispered to me, "It's just not Thanksgiving until you are here with us."

I knew exactly how she felt. I had never had a holiday like the ones I spent with her and her family last year and although I knew what day it was when I woke up that morning and while I was working, it was as if it wasn't really Thanksgiving until I stepped through the door of Aunt Dot's house. It wasn't Thanksgiving until I was there with Amelia and her family and this year they were my family.

Within seconds of releasing our embrace everyone returned to their duties, including Amelia. I would have been content to stay and help out, but beyond sampling the sweet tea for Aunt Dot, I was not allowed to lift a finger. It wasn't the women folk who ushered me from the kitchen, but Uncle Jim.

"Come on, son," Uncle Jim pulled me by the hand and carried on with chastising me, "This here's women's work and you don't need to be messing it up for the rest of us. Before you know it they'll be expecting us to wash dishes and set tables. You come on here in with me."

Like last year, we were again asked to hold hands with the person next to us and then we took turns telling what we were thankful for this year. Aunt Dot began, "I am thankful that we have added in number this year and not subtracted. That's good enough for me." She nodded at me, Amelia and Gabby as she spoke.

401

The speeches continued around the room. Mrs. Graham was thankful that her son had finally found a good woman that could tolerate his work schedule. Mr. Graham was thankful that Gayle could tolerate his mother. The whole room erupted in laughter at that one. We thought that Gayle was going to say that she was thankful for Mr. Graham, but instead she focused on Amelia.

Gayle turned to Amelia as she spoke. "I did not tell anyone, but I had a bit of a scare of my own this year. I found a lump, had a mammogram, yes, that hurt, but I am clear..."

Amelia gasped, "Why didn't you tell me?"

Aunt Dot and several others in the room including Mr. Graham just plain gasped.

Gayle looked around the room, "I did not tell anyone because I did not want you to worry needlessly."

"You didn't know it was needless." Amelia tugged Gayle's hand to call her attention back.

"You have enough to worry about," Gayle glanced at me and Gabby and reached for Amelia's ever expanding belly.

"That's no excuse!" Amelia was not happy.

"I'm sorry I didn't tell you, but I'm fine, Millie."

Amelia was standing next to Gayle so it was her turn to tell what she was thankful for after Gayle and she likely had something else in mind before Gayle's revelation, but not after that. "I'm thankful that Aunt Gayle does not have breast cancer. I mean, I am really, really thankful. And, next time she has news like that she better tell me!"

Everyone thought Amelia was done. I thought she was done because she looked to me as if she was passing the torch. Suddenly, it was as if a light came on in her head. As I opened my mouth to speak, Amelia started again. She reached to take Gabby from me and then spoke directly to Gabby, "I am so very thankful for you."

The whole room let out an, "Aww."

Amelia continued, "I am so thankful for your Daddy and I am thankful that you are both mine."

I leaned down and kissed Amelia's forehead and this time when she looked at me she really was finished, so I began.

I looked over to Bonnie. "Last year, Bonnie was thankful that Amelia was not married with children, so she could help with her children. I commented then that I was also thankful that Amelia was not married with children or this would be quite awkward for me. This year, I am glad Amelia is married and I am thankful that she made me a part your wonderful family. I am thankful for each and every one of you."

It was not long after everyone was finished cleaning up from dinner that we headed over to Gayle's. It was chilly outside that night and we found the heat in the apartment had been fixed since we first stayed there. With the exception of the heat and the addition of Gabby's playpen, the apartment was exactly the same. I still could not get over how beautiful it was and that it was in the top of a barn. There were horses in stalls just below us and to look at the place one would never know it.

Amelia fed Gabby her last bottle of the evening and rocked her to sleep while I showered. When I was finished, I found Amelia waiting for me in bed. There was music playing softly in the room. A song that Amelia had been playing a lot, "Me and You" by Kenny Chesney, was floating through the air. It was fitting of the mood.

Amelia was wearing a white lace nightgown that appeared to be made of gauze. It was long and flowing and, as sheer as it was, it covered any sign of the baby. Her hair fell in curls all around her face, neck and shoulders and she was fresh-faced having just taken off her make-up for the night. She was perfection and she exuded the feeling of home to me.

"You know, I meant what I said at dinner tonight." Amelia reached out her arms to me and I crawled into the bed and into her.

"I'm so thankful for you," she whispered to me just as I sealed her lips with mine.

It had been a few weeks since we had made love. Being completely intimate with Amelia had become more complicated by the pregnancy. Of course, there was always the initial fear that sex would somehow damage the baby, but everyone knows that's ridiculous. Beyond that, Amelia was plagued by sciatic nerve issues. She rarely complained and when she did she described it as having a cramp from her left butt cheek to her calf muscle in that leg. We had tried a couple of times, but I could tell that most any position caused her pain. I missed being wrapped up in her at every opportunity, but I would wait forever for her. I was not sure what made this night different, but tonight I had something else to be thankful for as Amelia gave into my touch.

Like the old Bellsouth telephone ad, I let my fingers do the walking and inched her nightgown up as I went. Lightly, I slid my hand up her leg. It was smooth as if she had shaved in anticipation of how our evening would end. I leaned into her hair and breathed her in, strawberries as always. I did not know what I would do if they ever stopped making that shampoo. Since I met Amelia, I could hardly see or smell strawberries without thinking of her and getting turned on.

"Would you mind?" Amelia asked as she pushed me to my back and climbed on top of me.

"Not at all." I am sure she was thinking that this would work better for us if she was on top and she was right.

Up on her knees she went and straddled me. The skirt of the nightgown fell around me and I could feel that Amelia had indeed prepared for this. I could tell by the feel of her skin against mine where I should have felt the lace of her underpants. Everything was smooth.

Despite the baby that was occupying a great deal of space between us, Amelia managed to lean over me and leave trails of kisses from my left earlobe to my Adam's apple. All the while kissing me, she eased her hands up my arms until she locked her fingers in mine over my head.

Amelia must have put the music on a timer because it cut off after about twenty minutes and then there was a stillness in the

404

apartment. Gabby was in her playpen asleep in the living room and we had left the door to the bedroom open so we could hear her. We aimed to avoid waking her and were quieter than normal. It was so quiet, I could hear the covers on the bed rustle a little as we moved in unison. I could hear Amelia's breathing increasing and I could barely hear the muffled sound of a horse neighing from the stalls below. The horse was almost distracting, but the sound of Amelia's release recalled my focus. I followed within what seemed like seconds and the last thing I remember of that night was Amelia's head on my shoulder and the feel of her beating heart against my skin.

The middle of the night I heard Gabby. I awoke instantly with her first whimper and found Amelia in exactly the same spot as I left her when I closed my eyes. Amelia hadn't moved a muscle while she slept. Her head was still on my shoulder and her arm was draped across me. I eased from under her and she hardly stirred and she certainly did not wake up. Thank goodness I heard Gabby because Amelia was out cold.

There was a plush rocking chair recliner in the living room of the apartment. It was way more comfortable than the one we had at The Jefferson. If I sat in the glider at our apartment to feed Gabby, I never allowed myself to fall asleep. I was always too terrified that I would relax, she would squirm and I would drop her. I am not sure what was going on with me. Was the recliner here that comfortable? Was I that tired? It must have been something since the next thing I knew, Gabby was snuggled up on my chest and Amelia was putting a blanket over the both of us.

"It's okay. Go back to sleep," she whispered.

"What time is it?" I asked while repositioning in the chair.

"Not quite 6:00 a.m."

"What are you doing up?"

"Our other girl is very active this morning." Amelia stood back up from spreading the blanket over us and I reached for her hand.

405

"Is everything alright?" I lifted my head and started to focus a little more.

Amelia took my hand in hers and placed mine over her stomach. "It is like she's rolling over. Feel that?"

I did feel it. It really did feel like she rolled over. I braced Gabby with my other hand and leaned up to try to get a better look. I am sure if there had been more light in the room, I would have seen a bulge move from one side of Amelia's abdomen to the next.

"She's getting big," I observed without thinking what that implied.

"Thanks!" Amelia stepped back and my hand dropped. Even though she whispered, I could hear the sarcasm.

Amelia turned to leave as I spoke. "I just meant..."

"I know what you meant." Cutting her eyes over her shoulder, she looked back at me.

"I was just..."

"Yeah, I know. Go back to sleep."

I raised more from the chair while guarding Gabby. "Are you mad with me?"

Amelia stopped and turned back as I stood to follow her. "No. I've got three more months. I know she's going to get bigger and I am going to get bigger. It's natural."

She stepped toward me, went up on her toes and I leaned down to meet her. She kissed me. "I'm going back to bed. Would you like to join me?"

"I'll be right there." I kissed Amelia again and then she turned back toward the bedroom. I placed Gabby back in her bed and I went to ours.

A knock at the door woke me and I glanced at the clock on the bedside table. We had slept until 9:00 a.m. The knocking came

406

in beats of three and whoever it was was on their third round of knocks.

Both Amelia and I sat up at the same time. Gabby was only seconds behind us and she was not happy.

"Get the door. I'll get Gabby," I told Amelia.

We were barely to our feet when I hear the voice of her aunt. "Are y'all up?"

It was Gayle and she was delivering breakfast. I could not hear the conversation between her and Amelia over Gabby's crying. I hurried to make a bottle with one hand while carrying and attempting to console Gabby with the other.

"Daddy's got you," I tried to assure her, "and he's hurrying."

Amelia returned with two plates of bacon, eggs and pancakes. It smelled wonderful, so wonderful that even Little One was licking her chops.

"I totally forgot what an early riser she is," Amelia described Gayle. "I told her I wanted to take you over to see the progress at Seven Springs and she's ready to go now."

"Can I get dressed first?" I searched the kitchen drawers as I matched Amelia's tone for being a little put out by being woken up.

Amelia just cut her eyes and smiled at me. She put the plates on the table and I put Gabby back in her playpen with her bottle. She was capable of holding it herself now. Then, we scarfed down breakfast and hurriedly began getting dressed.

I was shaving in the bathroom and Amelia was dressing Gabby on the bed, but the conversation had not stopped since Gayle left. It progressed from Gayle's timing to how work at Seven Springs was coming.

Amelia was finished getting dressed and I was just about there. Amelia looked through the bathroom door to me as she put a new diaper on Gabby. "I cannot wait for you to see the place. With everything else going on, I just didn't think of telling you the details of what all was going on at the Springs worth mentioning, but now that you're here, I can hardly wait for you to see it."

There was a light in Amelia's eyes when she spoke that exuded excitement. It made me think of the day I first laid eyes on her. I put down my razor and pulled my shirt over my head.

"Am I going to recognize the place?" I asked her as I handed her a fresh diaper for Gabby. "You didn't change anything about our picnic site did you?"

Amelia looked at me with concern. "Of course I did. There's a pergola there now. I warned you of that the day we had the picnic there."

"I really don't remember you saying that at all." Amelia was essentially done with Gabby so I scooped her up and whirled her into my arms. "You have to understand, I was a little distracted during that picnic."

Again, she looked at me curiously, "Distracted?"

"I mainly remember two things from that day. You told me you loved me for the first time and that was a staggering revelation for me. Secondly, you were straddling me and you smelled so good. I can still see you unbuttoning your shirt..."

Gabby said, "Da Da," and the moment came to a screeching halt. Both Amelia and I snapped our necks, whipping around to look at her. We were both looking to confirm what we thought we heard.

"Did she just say 'Da Da'?" I was dumbfounded.

"I think she did!" Amelia heard it too.

"Gabby, did you just say Da Da? Did you call Daddy?" I leaned over and scooped her up.

Gabby giggled and kicked her feet, but did not say a recognizable word. I begged her to say it again, but she just smiled and batted her big brown eyes at me.

Amelia stood at my side, "I love the way she looks at you. You know, she has never looked at me the way she looks at you. There's no mistaking how much she loves you."

I gave a sideways glance to Amelia. "She loves you too."

"Oh, I know. Well, more like I think she loves me, but I know she loves you."

"You are being silly."

"I'm not jealous ." Amelia draped her arm around my side and leaned into a side arm hug. "It thrills me that she loves you as much as I do."

Just as I kissed Amelia's forehead, Gabby said it again, "Da Da! Da Da! Da Da!"

"She's so cute and she has the personality of a little comedian." Amelia tickled Gabby in her ribs with an index finger and Gabby squenched her nose up and laughed like Amelia was the funniest thing in the world.

The knock at the door came once more. It was Gayle and she was past ready to go with us to Seven Springs. Our family moment was cut short, but I knew there would be plenty more despite whatever was ahead with the still looming custody battle.

The three of us rode with Gayle in her truck around the road to Seven Springs. I gazed out the passenger's side window and even as we pulled up to the gate, I could already tell a difference in the place. Trees had been trimmed, flowers planted and that was just near the gate.

"You mind getting that?" Gayle asked as she tossed me a key and gave a nod in the direction of the closed gate that was blocking the driveway.

I quickly jumped out and went to open it. I put the key in without looking at it more than just to pick up the lock. I was completely distracted by the landscaping. I glanced all around as I walked the gate open.

To the left of the gate was a barn. It wasn't new. I remembered it from the other time I was there. The difference in the barn was that it had new boards and a fresh coat of stain and new tin on the roof. The tractor under the lean to was also freshly sandblasted and painted a Smurf blue color. The last time I saw the barn it looked like it was about to fall in on itself and the tractor was rustier than the Tin Man before Dorothy found him. That wasn't the end of what all I saw.

When Gayle drove through the gate, my eyes followed behind the truck until it pulled to the side and parked, facing the old hotel building. The old hotel was exactly the same, not better or worse, just the same. Work was yet to be started on it and the landscaping near it was virtually untouched as well.

I walked to catch up with them to open the car door for Amelia. After all of our time together, I still opened doors for her. I knew that impressed her from our very first date, the trip to the Georgian Terrace. It really was the little things that Amelia noticed and she was impressed by attention to details and that could be seen all around the hotel.

I caught up with them before Amelia or Gayle could open the doors for themselves. It was a king cab truck and Amelia sat in the seat behind Gayle. I was able to grab both door handles and open them at the same time. I offered a hand to Amelia, but she was unbuckling Gabby from the car seat, so I offered a hand to Gayle while I waited for Amelia.

"What do you think of the place?" Gayle noticed me taking it all in. "Quite a bit of changes, huh?"

"It's looking good, but what's going on with the building?" I was curious because I thought they had met with a contractor already.

Amelia chimed in and I turned back to help her from the truck. "We hired a contractor out of Augusta. He's the best in the CSRA and came highly recommended, but he had another job to finish before he could start on the hotel."

"He agreed with me that the building has some problems, real issues..."

Amelia interrupted Gayle. "And he agreed with me that the place could be saved."

Gayle cut Amelia a look with a raised eyebrow signifying that she still did not like being usurped on the subject of tearing the place down. Amelia ignored the look and handed Gabby to me as she slid out of the 4x4 truck. Although it had running boards, it was a good bit higher off of the ground than what Amelia was used to in the old Chevy of hers. I shifted Gabby to one arm and offered Amelia a hand getting down.

As soon as her feet touched the ground, Amelia was on wide open. "I have so much to show you," she said as she pulled me along behind her. Gayle followed as well. Across the driveway we went and I could already see the pergola. It was on the exact spot where we had picnicked this very day last year.

I continued to survey the property as we walked down toward the pergola. The creek had been completely cleared off. There wasn't a single leaf out of place and the pine straw was only in beds. The wild azaleas were trimmed, the ferns were divided and replanted in a more organized fashion, and the grass was thicker than I remembered. A great deal of work and care had definitely been put into the place since the last time I had visited.

"Amelia, who did all of this?" I knew she had not been here all that much since the bombing, so I knew it wasn't her doing. I also knew that she had been to the springs so infrequently that the likelihood that she was hands-on supervising was slim as well.

Amelia did not skip a step when she said, "Dixon's done everything. It looks great, doesn't it?"

"It does look great! Did he do this all by himself?" I could not believe it. This wasn't just some planting or raking. This was done by someone with a talent for landscaping.

"Jay and I helped with the pergola, but I think Uncle Jim has been helping him a little with the yard. Although, yesterday, Uncle Jim said everything was Dixon's idea."

411

"Are you telling me he came up with all of this on his own?"

"I gave him a picture that I cut out of Southern Living magazine and he recreated it." Amelia pointed to the building ahead of us. "Aside from that, he came up with the rest all on his own. Who would have thought, right? I mean, I gave him some direction in the beginning and then each time I was here, he surprised me with how much above and beyond he had gone."

It did look like something that would have been featured in Southern Living. There were five columns that supported it and it was unlike any I had seen before. It was round.

When we arrived at the pergola Amelia asked, "How do you like the Wisteria?"

"It looks like it is beginning to climb," I observed as I stepped under the first beam. I knew the Wisteria had been planted earlier in the spring when the structure had been built and it really was starting to take off.

"I want all of the vines to grow up and around and connect. By next year we should have lavender blooms hanging from it."

The pergola looked more like a gazebo, but lacked the formal roof that a gazebo typically had. In fact, it could have been mistaken for a small outdoor stage and I commented on that as well as the structure itself.

"Where did you find all of the old stacked stone?" It wasn't just stacked stone, it was obviously old and weathered.

"Dixon scoured all of the property that anyone owns in the family and found old chimneys where buildings used to be. He pushed down the chimneys and hauled it back here and rebuilt the chimneys into these columns. What do you think?"

"I think everything is beautiful." I could see that Gayle was as proud of Amelia for making this place start to come back to life as I was. She did not say anything, but I could tell by the look on her face as Amelia spoke.

"My thoughts have always been that this would be where the bride and groom would stand when we host weddings out here. I also want it to be used as a stage when we do outdoor concerts and a seating area for guests of the inn when it isn't being used for the other two purposes."

Gabby started to squirm in my arms and fuss as I took in the view of the inn from the pergola. I tried to calm her, but wasn't having much luck. It was hard to focus with her and Amelia noticed.

"Aunt Gayle, would you mind taking Gabby. She probably needs a diaper change." Amelia was hardly finished speaking before Gayle reached for Little One.

"Come with me. We'll go get you some dry panties." Although Amelia and I never did baby talk to Gabby, Gayle made up for it. She always made such a fuss over Gabby that I was surprised she had not already taken her from me, but as soon as Amelia said the word, Gayle was off with her in a flash.

As Gayle walked away toward the truck with Gabby, Amelia stepped under the pergola and took my hands. She eased up to me. "Next Spring, we will christen this thing."

I smiled down at her, "Will we now?"

"Oh yes. We will."

I kissed her and the memories of this spot last year were fresh in my mind. Amelia pulled back from me and my mind went to images of the future. I had never thought much about my future until I met her and then I always imagined her in it. My future was her future and I was fine with that. I looked forward to it.

"Are you still planning for us to live out here?" I was curious if her plans had changed.

"If you are okay with that," she answered. I could tell she was dying for me to agree.

"I would live in a dirt hut in Timbuktu with you, so here is just as good of a place as any as long as I'm with you. ...And Gabby. ...And Sweat Pea."

413

Amelia looked to the meadow that stretched along the edge of the creek and between where we were and the barn near the gate. "Can you just picture the girls playing out here? They can put out blankets and have tea party picnics."

"I don't know if I want the girls having *picnics* out here anytime soon. I am well aware of where our picnic out here was headed." I raised an eyebrow at the word "picnic".

"Right," Amelia blushed a little. "Maybe they can just play with dolls or hide and seek around the property."

"There's an idea, but, Amelia, no matter what they play, I'm sure you will create a wonderful childhood for them here."

CHAPTER 22

I had been at the club since the early afternoon on Saturday. Even though I did not like to be away from Amelia, I knew she had some things to take care of at Seven Springs, so I went on into the club and participated in game day. On the Saturdays when Beth had Gabby, I had joined in watching college football in the bar with some of the members. I had a good time and it was good for me to schmooze with them on a social level from time to time. Anyway, Amelia took Gabby with her and went to meet Gayle to go over things with the general contractor for the old hotel at the Springs and I went to watch football and to work.

As far as the dinner shift went, things were busy until about 9:00 p.m. I was plating up an order for a four-top when Daniel came in and told me that I had a guest that wanted to see me. They were waiting in the executive dining room. The night had been virtually uneventful until that moment and then I could not wait to get home to tell Amelia about it.

In the weeks since Beth had rear-ended my Acura Legend and royally screwed the suspension, I had been driving the C10 pick-up truck that was Amelia's grandfather's. That night on the way home, I was so excited to get home to tell Amelia everything that I took the turn into the driveway at The Jefferson on two wheels. I felt only slightly bad about doing that because I knew Amelia would have been pissed if she had seen me abuse the truck like that. The reality was that concerns for the truck were the last thing on my mind right then.

I barely rolled to a stop underneath the carport before I snatched the keys from the ignition, grabbed the large manila envelope from the passenger's side and sprinted around to the front door of our building. I started calling Amelia's name as soon as I had the key in the door to our apartment. I took the stairs two, possibly three steps, at a time as I ran up them. I was so anxious to get to her and share my news that I wasn't even out of breath when I got to the top.

I expected to find Amelia in the living room, head propped on the back of the couch and law book still in hand, but fast asleep or just waking up. She usually tried to wait up for me, but in the last few weeks, that had become harder and harder for her. The pregnancy was sucking the energy right out of her and she would usually fall asleep studying and waiting on me, but the sound of me turning the key in the lock was her wake-up call. Several times I arrived upstairs to find her wiping her eyes and waking up.

Tonight she wasn't on the couch and she didn't answer when I called her name. A pang of panic ran through me and for a second my excitement was crushed and I could feel my stomach in my throat. I feared the worse.

I called her name again and the sound of a flushing toilet followed. It sounded as if it came from the master bathroom, so I rushed into our room, ready and waiting for her to come out. I had not thought to cut the light on in the room, so the whole place was pitch black except for what little light was coming through the French doors from the street light.

The bathroom door opened, Amelia flipped off the light switch in there and I said, "Have I got a surprise for you!" all at the same time.

She was surprised alright. Amelia screamed bloody murder. She did not expect me home for about another thirty or forty-five minutes and had not heard me come up the stairs or call for her. I did not expect her to scream in my face, so she startled me as well and I screamed, too.

As soon as I screamed she realized it was only me and snapped, "Unless you want me to squeeze this baby out right here, do not ever do that to me again!"

Amelia paused only to catch her breath and barely long enough for me to apologize, "You nearly scared the life out of me!" She huffed.

I could tell she needed to sit down, so I offered my arm and helped her to the bed. She was seven months pregnant at that time and by her own description, "as big as a hippopotamus." I thought she was as beautiful as ever, but she was starting to waddle a little when she walked. That night, she waddled over to the bed with my assistance and sat down. She panted as she sat there and tried to catch her breath.

"Are you okay?" I asked her. "I did not mean to scare you like that. I called your name when I came up the stairs."

"I'm sorry. Gabby's been asleep for about two hours. I've been reading and the whole building's been quiet tonight. I thought I was the only one in the whole place..."

I finished her sentence for her. "And then I came home and scared you half to death."

I sat down on the bed next to her and put my arm around her as I spoke. "I'm so sorry. Are you okay?" I asked her again.

A car went past and the head lights lit up her face just as Amelia looked up and smiled at me. "I'm fine and glad you're home." She pursed her lips and then admitted, "I don't like the feeling of being completely alone in the building. I know Gabby's here, but still."

I pulled Amelia closer to me and kissed her forehead. "I know, I know." I assured her.

We sat in silence for just a moment before I noticed the envelope still in my hand. "Oh," I said with a jump. "I have something to show you!"

I reached back and over around her to cut the lamp on.

"Oh my God, what?!" From the way Amelia responded, I think I may have startled her again.

I opened the envelope and handed Amelia the pages that were inside and instructed her, "Read this."

Amelia started reading, but I could not contain myself. "Joan came by the club tonight and gave this to me. I could hardly wait to get home to show you."

Suddenly Amelia jumped from the bed. "Dick relinquished his rights to Gabby! What? How? Why?"

I jumped up too. "I know. So many questions, right?"

"I can't believe it!"

"Notice," I pointed about one-fourth down the page. "This paragraph right here is an admission that he is Gabby's father." I emphasized the word "is".

Amelia cut her eyes from the page to me. "More like a sperm donor."

"Nonetheless, look there." I pointed three fourths of the way down. "He not only gave up his rights, but he assigned them to me."

I had been reading over Amelia's shoulder, but upon my last word she spun around to face me. She dropped the hand that held the papers to her side and demanded to know, "Why would he just give her to you? I mean, he already gave her, but why would he put any of this in writing? What does he want? What did Joan say?" Amelia had so many questions and she fired them off one behind the other in rapid succession.

I could not get a word in edgewise to answer her until she flopped back down on the bed. "Just tell me everything," she sighed, out of breath from speaking.

"Well, Joan showed up just as the dinner rush was slowing down," I began while I paced across the room and closed the curtains to the French doors. Amelia watched and listened attentively.

"Daniel came and got me. He just told me someone was waiting to see me in the executive dining room. A client was supposed to have come in to see about booking a wedding earlier and I thought that it was the client and she was just running really late. I never would have thought I would find Joan waiting for me."

I finished with the curtains and continued with both my trek back across the room and with my story. "When I finished plating up the entrees that I was working on, I left my apron and went upstairs. I turned the corner from the corridor into the executive dining room to find Joan instead of a client."

"'I can't stay long, but I've got what you asked me to get,' Joan said to me. Honestly, Amelia, I was so caught off guard that I had no idea what she was talking about, so she had to explain it to me."

Amelia rolled in the bed to get more comfortable and propped her head up on her elbow. I started getting undressed as she watched me and listened while I continued to give the play by play.

"Joan said that she had been working up the courage to demand that Dick sign off on this and tell him that if he didn't then she was going to tell their children all of his business, divorce him and take everything he owned. She explained to me that he had been running around on her for as long as she could remember, but she had always stayed with him for the sake of her children. She drew the line at him fathering a child with another woman."

I continued the conversation as I headed into the bathroom to cut the water on. I left the door open, but spoke a little louder so Amelia could hear me over the shower.

"Joan told me she was preparing to leave him this time. She gave me all those documents on him last month so it would not only help with our case against Beth, but so that it would be on the record with the court that he had run around on her and fathered a child. She was going to screw him good, Amelia."

I stepped into the shower and I could hear that Amelia was saying something, but I could not understand her. I stuck my head around the shower curtain. "Sorry, I didn't catch that."

Amelia got up from the bed and joined me in the bathroom. Once she was seated on the lid of the toilet she repeated herself. "I asked, 'Did she tell you what changed? Why she did not have to blackmail him and if she is still planning to leave him?"

"I don't know if she's going to leave him, but she said the one redeeming quality that Dick has is that he loves his children..."

Amelia huffed, "All of them, but Gabby?"

All lathered up, I stuck my head out again. "I know, that's what I thought, but the way Joan explained it is that he did this because he loves all of his children, including Gabby."

"How does she figure?" Amelia's voice was sarcastic. "If he loves her why are you the one fighting for custody of her?" Amelia also pointed out, "You're dripping everywhere."

I tucked back into the shower and went on, "According to Joan, about three weeks ago Dick took his car in to Rogers', you know, the garage in Greensboro that still has my car. Anyway, Dick needed a tire plugged and while there he saw the damage to my car from where Beth hit me that afternoon at Attorney Ellis'. He knew straight away that it was my car and when he got home that night he asked Joan if she knew that I had been in a wreck. Apparently word of what happened is all over the club. Praise told Joan all of the gory details of how Beth was supposed to be bringing Gabby back and was hopped up on something. Then, when Dick was telling Joan about seeing the car at the shop, he said the back had had a grenade go off in the trunk. Joan then told him, 'Yeah and Beth had her daughter in the car when she hit his car and the baby wasn't even strapped in!"

"None of their children were home for dinner. After Joan told Dick that Gabby was in the car with Beth, he ate a couple more bites of his dinner quietly then pushed his plate away. Joan could tell something was bothering him. He was pissed."

"She reiterated his redeeming quality to me at that point. It's always been Dick's opinion that you don't fuck around with kids, especially his."

Amelia interrupted me. "Joan used the word 'fuck'?"

"I embellished a little, but you get the point. Anyway, Joan said she quietly ate her dinner, but she could tell Dick was fuming. Clearly, there was more to it for him."

"You know, Dick still did not have any idea that Joan knew Gabby was his. She said she took a couple of big gulps of her wine and then asked him as sweetly as she could. She said, 'Dick, Gabby Hewitt is yours, isn't she?"

Before I could say anything else, Amelia was impatient and started with the questions, "She asked him out right? What did he say?"

Our conversation was going back and forth like banter then.

"He admitted it," I replied.

"No, he didn't!"

I heard her move and a loud thud. I think she nearly fell off of the toilet where she had been sitting. I threw open the shower to make sure she was alright. I found Amelia pulling her big pregnant self out from between the toilet and the wall. She clearly wasn't hurt, but definitely embarrassed.

"What just happened? Did you just break the commode?" I tried to joke with her.

"NO!" She tried not to laugh. "I adjusted my weight and in all of my excitement, the seat slipped and threw me into the wall."

I was trying not to laugh, but she was clearly surprised by Dick's admission and then to get slung off of the toilet was hilarious. I felt sorry for her, but it was funny.

Amelia scrambled to pull her nightgown back down and get her ass out of the crack between the wall and the toilet, but she wasn't having much luck.

"Dammit! Don't you dare laugh, Gabriel Hewitt! Get over here and help me up!"

"I'm sorry. I'm so sorry," I laughed while I apologized for laughing. "I can't help it. I'm sorry."

I didn't bother to grab a towel, I just stepped out and offered her my hand. I helped her up and I could see it on her face, she was genuinely embarrassed and I had made things worse. She wasn't laughing it off with me and I immediately stopped and changed my tone to match hers.

I apologized again, but as soon as Amelia was on her feet good, she thanked me and then left the room. I reached for my towel from the rack as I passed it and followed Amelia. I was not finished telling her what all Joan had told me, but that conversation was over for the time being.

"Amelia," I called after her, but she did not stop.

Slipping on the hardwood floor in my wet feet slowed me down from catching up with her and I wanted to make sure she was alright. Amelia was nearly across the living room to the kitchen when I caught up with her. Something was clearly wrong. I took her hand to stop her. I moved around to see her face and she hung her head.

"Amelia, are you crying?" I pulled her face into my chest as she nodded in the affirmative.

"Oh, no, what?" I said softly as I held her.

Her voice was muffled when she answered. "I'm big and fat and pregnant and clumsy and you're..."

I cut her off. There was no need for her to finish that sentence. "I am happy to be married to the most beautiful girl in the world."

I lifted her chin and there were tears streaming down her face. "Come on now, you know I love you just the way you are. Tell me you know I'm yours."

Amelia hung her head again.

"Always yours, Amelia. No matter what and you never have to worry about that."

I could feel her nod her head again and I could hear her sniffle.

I continued to hold her for a few more minutes until she pulled back. Her personality was starting to return to normal.

"I'm probably being ridiculous. I know I've only got a few more months like this and then I'll be back to normal."

"You know I would love you even if things never went back to what you consider normal, right?"

"I know." She seemed to say it reluctantly and I did not push her for a more sincere answer.

I offered to get her whatever she wanted from the kitchen. "Cheesecake, glass of milk, crackers, what would you like?"

Amelia's answer came out of nowhere, "I want Krispy Kreme doughnuts and a box of Tums."

"Uhh, talk about midnight cravings," I responded as I looked to the kitchen and back. I knew there weren't any in the house, so I'm not sure why I bothered looking.

"I don't know why I want them, but I would kill for one fresh off of the conveyor belt."

"So, I could not just run up to The Golden Pantry and get you one of the boxes from there?"

Amelia shook her head, "no," but responded verbally, "I need a doughnut like I need a hole in my head or another fifteen pounds on my ass." She rubbed her behind as she said the last half of her sentence.

"Get dressed," I told her as I started back toward the bedroom.

"What?" Her eyes got wide and she smiled a smile of delight and shock.

"We are going to find you a fresh Krispy Kreme doughnut." I went back to her and pulled her along with me.

"You are not serious," she protested.

"I am. We are going to Macon to get fresh doughnuts."

"The store in Macon closes at midnight."

I was still listening to her as I pulled a pair of jeans out of the closet for her and I responded as I set her tennis shoes out. "Then we're going to Atlanta. The one on Ponce is open twenty-four hours a day."

"You are crazy! What about Gabby?"

"We're bringing her with us, of course."

Amelia just stood there for a minute while I continued to lay out our clothes and start getting changed. Finally, she relented and started pulling on her jeans. "I can't believe we are doing this!"

"Believe it! Mrs. Hewitt, you need an adventure and a doughnut."

I was dressed in a flash, had Gabby's diaper bag, which stayed packed and ready to go, and Gabby in the car carrier while Amelia finished getting dressed. I pulled the blanket completely over the carrier to protect her from the night air and that was after I put one of the knitted caps that Praise made for her on. During all of that, the only move she made was to put her thumb in her mouth.

When Amelia finally emerged from the bedroom, she voiced concern over our adventure again. "You know it's quarter past midnight now and it will be nearly 3:00 a.m. before we get there."

I was not backing down. We were doing this. "I'm aware of that, so let's get going."

I started down the stairs with Gabby and Amelia followed. "Wait here and I will bring the truck around."

We listened to the radio and sang along all the way to Eatonton, but as we were turning onto I-20, Amelia finally brought up the subject of Dick and Joan again. Gabby was fast asleep in the carrier and at the end of five minutes of staring at her and singing to her, Amelia asked. "What made him sign the papers?"

"Joan said he wanted all of his children to be safe and loved."

Tears filled Amelia's eyes and she turned her head to the passenger's side window. This was the second time tonight that she had tried to hold back from me seeing her cry.

"Amelia, I know it's strange, but according to Joan, he did it because he loves her. Joan said he apologized to her for all of the lowdown things he had ever done to her and threw himself on her mercy. Joan had never seen him like this before. He was terrified that his other children would find out about Gabby and how that would affect them. Joan convinced him that the best thing to do for everyone, including Gabby, would be for him to sign over his rights. Joan said their youngest thrives on being the baby of the family and the apple of Dick's eye and it would just kill the boy to know his position in his father's family had been replaced. She also said that he was very domineering toward the boys and to her and they all had their issues with their father, but none of them had any idea that he ran around and it would devastate them. He knew they would be crushed. "

Amelia turned back to me, "She had him give her up to save her children?"

"Wouldn't you do anything, sacrifice anyone to protect your children?" I asked her and I could see the wheels turning in her head. "You would have done the same as Joan. You would have sacrificed one that meant nothing to you for the sake of three that meant the world to you. That's what any good parent would do. That's what Joan is to her children and we shouldn't judge her for that."

"I suppose you're right," Amelia looked back to Gabby and the tears were starting to dry up. "She's so sweet."

"And you can't fathom how anyone could ever give her up. I think despite everything, Dick gave Gabby up to protect her from Beth. To hear Joan tell it, he was livid at the idea of Beth having wrecked the car so carelessly while Gabby was in it with her. I know I have had my differences with him, but he could have just turned a blind eye to all of this and he didn't. I think he did the only decent thing he could do in this situation."

"I suppose you're right, but he doesn't know what he's missing."

I reached over and took Amelia's hand and pulled it across the cab of the truck to my lips. I kissed her hand. "I think he knows, but what's he to do? Ruin everyone's lives that he loves? He's nearly sixty years old and Joan's in her early fifties. This makes the most sense for them. Joan might forgive him again, but I don't see her taking his love child to raise and I don't see him being divorced and raising her alone and I sure don't see him marrying Beth."

"Part of what you are saying is that he took the easy way out," Amelia stroked Gabby's hair as she spoke.

"I guess that's one way to look at it, but I think in his own way he might have been giving her the family that he couldn't."

"Maybe."

"Regardless of his motives, I really hope I can beat Beth without having to use any of this." I glanced at her to see what she might think of what I had just said and she looked puzzled. I immediately began to explain what I meant.

"Amelia, look at me. You and I both know you are the only real mother of my children. I know that's important to you, but we have to think of what's best for Gabby in the long run. I don't want to crawl in the gutter with Beth and I think pulling this out in court and slapping her in the face with it should be my last resort."

There was a bit of exasperation in her tone when she replied, "Don't you think you crawled in the gutter with her the other day when you told Attorney Ellis to dig up her vet records? I'm not criticizing you. Lord knows I would have held her in the gutter and drowned her to protect you and Gabby months ago. I'm just saying, there's no place I wouldn't go to protect our family. If she wanted a fight at the gates of Hell, then I'm there."

"One day, when all the sordid details of Gabby's birth and everything about the custody proceedings comes out to her, I want her to understand that I did not take her from her mother. I never want Gabby to see her mother as a victim and if she ever does, I certainly don't want her to think that we were the ones that victimized her."

"You can't control what Gabby thinks and that could be years from now and why..."

"Because she's not like you, she's not old enough to see her mother for what she really is and as soon as she finds out that she's not ours, her real mother, Beth, will be a princess that will hold every little girl's fantasy. You were older and had time to know your mother, so there was no dreaming of her coming and taking you away to her fancy house with all of the dolls that you could ever want."

"You have given this a great deal of thought, but why? Why are you worried about what Gabby will think of Beth?"

"I can't seem to help myself. I think about it because I used to fantasize that there had been some sort of horrible mistake and that my parents would come for me. I convinced myself of a thousand scenarios explaining what had really happened and how they would come for me when the time was right."

"Gabriel, I'm so sorry. It was rare, but I would dream of my mother coming to her senses and coming for me. I was lucky that I had Granddaddy and Aunt Gayle. Life was good and I didn't dwell on her. They gave me a great life and it lessened the opportunity to miss her. You have to trust that we can give that to Gabby. And, Gabriel, I know we've only been at this parenting thing for a few months, but you are a great father."

"So you aren't disappointed in me?"

"Why would I be disappointed?"

"Because I have always said to you, 'Mess with the bull and you'll get the horns,' and I know you have been waiting for me to give her the horns."

"Sometimes the best way to catch flies is with honey."

"And sometimes you sound just like my grandfather."

"That's why you love me so much!" I smiled at her and she blushed. I loved that I could still make her blush after all this time.

We plugged on toward Atlanta. We were almost to Conyers where the grassy median was replaced by the cement wall, not far from where Amelia and Cara had gone to the horse park and seen the German Equestrian team the day of the bombing at Centennial Olympic Park. I'm not sure if she realized and I certainly did not bring it up.

Gabby had not budged since we loaded her into the truck and left Milledgeville. I wasn't that tired, but Amelia yawned every other breath.

"If you want to close your eyes for a little while, I'll be fine. I'm sure the smell of fresh doughnuts will wake you when we get there."

Amelia looked at me as if to seek assurance. "It's okay. You can go to sleep. I don't mind."

It wasn't even five minutes and she was slumped over on Gabby's car seat and fast asleep. I loved to watch them sleep. There were times when I would creep into Gabby's room and bring her back to our bed just so I could watch the two of them sleep. Watching them was one of my favorite things to do, so this situation made it hard to keep my eyes on the road.

As Amelia and Gabby slept, I was left with my thoughts. I thought about the first time I discovered that the Krispy Kreme on Ponce was open all night. I was in college and Beth had flown me down for the weekend. Beth had insisted we go to a party at one of her friend's houses.

The friend lived in one of the mansions along Ponce de Leon Avenue out toward Decatur. Short of Beth's parents' house, it was the largest house I had ever been inside. As much as I was in awe of the house, I was so out of place. The other party-goers looked like Ralph Lauren models and I lacked the self-confidence and the wardrobe to feel comfortable in that group. The only thing I was wearing that night that was my own was my underwear. Everything else was my roommate's, a pair of Calvin Klein jeans and an Old Navy sweater.

I wanted to leave from the moment we pulled into the driveway, but Beth was in her element. The driveway was long and cobblestoned. Driveways where I was from were often dirt paths to the house and even the most extravagant house I had lived in only had a concrete slab. This driveway was completely lined with every luxury car that I had ever dreamed of and I mean every one: Mercedes, BMW, Audi, Lexus and several varieties of Porsche too.

Beth kissed everyone that greeted her on the lips and that just added to my discomfort. With the exception of handing me her purse and her jacket, it was as if I was not with her at all. There were no introductions to the guys or the girls she greeted. They fell all over one another while I was not even an afterthought. I was bumped into by no less than fifteen different party- goers who were either intoxicated or high; either way, I was invisible to them and my date.

Looking back, this is the night that should have been the turning point for me and Beth. That should have been the night I ended things with her.

A true sign of a bad party for me is when I didn't even feel like drinking. I just wanted to go home and I didn't mean back to Beth's parents' house. I wanted to go back to my dorm room and be alone. I wanted out of Atlanta and off of that porch where I had been waiting on Beth to notice I was missing. When she did notice I was not at her side with her purse and coat, she finally came looking for me or them, I'm still not sure, but she came bearing what she thought was a gift.

I was sitting on the top step of the porch contemplating walking to the nearest MARTA stop and then making my way to the airport. I was working up the courage to take that first step when Beth flopped down on top of me.

"Hey, Baby, I brought you something," and then she kissed me awkwardly deep and hard before presenting me with a line of coke strewn across a tiny little mirror.

"What?!" I shrieked as I stood tossing her off of my lap. "I'm on scholarship with the fucking Navy! I can't be near that stuff! What are you thinking?"

"Don't be such a tight ass!" Beth snapped as she clawed her way to her feet. "What's the big damn deal?"

"The big damn deal is I could lose my scholarship and be dishonorably discharged!"

The decision I had been struggling with was suddenly made. I threw her coat and purse at her and I started walking. Down the steps, across the yard and past all of the luxury cars including Beth's, I went. I didn't even look back, but I could hear her screaming behind me.

"That's right, run! Drag your ass back where you came from!" she yelled after me.

I kept walking. I made it about four blocks before Beth pulled up next to me.

The window rolled down and Beth did her best to sound sincere, "Get in!"

I kept walking.

"Come on, get in. You are going to freeze." She had a valid point. My blood had been boiling over her, but now the cold was starting to get to me.

I shook off the chill and pressed on. Beth did not take the hint I was giving. She rolled along beside me until I couldn't take the cold any longer. It was just above freezing that night and I could see my breath.

"Come on, Gabe, get in!" she said once more.

There still wasn't an apology and I knew I would never get one, but, as usual, I caved.

"Did you do the coke?" I asked as I stopped and turned toward her car.

The little red BMW rolled to a stop. Yeah, she had the one from the latest Bond movie and the sound of an answer came through the window.

"Jesus! I'm not getting in the car with you driving and high!" I started walking again.

Beth put the car in gear and gave it the gas. I thought she was speeding off, but she only jerked it past me to cut me off. She pulled right in my path, right up on the sidewalk, jumped out and threw the keys at me. "Fine, you drive."

The keys hit me in the chest and bounced off. Again, looking back, that was the moment I should have left them on the ground and kept walking. I was a stupid boy. I picked up the keys and got in the car. Beth slunk back into the passenger's seat and not another word was spoken. I thought she passed out.

We were about a mile down the road when she perked up. "I'm starving! Pull in there!"

"It's 2:00 a.m."

"Look," she pointed and laughed, "Hot nuts now!"

With one hand, Beth pointed at the sign in front of the Krispy Kreme shop. The word "dough" was not working in the neon sign that was next to us at the red light. With the other hand, she reached between my legs.

"Pull around back," she panted.

I shook my head at the memory as I pulled into the Krispy Kreme shop that night with Amelia and Gabby sleeping in the truck next to me. I didn't need to relive the rest of the night with Beth. I was a stupid twenty-one year old boy, a stupid, stupid boy and I knew better, but I just never did better. I always took the easy way out when it came to her back then. There were some things I regretted about my time with her, but I could not regret it all because were it not for her, I would not have Amelia and Gabby.

I woke Amelia and we all went inside. Gabby woke up while we were removing her from the car and the three of us watched the conveyor belt bring around the freshly fried doughnuts and run them under the glaze. Gabby seemed as fascinated as Amelia and I. We satisfied that craving of Amelia's for fresh doughnuts and I never mentioned a word of my prior trip to that doughnut shop.

431

After the doughnut shop, we called Anthony at the Westin and took him breakfast. Since we were all the way down there, going by to see him seemed like the right thing to do. Anthony was working the night shift and was happy to see us. We hadn't seen him since our wedding. I still felt as if I had known him forever and would be eternally grateful to him for helping me find Amelia the morning of the bombing.

CHAPTER 23

Amelia was just over seven months along in the pregnancy and the Braxton Hicks contractions were coming more often, but nothing had been as scary as when we ended up in the hospital the night Beth wrecked my car. We tried to keep in mind that it was just her body's way of getting her ready for the birth of Sweet Pea.

The days counted down. We were going to trial since the judge refused to rule on the Motion for Summary Judgment and terminate Beth's parental rights. The culmination of the custody battle for Gabby was nearly upon us.

The trial was set for Monday, December 16$^{th}$, and on Friday we did trial prep at Attorney Ellis' office. It was the first time I had been to the office since the day Beth totaled my car and fled. The car was only three years old, an Acura Legend. They were supposed to be the cream of the crop of Hondas, but the way it hit the railroad tie that separated the parking lot from the lawn of the building, tore out the suspension and bent the frame. I would not have thought a rear-ender would have caused that much damage, but the car took a beating.

I went back and forth with the shop and the insurance company for nearly a month before they deemed it totaled. Roger's was the most reputable garage in Greensboro, but even Roger himself could not get the car to drive right again and he was rumored to be a miracle worker. He finally agreed that the car looked like it was aimed at a fifteen degree angle when it was driving straight down the road.

I liked the car. It was the closest thing to a new car I had ever had and only the second one that I had ever owned at all. Losing it was a blow, but that blow was softened by the fact that the pictures, estimates and repair notes that were laid across Attorney Ellis' desk that Friday afternoon would all prove useful in defending against Beth. The carelessness of the wreck, the disregard for everyone's safety including hers and Gabby's coupled with the damage to my car would just be more strings in the pile that would be the undoing of any ties she had to Gabby.

Amelia went with me to the appointment that afternoon and she attempted to participate in the preparation, but as politely as he could, Mr. Ellis shut her down at every turn. Finally he came out with it, "You know, you cannot come to trial on Monday, right?"

Although Amelia was visibly stunned, I was the first to protest. "I need her with me."

"Why would that be? You understand that this trial is to be held in front of a jury of Green County citizens? You realize you must appear to be one of them?" Attorney Ellis continued his questions.

Amelia was getting his point, but I was oblivious. "She has every right to be there."

"Ah, yes, let's talk about right. Do two wrongs make a right?" he asked.

"What?"

"Now, I am not judging, I understand every piece of evidence we have against Ms. Reed, but please let me explain to you how you," he paused for a second and looked to Amelia, "and Mrs. Hewitt appear."

Amelia must have been able to tell that I was about to go on the defensive and she grabbed my hand. I looked at her and she calmly shook her head in the negative to me and whispered, "Don't."

Mr. Ellis went on, "The everyday citizens of the county are not those you see on the boats around the lake. They are the ones you see in the churches on Sunday mornings and in the fields and factories on Monday through Friday. What do you think the jurors will see when they look at the two of you?"

Amelia stayed seated in one of the two guest chairs that were in front of Mr. Ellis' desk, but I stood and turned my back and ran my hands through my hair.

Amelia answered his question quietly, "He's right. I can't be there."

I whipped around to her, to both of them. "Excuse me?"

"Since you won't tell that Beth lied about you being Gabby's father, the jury has no option but to think that you got one woman pregnant and left her to get another, much younger girl pregnant. It won't matter that you married me."

All I could do was shake my head.

Attorney Ellis flipped through some pages that he picked up from his desk. "It is only by the grace of God that Ms. Reed's attorney has not called her as a witness. According to the pre-trial order, they have only listed her parents, her brothers and her doctor as witnesses."

Mr. Ellis tossed the paper down and threw up his hands. He looked to Amelia when he spoke again. "I don't know what to make of it. I would have put your name on the list first. You would have been the key to me making the jury believe he was a real scoundrel. On what other ground could she hope to have a standing?"

I was on the outside of a club of lawyers looking in. Suddenly, Amelia was the one on her feet.

"Perhaps she doesn't really want a standing. Perhaps she doesn't want Gabby at all. She's never really acted like she wanted her. Perhaps she's only putting up the appearance of a fight. As long as I have known her, she's only wanted Gabriel like a child that no longer wants a toy until another child picked it up. Also, from everything Gabriel has told me, she has a job, but she survives off of her parents' money. I would be willing to bet good money that her mother is the driving force behind all of this. They are paying for the lawyer; she isn't."

"You may be right, but what does that matter?" he asked and still I just looked on.

Amelia paced. "Her mother does not have the ammunition on Gabriel because she would have to have the ammunition on Beth."

"Ammunition?"

435

"As much as Beth has done to Gabriel, he has been the best friend she has ever had. He's never breathed a word to anyone in her family what they really raised."

"But she exposed his time in YDC."

"That was only a threat, to scare him into letting go of all of this."

"But he didn't let go." Attorney Ellis continued with his side of the banter.

"Right, and now here we are. I stand by what I said. She doesn't want Gabby, but her mother does."

"Do you think her mother even knows who the father of the child is?"

I interrupted. "Not a clue. I'm sure Mrs. Reed believes to the core that I am the father and she would be mortified to find out the father of her grandchild is a much older, married man. Oh yes, Mrs. Barbara Reed is the picture of Atlanta society and it's bad enough that Beth had a baby out of wedlock let alone one with a married man. Her husband might be new money, but she's old money and she would be embarrassed beyond repair. She's heard the rumors about her daughter for years, but refused to believe them and her husband has always fixed things so she wouldn't have to..."

Mr. Ellis scratched his head and shrugged. "I don't know how to fight this because I don't know what they have up their sleeves."

"I think we are as stuck as she is," I added.

I never thought I would hear her say it, but Amelia's advice was, "Kill them with kindness. If you go on the attack you risk alienating the jury for beating up on her, but if you don't pull out all the stops you risk them giving Gabby to her. Like you told us before, everyone's opinion is that a child needs their mother. Some still believe that even a bad mother is better than no mother."

436

The three of us shook our heads in unison. Amelia and I left there that afternoon no more prepared for trial than we were when we first walked in. Sure, we knew what evidence Attorney Ellis had to present against Beth, to paint her as a villainess of a mother, but we did not know how the use of that information would help or hurt us or if the use of it would be required at all.

I don't know how we managed to do it, but we managed to avoid the subject of the trial most of the weekend. I was nervous and talking about it wouldn't change that. Amelia had been banished from the courthouse, so maybe she thought she had contributed all she could at that point. Maybe Amelia was just as worried as I was and that was why she had avoided the topic all weekend.

We climbed into bed around 9:30 on Sunday night. She snuggled up to me and I could smell her hair as I laid my head against her neck. We laid there on our sides and in this position I could hardly tell she was pregnant at all. She curled her arm around mine and a leg across one of mine and we were entwined. We laid there in silence until I couldn't take it anymore. Enough time had passed that she could have been asleep, but I knew she wasn't.

"Amelia," I whispered into her neck. "Are you awake?"

"Yes." Her answer was a little louder and she rolled over to face me.

I brushed her hair away from her face. "I don't know what's going to happen tomorrow and..."

"And you are scared?" No man wanted to admit they were ever scared so it was comforting that Amelia took the words out of my mouth.

"I hate the thought of being there without you."

Amelia inched closer to me and we were tangled up in each other again as we laid there. "You are going to be fine. You'll have Daniel and Jay and Cara and Mrs. Allen. There will be so many people there to support you."

"It won't be the same without you."

437

"I promise, everything will be fine."

"You don't know that."

It was dark and I couldn't see a thing in there, but I could feel Amelia reach for my hand. She pulled it closer and placed it across her stomach. I could feel the baby kicking like a soccer player.

"No matter what happens, you will always have us," and she kissed me.

Amelia had a way of making everything better with just a kiss. It was deep and wet and I could have died in that moment. Her hand traveled from atop mine to caress my cheek and I pulled her as close to me as I possibly could.

It was cold and I was wearing a new pair of flannel pajama bottoms. Amelia had confiscated the button up shirt that came with the set and she was wearing it. As she had slid her hand to my cheek, I slid mine to her behind. I didn't forget the baby was between us, but I lost myself in her. I wanted her and by all account, I needed her.

I slipped my index finger into the hem of the leg of her panties at her hip and eased them around.

"Like old times," she sighed.

I laughed ever so slightly. I had thought maybe I should ask if she was up for what I had in mind, but I didn't. I comforted myself with the thought that she would tell me if she wanted me to stop and she seemed to be telling me just the opposite. Amelia arched her back and raised her leg up mine as I continued my trail around the hem. I could feel chill bumps on her skin.

"Gabriel, I love you no matter what the outcome tomorrow. This is where you belong," Amelia whispered as she climbed on top of me.

The moonlight lit her face. She was so beautiful and she loved me. Normally I would have been satisfied just to look at her, but not that night. That night I needed her more than I had ever needed her before, more than the night after the Delta Digital Christmas party last year.

I did not know what I did to deserve her. I spent a lifetime trying to forgive myself for what I had done to my parents and my sister and trying to believe that the opinion of my grandmother was not the only opinion anyone should ever have of me. I had searched all of my life for self-worth and it took finding her for me to feel as if I was worth anything at all.

I made love to her that night fearing it would be the last. I got us into this mess with Beth and Gabby and I could have ended it months ago when I figured out Gabby was not mine. I loved Gabby and I never thought about giving her up, but until that moment I had never thought about losing Amelia over her. I was terrified that if I lost the case for Gabby, it would break Amelia's heart and we would never be the same. She only came to love Gabby because of me and I would have no one to blame for this but myself. Amelia would have no one to blame, but me. I tried to do the honorable thing by Gabby, but if I failed, would it cost me Amelia?

\*\*\*

School was out for Christmas break, so I didn't bother to wake Amelia when I got up the next morning. She was so peaceful and still naked under the covers from the night before. I kissed her on the forehead and headed into the shower. I had every intention of leaving her in bed asleep.

I was midway of my shower when the smell of bacon wafted into the bathroom. A few minutes more and scrambled eggs and pancakes were floating in the air. When I finally made it out of there, I found a plate of bacon, eggs and pancakes along with a glass of orange juice waiting next to the sink for me.

I dressed as quickly as I could and took the plate to find Amelia. I wanted to make sure she saved something for herself and I needed to kiss Gabby good morning. I didn't have to go far. I found

Amelia sitting in our bed with Gabby propped up on her belly. She was reading the Cat in the Hat while Gabby held her own bottle.

I took a seat on the bed next to them. I cut the first bite of my pancakes and offered it to Amelia.

"No, thanks. I already ate," she replied.

I looked at them and they were a vision. I did not care what any jury would think, Amelia was the picture of motherhood and if people could not see that then they were fools. I watched them as I took bites of bacon and swallows of orange juice. Amelia watched me back and with a curious face.

"Do you own another suit?" She readjusted Gabby against her and rolled over to face me.

"Yes. Why?" I drew out the words as I had no idea why she was asking.

"That's the suit you wore to the Georgian Terrace. That was a good night."

"And..."

"I remember every detail of that night. It was perfect and I don't want a thing about it tarnished." She wiped a stray strand of hair from her eye and looked away. She shrugged as she completed her thought. "Not even that suit."

"You want me to change?"

"Only what you're wearing."

I finished breakfast and changed from my navy blue suit into my black one. I kissed the girls and was reluctantly on my way. It was a bright December morning, a week from Christmas and the decorations perched on all of the light poles on the way out of Milledgeville were just shutting off in the morning light. With this case looming over us, I just had not been able to get into the Christmas spirit no matter how many light poles I saw, how many parties we hosted at the club or how Amelia had decorated the apartment. I just kept thinking that this day marked the beginning of the end, no matter what the outcome.

I pulled into the parking lot outside of the Green County Courthouse in Amelia's grandfather's old C-10 pick-up truck just before 8:00 a.m.

"Shit! Shit! Shit!" I gritted my teeth and huffed out under my breath upon sight of Mr. and Mrs. Reed.

They were exiting Mrs. Reed's black BMW. J.J. was getting out of the back passenger's side and Mr. Reed was holding the door. I looked away before I saw Beth step out of the other back seat. Another black BMW, a smaller sedan, was parked right next to them and two men and a woman stood along the driver's side of it. They were all dressed in black from head to toe, suits pressed and brief cases firmly gripped in hand.

Across the parking lot I noticed Attorney Ellis and Joyce. They were behind his old Volvo station wagon pulling out box after box and stacking them on a set of mini hand-trucks. By the time I pulled up and parked along the side of them, Attorney Ellis was throwing his tattered old brown brief case on top of the heap and Joyce was strapping it all together with a neon green bungee cord.

His Volvo looked more like the "fishing car" of an attorney, but that was his everyday vehicle. His wardrobe looked like he was hosting a Wednesday night prayer meeting. His hair was not so much combed as it was blown dry with the windows down on the way there that morning. All of that being said, Attorney Ellis had come highly recommended and was known to be the best in the county, but compared to the guys in the suits across the parking lot I had to wonder.

I checked my appearance in the rearview mirror of the truck once more before I got out. It was too late to chance anything so I gathered my nerves and got out of the truck.

441

"Can I help you all carry any of that?" I asked them as I reached to help Mrs. Joyce with the little set of hand-trucks.

"Good morning, Gabe. Nervous?" Joyce asked.

Mr. Ellis was busy locking up the Volvo, but answered for me over his shoulder. "Of course he's nervous, but nervousness won't change anything, so you might as well leave that nonsense out here."

"Fish or cut bait, right?" I did my best to take his advice and tried cracking a little joke.

"That's what my daddy'd say," Joyce added as we all started toward the front of the courthouse.

As we walked, Attorney Ellis began to explain to me what to expect and the process of things. "This morning we'll take care of a few legal formalities and then start with voir dire, jury selection. It's not so much selection as de-selection, but I need you to pay attention. The judge will ask some questions. I'll ask them some questions and then her attorney will have a chance to ask questions. You can make notes. If there's anyone you like make a note and likewise for anyone you don't like. If you get a funny feeling, if they won't look you in the eye, if you get a good vibe from them, let me know. Okay?"

"Okay." I nodded in agreement and we approached the steps.

"After we have the jury picked, we'll do opening statements. We sued her so I'll go first. After opening statements, we will call our first witnesses. That means you followed by Mrs. Allen, Daniel and so on. Remember, just answer the questions as you did in your deposition. Only elaborate if I ask you to, but keep your answers to yes or no when they cross you. I am not telling you anything I didn't tell you already when you were at the office on Friday."

"Alright. And you will ask her questions about her deposition? How? When she didn't show up for hers?"

442

"That's going to be tricky, but that's for me to worry about and you to trust me on. It could just be that all of this is a formality. Keep in mind, these attorneys are handicapped by the fact that they were just hired and an extension was refused."

The first group of attorneys that the Reeds hired for Beth was the toast of Atlanta and they quit after the wreck and when she went missing. Attorney Ellis had already had a frank conversation with them when they were unable to agree to a date to make Beth available to be deposed.

"Between us," they told him, "we can't find our client."

That had been weeks ago and the following week a notice of withdrawal of counsel arrived from that firm and a week following that a notice of representation arrived from a firm of which Attorney Ellis had never heard. He inquired around and found out that the firm typically did real estate closings and remained on retainer for Mr. Reed's construction company.

I held the door for Joyce to enter first followed by Attorney Ellis. It just so happened J.J. Reed had lingered in the parking lot longer than the rest of the Reed family, so I held the door for him as well.

"May I have a moment, Gabe?" J.J. Reed has a soft voice and he always seemed so detached from the rest of the Reed clan that I was a little shocked to see him that morning.

I looked to Attorney Ellis before I answered. Mr. Ellis shook his head gently side to side.

"Now's not a good time," I politely replied.

"Well, it's good to see you despite the circumstances," he said as he hung his head and headed on inside the courthouse.

I had not seen J.J. in over two years. He was always the nicest of the Reed children. One would have thought that being the oldest, he would have set the standard, but judging by the way Beth and her younger brother turned out, the mold was broken when J.J. was made. He looked like them; same hair color, skin tone, eyes and tall, dark brown, fair with hints of freckles, green and cresting six foot three. Personality wise, he was completely opposite. He was kind for the sake of being kind. The other two, Beth and her brother Ari, were only sincerely nice to their parents and I think that was only because they didn't want to bite the hand that fed them. To everyone else they were only nice when it benefitted them. My opinion of them was further cemented in the fact that Ari, whose full name was actually Arnold Linton Reed, could not be bothered to turn out and show support for his sister or their parents during the trial.

There was something odd about the exchange, but I tried not to think anything of it. We walked down the corridor past all of the courthouse staff, jailers and those in orange jumpsuits milling about awaiting their arraignments. J.J. disappeared in the crowd ahead of us.

At the door to the courtroom, I held the door for Mrs. Joyce and Mr. Ellis. Joyce ran the hand trucks into the door and lost the whole load in the middle of the swinging doors. Papers and files went all across the floor and down the aisle a couple of feet. I had hold of one, but the other swung into the room and back and hit her as she bent over to pick everything up.

Beth was standing next to the two attorneys at the table closest to the jury box. Her mother was leaning against the railing that separated the galley from the area with the tables, straightening Beth's collar. Her father was whispering to J.J. when the commotion with our file boxes happened in the doorway of the courtroom. The entire Reed clan, with the exception of J.J., turned and snickered at Mrs. Joyce's misfortune. I stood and cut my eyes at all of them, gave them a real good "shut the hell up" look. Attorney Ellis noticed and took hold of my arm to reign me in.

"Save it for the stand." He turned his head away from them when he spoke, so there was no way of them knowing what he said.

I stifled my urge to do more than give them a look and I went back to helping with the mess of papers. Why did it take me so long to realize that everything about them grated on my nerves?

Once we had everything picked up, we continued to our table. Joyce stopped shy of the empty table on the left hand side of the courtroom. She looked at Beth's team as if they were in her way, but they did not even acknowledge her.

"Joyce, it's okay. We'll take that table. I don't mind them having that one." Attorney Ellis patted Joyce on the back as he passed behind her and proceeded to put the files he was carrying down on the empty table.

I followed him. There were three chairs at the table and they faced the judge's bench and the jury was to the far side of the room. I was pulling out the middle chair that he had gestured would be mine when he began to explain courtesies of the courtroom.

"Usually the one that files the suit gets the seat closest to the jury. Normally, I would make them move, but in this case, I want the jury to watch her. I think it will do them good."

The morning drug on and although my attorney had described the proceedings to me, he had not warned me how boring it would be. This was nothing like Matlock or Perry Mason. I would best describe it as a hurry up and wait situation.

Jury selection was painfully slow. At the get-go, Ellis leaned over to me and whispered, "If her attorney doesn't know any better than to think that he should go first, then he probably doesn't know what he's doing with the questions either. I'm going to let him go ahead and let him hang himself with the jurors."

No sooner had he stopped whispering in one ear did Mrs. Joyce start in my other. "If it is obvious to the jurors that her attorney doesn't know what he's doing, they will become annoyed with him. They'll feel like he's wasting their time and they won't like him. That's a good thing for us."

By the end of it all, I could tell you where each lived, which part of the county, where they worked, went to church and what denomination. Those answers were provided by the questions the judge asked. I also found out if they all had children, their ages, if they were married, what type of car they drove, where they were originally from, if they had family in Atlanta or business on the lake, if they knew any of the Reeds, me or our attorneys and a few other things. Their questions had gone on for an hour asking everything under the sun about the people in the jury pool.

No one knew me or the Reeds, all but two out of twenty-seven knew Attorney Ellis and Mrs. Joyce. Beth's attorneys made a motion to have the panel dismissed and another brought in as they felt they could not get an impartial jury from this group since they all knew Attorney Ellis. The judge simply laughed and waived his hand for them to carry on with their questions or sit down. Evidently, everyone in the county knew my attorney.

When it was his turn to ask questions, Attorney Ellis began by introducing himself to jurors numbers three and eighteen, the ones who had previously raised their hands to signify that they did not know him. The whole panel then broke up in laughter.

"I appreciate your service today and I'm only going to ask y'all a few more questions," he started. He gestured to me, "This is my client, Gabriel Hewitt. Do any of you have a problem with primary custody of a child being granted to a father?"

No one in the jury pool raised their hands.

After waiting about thirty seconds, Attorney Ellis continued. "Does anyone have a problem with a father being granted sole custody?"

There were rumblings from Mrs. Reed to Mr. Reed, but no one in the panel raised a hand.

He posed another question, "Has any one here used recreational drugs in the last year?"

No hands were raised.

"We aren't here to judge you and this information is not to persecute or prosecute you. It is only to determine if you are the right person for this case," he explained.

Still no hands were raised.

"Any recreational drug use in the last five years?"

Juror number twelve's hand went up and Joyce marked his name on her list.

"Anyone in the last ten years?"

Jurors two, eight and eighteen raised their hands and Joyce noted it.

"Anyone think that drug use around children is acceptable?"

Rumblings again came from the Reeds. Mr. Reed leaned forward and gave a stern look to Beth's attorney. That look led to a quick shout of "Objection!"

The objection was over-ruled by the judge and the attorney sat back down disappointed.

"Just a few more questions," Attorney Ellis began again. "Have any of you ever been in a car accident?"

Thirteen hands went up and Joyce marked all of them.

"Good, good. How many of you were not the cause of the accident?"

Three hands went down.

"Alright. How many of those of you left were victims of hit and run?"

The words were barely out of his mouth before the opposing counsel screamed, "Objection!" again.

The judge called them to the bench. Attorney Ellis told us when he came back that he was lightly chastised, but not to worry.

The judge then instructed the jury to disregard Mr. Ellis' last question. Attorney Ellis did not mind. In fact, his words were with a low chuckle, "Can't un-ring a bell."

He stood before the entire panel once more, "Any of you good people believe that a mother's rights should never be terminated?"

"Terminated?" Mrs. Reed screamed from her seat in the pew across the courtroom. She was then warned about outbursts and informed that she would be removed if she had another. She settled back down, but not without a frenzy of whispering among her and the other members of the Reed party.

In response to Attorney Ellis' questions about termination of a mother's rights, only one hand went up. Juror seven raised his hand.

"I have no further questions."

Within ten minutes, the jury was struck and we had a panel of one retired man, two retired grandmothers, a teacher from the elementary school in Greensboro, a stay at home mother and a worker from the power plant in Milledgeville. The retired man was the only man on the jury panel.

I was initially concerned about having almost all women, but Joyce calmed those concerns, "Women are almost always more critical of other women than men are."

After the jurors were struck came the opening statements. Again Beth's attorney stepped forward to address the court first. Joyce looked at Attorney Ellis befuddled. The judge even looked at Attorney Ellis, a look questioning if he wanted the judge to intervene and have Beth's attorney return to his seat.

"Do they have no idea of courtroom etiquette or are they trying to step on your toes?" she leaned around me and asked him.

He pulled out a fresh notebook as he answered. "I don't know, but I don't mind having the last word."

Joyce smiled and I just sat there wondering what argument Beth's attorney was about to put up.

He was a tall man with salt and pepper gray hair. He had thick, black rimmed glasses which he adjusted as he approached the podium. He reminded me of an older Clark Kent. He placed a legal pad on the podium and began to address the jurors directly.

"Good morning," he announced and the six jurors reciprocated.

"I'm Bill Ayers and I have the honor of representing Ms. Lizbeth Reed. Beth is the mother of a five month old daughter, Gabriella Grace Hewitt." He gestured in my direction, "Mr. Gabe Hewitt is the father. They call her Gabby and you'll hear a great deal in the next day or so about baby Gabby and it is your duty to decide the best custody arrangement for her. We will try to keep this as brief as possible because we understand your time is valuable, but please understand baby Gabby is "valuable" to Ms. Reed and her family and we ask that you award primary physical custody to Ms. Reed."

Mr. Ayers then turned and went back to his seat. While Joyce and Attorney Ellis whispered across me about how weak of an opening argument that was I glanced back to the row where the Reeds were seated. It appeared that they knew it was weak as well.

Attorney Ellis stood and from right there next to me, he began to speak. He didn't bother going all the way to the podium before he started his opening.

"Good morning, again."

This time the jurors just nodded in response. They all knew him so there was no need for another introduction so he began by introducing me.

"My client here," he motioned to me at his side, "is Gabriel Hewitt. Mr. Hewitt is a former Navy Officer and is now the food and beverage director at Port Honor out on the lake. He's an upstanding member of the community, but you might hear over the next day or so that Mr. Hewitt served time in a youth detention center while he was a teenager and he did."

I didn't realize he was going to throw us on the sword from the get go like that, but I did my best not to appear fazed as he approached the podium and continued.

"Now we can spend time explaining that or you can understand that like the rest of us, Mr. Hewitt did something in his youth that he wasn't necessarily proud of. He served his time back then and rose above all the challenges of his youth. You will hear from friends and family to that regard. You will hear what a good man and good father Mr. Hewitt has turned out to be."

"You will also hear about Ms. Reed and that she has not risen above. You will hear that Ms. Reed shows a blatant disregard for the law. You will hear that Ms. Reed continues to make poor decisions that jeopardize the safety of those around her, including her daughter. We do not challenge Ms. Reed or her family's love for her child, but we do challenge whether Ms. Reed is fit to care for Gabby."

"We ask that you listen to the evidence carefully. We know it is a difficult decision that we are asking you to make, but one that we are compelled to ask you to make. We feel that after listening to the testimony and the facts, at the end of this case you will know as I do, that sole primary and physical custody of Gabriella Grace Hewitt rests with Mr. Hewitt. Thank you for your time and your service."

Attorney Ellis returned to the chair next to me. Never once during his statement did he say that I was Gabby's father. He said that I had turned out to be a good father, but he never referred to me as Gabby's father.

Attorney Ellis' behind was barely in the chair before the judge asked the attorneys, "Which one of you is going to call the first witness?"

Attorney Ellis looked to Mr. Ayers who looked puzzled by the question. Ultimately, Attorney Ellis granted Mr. Ayers the opportunity to call his first witness. He called Beth's mother, Mrs. Reed.

They went through all of the formalities of swearing her in and background information and then it went on from there. He essentially gave her free reign to tell how she knew me and her opinion as to who should have Gabby. Of course she said Beth should be given custody of Gabby and she went on and on about how much everyone in the family loved Gabby. The whole thing did not last more than ten minutes and Attorney Ayers was finished with Mrs. Reed and Attorney Ellis began his cross.

After his introduction, Attorney Ellis' first question was, "Mrs. Reed what is your granddaughter's date of birth?"

Mrs. Reed pressed her skirt to smooth it across her lap as she repositioned herself and answered. "July 1, 1996."

"And is it true that you did not call Mr. Hewitt to come to the hospital for the birth of Gabby until two days later?"

"Well..." she stuttered.

"Yes or no, ma'am," he pressed her.

"Correct."

"You told the court just moments ago that your daughter lived with Mr. Hewitt prior to the birth of the child. Is that correct?"

"Yes. They were engaged." I shook my head in disagreement of her statement. Beth and I were never engaged. She noticed me and added to her statement. "He gave her a ring."

"If that was the case, why would she not call him to the hospital when she was in labor?"

"It was an oversight on my part."

"An oversight? As in, you forgot to call who you thought was your future son-in-law to the birth of his child? Was it also an oversight that you did not correct him when he believed the child was born on July 3rd and not July 1st?" Attorney Ellis had successfully painted Mrs. Reed as a fool.

"Well, I..."

"Earlier you told the court that your daughter wants her daughter to come and live with her and she wants primary custody of Gabby. Is that correct?"

"Yes."

"And did your daughter not want Gabby the day she was released from the hospital and you turned her over to Mr. Hewitt?"

"She was suffering from post-partum depression. She wasn't herself."

Attorney Ellis quickly turned back to the table and thumbed through a stack of papers that he had labeled, Northside Hospital. He pulled out three copies of pages.

"Your Honor," he addressed the judge as he turned back toward the witness stand. "May I approach the witness?"

As the judge granted permission, Attorney Ellis first approached Beth's attorney and handed him a copy before continuing on to Mrs. Reed.

"I am about to hand the witness what I have marked as Plaintiff's Exhibit 'A-1'. Mrs. Reed, if you will direct your attention to the highlighted portion. Would you please read that aloud?"

Eventually, the judge directed Mrs. Reed to read the passage, "Patient tests positive for cocaine."

"And who's medical records are these? If you would read the name at the top of the page..."

"Patient ID Number 1596723." She tried to be coy, but he was not having it.

"The name of the patient is right next to that number. Please read the name of the patient."

"Lizbeth Margaret Reed," Mrs. Reed answered with distain.

Attorney Ellis looked to the judge, "Plaintiff would like to publish these to the jury."

"Granted," the judge stated.

After submitting the document to the jurors, Attorney Ellis returned to our table and grabbed another set of copies from the Northside stack. He went through the same process regarding how Gabby came to be turned over to me. He had Mrs. Reed read pages that detailed how the Department of Family and Children's Services visited Beth in the hospital and refused to allow Gabby to be released to her when she was discharged from the hospital due to her drug use.

"So, it wasn't because your daughter was going to your house to recuperate that kept Gabby from being with her after their release from the hospital?"

Reluctantly, Mrs. Reed answered, "No."

Attorney Ellis also had Mrs. Reed testify to Beth's arrests after presenting her with police reports and having her read from the reports. He even revisited her statement about how I had given Beth an engagement ring. He questioned her as to whether she had heard that I had given Beth  my mother's wedding set and after she acknowledged that as being the story she was given, he presented her with the police report detailing the wedding set as items that were stolen from my home last December.

Attorney Ellis changed his line of questioning and really got to the point. "Mrs. Reed, do you love your granddaughter?"

"Yes, of course, more than anything," she blotted tears from her eyes as she answered.

"Enough to put the child's health and happiness above the wants and desires of your daughter?" he asked.

Mrs. Reed was speechless. Her face was blank with shock at his question. She looked at Beth and back to Attorney Ellis.

"Do you love your granddaughter enough to let her go?"

"I love my granddaughter and I would never allow anyone to harm her!"

"Mrs. Reed, would you not consider abandonment harm?"

Mrs. Reed looked to Beth's attorney, the one Mrs. Reed herself was footing the bill for, to save her, but he said nothing. No objection came from that table.

Attorney Ellis repeated his question, "Mrs. Reed, do you consider abandonment as harmful to a child?  Please answer the question."

"Yes!" She snapped at him.

"No further questions."

Attorney Ellis released Mrs. Reed from the stand in shame and in tears. She immediately fled the courtroom and J.J. followed. I almost felt bad for her. She had always been kind to me, but she was the perfect example of how nice people are perfectly capable of raising completely rotten kids.

The next witness Beth's attorney called to the stand did not fare any better than Mrs. Reed. It was the housekeeper and nanny that raised Beth and still worked for the family. Her name was Ms. Braun and she was German. I think her first name was Peggy, but Beth called her Eva, as in Hitler's mistress, even to her face. Mrs. Braun took it all in stride and probably was the only person next to Mrs. Reed that actually loved Beth unconditionally.

On direct, Ms. Braun did her best to convince the jury that Beth was a nice girl, at worst just misunderstood. On cross, however, Mr. Ellis had her admit that she was the one that took care of Gabby on the days when Beth had visitation. He had her agree that Beth was uninterested in Gabby. He also questioned Ms. Braun about the way Beth treated her pets.

"You have been with the Reed family for twenty-six years. In that time, how many pets has Miss Reed owned?" Attorney Ellis asked her.

In a pensive voice she answered, "Eight."

"How many were dogs and how many were horses?"

Again, she was hesitant in her answer. "Five dogs, two horses and one guinea pig."

"And of those five dogs how many were puppies when she got them?"

"All of them."

"How many does she still have?"

"None."

"What was the name of her most recent dog?"

"Beatle."

"Can you tell the court what happened to Beatle?"

Ms. Braun raised an eyebrow, but did not answer. She looked to Beth and her attorney as if she needed to be saved from having to answer the question. Beth's attorney tried to object, but the judge shut him down and instructed Ms. Braun to answer the question.

"He died."

The questioning went on and Ms. Braun was presented with the vet records that detailed how Beatle, the six pound Yorkie puppy, died from blunt trauma to his abdomen. Like Mrs. Reed, Ms. Braun was forced to read from the records presented to her. It did not take much to read between the lines of what the records said and understand that the poor pup had been kicked.

"Ms. Braun, would you say that any of Miss Reed's dogs died of natural causes?" Attorney Ellis asked as he laid the stack of veterinary records in front of her insinuating that the answer was in the records and he could verify her answer if he chose to do so.

Ms. Braun tried to soften the answer by stating that she could not recall any pets that were with the family more than two years. Shortly after she answered, she was dismissed from the stand. Mrs. Braun left the stand in tears clearly guilty of having inadvertently betrayed Beth.

The last witness of the day to be called to the stand was Beth's therapist. Mrs. Reed left the courtroom during his testimony. Like she had done during her other witnesses, Beth stared off at the wall. She looked as if she were sedated, only moving enough to blink and give the occasional eye roll.

Dr. LaRoy had a long list of credentials including a PhD in Behavioral Science from Emory, but not an M.D. from Emory. He testified that Beth had done two stints of rehab at his clinic. One stint was as a result of the recommendation from DFACS upon her release from the hospital after having given birth to Gabby. The other stint began two days after she totaled my car. He claimed she voluntarily committed herself to the programs each time in order to get clean for the sake of her daughter.

When Attorney Ellis got a hold of Dr. LaRoy, he came off like a head shrinking charlatan. Figuratively, Attorney Ellis beat him about the head with the knowledge that his first treatment of Beth had been unsuccessful as evidenced by her committing herself to another round of rehab within four months of the first.

"Who's to say this round of treatment was more effective than the first? Can we trust Miss Reed with a baby? Can we trust her not to kill the child the next time she has a bad day, falls off of the proverbial wagon and decides to ram someone else's car?" He asked the questions in rapid fire succession, preventing Dr. LaRoy from answering.

In reality, they weren't meant to be answered. Everyone understood that he asked them just to give the jurors something to think about. Beth's attorney tried to stop him, but only succeeded in having the judge order the jury to disregard the last questions asked by Plaintiff's counsel.

"No further questions," Attorney Ellis released Dr. LaRoy.

I watched as Attorney Ellis returned to take his seat at the table beside me and Joyce whispered to me, "Remember, can't un-ring a bell. Just look at the jurors' faces."

Joyce had a point. They were all shaking their heads back and forth, answering the questions, "no".

Shortly thereafter, the jurors were released for the day. I helped Joyce and Attorney Ellis carry the case files back to his Volvo station wagon. We lingered in the parking lot and discussed the strategy for the following day. We fully expected Beth to be called to the stand first thing the following morning as they did not have anyone else left on their list of witnesses.

That night I gave Amelia the complete play-by-play. I held Gabby and fed her a bottle as I recounted the testimony of each witness.

"I wish you could see it," I told her. "I think this might be a slam dunk. You should see the jurors."

"I sure hope so. I am so ready for all of this to be over."

CHAPTER 24

"Would you please state your full name for the record?" It was 9:00 a.m. and the second day of Gabby's custody trial began with Beth's attorney calling her to the stand.

"Lizbeth Margret Reed. Everyone calls me Beth." She sounded so sweet. I had heard her like that before, but I knew it wouldn't last. She just wasn't capable of being nice for very long.

Mr. Ayers appeared more prepared today as he stood before her with a legal pad with questions and notes written all over it. He began by having Beth provide a history of our relationship. She gave a timeline starting from the moment she gave me directions in the airport that day way back when I was in college.

"He was the most polite boy I had ever met." She complimented me. "I fell in love with him instantly."

"And is he still polite to you?"

"No." A tear rolled down her face. I had never seen Beth cry before. I had seen her give a performance before, but nothing like this.

"Would you elaborate?" He coaxed her on and her mother looked at her with reassuring eyes also urging her to continue.

Beth turned her head to the jury and delivered a line. "He found someone new. I told him I was pregnant and he was through with me."

"That is a lie. She lied!" I gritted my teeth and tried to keep my words to a hushed tone, but still I gasped and Joyce grabbed my arm to restrain me.

Beth went on. "We had been together for eight years. I waited on him while he was overseas in the Navy. I helped get him the job at the club and I thought we were getting married. He had a rough childhood, but I forgave him when he was cruel to me and he could be cruel. I thought he needed space. He said we were just on a break. I thought he loved me. I thought..."

Beth dropped her head in her hands. What a show she was putting on, Oscar-worthy. I looked to the jurors and I feared we were losing them. There was one that was rolling her eyes, but the others were leaning in as if to pay close attention to what she was saying. All of our work from the day before appeared to be coming undone. I could feel myself sweating.

"He found someone younger, much younger and I was pregnant. I did some stupid things. I realize that now. I'm sorry, Mommy. I'm sorry you have to hear this." She looked to the audience and locked eyes with her mother. Tears were streaming from Mrs. Reed's eyes as Beth told her lies.

"I'm so sorry. I was weak and there were moments when I wasn't sure if I wanted to be a mother, a single mother. I was so hurt and betrayed. I thought about harming myself. Yeah, I tried cocaine. I didn't know what to do. His girlfriend was there when I told him and she's a sweet, very young girl. She tried to do the right thing and she let him go. I thought he was going to do the honorable thing then. He even invited me to move in with him toward the end of the pregnancy. We had a horrible fight right before I gave birth. He was cruel to me and I didn't want him there when I gave birth, that's why I didn't call him. It's why I didn't call my mother. I didn't want her to be disappointed in him. My family loved him. They didn't know."

She called *me* cruel and insinuated that I drove her to do drugs. The nerve of her! I could feel the veins coming out in my head as she told one bold faced lie after another. I could do nothing but sit there and listen and watch the jurors as she explained everything away. Her attorney kept her on the stand for almost an hour and a half before Attorney Ellis was given a crack at her.

"Miss Reed, you mean to tell me that you want these good people to believe that you took drugs during your pregnancy because your feelings were hurt?"

"Well, it's not that simple. He was everything to me and," Beth glanced to the jury box and locked eyes with one of the women, "you know how it is. My heart wasn't just broken, it was shattered. I was crushed. I didn't know what I was going to do. Sometimes we do foolish things over our fragile hearts."

460

Attorney Ellis was smart. He moved to get between Beth and the woman before the woman could become further sucked into Beth's lies.

"Miss Reed, if you could keep your answers to 'yes' or 'no', that would be helpful," he advised her before asking the next question.

"Are you currently employed?"

"No."

"So you have no means to support a child?"

"My paren..."

He cut her off, "Yes or no, Miss Reed. You have no means of your own to support a child, isn't that correct?"

"I live wi..." Beth started and he cut her off again.

Attorney Ellis turned his attention to the judge. "Your honor, would you please instruct the witness to limit her answers to 'yes' or 'no'?"

The judge granted Ellis' request and instructed Beth to limit her answers. For a split second, I could see the act drop and a look of distain crossed her face. It was only a flash and then she was back in character.

"No," she said sweetly.

Mrs. Joyce leaned over to me. Her voice was so low that I could barely understand her. "Butter really wouldn't melt in her mouth, huh?"

I barely turned my head and raised an eyebrow in response as Attorney Ellis continued with his questions to Beth.

"Is it true that you were fired from your last job as a reporter with WGGA in Atlanta?" He asked as he returned to the table and sifted through a stack of documents he had labeled "employment".

As Beth provided a reluctant, "Yes," he pulled out a couple of pages from the stack.

"Miss Reed, isn't it true that you were fired because on June 4, 1996, you failed your second random drug test?"

"I don't recall that that's why..."

"May I approach the witness?" Attorney Ellis asked the judge.

The judge nodded in the affirmative and Attorney Ellis approached Beth. "Miss Reed, if you will look at the pages labeled Plaintiff's Exhibit W-1."

Joyce leaned to me. "Her attorney really is incompetent. He should at least try to object."

I glanced in the direction of our opposing counsel and he did not budge.

Attorney Ellis handed Beth a page from the stack of employment records and she looked at it. "Would you please read the highlighted portion and let me know if that helps your recollection?"

Beth pushed the page back toward him refusing to look at the page, but he didn't pick it up.

"Miss Reed, do you see the date highlighted at the top of that page?"

"Yes."

"Would you mind reading the date at the top of the page?"

"March 15, 1995"

"And farther down, what does the highlighted portion say?"

"Drug screen failure." As she read the line, he walked over and stood at the corner of the jury box.

"I'm sorry. I could not hear you. Would you mind reading that once more and a little louder?"

"Drug screen failure!" Beth said a little louder and with just a little bite in her voice. She was starting to have a hard time playing nice.

"Drug screen failure," he repeated as he looked at the jurors and shook his head. "Miss Reed, were you pregnant on March 15, 1995?"

"No."

"But you just said you took drugs because he dumped you for a younger woman when you were pregnant, correct?"

"That's not..."

He shut her down again, "Yes or no, Miss Reed."

I was giddy inside. The look on Joyce's face was as if she was giddy inside too. Beth was not giddy. She tried to keep her composure, but she was slipping.

"Miss Reed, your mother said that you and Mr. Hewitt were engaged and that he gave you a ring is that correct?"

"Yes."

"And you showed your mother the ring you received from Mr. Hewitt?"

"Yes."

Attorney Ellis left the spot where he had been standing near the jurors and made his way back over to the table where he thumbed through to the police report from the time Beth broke into my house right before Christmas of last year.

"Was the ring that he gave you a part of a set that belonged to his mother?"

"Yes."

Again he asked permission to approach and permission was granted. "Miss Reed, would you mind reading the highlighted portion of this document? In fact, let me just tell you that this is a police report from when Gabe's house was broken into last December."

Beth looked at the report and then answered, "Do you want me to read the whole paragraph?

"Yes, the whole paragraph. Aloud."

"I got it," the real Beth was starting to shine through as she spoke.

Beth looked over the page, reading silently before she read it out loud. "Items missing from residence: One vintage diamond wedding set, three carat total weight with estimated value of $18,000."

"Do you maintain that Mr. Hewitt gave the set to you, because as you just read, he reported them to the police as having been stolen in a break in? And that wouldn't happen to be the wedding set you are wearing right now, would it?"

Beth quickly folded her right hand over her left. "He gave them to me!"

"And you just broke in his house to take back what was already yours? Is that what you are trying to tell us?"

"Well, yes."

"So you admit you broke into his house?"

"What? No! No!" Attorney Ellis turned his back on her and walked back to the corner spot by the jury box as she struggled to retrieve her admission. She was back-peddling something fierce.

"Miss Reed, which is it?" he turned back and asked. "Never mind. Miss Reed, what were the circumstances of the day you last saw your daughter?"

464

Her head spun at the change in the direction of the conversation and Beth struggled to switch gears. She thought for a moment before she answered. She was surely trying to figure out a way to sugar coat the fact that she totaled my car. "I was not myself."

"How so?" Back to our table he strutted.

"I didn't feel well." She would not even look at him when she replied.

"Would you tell us the outcome of your 'not feeling well' that day?" His tone was that of mocking her when he repeated her words, "not feeling well" as he sifted through the case file and pulled out the accident report from the day of the wreck.

"I had an accident."

"Could you describe the wreck?"

"I really can't recall the details."

Each time he approached a witness to provide them with a document, Attorney Ellis asked permission of the judge. This time was no different and, as usual, permission was granted. He provided a copy to Beth's attorney, who made a motion to try to keep the documents out, but was denied. Attorney Ellis then proceeded to the witness box with the accident report in hand. He presented it to Beth and, like all of the other documents, he had her read portions that he had highlighted in advance.

He instructed her to read the date of the report and she did. After that, he instructed her to read a portion on the following page.

"Right down there." It looked like he pointed about a third of the way down the page. "Where it says 'narrative'. Does that help your recollection?"

Beth rolled her eyes, but did not give a verbal response.

"Miss Reed, would you say that's a fair assessment of the wreck? That Baby Gabby was in your car when you entered the parking lot of my office and you slammed into the rear of Mr.

Hewitt's car with such force that it caused, what does it say there? Significant rear-end damage? Is that what it says?"

"That's what it says." I'm not sure if the jurors saw Beth's jaw clinching, but I did.

While she was answering, Attorney Ellis went back to what must have been his favorite spot near the far end of the jury box. "I'm sorry, I didn't quite hear that. Would you mind repeating it?"

"That's what it says!" She raised her voice significantly. True Beth was about to make an appearance.

"If I could direct you to the notes section, Miss Reed, doesn't it also state that Baby Gabby was not strapped into the car seat?"

Beth rolled her eyes and after some discussion, the judge instructed her to answer the question verbally and loud enough that the jury could hear her.

"Yes!"

"And, the next line says that vehicle one fled the scene. Miss Reed, would you mind telling us which car is vehicle one?"

Beth straightened up in her chair and gave him a real eat shit look. "A white BMW."

"Miss Reed, don't you own a white BMW?"

"You know I do."

"And you fled the scene of the accident that day leaving Baby Gabby with us and not knowing if she was injured?"

"OBJECTION! OBJECTION!" Her attorney was on his feet screaming.

Attorney Ellis whipped his head around. "Objection? It's about time, but for what? Oh, never mind I asked."

Before the judge could intervene, Attorney Ellis turned back to Beth. "Miss Reed, what color are your eyes?"

Beth was visibly taken aback by the change of topic and he repeated the question. She answered timely when he asked the second time. "Green."

"And Mr. Hewitt's, what color are his eyes?" He walked over and stood next to me drawing the jury's attention to me.

I did not want this to come out. I told him specifically that I didn't want it to come out. I didn't want the revelation of Gabby's true paternity to be on the court record. I was getting nervous. We had talked about this and he assured me that he understood.

"Blue." The most curious look was on Beth's face when she said the word.

Attorney Ellis did not look at Beth when he asked her what color Gabby's eyes were. He looked at juror number three, the biology teacher from Green County High.

"Brown," Beth replied. Beth was completely oblivious to where this line of questioning was going and so was her attorney as he did not object once.

I could see the light go off in juror number three's head. Our eyes met and I knew she knew and she knew I knew. I gave a slight nod of my head in acknowledgement. I am sure her head was turning the same way Gayle's and Jay's were the day they found out. The question they had was the same question she had. "What man would fight for a child that wasn't his?" Hopefully, this juror would come to the same conclusion that they had come to, a good man. Hopefully, she could convince the rest of the jurors of that too.

"Miss Reed, you said you waited for Mr. Hewitt while he was overseas in the Navy?" Attorney Ellis did not miss a beat with his series of questions.

"Yes." For someone who started off their testimony thinking they were going to out-smart everyone, she sure was clueless as to what was going on.

"So you were faithful to him?"

"Yes."

"And this last year, were you faithful to him?"

"Yes."

"And you have green eyes, he has blue and your daughter has brown?"

Beth was growing impatient with his questions and her answers were starting to snap, "Yes!"

Attorney Ellis looked to the biology teacher and she was leaning in attentively.

"Miss Reed, do you love your daughter?" He changed the subject again leaving Beth's head turning.

"Yes, yes, of course!"

"And you want the best for her?"

Beth looked to her mother before answering. "Of course."

"Would you consider a life with someone who abuses drugs and has multiple arrests better than someone who has served our country, has no arrests and no history of recreational drug use?"

"Objection!" Attorney Ayers was starting to earn his money.

The objection was sustained.

"Miss Reed, you want this jury to believe you love your daughter and would never abandon her?"

"Yes."

"You would never abandon her again, you mean?"

"What? I never..." She raised her voice.

"Are you now saying you never abandoned your daughter?"

"I left her with her father and he has twisted this!" She was on the verge of snapping.

"Right, but did you call even once to check on her? Did you return any of his calls?"

Beth glanced to her mother, but her mother was distracted whispering with her brother.

Attorney Ellis did not allow the silence to continue as Beth cultivated an answer. He picked up speed with his questioning. "Miss Reed, your daughter was almost six weeks old before you showed up again. Is that your idea of responsible parenting?"

"I told you I left her with her father!"

"And to you it is perfectly acceptable and normal for a mother not to call and check on their infant child as long as they are with their father? That's not abandonment?" His sentences were long, but they were quick.

"No, he's her father!"

"But, if he wasn't her father, would that fit your definition of abandonment?"

The speed of his questions paid off and she answered as he had intended her. "Right."

"No further questions."

Attorney Ellis started back toward his seat next to me and Beth got up from the chair in the witness box. He looked up at me and it was as if he remembered something he had forgotten to ask her. He whipped back around. "Sorry, one more thing, Miss Reed. May I have my client's mother's wedding set back?"

Attorney Ellis held out his hand and Beth looked stunned. The words, "How dare you?" were written all over her face. Right there in front of everyone she tugged at her finger until she snatched off the rings. She was not classy enough to just hand them to him as she walked passed. She threw them at me in style of a grand gesture.

Attorney Ellis returned to the seat next to me with a giant smile on his face. Joyce quickly gathered up the pieces to Mother's

469

wedding set. Beth glared at the three of us as she crossed the distance between the witness stand and her seat.

Once back in her chair, Joyce reached behind me and patted Attorney Ellis on the back. "Good job, Jack."

"I agree. She's been had and she doesn't even know how bad," I praised him.

The judge released everyone for lunch and we were to return at 1:30. Yesterday, we ended up at the same restaurant as the jury and the Reeds, so today we walked back to Attorney Ellis' office where a catered lunch was waiting on us. His office wasn't far from the courthouse and Cara, Jay, Daniel and Mrs. Allen joined us. It was a working lunch where we were all thoroughly prepped for testifying that afternoon.

My entourage and I were on our way back through the courthouse to the courtroom when I was approached by Beth as we attempted to pass by the restroom doors in the hallway. There was no one else with her. She really had some nerve.

She turned up a nostril as she spoke to me, "If you think you're going to just take my child, you are wrong! If you think you're going to be free of me, you're wrong about that too!"

I should have kept walking because what I didn't notice was the jurors filing in behind us. Instead of ignoring her, I responded. The thought of never being free of her struck a nerve. By the time I was done with her, everyone in the place knew that I despised her.

"If you ever think of speaking to me in the future, don't. If you see me coming, go the other direction. Do not approach me. Do not look at me. Do not talk to me. I want nothing to do with you. I despise you on every level, with every fiber of my being. Any redeeming quality that I thought you had, you destroyed the day you wrecked the car with Gabby in it. You lie, you cheat and you scheme and if I never see you again, it would be too soon. And, if by some misfortune, you're granted custody of Gabby and anything ever happens to her, if one hair on her head is harmed, I will spend every waking moment of the rest of my life making you suffer. If you don't believe me, just try me."

470

As if she did not hear me at all, Beth reached for me. She went to touch my face and was opening her mouth to speak. That's when I took her by her wrists and nearly lost it. "Are you out of your fucking mind?" I clinched my teeth and hissed at her. I slung her hands away from me and she was speechless. "Don't you ever touch me again!"

I could hear her as Jay and Daniel pulled me away. "But Gabe..." She was intent on following us, but Jay warned her off and the three of us continued to the courtroom.

Mrs. Joyce was in the restroom and Attorney Ellis had gone ahead of us to the courtroom, so both of them missed the exchange in the hallway. The rest of the Reed family was seated in the courtroom with some of Mrs. Reed's friends who had come down for moral support when we walked in the room. They had missed everything, but unfortunately, Beth's attorney had not missed a thing. As soon as the judge took the bench and before he called in the jury, Mr. Ayers demanded a mistrial on the basis that the jury had witnessed everything in the hallway and had been tainted.

"Tainted how?" the judge looked down from the bench and asked him. "Seems to me that Mr. Hewitt is the one that might have reason to be worried now."

The judge did not spell it out, but my attorney gave me an earful about how I had just provided them with the possibility for an assault charge against me for laying hands on her. "You should have kept walking. You may have undone our entire case."

I dropped my head to my hands, "I'm so sorry. I don't know what got into me."

"Let's just see about doing damage control." He shook his head. I think he was disappointed in me.

The first witness called for my case was Mrs. Allen. She testified that I had hired her to watch Gabby while I was at work.

"What do you think of Mr. Hewitt as a father?" Attorney Ellis asked her.

Mrs. Allen began by wiping her brow and explaining how she first came to know me. "My grandson worked for Mr. Hewitt in the restaurant at Port Honor as a dishwasher. He hired Rudy knowing that he really didn't have reliable transportation of his own. They struck a deal that if Rudy could always find his own way to work, then Mr. Hewitt would see to it that he got home safely even if he had to drive him himself. From day one, Mr. Hewitt encouraged Rudy to save his money and get his own car. Rudy said he told him, 'A man should never have to rely on anyone but himself.'"

"In those months, Mr. Hewitt held true to his word. He made sure Rudy had a ride home and there were several times that Mr. Hewitt brought him home himself. After about six months, Mr. Hewitt called Rudy into his office and he wanted to discuss how much Rudy had been able to save since he started working there. I hate to tell you all this, but my poor boy has had to help out with some of the family bills in caring for his little brothers. No teenager should have such responsibilities. Rudy had only managed to save $100. Mr. Hewitt went on to explain to Rudy that one of the club members was selling a car. It was a 1984 Cutlass Supreme. They wanted $600 for the car. He took Rudy to look at the car. Mr. Hewitt looked over the engine and everything. He had Rudy put $100 down on the car and he financed it for him. He even allowed him to pick up some extra work around the club to pay the car off faster. He also taught the boy to drive."

"So, as for what I think of him as a father? Well, he's the best father my grandson has ever had."

"Thank you, Mrs. Allen, but have you had any specific occasions to witness Mr. Hewitt as a father to baby Gabby?"

"He calls her 'Little One' and I've never seen a man more in love with a child. She had colic for a while and she was inconsolable. There were times when the poor thing would scream for hours, but never once did he even appear the slightest bit frustrated with her. If he didn't love every second with that child, I would never know it. There was one time in particular that I could not get her calmed down and he came home and sat with her on the dryer with it running just to sooth her. There's not a soul on Earth that could love that baby more."

"Mrs. Allen, have you ever met Miss Reed before today?"

Mrs. Allen had been prepped not to roll her eyes at the mention of Beth's name, but she could not seem to help herself before she was on the witness stand or now that she was there. Her whole demeanor changed as she started to relay the story of meeting Beth.

Mrs. Allen described the day that Beth was last arrested at the house on Snug Harbor. That was the last line of questioning that Attorney Ellis had for Mrs. Allen and the line of questions with which Attorney Ayers began. He didn't rattle her. She was very detailed in her answers. Unlike his witnesses, Mrs. Allen was great on direct and did not fall apart on cross.

Our next witness was Daniel and he was asked to give his version of the events of the day that Beth got arrested at the house at Snug Harbor for the second time. His story matched Mrs. Allen's to the letter.

"I didn't see Beth, Miss Reed, enter the house. I was in the garage when she first came in and what I didn't see, I heard."

"So you heard..." Before Attorney Ellis could finish the question, Daniel finished it.

"We were packing up the house and I had gone to the garage to load some boxes in Gabe's car when I heard her calling for him, demanding to know what the meaning of, well, the meaning of him moving. I heard them arguing. I heard her threaten Gabe. I heard her being her usual self." One could tell by Daniel's tone that the phrase about "being her usual self" was not a compliment.

"And this sort of behavior was not necessarily unusual?"

"She's demanding to say the least."

"Would you say that Miss Reed was typically rude to Mr. Hewitt?"

"Rude? That's an understatement. She typically treated him like dirt beneath her feet."

473

"Did Mr. Hewitt refuse to allow Miss Reed to see the baby?"

"None of us, including Gabe, knew where Beth was since she had given birth to Gabby. One would have thought she would have asked to see Gabby straightaway, but she didn't."

"Are you saying that a mother that had not seen her child since she was five days old did not ask to see her..."

"No, her only concern seemed to be that she had lost control of Gabe. In fact, she did not ask about Gabby until after Gabe pointed out to her that she hadn't asked. I believe his exact words were, 'How dare you show your face here and not ask about Gabby.'"

"Then what happened?"

"She asked about Gabby and he reiterated his demand for her to leave the house."

"And did she leave?"

"No."

All the while Attorney Ellis went back and forth with Daniel, he stood at his favorite spot next to the jurors in the corner of the jury box and at the back end of the table where Beth and her attorneys were seated. He did not block the jurors' view of Beth. In fact, as much as the jurors were watching the to and fro between the two of them, they were also taking glances at Beth. I took a few looks at her as well. As usual, she had a far away, unaffected look about her, as if they were talking about someone else entirely.

Attorney Ellis continued with his questions, "And where were you during all of this arguing between Mr. Hewitt and Miss Reed? Surely you did not hear all of this from the garage?"

"No, when I first heard their elevated voices through the garage door from the kitchen, I came inside."

"So they were in the?" The fluctuation in his voice indicated the question without him finishing the sentence.

"The living room."

"And you heard them all the way out in the garage?"

"Yes, sir. I had left the door open from the kitchen because I was going right back in and when I heard her first scream at Gabe, I went back inside."

"But you didn't go all the way into the living room."

"I didn't really know what to do. I didn't want to get in their business, but..."

"Did you fear that Miss Reed might hurt Mr. Hewitt?"

"She did end up hurting him."

"She did?"

"Yes. She put a gash in his shoulder with a golf club that required him to get stitches at the ER that night."

"So you saw her physically attack him?"

"I did."

"And did you intervene?"

"I was about to. I mean, she was going crazy swinging the golf club at him and everywhere, so I was afraid and then, well, you know what Mrs. Allen did. She just told you before about drawing her gun. Thank goodness she was there, Mrs. Allen that is." Daniel glanced to Mrs. Allen as he spoke of her and the jurors looked with him.

The remainder of Daniel's testimony revolved around what sort of father he thought I was. He was full of compliments as to my parenting skills and my attentiveness to Gabby.

Attorney Ayers was quick to pounce as soon as Ellis said he had no further questions for Daniel. His first question, "Is it true you are a homosexual man?"

475

The whole courtroom gasped and Attorney Ellis was on his feet, "OBJECTION!"

"Sustained!" the judge ruled.

"I withdraw the question." Attorney Ayers cut his eyes to the jury. Apparently he knew a thing or two about not being able to un-ring a bell too, but he wasn't done ringing it. His next question was equally below the belt, the Bible belt. "Have you and Mr. Hewitt ever been lovers?"

"OBJECTION!" shouted Ellis.

"Sustained!" the judge was commanding, but didn't raise his voice.

"Withdrawn." Again, he just cut his eyes at the jury and they were looking uncomfortable just as he had intended.

Attorney Ayers had hit a nerve with Daniel and gay or not, Daniel came out swinging. "Why are you so concerned with my sexuality? Are you looking for a date? Thank you, but I am taken."

Two of the jurors on the front row snickered, but the rest shook their heads. The damage was done. Two steps forward one step back, I hoped it was only one step back and all of the good he had done for the case had not been undone.

Attorney Ellis eased over against me. "We can't put Jay on the stand now," he whispered.

"I know," I conceded.

"I have Joan listed on the witness list. I think we should call her..."

"And what? You have planted the seed that Gabby's not mine and what if they don't see the point in giving a child to someone who's not her biological father when her mother is somewhat trying to fight for her?"

"I don't think it will be like that."

"No!"

"Have it your way, stubborn..."

"Stubborn ass, I know."

As Attorney Ellis and I finished our whispering, Beth's attorney was finishing up with Daniel. Daniel was beginning to stand up when Attorney Ellis asked to redirect and was granted permission.

"If you are gay and I'm not asking or insinuating anything, would that prevent you from knowing a good father when you saw one?"

"I wouldn't think so," Daniel replied.

"And likewise, do you think such would prevent one from recognizing what a not so great mother looked like?"

"No."

"And, would such a condition prevent one from being able to tell the truth?"

"In my opinion, absolutely not."

"So, even if you were gay, you would still know what you saw that day in Mr. Hewitt's house?"

"Right."

Attorney Ellis then released Daniel after Beth's attorney said that he had no further questions.

I tried to get a reading on the jurors, but they were stone cold poker faces. Some watched Daniel as he left the witness stand. Some watched Beth, but only one made contact with me. The one that I seem to have connected with was the high school biology teacher. I wasn't sure that any others might rule in my favor, but I was pretty sure about her. I was pretty sure she knew what was what and despite that, I didn't want that on any court transcript. I was fine if any of the jurors figured it out on their own and still awarded Gabby to me.

The judge gave us a break after Daniel was released from the stand. As soon as the jurors began to make their way to the jury room, Mrs. Reed and all her girlfriends huddled around Beth, congratulating her on the small victory of Daniel having been discredited. It almost made my stomach churn. I didn't want to hang around for the love fest, so I took that opportunity to call Amelia since I had not had a chance to call her while we were at lunch. As I suspected, she was beside herself with worry. Her mind was running away with her as to why I had not called already.

I gave Amelia every detail I could think of in the amount of time I had. I told her about Beth's testimony, Mrs. Allen's and Daniel's. She had a million questions and she was not happy with very many of the answers. In fact, to say she was unhappy was an understatement. She was furious.

"So they made a big deal about Daniel's sexuality to discredit him and now you can't use Jay." I could hear her shaking her head in disgust through the phone. I could also hear Gabby fuss a little in the background. "Shhh. Shhh, baby. Mommy and Daddy are talking."

"Amelia, you need to keep calm for her sake and yours, but you are right about Jay. We might get away with me having one gay friend, but two might be pushing it."

"That's just a low blow, you know. She can't win the right way. Honestly, this is just as bad as cheating, but I suppose that's all she knows!" Amelia let out a huff and again I could feel her fury.

"I know, but what can we do?" I sighed. I felt like my hands were tied, but I tried to assure her as much as I could. I knew that beyond the pure hatred she had for the situation and for Beth, Amelia was scared. I was scared too.

"Call Joan! You can't keep a secret like this anyway, so shine the light on it from the get go. I know you are worried about this all being on the court record and Gabby being faced with it, but you need to get past that. You are afraid of it being in black and white that her mother was unfit and neither of her parents really wanted her. Well, Gabriel, there are worse things in life than being raised by people other than your biological parents. We will not let this define

478

her, so you need to rip off the Band-aide that's holding Beth's parental rights in place. Call Joan as a witness!"

"Stella's up next. I'll think about calling Joan." I leaned my head against the wall at the far end of the hallway in the courthouse where I had found a quiet spot to make the call. No one was around to hear me, but for a few minutes, there was nothing to hear. What else could I say to her right then to make her feel better about any of this? We just sat there on the line with one another.

I was just about to tell her that I loved her when Amelia finally broke the silence and asked "Is Jay still there?"

I was surprised by her question. I'm sure I sounded a little deflated. "He just left."

"Okay." I could hear a definite shift in her mood. "I know you've got to get back in there, so I'll just get the rest of the details from Jay and that should tide me over until you get home tonight."

"Alright. I hope we get out of here by 5:00 p.m., if so, I should see you and Little One around 6:00."

CHAPTER 25

Court was back in session at 2:30 p.m. and the next witness was Stella. She said as many great things about me as she could, but she was obviously nervous. Despite her nervousness, she held her own when being cross examined by Beth's attorney. The best thing she said about me was, "All fathers should dote on their children the way he dotes on Gabby. I can guarantee that that child will always know and feel love as long as she is with Gabe."

At 3:00 p.m., I was sworn in on the witness stand. I was our last witness and I was as nervous as any of those that had gone before me, but I took comfort in the fact that there was a light at the end of the tunnel.

Attorney Ellis and I had a lot of ground to cover and we started with my history with Beth. I answered questions regarding how we met and continued on to what our relationship was like over the years.

"Miss Reed said the two of you have been together for eight years, is that true?" Attorney Ellis stood at the podium with his pile of notes detailing question after question. This was just among the many we had gone over in his office on Friday.

"No. Her math is wrong as well as her perception. I met her when I was nineteen so that means we have known one another for ten years. We were only 'together' for about four years."

"And when did your relationship change?"

"When I was sent overseas to serve my time in the Navy right after I graduated college."

"How did you leave things with Miss Reed when you left?"

"We had a discussion that our relationship had run its course. We agreed that we had done the long distance thing long enough and that we both wanted more out of life than to be tied to someone who was rarely around. In all honesty, we just weren't a good match and I thought we both knew that at the time."

"So you thought it was a mutual decision to break up?"

"I know it was a mutual decision."

"Tell me about the pact." Attorney Ellis carried his legal pad with him and moved to that special spot he had at the corner of the jury box.

As he instructed me, I glanced at the jurors every now and then and I tried to make eye contact. He had told me that I needed them to like me and I was to use what God gave me, bat my eyes a little at the ladies. I wasn't comfortable with that. Selling myself on my looks had never been my style. I did make eye contact with them, but nothing more than a couple of seconds.

"It was just something silly. We were just being drunk college kids one night and Beth made me agree that if we weren't married by the time we were thirty then we would get married. I didn't think she was serious."

"What do you think now?"

"I think it's still a silly pact."

"But do you think Miss Reed thought it was a silly pact? More to the point, do you think Miss Reed loved you and that you led her on?"

"God, no." I ran my fingers through my hair, that thing I did when I was nervous, and I glanced to Beth as I answered. "She might have thought she loved me at one point, but it's not love. It's more like a need to possess something that she has for me."

The questions continued and we covered how Beth came to live with me prior to Gabby's birth. "She showed up four weeks prior to her actual delivery date, suitcase in hand and told me we were on baby watch."

"Where had she been before coming to your house?"

"At her parents' house in Atlanta."

"So you weren't living together all along?"

"No. She lived in Atlanta sometimes and sometimes at her parents' lake house. She kind of went wherever her parents were. Anyway, she said her parents were going on a Mediterranean cruise and she could not stay home alone. What was I to do? I let her in. I thought it was only for a week, but then she didn't leave."

"And then what?"

"I was working at the club and when I came home one night, she was gone."

"Did you think anything of that? Did you wonder where she went?"

"No. She left a note saying she was going to her parents, so I figured she went home. Then, three days later, her mother called and said she had had the baby."

Attorney Ellis had me briefly describe the circumstances of our relationship after I returned from the Navy.

"We remained friends while I was in the Navy. Beth knew I had no family and she would invite me to her family's home when I had leave."

"Were there ever any instances when you were more than friends?"

"There were a couple of instances when we went back to familiar ways, but with no expectations." I tried to gently say that we had sex on a few occasions, but nothing regular or with strings.

"Were you and Miss Reed an item when she got pregnant?"

"No. We were friends."

We moved on from that line of questioning as I had explained to him that I was not sure if I had had intercourse with her in the time period when she became pregnant with Gabby. I told him about the night we got drunk at the club and I woke up at her parents' lake house not knowing how I got there.

"Tell me about the day you took Gabby home from the hospital. How did you come to have charge of her care?"

"I brought the car around and Mrs. Reed put Gabby in the car seat in my car. I thought she was going home with Beth and Mrs. Reed. I was even a little scared that Beth and Gabby were going to come home with me, but instead Mrs. Reed said that Beth needed to recuperate."

"Did you know about Miss Reed's drug use at that point?"

I first looked at Beth and then to the jurors when I answered. "I knew she had done drugs in the past, but I had no idea that she was doing anything while she was pregnant."

During all of my testimony, Beth stared blankly at her hands as if she was admiring her nails and sometimes she just stared off at the floor between her table and the witness stand. At no point did she look like she was paying attention to what I was saying, let alone as if she was affected by my words.

Attorney Ellis went through the whole asking permission to approach the witness stand procedure and then presented me with portions of both Beth and Gabby's medical records from the birth. He had me read portions indicating the types of drugs in Beth's system while she was pregnant. He also introduced the pamphlets that Gabby's pediatrician gave us about babies born to mothers on drugs.

"Did you ever suspect or notice any symptoms of Gabby having issues as a result of Beth's intrauterine drug use?"

I looked at Beth searching for a reaction as I spoke. "We were worried that she was exhibiting symptoms. It scared the life out of me because we went from having a sweet baby to one that we could not console or satisfy. When I tell you she cried, I mean she cried and cried and cried. There were days that were filled with her screams. It was as if something was terrorizing her. As it turned out, she just had the colic and she's fine now. We were very lucky, but Gabby was the real lucky one. We were told that she may not show any symptoms and so far so good, no more colic."

Attorney Ellis asked me about what Gabby's pediatrician told us about the long term prognosis for Gabby and any long term effects of Beth's drug use, but Attorney Ayers objected. The judge ruled in his favor and agreed that I could not tell what the pediatrician said as it was hearsay. Attorney Ellis was not deterred. He whipped out Gabby's medical records, introduced them and proceeded to ask me to read them and tell what the doctor said about the long term effects.

"It says we may not notice any effects until her school age years." I looked up to the jurors when I finished and several were shaking their heads.

"And you interpret that to mean it may affect her learning abilities?" He looked to jurors as well.

"Yes, that's what I understand it to say."

The questions kept coming and it was approaching 4:00 when he asked me about the day Beth attacked me in my house. I told the same story that Mrs. Allen and Daniel had told, except it was more from a first person, receiving end, point of view. Attorney Ellis introduced my medical records as an exhibit and we discussed how many stitches I took to my shoulder at the ER. We also talked about what led to the fight and how wild Beth went.

"Is this a photo of how your shoulder looked after the stitches on the day of the assault?" He handed me the photo.

"Yes, it is." He took it back from me and then gave it to Beth's attorney and then to the jury.

"Do you think she was on something that day?" He asked as the jurors passed the picture among themselves.

"I have no idea, but I wouldn't doubt it. I'd never seen her lose her mind like that before. I'm not sure what would have happened to me if Mrs. Allen had not been there to subdue Beth."

Attorney Ellis then presented me with the police report from that day. "Did you file this report on Miss Reid?" As he asked his question, he turned his back on me and walked over and stood in front of the jurors.

484

"Yes." I answered. The way he positioned himself was in such a manner that when I answered I was looking at both Attorney Ellis and the jury.

"And it says here she was charged with assault?"

"Yes."

"Did you witness her arrest?"

"Yes."

"This was not her first arrest, correct?"

"Correct. She was arrested for breaking into my house in the middle of the night last year. No, let me correct that. She broke into my house, but she was ultimately arrested for DUI."

"Do you know if either of these cases have gone to trial yet?"

"No, I don't know."

Attorney Ellis returned to our table and Mrs. Joyce handed him another set of documents. He proceeded to question me as to the documents, indictments against Beth for the DUI and for the assault. Once those were entered, he tendered them to the jury and they passed them around as well.

The next series of questions had me reiterate what Beth had said about the break-in at my house when my mother's rings were stolen. "You filed a police report last December concerning a theft at your house, is that correct?"

"Yes."

"And you reported items stolen." He handed me a copy of the police report from the break-in. "And the items you claim were stolen, could you read that off to the jury, the items that were stolen?"

I took the report and flipped to the second page. "Yes. It says, a woman's wedding set, gold bands with three carat total weight in diamonds. There are a couple of other items that are listed, but that's the main thing."

"But Miss Reed said you gave the set to her. Did you forget that you gave it to her?"

"No. I never gave that set to anyone."

"And were you ever engaged to Miss Reed?"

"No. We were never engaged."

"Not even after you found out she was pregnant?"

"No."

"Why is that?"

I am sure I looked puzzled by his question. That was not a part of the prep and I was a bit thrown by it. The first thing that entered my head as an answer was what Amelia had said that night at the bar in Milledgeville. The night that I knew I had to have her. Before I really realized what I was saying, I repeated almost verbatim the answer she gave that night about her expectations if she found herself pregnant and unwed.

"I was not in love with Miss Reed and I don't believe people should get married just for the sake of a child. Not that I see Gabby as a problem, but an unexpected pregnancy followed by an unwanted marriage. Wouldn't that be like compounding one problem with another?"

Attorney Ellis moved so that he could make eye contact with the juror that was the biology teacher. "Gabe, what color are your eyes?"

"Blue."

"And Miss Reed's?"

"Green."

"And Gabby's?"

"Her eyes are brown."

486

"Gabe, do you love Gabby?" When he started that question I was afraid he was going to say "love her like your own" and let the cat fully out of the bag.

"More than anything," I replied as I looked dead on at Mrs. Reed in the audience before turning my gaze to the jurors. I had not looked at Beth's mother until that point and I don't know what made me look at her then. Perhaps I wanted her to know I loved Gabby as much as she did. I don't know. Regardless of what I tried to communicate, she looked away to her blonde friend that was seated next to her. She whispered to the woman as they each looked at me and rolled their eyes.

"And you would do absolutely anything for Gabby?"

"Yes, anything."

"No further questions." Attorney Ellis was finally finished with me.

Beth's attorney was quick to approach the podium and start with his questions. "What is the nature of your friendship with Mr. Daniel Redmond?"

"We are friends." I responded with skepticism.

"Friends, okay. You mentioned that you and Miss Reed were just 'friends' for the last few years. Is that correct?"

"Correct."

"And you and Miss Reed continued to be intimate even after you were just 'friends'?" He emphasized the word "friends".

"I know where you are going with this and if you are trying to insinuate that Daniel and I sleep together, you are way off base!" He was getting under my skin and I tried to keep my emotions in check, but I was having difficulty with that.

"So you don't sleep with all of your friends?"

"Of course I don't sleep with all of my friends."

"Mr. Hewitt, is it true that you are a newlywed?"

"Yes."

"So while my client had just given birth to your child and, for all you knew, was recuperating, you married someone else?"

"I did not get married until after Beth came back, assaulted me and well after I had filed the petition seeking full custody of Gabby."

"Mr. Hewitt, you want these good ladies and this good gentleman of the jury to believe that a man who surrounds himself with homosexual men, who would not marry the mother of his child, but marry another young girl, and sue said mother for sole custody of the newborn is more fit to raise the child than the child's own mother? Mr. Hewitt, would you consider those to be good moral characteristics to teach a child?"

"First of all, what I aim to teach my child is that people should be judged on their deeds and actions and how they treat others, not by their sexuality. Secondly, I had no idea where Beth was. She and her mother left Gabby with me and then did not have the decency to call and check on the poor child. I left messages for them. I could have used some help, but they did not even bother to return my calls. So as far as I am concerned, all of this caring they want these fine ladies and gentleman to think they have for Gabby, it is a load of crap. They no more care for Gabby than they care for any of the pets Beth has been given and abused and even killed over the years."

Attorney Ayers opened his mouth to start his next question and I cut him off.

"One more thing, yeah, I want them to know that I am more fit than a woman who has been arrested several times, who rear-ended my car to the point that it was totaled while Gabby was inside, and..."

This time, he cut me off. "Mr. Hewitt, if you would limit your answers to 'yes' or 'no'. That would be great."

I looked at the jurors as I rolled my eyes and shook my head in dismay.

"Mr. Hewitt, isn't it true that Miss Reed only attacked you after you denied her access to her baby?"

"No."

"You deny that you refused to allow her access to Gabby?"

"No."

"But you just said..."

"She only demanded to see Gabby after I pointed out that she hadn't asked to see her. She was already acting hostile and there was no way someone in her frame of mind needed to be around a baby at that point."

"And you are an expert on babies?"

"I am an expert on *that* baby." The jurors laughed at my response.

Attorney Ayers continued with another twenty minutes worth of insignificant questions. Until I guess he got tired of not getting anywhere with me. "One more question," he said. "Why is your attorney so concerned with everyone's eye color?"

"Why don't you ask your client?" I looked at Beth and she rolled her eyes and looked away.

"I am asking you."

I held my ground. "And I am telling you to ask your client."

"Mr. Hewitt, I can have the judge compel you to answer."

I thought about what Amelia said. There's no need trying to keep a secret like this. It's bound to come out. Her parting words to me during our last call was for me to call Joan and get it over with.

The judge looked down from the bench and raised an eyebrow at me. He was seconds away from telling me to answer the question when I decided to take the bull by the horns and let the chips fall where they may. I had been so scared of what would be on

489

the record that I had not thought about what I could put on the record until that moment.

"The reason he is interested in our eye color is that basic ninth grade biology teaches us that the likelihood of a mother with green eyes such as Beth and a father with blue eyes such as mine are highly unlikely to have a child such as Gabby with brown eyes. There's no doubt that Beth is Gabby's mother, but just based on that simple high school level DNA test, I am not Gabby's biological father."

I looked to Attorney Ellis and he gave me a nod to keep going. I remembered what he said about un-ringing a bell and I added, Gabby's biological father is Richard Thompson, the married manager of Port Honor."

"LIAR!" Beth jumped to her feet and screamed while her attorney's mouth dropped open. He had not seen that one coming. Beth's mother's stuffy tennis friends had not seen it coming either. Beth immediately turned to her mother and threw on the tears, "He's lying, Mommy! He is the father. There's no one else."

Mrs. Reed gave an understanding nod of her head and a pursed smile. Mrs. Reed's friends took her hands to console her, but Beth's father looked away and her brother just shook his head as if he knew that every bit of what I was saying was true.

"Mr. Ayers, you will kindly control your client. Another outburst and she will be removed!" The judge banged the gavel a few times as he gave his warning.

Mr. Ayers took a brief moment to try to settle Beth, but he wasn't having much luck. She did not scream again, but there was some definite pounding on the table in front of her and hushed threats exchanged between them.

Beyond Beth, I could see the puzzled look on her mother's face. Clearly this was the first she was hearing of any of this. I also looked to the jurors. The biology teacher was telling one of the others, "I knew it!" I could hear her as well as I could hear my own thoughts. Another juror was covering her mouth as if this was as shocking to her as it had been to Mrs. Reed's friends.

Mr. Ayers turned his attention back to me and the judge and Beth turned her attention to her mother. I am sure she was trying to do damage control; trying to convince her mother that I was not telling the truth.

"I move for a directed verdict in this case in favor of my client since Mr. Hewitt has no grounds for suit against my client considering he has admitted that he is not the child's father." Attorney Ayers was clearing his files from the podium as he spoke. He clearly thought the case was over, but he was wrong.

Attorney Ellis was on his feet in a flash. "Your honor, may I approach?"

The judge agreed and the two attorneys approached the judge's bench. "Your honor, he has admitted that he is not her biological father, but he is the only father the child has known. He is the person who was given the child by her mother and her father. It would be detrimental to the well-being of the child to take her from the only family she has ever known and place her in the home of virtual strangers. Furthermore, the biological father has signed his rights away to Mr. Hewitt."

I just sat there and listened as Mr. Ayers tried to argue, "Surely there is no case history allowing a child to be given to a non-relative."

"Actually there it is, and it is called an adoption," added my attorney as he laid the signed waiver of parental rights on the desk in front of the judge. "We are also prepared to call a witness to verify the authenticity of this document and the wishes of the father."

"Do you plan to call the father?" the judge asked.

"No, I plan to call his wife," Attorney Ellis explained and again Attorney Ayers' face was priceless. He really did not know what else to expect from this case.

This time, the unrest came from the audience and it was Mr. Reed that was on his feet. "Ayers, are you going to stand for this?! For the love of God, do something man! Shut this down!"

Several beats of the gavel rang out through the courtroom as Mr. Reed made his demands and the judge commanded order. When Mr. Reed was finally finished, the judge ordered him removed from the courtroom and both of the Reed women were in tears. Mrs. Reed was visibly embarrassed and Beth; she was crying, but I'm not sure why. Was she still acting or was she afraid that she might actually be breaking her mother's heart? Who was I kidding? Of course it was an act. She had bragged to me so many times that her mother was a fool for her that I could not even keep count.

There was some argument between the attorneys as to whether Mrs. Thompson, Joan, could be called. In the end, the judge ruled in favor of my attorney. We were sent to recess so we could get Joan to the courthouse. Joan had not wanted to be involved, but said she would if we absolutely had to have her and as it turned out we did and she came straight on.

In the moments between my phone call to Joan and her arrival, Attorney Ellis and I hurriedly made a list of questions for him to ask her. He told me that his trials didn't usually go like this. Usually everyone had been deposed prior to trial and therefore he knew the answers to all of their questions in advance and the trial was really just a show for the jury. It was most certainly an opportunity to master his skills of flying by the seat of his pants.

When Joan arrived, Attorney Ayers tried again to persuade the judge to prevent her testimony, but his attempts were in vain. Joan was promptly sworn in and the foundation was laid.

"Yes, I am married to Richard Thompson, III, have been for twenty-nine years," Joan replied after stating her name.

"Mrs. Thompson, I am going to get straight to the point. How do you know the defendant, Miss Reed?" Attorney Ellis gestured toward Beth as he finished the question.

Joan looked to Beth as he had intended and she began to explain, "I have known Miss Reed since she was in her late teens when my husband took the job at Port Honor as the general manager. She was in her late teens at the time and she used to come to the club with her parents who are members."

"So you have known her for about ten years? Would that be about right?"

"Yes."

"And do you know her on a personal level or just through your husband's business at the club?"

"Beth first dated by oldest son while they were in college. They both attended Emory."

This was a revelation to me and I looked to Joan and then to Beth. Joan caught my look and expounded upon her statement, but Beth only rolled her eyes.

"They dated for about six months. I believe Miss Reed was a sophomore in college at the time. My son ended it when he found out that she had a steady boyfriend that was out of state."

"Mrs. Thompson, did your son ever acknowledge who the out of state boyfriend was?"

"It was Mr. Hewitt, but he did not tell us that until after my husband had hired Mr. Hewitt as the chef at the club."

"And, have you been acquainted with Miss Reed on a personal level since?" Attorney Ellis continued.

"Unfortunately, yes. She became involved with my husband."

While Joan was answering the question, Attorney Ellis moved to the corner of the jury box where he had spent so much time in the last two days. Once there he turned back, "Mrs. Thompson, I know this may be a difficult subject for you and I apologize, but I have to ask. Do you mean to tell us that your husband was having an affair with Miss Reed?"

"That is exactly what I am saying." Joan shifted in her seat and looked directly at the jurors who were looking back and forth from her to Beth. Beth turned her head away from the jurors when they looked to her.

493

"And you know this how?"

"All of my friends were talking..."

"Objection: Hearsay!" Attorney Ayers interjected.

"Sustained," the judge replied.

"Did you ever have reason, beyond what your friends were saying, to suspect they were..."

"Well, I caught them. Mr. Hewitt asked one of his staff members to run a tray of food up to the inn one afternoon, but since I was going that way on my way home, I volunteered to drop off the tray. I pulled into the parking lot up there and found Dick's car. I shrugged it off because he often had meetings up there with the manager of the inn. The inn manager was a friend of mine and she knew what Dick was up to and she sort of orchestrated me catching him. After I put the tray..."

The movement of Beth's chair distracted everyone in the room including Joan and she stopped her story. Beth was reaching back to assure her mother that all of this was a lie. Mrs. Reed did not look as receptive to her daughter's excuses and lies this time, but she reached out her hand to her daughter anyway.

Joan began again, "Deborah, the inn manager asked me to go with her downstairs after I put the tray in the refrigerator. She told me she wanted me to look at the carpet in the men's locker room with her to see if I thought it needed replacing or just cleaned. I believed she needed my help, so I followed her to the locker room. No one was supposed to be in there, but the carpet we were supposed to be looking at was strewn with my husband's clothes and those of a woman, and there was panting, heavy panting, coming from the sauna. That's when Deborah stepped aside and I looked into the sauna and found my husband in the throes of passion with Miss Reed."

"You are a lying bitch!" Beth exploded forward nearly all the way across the table in front of her.

"Mr. Ayers, control your client!" The judge raised his voice and boomed.

494

Beth was fuming. I could hear her huffing and puffing as Mr. Ayers whispered something to her. All eyes were on her, but Attorney Ellis continued as if nothing was going on and Joan somehow did the same. "Did they see you?"

"No. I ran out of there."

"Can you tell us exactly when this was?"

"Oh, I will never forget that day." She emphasized the word "never" as if it had five syllables. "It was October 2, 1995."

After Joan answered he seemed to change the subject with his next question. "And you're a mother, right?"

"Right. Three children."

"So three pregnancies and that would make you pretty knowledgeable when it comes to calculating due dates?"

"I suppose."

"Then let me ask you, does it stand to reason that if conception took place on say, October 2nd, would July 1st, be a viable due date?"

"Oh, yes. Most everyone thinks a pregnancy is nine months, but most pregnancies are closer to ten months."

"I know this is a sensitive question, but I have to ask. Do you think it is possible that your husband is the father of Gabriella Grace Hewitt, the child Miss Reed gave birth to on July 1, 1996?"

"It is more than possible. From what I have found out, the encounter I witnessed, it wasn't a one-time thing. I hate to say this, but the fact is my husband fathered a child with another woman. "

This revelation was more than Beth could take and again she flew from her seat. Her chair went flying and hit the rail behind her. It made a God-awful slamming noise and her mother who was sitting directly on the other side of that rail jumped up and back as if that chair had come straight through.

495

Beth grabbed every file folder that was on the table in front of her and in one swoop, she slung every last file and piece of paper across the courtroom in front of her. "I did not have an affair with your sorry ass husband!"

That's when Joan responded directly to Beth and her antics. Joan stood and announced to the entire room as she threw a page of her own at Beth, "Here's the DNA test that proves it. That's right, a sample of your child's hair matched against my husband and Mr. Hewitt." She cut her eyes at the jury, "Unlike Miss Reed, science doesn't lie."

"You are a bitter old crone!" Beth screamed at Joan.

Joan whipped out another piece of paper and flung that in Beth's direction as well, "And, this is The Assignment of Parental Rights that my husband signed over to Mr. Hewitt. Just so we are clear, he wants nothing more to do with you or your child, but he does want his child to have a better upbringing than the one you have clearly had."

Beth's mother gasped at the insult. Anyone could tell by the look on her face, she was embarrassed beyond belief and nearly sick over it. Tears were forming in her eyes, eyes that had now been opened to how the rest of the world viewed her daughter.

The judge was hammering that gavel of his on the desk like an entire construction crew. "Order! Order! Bailiff, please remove Miss Reed. I will no longer tolerate her disrespect to my courtroom. Mrs. Thompson, if you do not take your seat, I will hold you in contempt."

Beth was forcibly drug from the courtroom by two bailiffs, but she was kicking and screaming. She put up a good fight even without the golf club that she used on me. Finally, the larger of the two just bear hugged her and picked her up and carried her out.

Beth's mother stayed seated in the pew right behind the chair where Beth had been seated throughout the trial. This was a woman that would normally argue with anyone who said a cross word about her daughter. I had seen her defend Beth on a number of occasions against both of her brothers when they made accusations that could have exposed Beth's true nature, but this time she didn't move. She didn't even look when Beth screamed for her. She stayed seated with her head in her hands, sobbing and her friends tried to console her.

Five minutes later and court was adjourned for the day. I looked for Beth in the hallway as I left the courtroom, but I didn't see her. I don't know what the bailiffs did with Beth once they got her in the hall. I don't think she was arrested. I wasn't looking because I cared. It actually warmed my heart to see her removed like that from the courtroom, but despite that, it did not warm my heart to see her mother shattered.

Just when I was done looking for Beth and heading across the courthouse parking lot to the truck, I saw her. J.J. was holding the car door for her as she got in. Even from that distance, I could see her face was streaked with make-up and she had been crying. If this were football, my fans would be on their feet screaming and doing dances in the stands. I had not scored the touchdown against her yet, but it was third and goal and I was going for it.

CHAPTER 26

I had not left her side since we arrived at the hospital and I didn't want to leave her then, but Jay insisted on buying me lunch and Amelia insisted that I let him. They both knew I hadn't eaten breakfast that morning and I was starving.

"It feels like she's coming any minute, but you heard what the doctor just said, she hasn't budged. It could be hours. Go on, get some lunch." Amelia glanced around the room at the monitors and the IV that she was hooked up to. "I'm not going anywhere," she added.

"Okay, but if you need me, if anything changes, you will send someone to get me," I made her promise.

She shook her head in agreement and I leaned down and kissed her head. I also apologized to her again for our fight earlier.

"It's alright, Gabriel. You didn't make me go into labor. Sweet Pea just has a mind of her own," she assured me as she patted her stomach.

Tears filled my eyes. I couldn't help blaming myself and it didn't help that I knew Amelia was scared. Baby girl, as she called her, wasn't due for another two months, but Amelia was in full blown labor and the early report from the doctor on call at Oconee Regional was that he didn't think they could stop it. The doctor had given us a rundown on risks to the baby due to her early arrival and I tried to hide my fear from Amelia, but I was worried. I think that's another reason why Jay wanted to take me to lunch. He knew I needed to get what I was feeling off of my chest and not to Amelia.

"I don't want to leave you alone," I protested.

"Go on, get some lunch and get back here to hold my hand through this and don't worry. Aunt Gayle should be here any moment."

"The quicker we go, the quicker we can get back," Jay told me as he opened the door and walked into the hallway to wait for me.

I followed, but only because I knew if I didn't get something to eat soon, I would not be of any use to Amelia.

As Jay and I walked down the hall to the cafeteria, I replayed the fight in my head and I thought about all of the signs I missed.

\*\*\*

"Amelia! Where are you?" I screamed as I ran up the stairs. I had been to court that morning and was now home.

Amelia was in the nursery changing Gabby and I'm sure she heard me stomping up the stairs two at a time. She quickly finished with Gabby and put her in her crib so she could come and see what was wrong with me.

"What is it?" she asked just as I appeared in the living room door.

"Beth signed over her rights to you and me. Do you know anything about this?" I'm sure I sounded pissed and this was not the reaction she had expected.

Amelia just looked at me. Of course she had something to do with it, but suddenly she was afraid to admit to it. I guess I should have been happy that this was over no matter how it happened, but I wasn't.

"You did! Oh my God, Amelia!" I threw my hands to the sides of my head and paced back and forth.

I did not know it until we arrived at the hospital, but the entire time we were arguing, she was having contractions.

"Flippin' Braxton Hicks again, fine timing," she thought as I went at her with my accusations about her involvement in Beth's decision to give up Gabby completely and dismiss the case. She said it started out as a twinge, but steadily became the most fierce twinges yet.

I should have noticed something was wrong with her. I could see her rubbing her back, the origin of the pain, as she snapped back at me, "I'm guessing you aren't happy!"

499

"No! I am most certainly not happy! I could have beaten her!"

"And now you have!" She said, holding her breath as the pain shot through her again, while she tried to convince me that I had won.

"I didn't beat her. You, you..." I walked off and left her standing in the living room. "I am furious with you, Amelia!"

She followed me into our bedroom. "Furious for what? Because I got rid of Beth once and for all? Because I secured Gabby's future and ours or is your pride hurt because all of this was just about beating her?"

While we waited for the anesthesiologist to come and put in the epidural, she told me that just as she entered the bedroom, she started to become aware that it was nothing that could be called a twinge. This was a full blown, slicing feeling that went through her back and all the way around. Her belly was tight and it took her breath. She even described holding her breath through the pain and bracing herself against the door jam while it passed.

"I could have won the honorable way, the legal way, but you? Amelia, what did you do? Did you pay her? What?" I was changing out of my suit as I continued to scold her. "You let me go there and sit and wait this morning. You let the judge's secretary tell me and you did all of this after I told you everything last night. I told you last night that I was going to win and you didn't believe me?"

"Yeah, I paid her and she was all too eager to take the money! And, it was all in motion before you told me anything last night, before you even made it home, but there was no need telling you because the release, dismissal and the relinquishment of her parental rights weren't filed until after you left for court this morning. I had to let you go just in case she changed her mind and they didn't file the documents. So, calm down. I solved the problem."

"And you didn't discuss this with me? How much did you..."

"I gave her a million dollars."

500

"You paid a million dollars for Gabby? Where did you get that kind of cash?"

"I had Attorney Bell sell the timber on some of my land."

"Jesus! I don't know you at all. This was days in the works and you didn't say a word to me."

"I didn't realize it was all about winning against Beth. I thought it was about securing custody of Gabby and I did that. I did what I had to do to save our daughter. It was only a back-up plan and then you said at lunchtime yesterday that you weren't sure which way it would go. I wouldn't have gone through with it, but you said..."

"And then last night I told you everything was going to be fine. I gave you every last detail and you said nothing." I wasn't calming down and we were going at it pretty good. I was blinded by my fury with her and I didn't notice.

While I went into the bathroom, Amelia started timing the length of time between what she feared was the real thing, labor contractions. When I came back into the room, I found her slumped over and breathing hard. She was clutching her stomach and doing her best to breathe through the contraction.

"Amelia, are you alright?" I softened my voice. Seeing her like that, I knew something was wrong.

She let out three huffs before standing back up right and tossing me her watch. "Time it starting...Now!"

"What?" I asked as I caught the watch.

"If it is closer than five minutes apart, we have to get going." She swallowed hard and I could see sweat starting to bead on her forehead.

At first, I thought she was just having another bout of Braxton Hicks, but this did not look like any of the false labor she had had in the past. It started to dawn on me and I asked, "Do you mean..."

Amelia knew what I was getting at. "I think so," she replied before I even finished my question.

"But it's not time yet. You have two more months." I dropped to my knees in front of her. I paid close attention to the second hand on her watch and I waited with her until the next one started to come on.

"Oh. Oh. Oh!" She bit her lip and tried to grin and bear through it.

"Four minutes. Oh shit, Amelia! It's not time yet! She can't come this early!" I gripped the sides of her legs and looked up at her. I was starting to panic.

Amelia placed her hand in my hair and lifted my face from staring at the watch. "Gabriel, you have to go get Stella to watch Gabby. Please go get her now."

"Okay!" I jumped up and ran all the way to Stella and Travis' door.

I wailed on the door and Stella appeared within seconds. "Thank God you're home!"

Stella was polite, but put off by my greeting. "Hello to you too, Gabe."

"Sorry, but Amelia appears to be in real labor this time. The contractions are at four minutes apart. Can you watch Gabby for us?"

Stella didn't even respond verbally. She pushed past me and ran up the stairs. I followed. She ran straight for Amelia who had now managed to pull her suitcase out of the closet and was nearly doubled over and swearing.

"Millie?" Stella said with such intonation as to imply that she was asking if Amelia was alright.

"Uh huh?" Amelia grunted as she white-knuckled the sides of the suitcase.

Stella whipped her head around to me. "I've got Gabby. Take Millie and go! I'll finish packing her suitcase and Travis will bring it. Just go!"

The contraction passed and before the next one came, we made it to her car. We were going to the hospital to have our baby in her dad's Corvette. Amelia told me that even though she never knew her father, there were times in her life when she could feel him with her. The ride to the hospital was one of those times. While she was feeling cramped with a ghost in the car with us, I was feeling cramped thinking about how we were going to get a baby home. Since my Acura had been what we considered the family car and it had been totaled, I had promised Amelia a new car for her birthday, but I got distracted with the custody trial and had not gotten around to buying another car. We were supposed to have another two months before the baby came and we hadn't gone any place where we needed to both go and take Gabby, so I had not felt rushed to buy anything. In this moment, I felt rushed.

The contractions were coming harder each time. The hardest one came in the car and Amelia clutched the armrest on the door of the car. We sped toward Oconee Regional on the other side of Milledgeville from The Jefferson.

"We have got to get a new car!" Amelia screamed and nearly scared the life out of me.

"Shit! Amelia!" I jerked the wheel and barely missed an on-coming car.

Amelia huffed, "Ahhh. Whoowww. Hhhhh. Sorry."

I took the turn into the parking lot of the hospital on what felt like two wheels and I was scared. I was scared because she was coming early. Had her lungs developed enough? I wanted to be brave for Amelia. I knew she was scared too. I could see the tears building in her eyes. I'm sure my driving scared her, but that paled in comparison to the fear she had if she was thinking the same thing I was. Sweet Pea was coming two months early. We hadn't toured the hospital or taken a birthing class or settled on a name for her or anything.

503

"I know, I know. I'm sorry. I promised you a car for your birthday and then we got caught up in getting ready for trial. Oh, Amelia, I'm so sorry for fussing at you about Beth." I reached over and took her hand as I pulled into one of the parking spots marked for emergencies. The spark was there and it was still like ringing a bell all the way to my core.

"I'm so sorry I disappointed you." She hung her head against the passenger side window. Even though I could not see her face, I could tell by the way she was squeezing my hand, that she was having another contraction. They were coming faster, about three minutes apart.

She gathered her wind and apologized again. "If I had not paid her off, you would have won on your own and I stole that from you, and we wouldn't have fought today and now..."

She started to full on cry. "I'm so so so so sorry! Please forgive me. Please. What if something happens to..."

I didn't want her thinking like that. "Amelia, no, no, we're going in there right now and everything's going to be okay. I'm going to get out of the car and come around and get you. We'll do this together. Nothing's going to happen to her." I leaned over and gently pulled her face from the window. I kissed her. "I will love you forever, no matter what. It's me that's sorry about our fight, but let's forget about that and get you inside and have this baby."

\*\*\*

Jay and I walked down the hall looking for the cafeteria. As many times as I had been to Oconee Regional in the last year, I should have been an expert on the place. I should have known right where the cafeteria was along with everything else, but I didn't. Until that day, my expertise had been confined to the emergency room, radiology department and the orthopedic office across the street.

Jay had arrived at the hospital about five minutes behind us. In fact, he got Amelia into a wheelchair as I checked her in. Both Amelia and I were glad to see him. As it turned out, he had been home when I was wailing on Stella and Travis' door. He didn't realize what was up, but got concerned when he heard all of the

504

running up and down the stairs and the Corvette peel out of the driveway at the apartment. He immediately ran upstairs to find Stella who told him what was going on. He came as soon as he heard.

"I think it's right down here," Jay said as he led the way.

I reached up and touched his shoulder. Jay stopped and turned to me.

"Thank you for coming down here today." I thought about what I should have said to Amelia that morning and I said it to Jay. "I know you had something to do with us getting custody of Gabby and I'm going to tell you what I should have told Amelia this morning, 'Thank you.' I was a stubborn ass this morning and I picked a fight with her."

There was so much more that I wanted to say, but my emotions got the better of me. I could not push out the what-ifs. What if something happened to the baby? Could Amelia forgive me? What if something happened to Amelia? What if something happened to both of them?

Jay tried to change the subject. "Amelia told me you have this phrase about the bull and getting the horns. You fought because Amelia took the bull by the horns."

"I wanted Beth to get what was coming to her so badly I could taste it and then this." I shook my head. I was at a loss for words. I wiped the tears from my eyes.

"You know, Amelia only did all of this to protect Gabby. She has a way of protecting those she loves, no matter what the personal cost to her. She gave me the cash, but she also gave me every bank card she has and told me to empty every account if I had to, but I wasn't to come back without the documents signed."

I covered my mouth. I knew roughly how much Amelia had in the accounts from the day she showed us the ledger. It was a lot and she was willing to wipe it all out just to save Gabby. I couldn't believe it.

Jay leaned up against the wall next to me. He gave me a nudge. "You wanna know how much money Beth took for Gabby?"

I nodded my head "yes", but I wasn't sure I really wanted to know the answer. What if he had wiped out all of the accounts and Amelia had given away her entire fortune to Beth? Before I could think anything more about it, Jay answered.

"She got about ten grand."

I had been staring straight down at my shoes, but when he said 'ten grand' I nearly broke my neck whipping around to get confirmation of that and to see the look on his face.

"I called Amelia from the pay phone in front of the Greensboro Post Office after I caught up with Beth in the hallway, after the bailiffs threw her out. As they were about to drag her away, she asked to use the restroom, said she had to pee. They let her and while they weren't looking, I walked right into the ladies room and made the offer."

"Of course Amelia was impatient and wanted to know if Beth signed it. She didn't sign it right then, but she was sure 'nough interested in the money. That was the most money I had ever seen, a million dollars, and I could not believe I was offering it to the most awful person I had ever met, but I did like Amelia asked. I wouldn't have done it if I hadn't understood Amelia's motive and agreed with her. I would have done the same thing for Gabby if I had that kind of money."

"Oh, Amelia was frustrated. 'Will she just take the damn money and get out of our lives already?' Amelia demanded to know, but I calmed her down."

"I told her to calm down. I knew Beth would sign it, but I didn't think she was going to sign with her attorney and her parents waiting right outside, not with her mother already looking devastated. Plus, if she had no interest in it, she would have told me to go to Hell for even suggesting such a thing."

"Along with the money was a one way ticket to Italy. How soap opera like, right? The ticket to Italy was my idea. My grandmother would have been on the edge of her seat of her couch tuning in to see how this one turned out. You probably don't know, but I'm a soap addict. Sorry."

"Anyway, as I hung up the phone with Amelia, it occurred to me how it would work out in soap opera world and it wasn't a bad idea, but I needed some help to make it happen. I dialed Port Honor. I found Jerry and he agreed to help me. I rushed straight there. If Beth called me, I needed to be ready."

I just looked at Jay wondering what he did. I knew we needed to get back to Amelia. I wanted to hear the rest of the story, but I was getting antsy. Doctors and nurses and other visitors to the hospital passed us and Jay summed up the rest of the story.

"Somewhere over the Atlantic, on a flight to Rome, a blonde woman probably just screamed bloody murder when she opened her carry-on bag. What goes around comes around and I know you wanted to be the one that brought it around to Beth. I understand that. I mean, after everything she's done to you, I can imagine that you wanted to see her face when she got her own, but rest assured, she knows she's been had and she probably thinks you had something to do with it."

I let out a slight laugh.

"With Jerry's help, we replaced the contents of each bundle of bills with cut up newspaper in the middle and a hundred dollar bill on the top and bottom of each stack. I left three bundles alone, nothing but real money and that's what I handed her to count. It also helped that I booked her on a flight that she had to rush to get to. Oh, and it helped that she was blitzed out of her mind and her brother, John, Jr. or J.J. or whatever they call him, he practically held her hand as she signed. If you ask me, I'd say he was the driving force behind the decision. He might have been as much of an accomplice to Millie's plan as I was and they don't even know one another. Yeah, when she opens that duffle bag and sobers up enough to start counting the money, she'll know she's been had."

I laughed openly then. "So you told her she was getting a million and you gave her somewhere in the neighborhood of ten thousand."

"Yeah, I was going to bring the rest back to Millie this afternoon, but here we are. Come on, let me buy you a Coke and a sandwich before you pass out on us." Jay then started down the hall and I followed again all the while shaking my head at what they had done to Beth. It was priceless and, yes, I would have loved to have been a fly on the wall when she figured out she did not have a million dollars. Beth messed with the bull and Amelia gave her the horns, by golly.

*\*\**

There wasn't an empty seat in the waiting room. It was filled with everyone we knew. All of the residents of The Jefferson were there, except Stella and Travis. Stella was taking care of Gabby for us and Travis had come and dropped off suitcases for us and then returned to help Stella.

All of Amelia's relatives, Aunt Gayle, Aunt Dot and Uncle Jim, Aunt Ruth and her kids were there as well as Jay's parents, sister and his Aunt June. They had started trickling in within fifteen minutes of Amelia and I arriving at the hospital that morning and had been waiting ever since.

It was five minutes after midnight and I was still in my scrubs when I walked out to the waiting room. "George-Anne Marie Hewitt is here!" I announced. I was the one that officially named her. I would have given Amelia anything in the world she wanted so naming the baby exactly what she wanted was the least I could do after what she went through to get George-Anne into the world.

Amelia's Aunt Gayle just squealed with delight. She had been in the room with us all day, but could not come back with us to the operating room.

Everyone was talking at once. Many were saying "Congratulations," but Jay's Aunt June was the first one I understood to say something else and she asked, "How's Amelia?"

"She's fine. She's in recovery and I mean she took this like a champ." I was so proud of her and I am sure that was evident in my praise.

"Gayle said that she was in labor all day and the baby wouldn't move, so she had to have a C-section," her Aunt Ruth wanted confirmation. She and her group of the family were some of the last ones to arrive at the hospital before Amelia was rolled back to the operating room.

"That about sums it up. It was a case of the baby wanting to come, but just couldn't seem to make it happen on her own. I just can't imagine what Amelia went through." I shook my head and shrugged my shoulders.

Dixie added, "She's always been a tough girl." Her brother, Dixon, nodded in agreement.

There was a moment when everyone seemed to get a little quiet. I am sure they were just formulating their next questions, so, I seized the moment to start answering as many questions as I thought they would come up with to ask. "They took the baby back to the intensive care nursery to have her cleaned up and looked over by the pediatrician. I don't want to think about it and no one has mentioned it to Amelia, but George-Anne isn't out of the woods."

Gayle's hand shot to her mouth and Aunt Dot immediately grabbed hold of her for support.

"Her lungs aren't as developed as they would like for them to be and she is struggling just a little to breathe on her own." I tried to be brave as I described the baby's condition. I didn't want to worry them. I was assured that the odds of George-Anne being just fine were better than not.

"She weighs three pounds, six ounces so she needs to gain weight, but babies born at her gestation cannot suckle on their own. I have been assured that the doctors here are perfectly capable of handling this sort of thing and George-Anne will be right as rain within a few weeks."

"A few weeks?" three of the women shrieked together.

"It is very late, so please don't hang on my every word, we will know more tomorrow, but for now it is my understanding that they need to get her breathing on her own with no effort, her weight up to four pounds and have her mature enough to eat."

509

"So they have promised she will be alright?" Jay's Aunt June asked from toward the back of the pack.

"They haven't promised anything, but they say that everything looks normal and they expect her to be just fine. She's a little jaundice, but other than that she looks perfectly normal, just tiny. She even has a tiny little streak of blond hair, almost a Mohawk."

"A blonde Mohawk?" Aunt Dot questioned.

"Right, already a bit of a rebel, I'd say," Uncle Jim added.

I almost laughed at his statement, but I held back and carried on. "Amelia is in recovery and should be back in the room in about an hour. It has been a long day for everyone and I know I speak for Amelia as well as myself when I say this, thank y'all for coming. Your love and support mean the world to us and just knowing you were here helped get Amelia through this. Please keep us all in your prayers."

I started to tear up myself as I made my request. I pushed my index fingers to the center corners of my eyes to push down the tears. I had to look away from Gayle because she was doing the same thing.

Gayle came up and hugged me then. "When do you think they will let us see her?"

"I know you are dying to see the baby, but the nurses told me to ask you to go home and get some rest and I think that's for the best. I'm not trying to run y'all off, but I know you are tired and from what I gather, there's not going to be anything to see here tonight. I know Amelia will want to see every one of you tomorrow. Any of you that don't want to make the drive back to Avera tonight are welcome to stay at our place."

I handed Gayle my keys. "I'm not going anywhere tonight so you can take these and let yourself in and anyone else that wants to join you. I'm sorry about any mess in the apartment, but we just ran out of there this morning. I will call Stella and let her know that y'all are coming."

I also went ahead and made arrangements with Stella and Daniel to trade off responsibilities with Gabby until I got back home.

Everyone gathered their belongings and started saying their goodbyes. Aunt Dot agreed to stay over at The Jefferson with Gayle, but Aunt Ruth and her kids decided to make the trek back home since they didn't bring a change of clothes.

Jay left with his Aunt June and they promised to be back tomorrow, but not too early. He had waited with us all day and never left our sides. Jay was excited about being an honorary uncle and I was excited for him. He already filled in as uncle for Gabby so it was only natural that he would be an uncle to George-Anne as well.

As Jay walked away with his aunt, Gayle and Aunt Dot approached me to bid me good night. Before they could say anything, I had something I felt I needed to say to them.

"Not too long ago the three of us stood in another hospital waiting on Amelia, but with far different circumstances. That day you told me that I had ruined her life and I hope you don't feel that way about me still. I hope this hasn't ruined her life because this day, short of our wedding day, this is the happiest day of my life. I love her so much and I hope you know I would never do anything at all, not ever, to hurt her or our two girls. I hope I am a husband and father that she can be proud of and the very opposite of what you thought of me that day..."

I am sure I would have continued on, but Gayle grabbed me and hugged me for all she was worth. "Gabriel Hewitt, you are one of the best men I know and I am so sorry I did not realize that back then. I apologize if I gave you a moment's grief, but..."

I cut her off, "But you were just looking out for your girl like I'm going to be looking out for mine."

Gayle leaned back and there were tears in her eyes. She couldn't speak for a moment. She just shook her head in agreement. "You are one of the best men I have ever known and I am so thankful that Amelia has you."

Gayle and Aunt Dot were the last ones to leave and I walked them to their cars before I went back in to find the room that was assigned to Amelia. I was alone with my thoughts for about forty-five minutes before they brought Amelia in. She was asleep and they just wheeled the bed right in. Although her body had been through Hell that day, she was more beautiful in that moment than I had ever seen her before.

I leaned over and kissed her forehead. I brushed the hair from the edge of her face. "You are the mother of my children and they are perfect. I love the three of you with all my heart," I whispered to her.

Amelia barely mumbled back, "I love you, too."

It had been a long day and both of us fell asleep not too long after they brought her back to the room. Amelia was as snug as one in her condition could be in the hospital bed and I was in a chair that I had pulled over to the side of the bed. I was holding one of her hands and slouched over the side of the bed with my head against her leg as my pillow. At 4:00 a.m., Amelia awoke with a start.

"Gabriel!" Amelia jerked my hand. "Where's the baby and why haven't they let me hold her?"

I struggled to come to, but when she nudged me again, I realized she was in a panic. "Gabriel, where's George-Anne?"

I had hoped to wait until the morning, until Gayle had made it back to the hospital before giving the details of George-Anne's condition to Amelia. I knew that in a time like this a girl would need her mother and in Amelia's case, Gayle was the closest thing she had to a mother. I didn't know where to begin.

"Gabriel, what's wrong? Did they let you see her?" Amelia asked as she scooted over in the bed and made room for me to sit next to her.

I eased into the spot beside her as gently as I could. Amelia was still hooked up to a morphine pump, but I didn't want to risk bouncing her around and causing her to feel any pain from the surgery.

"Yes. Don't you remember the doctor showing her to us?"

Amelia leaned up so I could put my arm around her and she could lay her head back against my chest. I could feel her whimper a little when she answered. "I don't remember what she looks like," she cried.

"Hey now, no tears. This is a happy day and you were so drugged up that I'm surprised you remember your own name. Don't be so hard on yourself." I tried to comfort her, but it didn't seem to be working.

Amelia switched the subject and I was almost relieved, but the crying continued, "I didn't say goodbye to Gabby when we left this morning."

"I'm sure she's fine and probably didn't notice." I caressed her head as she cried.

"She didn't notice I left her?" She was hurt that I had implied Gabby wouldn't miss her. I had never seen her like this before. She was clearly hormonal.

I didn't know whether to assure her that Gabby missed her and risk her crying over the guilt of leaving Gabby or try to convince her that Gabby was fine with Stella or would she get upset and think that I was saying that Gabby didn't need her. I decided my best bet would be to change the subject back to George-Anne.

"She has a blonde Mohawk." I started with a detail about her that might lighten Amelia's mood.

"She has what?" Amelia cocked her head to look at my face.

"You heard me right, a blonde Mohawk. Your Uncle Jim says we are in for trouble with this one."

It was working. Amelia laughed slightly and grabbed the area of the incision to limit the movement.

"She's tiny, but the doctors believe she is going to be just fine in a few weeks. She just needs some help to mature. You are going to be able to see her later in the day, but I want you to prepare yourself. She was born early, but she's going to be fine. I don't want to worry you, so I'm going to let the doctors explain everything to you so that I don't give you wrong information."

"What if..."

Before Amelia could continue on with her question, I stopped her. "We are not going to live on 'what ifs'. We will live on hope and faith and nothing less; hope and faith that George-Anne Hewitt will be just fine. She's part you and part me and that means she is a fighter and a survivor."

Amelia let out a deep sigh and agreed to do her best to try.

Daylight came and Amelia was officially introduced to our daughter. A little after 9:00 a.m., Gayle and Aunt Dot were back at the hospital and Amelia was allowed to walk down to the NICU. Gayle was allowed to go with us. The three of us were made to scrub up and wear gloves before we were allowed to go in.

Even though I knew what to expect, I teared up at the sight of our tiny girl. She wasn't in a crib, but an incubator. She was sleeping, but she was so pitiful looking. There were so many tubes and the diaper they had on her looked as if it had swallowed her. She also had on what looked like goggles. We were told those were to protect her eyes during the phototherapy in the incubator. She looked like she was in a Tupperware box under a heat lamp. I think even the strongest man would have done as I did. I tried to be strong for Amelia and I prayed she didn't look back at me. I was afraid that if she saw me, she would surely lose it and I didn't want that for her. I did not want that to be the memory she had of first seeing our daughter.

There was no discussion on the subject, Amelia was the first of us to reach in and touch her. There was a chair that had been pulled up next to the incubator that held George-Anne. Amelia took a seat in the chair and reached in cautiously. Amelia finally rested her head against the side of the incubator and just stared at the baby. She was careful not to disturb any of the tubes as she caressed the baby's tiny body.

Amelia whispered to her, "Hey, sweet baby. It's Mommy and Daddy and we love you so much. And, Aunt Gayle is here too and there are so many other people that can't hardly wait to meet you. I know it's a lot to ask, but Mommy needs you to fight hard and get stronger so everyone can see what a sweet, pretty girl you are. And smart, I bet you are going to be so smart. Mommy is asking you nicely to please fight hard, get bigger and stronger so you can come home and meet Gabby. She's your sister."

Gayle and I stood behind Amelia each of us with a hand on one of her shoulders. We just listened while Amelia begged and willed George-Anne to survive.

Although Amelia was released from the hospital within four days of giving birth, George-Anne wasn't released right away. Christmas came and went and for the next two weeks following George-Anne's birth, Amelia spent almost every hour of every day at her side. So that Gabby wasn't neglected or felt she was forgotten, Amelia convinced the nurses to allow her to bring Gabby in with her when she came to visit George-Anne. Her argument was that if the babies weren't contagious and neither was Gabby, then what was the problem? It also helped that the money that Jay was supposed to give to Beth, he gave back to Amelia. Amelia then used part of it to make a sizeable donation to the hospital.

Amelia sang to the girls and told them one story after another. The nurses said they had never seen a young mother like Amelia more devoted to her children. She made friends with all of them on all of the shifts.

Most of the time that Amelia was camped out with the girls at the hospital, I was with her. When I wasn't there, I was at work. Everyone at the club asked about Amelia and George-Anne. There had been baby showers planned for Amelia, but because she delivered two months early they had not occurred. However, as soon as I returned to work, gifts from staff and club members poured in. Praise knitted a cap and sweater for her. Mrs. Lockerby brought in what seemed like a year's supply of diapers and others brought in formula and clothes. A few people brought things to me once they heard I had Gabby, but nothing like this volume.

I was sitting in my office one afternoon making out the schedule for the next week when a knock came at the door. My office was like a fishbowl with glass all around it and I don't know how I didn't see him walk up, but I didn't. Responding to the knock, I looked up. It was Dick.

There was an extra chair in my office, but Dick did not take it. He remained standing. As if the situation was not awkward enough, he was nearly seven feet tall and he towered over me regardless of whether I was standing or sitting as I was then.

As I took in his size standing there in the doorway, two things came to mind. Joan told me that he was half the man I was when she handed over the custody papers that he signed. For whatever reason, the sight of him and that memory amused me and I had to stifle the urge to laugh.

In shutting down my amusement, it also occurred to me that Gabby stood a very real chance of being a very, very tall woman. Her mother was millimeters shy of six feet tall and Dick was at least six foot eight.

"Gabe," Dick shuffled his hands in his pockets as if he was discretely adjusting himself as he said my name. "I know it's been uncomfortable between us."

Talk about the understatement of the year. I had wanted him dead on a number of occasions and contemplated killing him myself on at least two of those occasions.

I could not help myself, "'Uncomfortable' is not exactly the word I would use."

"Point taken." He hung his head. His body language suggested he might actually be ashamed and nervous. He did the shuffling of his pants with his hands in his pockets again.

"Well, I just came down here to say that if you need any time off due to your daughter and all, you can take as much as you need. Your job will always be here for you."

I did not see that coming. This was a side of him that I had never seen before. For a normal boss, this would have been very kind and generous, and maybe Dick was being just that or maybe it was just the manifestation of his guilt over Gabby. Who knows, but

516

before I realized it, I thanked him. By the look on his face, I could tell he was taken aback by my gratitude.

After I thanked him, he turned to leave and I turned back to my paperwork. I barely had my eyes back on the schedule when I heard Dick clear his throat. I looked back and he was in the doorway again.

"Look, I don't know how to say it. I mean, how does a man apologize for being an asshole his entire life?"

I said nothing and just shrugged my shoulders. I did not know what to make of any of this.

"Joan has left me and I deserve it. My children aren't fond of me and the only decent thing I have done lately is sign over the parental rights of my illegitimate child to another man to raise."

Dear Lord, I did not want to be his confidant, but it appeared that train was leaving the station and there was nothing I could do to stop it. How I prayed for the phone to ring or for someone else to walk up and need me, save me.

"I know I can't be her father. I've abandoned that task to you, but if she ever needs anything or if you need anything, all you have to do is ask and I will make it happen or die trying. I know my word is worthless to you, but I give you my word anyway."

Dick seemed genuine, but he was right. His word was no good to me, but the one thing I would ever want from him, I took that moment to request.

"All I want is for you to never interfere in our lives. If you ever think of claiming Gabby, put her first and understand that I'm the only father she's ever known."

I stood up from my chair and extended my hand. "I give you my word that I will tell her who her real father is when she is old enough to understand. And, for her sake, I will not lie to her, but I will paint you in the best possible light."

Dick took my hand and shook it. "This might be the one true gentleman's agreement that I have ever fully intended to keep. I

517

know I don't have the right to ask, but would you mind telling me how she's doing from time to time?"

I knew I really didn't owe him anything, but promised to provide him updates.

"I would appreciate that," he said. "I'll let you get back to work now and I meant it about the time off. If you need it, take it and we'll figure out something around here."

That night at the hospital, I told Amelia all about my conversation with Dick. Her only response was, "That's more concern for Gabby than Beth showed throughout the entire trial."

***

George-Anne Hewitt was released from the hospital on January 9, 1997. It was exactly three weeks after her birth. She weighed four pounds and thirteen ounces. She was sixteen inches long.

The doctors and nurses at Oconee Regional Medical Center had worked a miracle with her. What they had not told us was that when she was born, they didn't really expect her to pull through. Where we gave them credit for saving her, they gave Amelia credit. Many fully believed that Amelia willed her to live and she did.

I had promised Amelia a new car for her birthday and I was running behind on that promise the day she went into labor and we sped across town in the Corvette. Today, I had fulfilled the promise and her eyes lit up when I pulled up to the front door of the hospital to take them home.

Amelia almost didn't recognize me at first. I was driving the very model of Toyota 4Runner that she had admired in a Southern Living magazine the week before. I had the dealership in Milledgeville order one with all of the bells and whistles and the same color as the one in the ad, Sunfire Red Pearl with gray interior. It was every bit as modern as my Legend had been and bigger.

I pulled up in front of Amelia. She was holding George-Anne in her carrier, one identical to the one we had for Gabby. I jumped out and ran around to open the passenger side door for her. Gabby was in the passenger seat behind the driver's seat and I had installed the base for George-Anne's carrier in the seat on the opposite side.

Driving the four of us home from the hospital that day, I remembered every moment. The new car smell was not nearly as overwhelming of the feelings I had that day. A song called "Oh What a Thrill" was playing on the radio. It started just as we were pulling out of the parking lot of the hospital and it really got me thinking.

I looked around at each of my girls. Amelia was by my side and ooh-ing and ahh-ing over the dashboard, leather seats and the overall newness of the vehicle. I remembered the nervousness of first meeting her. The feelings I had for her were immediate and I was amazed as I looked back to our girls. I just could not believe things have come to this.

"I've never had a new car before," she commented as she ran her hand across the dash. I was lost in my thoughts and hardly heard her.

In the rear-view mirror, I looked back to Gabby. I could hear her laughing as she batted at the toy that hung across her carrier. Each time she swatted, Pooh Bear did flips like a gymnast on the uneven bars and Gabby squealed with delight. She was so pretty. Her brown hair was coming in thicker and her skin was still smooth like porcelain and had a hint of olive, like the lightest of natural tans. Her coloring was like Dick's and the shape of her face was round like Beth's, but she wasn't chubby. She was perfect and even though I was reminded every time I looked at her that she was not biologically mine, she was mine in my heart and I couldn't have loved her more.

In those first days, when it was just me and Gabby, I could not believe God trusted me with her, but I am so he they did. I was so scared. For everything I fumbled over, I knew somehow I would make things better for her and now here we were. Things were better.

From Gabby, I looked to George-Anne. She was snug and asleep in her carrier when I took her from Amelia and loaded her into the car. From what I could tell, she was still fast asleep. When I looked between the seats to get a glimpse of her, all I could see was the top of the crocheted cap that Praise had made for her. It was an exact replica of the one she had made for Gabby. The only movement from George-Anne was the slight up and down of the cap as she breathed. Under the cap was still signs of a blond Mohawk. The jaundice had gone away and her coloring was fair like mine and Amelia's. She was a little wrinkly, bundle of sweetness. Holding her the first time was breath taking.

Each of my girls was perfect in their own way. Both babies were blissfully ignorant as to what Amelia and I had been through to have them.

Never in my wildest dreams would I have ever thought this would be my life. As I took in the sight of each of them, I knew I was living a dream and despite everything, I loved every minute of it. I had found myself in them. They were the biggest thrill of my life.

Dear Reader,

Thank you again giving your time to my books. I hope you enjoyed <u>Port Honor</u> and <u>In Search of Honor</u>. I hope you enjoyed Gabriel's story.

I thought I would go ahead and let you know that I am not completely finished with Amelia and Gabriel, but I am going to take a little break from them. In the next book in The Port Honor Series I plan to answer the question, "Why didn't Aunt Gayle ever get married?" If you think she was she so devoted to raising Millie that she never thought of a life for herself beyond that, you're simply mistaken. I hope this peaks your interest and you will continue to give your time to my writing.

Please check my website, www.tsdawson.com, for upcoming release dates and events. There is also a link for you to contact me on the website. I encourage you to please email me via this contact; let me know how you did or did not like the books. I cannot communicate how I love hearing from my readers (I really, really love it!) And, if it is not too much trouble, please leave me a review on Amazon.com. I love reading those as well. Your feedback and reviews allow me to know what I am doing right as well as what I need to improve upon and this information is invaluable.

Thank you again and please know that I appreciate all that you do. I could write until the cows come home, but without you, I cannot be successful.

Sincerely,

TS Dawson